First comes marriage... Then comes Murder

A Women of Wynton's Mystery

DONNA MUMMA

ISBN 979-8-89151-175-0
Adobe Digital Edition (.epub) 979-8-89151-176-7

Cover artwork by Alessandra Fusi

Published by Barbour Publishing, Inc., 1810 Barbour Drive, Uhrichsville, Ohio 44683, www.barbourbooks.com

Our mission is to inspire the world with the life-changing message of the Bible.

Printed in the United States of America.

Dedication

To my amazing family
A big, wonderful crowd of readers and storytellers

Chapter 1

Vivien

Many around Levy City believed Vivien Sheffield needed to retire. Maybe her hair was turning grayer by the day while her middle grew more grandmotherly. But she didn't have the time to worry over other folks' opinions when she had a salon teeming with brides and their mothers.

It was February, the month of love. All the girls wanted white weddings, and 1956 was promising to be her best year yet.

A bevy of bridesmaids clad in Mamie Eisenhower pink chiffon gowns twirled around the fitting area in the back of the salon, gushing to one another about how darling they all looked. Their ear-piercing squeals burrowed into Vivien's ears.

Her longtime assistant, Mirette, chased after one girl refusing to stand still long enough to pin the gown's hem. The look on her dear friend's face broadcast it was time to corral all this feminine chaos back into a stable of sanity.

"Ladies." Vivien tugged the nearest bridesmaid's arm and stopped her in her tracks. "Line up here so Mirette and I can get a good look at you. No more running around like a bunch of wild rabbits."

While the girls scrambled into place, whispers from acetate linings in the gowns replaced the squeals. Mirette pushed back a silver curl dangling over her glasses, then moved to a chair. She held her measuring tape in one hand and her tomato-shaped pincushion in the other, then nodded to Vivien.

Vivien motioned to the first girl in line. "Go get pinned." She looked at the other girls. "Y'all stay put until Mirette's checked your measurements."

"Yes, Miss Vivien," they chorused.

"And when I'm measuring, don't start wiggling. Y'all hear me?"

Mirette unwound her measuring tape.

Vivien hoped the girls heeded Mirette's words. If one moved around too much, her assistant wasn't above giving a little poke with the needle to make her point clear.

The bride's mother, Merilee Bell, came bustling from the dressing room where her daughter was trying on her gown. "Vivien, Mary Hadley's not happy."

Merilee clicked her tongue against her teeth as if this whole affair annoyed the stew out of her. "This is the fourth fitting. Why can't you get this wedding gown fixed to suit her?"

Her square black patent leather purse flapped against her hip as she crossed her arms and stared over the rims of her cat-eye glasses. "I was talking with Lenora Baker the other day, and she said Cathy had no trouble when you made her dress last year."

Cathy was a dream bride. She loved her gown and took what it stood for to heart.

Mary Hadley came into the salon with one wedding goal in mind. To outdo every other bride in the county. She'd demanded a custom-made gown with yards and yards of lace, pearl accents, embroidered flowers with sequins in the middle, and quite possibly the widest satin skirt the South had seen since the War Between the States.

"I'll talk to her. But"—Vivien stared Merilee straight in the eyes—"no more big changes. Mirette and I have reconstructed her gown three times. We have other brides to work with."

Merilee drew in a loud breath through her nose and started swelling like a toad. "If—"

Vivien held up a finger and stopped her from going on. She pointed to one of the nearby white bucket-style chairs set aside for the mamas during fittings. "Have a seat, and I'll get her sorted out."

She entered the dressing room and found Mary Hadley standing in front of the mirror, picking at a lace ruffle. Her jet-black pin curls framed her face, setting off her cat-green eyes.

"Mama says you're not happy."

"Miss Vivien, I feel like I'm wearing cheap lace curtains." She flicked the ruffle from her fingers and wrinkled her nose as if she'd been asked to eat live worms.

"You asked for six rows of Chantilly lace on the skirt. That's what Mirette and I gave you."

Her reflection in the mirror eyed Vivien as she fingered one of the flowers sewn onto the neckline. "These flowers are tacky."

Vivien paused. Mary Hadley had demanded the flowers be added at her last fitting because the gown didn't match her springtime wedding date.

Kind words trampled down wrath. And truth set folks free. "Mirette and I spent two weekends making those flowers and came in an hour early for days to get them sewn on the dress in time for this fitting."

No matter how snippy a bride might get, they loved her as if she were their own and worked hard to make her wedding dreams come true. She and Mirette attended more bridal and baby showers than any two women in Levy City.

Mary Hadley seemed destined to become the first they would shower with rice at the reception and wave a permanent goodbye to when she left for the honeymoon.

"We'll remove those flowers. The lace, and everything else, stays." Vivien left the dressing room.

The line of bridesmaids stared as she walked past them. Merilee stood and blocked Vivien from taking another step. "Is she happy now?"

"Perfectly." She moved around Merilee and walked into the sales floor of the salon where the next thing on her to-do list waited.

Robbi Dever, the author of the column The Juice in *The Levy Times Commercial*, was there to observe Vivien and Mirette for an upcoming column. She'd insisted on showcasing Miss Vivien's salon in the paper to increase interest in Wynton's upcoming Bridal Week celebrations in April.

Vivien couldn't see starting this early as helpful, and suggested they wait until March. Robbi went to Mr. Wynton, owner of the store, and he asked Vivien to comply.

She rose from the soft cushions. "You sure didn't pick this dainty couch for a big-boned gal like me, did you?" Robbi's cackling laugh rang through the salon as she unfolded her almost six-foot frame to her full height.

Robbi gazed around the salon. "I hardly recognized the place when I came in. You and Mirette have transformed this salon."

"We decided to spruce things up before Bridal Week." Vivien looked across the space. "We added the gilded-framed floor-length mirrors, called in the store's carpenter to build these small, polished teakwood platforms in front of them, and arranged the different sitting areas so brides can model potential gowns for their mamas and friends."

Vivien pointed to the wall opposite where they stood. "He also built those display racks with the open doors so they'd each look like an open armoire. We hang the gown samples in there now."

Robbi raised her eyes to the ceiling. "Crystal chandeliers too?"

"Mr. Wynton donated those, plus the new rugs."

Robbi dug deep into her large alligator purse and pulled out a pen and notebook. She flipped the notebook open and scribbled something on the page. "What do you call this shade of blue on the couches and the rugs? I'll specify it in my article. My readers will want to run right out and find upholstery in the same color."

She leaned close and Vivien caught a faint whiff of Estée Lauder's Youth Dew. "You are one of Levy City's biggest trendsetters, you know."

"I ordered the couches through the store," Vivien explained. "The background color was called Cloudless, and the pattern on the upholstery is Lavender Cornflowers. The rugs are a darker, contrasting color called Ocean."

"Right. Those little beige stars in the carpet make even my big size 11s look lavish when I'm walking across." Robbi pressed her low-heeled loafer on the rugs as if to prove her point. "I'll stay out of the way and observe you doing what you do. Give my readers a little window into your day."

"That might be a bit boring."

"Nonsense," Robbi insisted, plopping down on the couch. "My readers will have a bird's-eye view of how Miss Vivien operates. They'll eat this up."

"Robbi, the entire female population of Levy City has seen me work. I've been a part of almost every wedding here for over twenty-five years."

"Oh pooh. You're too modest. I want them to see all the little things you do behind the scenes that make you"—she held her hands wide as if she were about to shout Hallelujah—"*Miss Vivien.*"

The salon's front-door chimes sounded. "Vivien Sheffield, where are you?"

"Excuse me, Robbi." Vivien met Ruth Gaskin, the mother of another one of her upcoming brides as she entered the center of the salon. "I'm right here, Ruth."

Ruth's face darkened to a deep crimson. "How dare you stab me in the back."

A gasp sounded behind Vivien. Mary Hadley's bridesmaids had bunched together in the doorway of the fitting room to watch the spectacle. She gestured for them to return to the fitting area. "Go make sure Mirette's finished with you, then change into your regular clothes."

When they lingered, she shooed them away. "Go on now."

They turned slowly as a group, murmuring among themselves.

She turned back to Ruth. "What's going on?"

If eyes could shoot fire, Ruth's would have burnt Vivien to a crisp. "You told my Stacia to marry that horrid Fred Patterson. Vivien, you know that boy comes from nothing and has no prospects other than working for his father in their tiny orange groves outside of town."

"I never said such—"

"What are we going to do with her gown, Vivien? The presents everyone sent?"

Ruth opened her purse and fumbled around inside until she produced a hankie. "We put a sixty-dollar deposit on the community center for the reception. And you know they won't refund it. I canceled Cameron's Catering because they kept adding new charges on everything I asked for. My sisters and I decided to make the food ourselves. Our freezers are packed, and now it's all going to go to waste." She buried her face in her hankie.

From the corner of her eye, Vivien noticed Robbi scrawling away in her notebook. She couldn't help that now.

"Ruth, you're not making a bit of sense."

She raised her face from her handkerchief. "My daughter called me at the break of dawn from somewhere in the middle of Georgia, telling me she eloped with a grove boy you told her to marry."

Mary Hadley, now dressed in her street clothes, marched from the fitting area. Her bridesmaids trailed behind her. They gathered in a long line across the salon floor, looking as if they were ready to play Red Rover.

Mirette stepped through the crowd and came to Vivien's side. "Do you have aspirin in your desk drawer?" she whispered.

"Not nearly enough."

The entrance chimes trilled, and Lenora Baker came into the salon. Her normally well-coiffed hair frizzed around her face, and her cheeks were drained of color.

Vivien rushed to her side. "Are you all right, Lenora?"

"Cathy. . .the police. . .she's dead."

As shocked gasps erupted from the bridesmaids, Robbi Dever sprang to her feet. "I'm sorry Miss Vivien, but the news never stops, and I have to chase this story."

She ran to the door and then scurried out to the elevator.

Vivien hugged the sobbing Lenora. "I'm so sorry."

The words tasted hollow and sour, but what more could she say at a time like this?

Nothing but a silent prayer for a mama's shattered heart and the loss of a dear, sweet girl.

Chapter 2

Audrey

Audrey Penault pulled her red T-Bird into her designated parking spot in Wynton's garage. The store's parking guard, Nelson, waved to her as she gathered her satchel and purse.

She held out a bag of cinnamon twists from Tiner's Bakery and a thermos of coffee. As Nelson took them from her, a half grin crinkled his brown face. "You're running late."

Audrey pulled on brown gloves that matched her brown wool suit, then settled her brown felt Juliet cap over her dark hair. "There was some kind of commotion over in Pine Acres. Sheriff Youngblood and his boys were directing traffic out of the neighborhood down to Platt Street. Took me forever to get here."

She buttoned her brown suit jacket around her waist, then smoothed the black velvet-trimmed lapels of the jacket. "I'd better get going. I'm supposed to meet with Mr. Wynton in ten minutes. Get some sleep when you get home, Nelson." Audrey hurried away as Nelson sat down in his resting chair to enjoy his breakfast.

When she reached Wynton's executive suite on the seventh floor, her boss's door stood open, his sign he was waiting for her. "Come on in, Audrey," he called.

She set her purse and satchel in her chair, then grabbed her steno pad and a pencil.

When she entered his office, she took the chair in front of his desk. It was then she realized she'd forgotten to remove her hat. Mr. Wynton was going to think she was a complete mess today. "I'm sorry for being late."

"I heard there's something going on in Pine Acres." Mr. Wynton slipped his black horn-rimmed glasses from his face and rubbed his eyes. "Did you look over the financials I sent home with you?"

"Yes sir."

"Thoughts?"

Audrey recalled the figures she'd studied the night before. "Christmas sales looked strong. Toys, Children's Apparel, and Ladies Sportswear recorded great numbers. Men's Apparel was down. Furniture and Housewares had a slight uptick. Several men in Levy City bought the Mixette, Hamilton Beach's handheld mixer, for their wives this year."

He nodded. "Thanks to you and Miss Vivien, the showstopper gown from the holiday fashion show was a big hit, but overall, the sales in Better Dresses took a big drop. Guesses as to why?"

Audrey paused. "Honest opinion?"

He nodded.

"The dresses our clothing buyers chose last year exceeded the average Levy City budget. Our ladies made their own dresses at home."

Mr. Wynton leaned back in his chair. "How so?"

He'd never drilled her like this before, but she wasn't going to let him have even an inkling this made her pulse jumpy.

"As I went over the numbers last night, I noticed a large rise in sales of fabric and patterns in our sewing department between October and January first. I dug into the invoices and saw a larger than normal percentage of the sales were for the more formal fabrics—taffeta, silk, and velvet. We sold more faux rhinestone trim, pearl buttons, and yards of velvet and satin ribbons than previous years. The bestselling patterns were McCall's for Misses evening or day dresses. All materials for making an evening gown or cocktail dress."

His wide smile crinkled the corners of his eyes. "Nothing at Wynton's gets past you, does it?"

"Just doing my job, sir."

"Come with me." He pushed back his chair and rose.

Audrey closed her steno pad and slid her pencil into the binder on the top.

As she followed Mr. Wynton from the office, he motioned to her desk. "Leave your pad. I want to show you something, and I won't need notes."

He walked across the outer office and held the door open for her. "Let's go for a walk."

Audrey glanced at the pile of paperwork on her desk. There were memos to type, the latest financial reports needed to be filed, and she needed to make carbon copies of the agenda for the afternoon board meeting.

Mr. Wynton beckoned for her to join him. "That will still be there when we get back." Which was precisely the problem, but she'd not go against his wishes.

He led her to the end of the corridor and down a second hallway until he stopped in front of an office at the very back of the seventh floor.

Audrey had only been this deep into Wynton's top floor a handful of times. She'd stored supplies for Wynton's annual Back-to-School Fashion Show and a Valentine's charity dance the local Rotary Club hosted in a nearby spare room.

He pushed against the door with his full weight until it opened wide enough for him to squeeze through. Once inside he stuck his head out. "Give me a minute to move some things. I don't want you falling off your heels in here."

The last thing his heart needed was him lifting and sliding boxes around. Audrey ignored his directions and eased around him into the room.

She met his irritated glance. "You know your heart's not ready for this. If I have to, I'll walk in my stocking feet and leave my shoes in the hall."

A deep sigh escaped him. "My heart's never felt better. It does a man good to stretch his muscles every once in a while."

"Not when I'm the one who's accountable to his doctor. He fussed at me for twenty straight minutes over the phone when you snuck off by yourself to go fishing last weekend."

He grunted in disgust. "He's just mad I didn't invite him."

Audrey hid a grin and focused on the chaos in the room. Stacks of unopened boxes stood in columns against the left wall, while dresses, coats, and men's trousers hung on racks pushed against the right wall. Opened wooden crates filled the center of the room, with clothes spilling over their edges, and others lying on the floor in heaps.

"It looks like a hurricane blew through here."

Mr. Wynton moved to the desk wedged into the corner of the room. He sat on the top and dangled his long legs over the edge. "Do you see anything worth salvaging for the store?"

Audrey surveyed the space and added up a quick estimation of how many thousands of dollars lay scattered about. Far too much to consider a write-off.

She shuffled her way to the nearest open crate and lifted out a filmy white blouse with a Peter Pan collar. "I saw something very similar to this in the Sears catalog last year. It's still a popular style. We could put this out in a summer fun sales promotion in May when the weather warms up." Audrey set the blouse aside and dug farther into the crate.

"There are several cotton sunsuits and sundresses in here as well. We could do a complete cross-promotion, with sunglasses, sandals, straw bags, and sun hats—even kids' swimsuits. We could use the slogan 'School's out, the sun and fun are calling.'"

She continued. "Set the display right up front near Ladies Sportswear, and bring in some of the sand buckets and shovels from Toys to get the kids excited."

"You pulled all that out of your hat just now?" Mr. Wynton pointed at her head.

Audrey smiled as more ideas swirled. She glanced around. "I could take a few items home and design several different campaigns." Audrey pointed to a crate sitting along the far wall. "Some things in there would go in a bride's trousseau. We could put those out during Bridal Week."

She shifted her attention to a clump of clothes hanging on the rack. "We have men's sportswear there, and I could come up with something for Valentine's Day and Father's Day. 'Go beyond just a tie for Dad this year.'"

She looked through the mass of merchandise before her. "I could go through those unopened boxes along the wall after work tonight, take inventory, and get it out on the floor as soon as possible, even if it's just clearance." She would find a way to sell all of this, whether in the main store or Wynton's bargain store on Latham Street.

The sound of a drawer opening called her back from her retail thoughts. She spun round to see Mr. Wynton pulling out a white box wrapped with a bright purple ribbon. He held it out to her.

"This is for you."

Audrey put the clothes back in the crate and took the box. The narrow package was heavier than she expected, and she took her time untying the bow. When she lifted the top and peered inside, she scowled. "I don't understand."

Mr. Wynton slid off the desk and lifted the wooden nameplate from within the folds of silver tissue paper. He ran his finger across the writing printed on the gold plate in front:

AUDREY PENAULT
Senior Buyer Ladies Fashions

"In less than five minutes, you've sorted this mess into at least three sales campaigns with guaranteed success. No one in this store understands retail better than you."

He cleared his throat. "Audrey, you've been my right arm through the worst period of my life." His voice trailed off.

His jaw clenched, and Audrey knew he was reliving the memories of his only child John T.'s betrayal and death, and his daughter-in-law Cissy's responsibility for the murder of his son plus some of his employees when she attempted to steal the store from him last year.

His Adam's apple bobbled as he swallowed back his emotions. "You're meant for bigger things than sitting behind a desk, answering my phone, and scribbling down my ramblings," Mr. Wynton said as he looked unwaveringly at Audrey. "That business degree hanging on the wall in your house demands it."

She went to protest, but he held up his hands. "It's done."

He tilted his head toward the door. "I've arranged for your name to be printed on the window later today. Go back to the executive suite, clean out your desk, and move in here. There's an empty box in the coat closet for that specific purpose."

A swirling fog clouded her brain until one thought pushed them away. "If I leave you today, you'll be without help."

He smiled. "Personnel is sending me a temp before noon."

There was no way on the good, green earth a new girl could catch on to all that needed to be done to keep Mr. Wynton's office running smoothly. Not just anyone could fill the position of Mr. Wynton's executive secretary.

She squared her shoulders and faced her boss. "I'll take this job on one condition."

He raised his eyebrows and crossed his arms. "Which is?"

"I train my replacement. I'm not leaving the executive office until I'm satisfied you're in capable hands. The store depends on that." She sealed her statement with a sharp nod. "Those are my terms."

Mr. Wynton rubbed his chin and stared at her a moment. "I need you in your role as a buyer today."

"Then I'll do both, until the new girl has the hang of the office."

"Audrey, Fashion Week is coming up in New York in three weeks. After that, I'm sending you to Chicago, then down to Tampa to look at what Maas Brothers is doing, and on to Burdines in Miami. You'll be going to Harrods in London, and Fashion Week in Paris later in the year. No one can do both jobs at once."

She'd never argued with or contradicted him. But this time she dug her heels in the rug and looked him straight in the eyes. "I'll find a way to make it work."

The room went quiet as they squared off against one another in a silent standoff.

"Not even you could find enough hours in the day to do both."

She flashed her twenty-four-karat smile. "Are you certain about that?"

Mr. Wynton sighed and thrust his hand toward her. "Deal."

Audrey took his hand in hers and gave him a firm shake.

A sideways grin spread across his face. "I need to have a talk with the person who taught you how to negotiate."

"I learned from the best."

"No ma'am. You came by that stubborn streak of yours naturally. Your daddy would have loved seeing his little girl put me to shame."

Her cheeks burned at his compliment. "Thank you, Mr. Wynton."

Daddy would have been proud of her. Far more than her mother. She'd seen Audrey's pursuit of a business degree and love of the retail world as a waste of time. At their last meeting, while Audrey was still in business school, her mother quipped she was wasting all her best assets on books.

A knock on the door interrupted her musing. One of the store's security officers peeked his head into the room.

"Mr. Wynton, there's a situation in Miss Vivien's salon."

Audrey's heart skipped a beat. "What's happened?"

"Lenora Baker is there, and she's had a breakdown of some sort. Her daughter Cathy was killed this morning."

Audrey looked to Mr. Wynton. He nodded and gestured toward the door. "Go. I'll lock up and meet you there."

She scooted around the officer and ran the entire way to the elevator. One thought marched through her brain over and over as she pressed the button for the fifth floor and waited.

Not again. Please God, not more murders.

Chapter 3

Gigi

Gigi Woodard played peekaboo with a sweet little girl who'd pressed her face against the candy case while her mama looked at nylon stockings in Ladies Accessories. She'd be tasked with wiping the tot's fingerprints from the display, but at least it gave her something to do.

Business had slowed down since the Christmas rush ended. Some days she yawned more times than she rang up a customer, but it still beat slinging hash and wearing those awful hairnets in Wynton's cafeteria. Being a clerk in Florida Delights and selling saltwater taffy, orange-flavored gumdrops, and other Florida-inspired treats was the best job she'd ever had.

She gave the glass a final quick swipe and returned the cleaner and cloth to the shelf behind the counter. Her boss, Mr. Spell, surveyed her work, then nodded his approval.

"I'm afraid that little girl may be our only hopes of a customer today."

Gigi gazed across the open space of Wynton's first floor. "There are a lot of shoppers today. Maybe some little kid will talk their mama into buying them some candy."

"Mamas don't buy candy this close to Valentine's Day." He released a long sigh. "It's the same every year. By the end of February, I'm back to running this department myself."

By himself? "What does that mean?"

Mr. Spell shrugged. "I always get extra help sent to me in November to get through the holiday fruit-shipping season, only to lose them by Valentine's Day when business drops."

She gripped the edge of the counter. "Do they get moved somewhere else in the store?"

"I've never seen any of them again."

Gigi resisted pounding the countertop with her fist. This couldn't be. Mr. Wynton told her last year he looked forward to seeing her rise, that she was going to be a valuable asset to the store. Why would he put her in a dead-end job after making such a promise?

She had to find Audrey and ask her if she was being fired. If anybody would know, it was Audrey.

Gigi checked her watch. "Mr. Spell, may I take an early break?"

He brought the Out to Lunch sign from under the counter and set it down by the register. "Let's both go."

Gigi hurried to retrieve her lunch bag from the employee locker room, then rushed up the back stairs to the seventh floor. The executive suite was empty when she entered.

Strange. Audrey rarely left her desk, often eating her salad lunch while she worked.

As she searched for a piece of paper, her heart nearly left her when a male voice called to her. She looked up to see Mr. Wynton in the doorway and stood ramrod straight, her cheeks burning as if she'd been caught stealing.

"I was trying to find a piece of paper to leave Audrey a note."

Her fear bubbled like a fizzy Coke as he stared at her. "Mr. Spell said I could take an early lunch."

A muscle twitched along his jaw. "Come with me."

Gigi walked to the door. Was this the big firing Mr. Spell had warned her of? Mr. Wynton might believe she wasn't worth keeping in the store if she could take time from her department to pass notes with Audrey.

She wasn't one for being patient, even if the news was bad. "Am I in trouble?"

Confusion sparked in his eyes as he motioned for her to pass into the hall. "Audrey's in Vivien's salon. There's been a. . .situation." He closed the office door behind him.

"What's going on?"

"I'm not sure, Gigi, but we'll find out together when we get there."

He took her elbow and walked her to the elevator. Mr. Wynton pressed the button for the fifth floor. When the car arrived, he waited as the operator pushed the latticed gate back, then bowed to her. "After you."

She ducked her head and scooted in. Gigi loved his formal, gentlemanly ways, but for some reason they always made her feel special and unworthy at the same time. Her mind reeled with what could possibly be so wrong in Miss Vivien's salon. If both Mr. Wynton and Audrey were needed, it must be a doozy of a problem.

The elevator jolted to a stop on the fifth floor. They stepped out to see a flock of young women standing together in a circle, all talking over one another. A dark-haired girl standing in the middle of them raised her voice and shushed the group.

"Keep by the phone today, girls. I've got to talk to Mama about all this, and I'll call y'all tonight to let you know what time to come over and hear what we've decided."

The girl in the middle narrowed her eyes and glared at Gigi and Mr. Wynton as they walked past. She gathered her friends closer and said something to them in whispered tones that caused the entire group to turn and stare.

Since she was with Mr. Wynton, Gigi bit back the hot words pushing to erupt from within. She'd seen that same you're-not-one-of-us look many times when she served certain employees in the cafeteria, and it always got her dander up.

When they reached the salon's entrance, a much older woman, puffed up like an angry rooster, barreled out the door and bumped into Gigi. She humphed as if the encounter had been all Gigi's fault, then rushed to the group of girls.

Gigi glanced over her shoulder at the group. "Poor Miss Vivien. That doesn't look good at all."

Mr. Wynton guided her into the salon with his hand at the small of her back. "No, it doesn't."

Miss Vivien sat on one of the newly added couches with her arm draped around a woman who was sobbing into her hands. She'd once told Gigi that part of her job included comforting mamas who were sad about their little babies getting married.

This mama was downright distraught. Miss Vivien seemed to be crying too.

Mr. Wynton walked to another area where Audrey and Mirette were talking. Gigi followed because she had no idea what else to do.

"Any news?" he asked in a hushed tone.

Mirette laid her hand against her cheek and shook her head. "All insanity broke loose. Merilee Bell and Mary Hadley were fussing about her dress, then Ruth Gaskin came in and blessed Vivien out because her daughter eloped last night and it was somehow Vivien's fault."

Mirette dabbed at a tear trickling from the corner of her eye. "Then Lenora Baker came in and told us Cathy was found murdered this morning. And of course, Robbi Dever was here for the entire spectacle."

Gigi whistled. "All that happened this morning?"

"Honey, all that happened before ten thirty."

Gigi stole a glance at the scene on the couch. "How's Miss Vivien?"

"She's been by Lenora's side since she came in. It's been a 'single box of tissues' crisis so far, but I'm still a bit concerned."

"I expect we'll be hearing from Merilee later," Audrey added.

Mr. Wynton nodded. "She almost bulldozed Gigi when we came in."

Gigi stretched to her full height. "Acted like it was all my fault."

Mirette smirked. "Join the club."

Mr. Wynton pulled the conversation back to the problem at hand. "Have you heard anything about what happened, Mirette?"

"Lenora said Cathy was bludgeoned to death with a silver candlestick. Her husband Joe is out of town on a business trip. Sheriff Youngblood said they're trying to get in touch with him. Miss Lottie Warner saw their front door standing open early this morning when she was out walking her dog. She went up to see if anything was amiss and found Cathy."

Gigi gasped. "Poor Miss Lottie. She's such a gentle soul. This kind of thing will just crush her."

Then a new thought hit her. "Mary Jo lives a few blocks from Miss Lottie. She's probably heard by now. Her little girls are going to be scared all over again, after what happened to them last year."

Mr. Wynton's face darkened a bit. "This city isn't ready for another round of something like this."

He stuck his hand in his coat pocket. "It appears you ladies have this under control." He turned to Audrey. "Let me know if I'm needed."

"Yes sir."

Mr. Wynton bowed to them all. "Ladies."

Gigi was the first to speak after he'd gone. "What can we do to help?"

Mirette shook her head. "Nothing. We've got a bride coming in at one to look at gowns. Until then"—she peered around Gigi to where Miss Vivien and Lenora sat—"looks like Vivien has her calmed down."

Gigi swiveled around to see them rising from the couch. Miss Vivien said something to the mother and walked over to join them.

"I'm going to drive Lenora over to her sister's. Her brother-in-law is off today, and I'll bring him back here to pick up her car." She took a quick look at her watch. "I'll be back for the one o'clock."

She patted Gigi and smiled at Audrey. "Thanks for coming up to check on me."

She went into the fitting rooms, returned with her coat and purse, and walked to the couch. "I'm ready, Lenora. If we don't get you over there quick, Glenna's going to come searching for us."

Lenora swayed as she stood, but Vivien slipped her arm though Lenora's and led her from the salon to the elevator.

"That was kind of you to come, Gigi. How did you hear about what happened?" Audrey asked once the other women were gone.

"Mr. Wynton found me in your office. I was trying to leave you a note. He told me something was wrong here in the salon and I needed to come with him."

"I love y'all, but I've had enough excitement and people for one morning. I've got to sit down and get me some quiet after all this madness." Mirette headed for the back of the salon, her message for Gigi and Audrey to leave made clear.

Audrey tilted her head toward the entrance. "Let's go."

Once they were outside the salon, Audrey pointed toward the door to the stairs. Since she was still on a break, and could use the exercise, Gigi agreed and walked ahead to hold the door open for Audrey.

"Why were you leaving me a note?" Audrey's voice bounced off the walls in the stairwell.

Gigi's cheeks grew warm. "I thought I was being fired."

"Why would you think that?"

"Mr. Spell said every year his clerks get fired by the end of February. You know I just moved into a new apartment because my other landlord died. I can't afford to live in the new place without this job."

"Mr. Spell is partly correct. Florida Delights doesn't need you anymore. But before you let your heart sink to your feet, listen to me. You're not being fired."

"Then where am I going?"

"You're being moved to a permanent position."

"Back to the cafeteria, right?" Gigi touched the edge of her scalp as she remembered the strangling grip of the hairnets smashing her blond pin curls to her head. Then the scents of meat loaf, steaming vegetables, and cleaning solution came back, making her stomach lurch.

In spite of Audrey's scolding, her heart and her hopes dove straight to her feet. She'd never be more than a waitress and was an idiot to hope for something better.

Gigi swallowed back an apple-sized lump of disappointment. No more wearing her new suits and cute hats to work. The navy-blue one with the straight skirt that she'd worn today was her favorite. She'd put two new blouses to match it on layaway a week ago.

What a waste. She'd be in the waitress uniforms again.

At least her suits wouldn't go to complete waste. Since Kenny had slipped into another mood and refused to leave the house, she'd been attending church with Mary Jo and the girls. Her suits fit right in at Levy City Baptist. At least wearing them once a week beat opening her closet every day and seeing them hanging there unused.

Audrey called her name, and Gigi snapped back to the conversation.

"You're not going back to the cafeteria. We've got something else in mind for you."

"Gift wrapping down in the basement, right?"

Audrey's lips wiggled as if she were holding back a grin. "We both know you don't have the patience or inclination to be a gift wrapper."

"What's left then? Furniture? Household Furnishings?" She paused as another thought hit her. "Please tell me it's not Housewares. I'd be terrible at the cooking demonstrations." Gigi shivered at the thought of being on display up on the fourth floor. Faking smiles as she tried to show off the latest in pots and pans, while filling the room with black smoke because she was burning everything.

"I may have worked in restaurants all my life, Audrey, but I can't even cook toast without turning it into a scorched brick."

Audrey sighed, giving the same look Mama always did when she grew tired of trying to convince her daughter life wasn't all bad. "You're not going to the fourth floor."

She stopped walking at the second-floor landing and faced Gigi. "Edie got engaged at Christmas and won't be coming back to the store. You're being moved to Cosmetics to fill that vacancy. You start next Monday."

Cosmetics was one of the most prestigious positions in all of Wynton's. Even Gigi knew much of the store's profits came from that department and Ladies Wear.

"Aren't you afraid I'll mess it up?"

"No. You will be one of our best salesgirls, and I don't want to hear anything else from you otherwise."

Audrey continued down the stairs. Her straight back and lifted chin broadcast she wouldn't hear anymore of Gigi's objections.

Gigi stood at the landing. The looks from the girls in the group outside the salon came back to her. Their silent message had been oh so easy to read.

You aren't one of us.

Two of those girls worked in Cosmetics.

Chapter 4

Mary Jo

Another clump of goose bumps rose on Mary Jo Johnson's arms as she swayed in the swing alone on her front porch. She'd bear the cold for as long as she could stand just to soak in the quiet of the night.

Tears dropped from the corners of her eyes, and she soaked them up with an embroidered linen hankie. She'd meant no harm.

The hook, as Kenny called it. If only she'd thought a little longer before she'd ordered the prosthetic arm through Wynton's. Realized how he might react. Maybe eased him into the idea rather than springing the thing on him with no warning.

Maybe, maybe, maybe. She was sick of *maybe* and tired of trying to keep everyone happy.

The loss of his arm in the construction accident last year had broken his spirit. He grieved because she was now the breadwinner for their family. In the mornings as she hurried to dress for her job as a clerk in Ladies Accessories at Wynton's, she'd see Kenny's anger flare, as if she were now working to pour salt in his wounds and taunt him rather than to keep their family afloat.

And the outright fit he'd pitched at the doctor's today, refusing to consider attending the training on how to use his artificial arm. Her cheeks still burned with shame at the words he'd spewed all through the office when he stormed out. She had to stay behind and bear the brunt of the doctor's rebuke as he told her to make Kenny move on.

She squeezed the swing's wooden armrest as her head throbbed.

Before God, her parents, and his, she'd vowed to stand by Kenny for better or worse. But Kenny had spent another day refusing to speak to her or their daughters, and she couldn't calm the fears as they raced through her mind. How much more of the worse could she take?

Her oldest daughter, Carrie Rose, opened the screen door and peeked around to meet her mother's gaze. "Mama, why are you out here?"

"You shouldn't be out of bed." Mary Jo planted her feet on the wooden planks of the porch's floor and pushed up from the swing. The old boards murmured groans into the night's silence as she made her way to the door.

Carrie Rose held the door open for her, and Mary Jo stroked her girl's silky cheek as she walked by. Her sweet seven-year-old was trying so hard to be helpful in hopes her actions would bring her daddy's fun side back.

"Penny and I heard the back door open. We were worried about you."

Mary Jo shut the front door and turned the lock. "Thanks, sweetie."

Forcing a smile she did not feel, she took her daughter by the hand. "How about I read some more of *Cinderella* to help you two fall back asleep? I'm in the mood for some happily ever after."

Both girls were slumbering by the time Cinderella left the ball and lost her shoe, so Mary Jo closed their book of fairy tales and laid it on the table. As she turned out the light, the phone rang and she rushed down the hall to the kitchen, noting the glow of the lamp in the living room. She glanced and saw Kenny stretched out on the couch, his breath coming in muffled snores. The edge of the blanket fell away from the empty sleeve of his shirt. It had been a year since he'd lost his arm in the construction accident. Scars covered the wound left behind, just as bitterness enveloped Kenny's heart and mind.

She could only pray a good night's sleep might help to bring him out of his latest mood.

Mary Jo caught the phone on the fifth ring. "Hello?" She whispered into the receiver to ensure she didn't wake the rest of her household.

"How's your day off been?" Gigi asked from the other end of the line.

Mary Jo choked back a lump of tears in her throat. "I'm so tired, Gigi."

"What's the matter? You sound terrible."

She rubbed her forehead. "Kenny hasn't spoken to me in over a week now. The girls know something's wrong, and they're trying so hard to be perfect to make Daddy happy."

"Oh Mary Jo, I'm so sorry. What put him in a dark funk this time?"

"I finally told him about my order."

Gigi went silent a moment. "Sounds like that went over like a lead balloon."

"Greg from Deliveries told me last week the prosthesis is due to come in any day now. I had to tell him I'd ordered it. I couldn't just bring it home and hand it to him."

"I guess not."

Mary Jo grabbed a wet rag from the sink and wiped away a spot of gravy that must have dripped onto the stove when she'd served supper. "The doctor told him the hospital has a program to help veterans like him learn to use prosthetic arms, but Kenny wouldn't hear of it and stormed out."

"Give him time. He'll come around."

"Hope so." Mary Jo rinsed the rag and hung it over the side of the sink. "How did things go at the store today?" She didn't much care about Wynton's at the moment but needed something else to think about.

"Wild. Did you hear about Cathy."

"Cathy who?"

"You don't know yet? Miss Lottie found Cathy Stevens dead this morning. She was murdered."

Ripples of fear shocked her heart. "At her house?"

"Yes," Gigi screeched. "Cathy's mother came into the salon after the police told her and promptly fell to pieces. Even Miss Vivien got shook up. I can't believe you haven't heard."

Mary Jo pulled a chair out and sat down at her kitchen table as a wave of dizziness overtook her. "I've been over at my parents' house most of the day. Daddy wasn't feeling well, and Mama called me to help. The only time I left was to go get the girls from school, but we went back to my parents' house. I didn't get home until after dark."

"Let me fill you in on the details then."

There was no way she could take on any more drama tonight. And the last thing she wanted to know about was a killer running rampant in town. "Please don't, Gigi. I'm too tired to hear all the gory details right now." She yawned as she spoke her last word. "What was your other big news?"

"I'll tell you at lunch tomorrow. You need to get to bed. I can hear your eyelids drooping from here." Gigi giggled at her joke.

"Thanks, Gigi. Bye."

Mary Jo rose and put the receiver back in the phone's cradle.

She sat back at the table and laid her head against the cool Formica surface. If only she could drift into a fog where no prosthetic hooks or angry husbands or murders existed.

The phone jangled again. Was there to be no peace tonight?

Mary Jo rose and answered the phone. "Gigi, whatever it is—"

"Where have you been? I've been trying to call for hours."

Her muscles tensed at the sound of her mother's voice. "I haven't been on the phone that long, Mama. A friend from the store called me."

"Can't those people leave you alone for a day?"

"This isn't like you, calling so late. Is something wrong?"

"I need you to come over here and help me with your daddy."

"Mama, it's late, the girls are in bed fast asleep. I'll run by tomorrow after I get off work."

"I need you here now. Your daddy's not able to settle down and go to sleep. I want you to come sit with him."

Mary Jo rubbed the back of her neck. "If you're worried, call Dr. Hall. He told you earlier not to hesitate if Daddy got worse."

"We don't need him here, charging good money just to pull out one of those vials of cough syrup from his bag and then pour the mess down your daddy's throat. We've got plenty left over from his visit today."

Mary Jo leaned her forehead against the wall next to where the phone hung in the kitchen. "I can't come, Mama. I have to get up early to go to work."

"If your husband would—"

She could not stand that conversation again tonight. "Please call the doctor if things get worse, Mama. Good night."

Mary Jo hung up before her mother could respond. Guilt bubbled up as she tiptoed down the hall to her room. She'd been taught her whole life to honor her father and mother, but tonight she was just too tired to take on anything else.

Once in bed, she stared at the ceiling as her brain bounced between her to-do list for the morning and the news of Cathy's death.

For better or worse. Honor thy father and mother.

Her eyes slid shut as one last Sunday school lesson came to mind: *Do not murder*.

But someone in Levy City must have forgotten to read that one.

Vivien covered her mouth as another yawn escaped her. If her count was correct, this was the fourth in the last ten minutes.

"Good grief, Vivien, you yawned so wide your head disappeared," Mirette said as she pulled pins from the gown on her dress form and pushed them back in her pincushion.

"I don't think my head hit the pillow until after one this morning."

"What in the world were you doing up that late?"

"My phone started ringing the moment I walked in my front door and didn't stop until after eleven thirty."

"Why were you so popular last night?"

Vivien walked to her desk and closed her schedule book. "First call was Merilee. She and Mary Hadley decided to take her dress to someone else to fix the problems that we don't have the talent or desire to correct."

Mirette cocked her head to the side. "Is that right?"

"Mm-hmm. I don't know why they don't fix whatever it is she's in a snit over themselves. Mary Hadley sews well."

"There isn't another seamstress in the state who'll touch that dress this close to the wedding. I wonder who she's talking to then?"

"Your guess is as good as mine."

A knock on the deliveries door in the back of the fitting room interrupted them.

"Who could that be?" Mirette made her way to the door.

"I don't know. I told everyone we were going to Cathy's funeral this afternoon." Vivien pulled her black pillbox hat from her desk drawer and smoothed out the dotted-swiss veil. The hat best matched the black crepe dress she'd picked to wear for the day.

Mirette returned with Rafe, one of Wynton's delivery men, following behind her with two boxes stacked on his dolly. "Where do you want Rafe to leave these?"

Vivien pointed to a spot beside her desk. "Put them here for now. We're not coming back after the funeral, so we'll unpack them tomorrow morning."

Rafe swiped a bead of sweat from his brown forehead and wheeled his load to the intended spot, where he set the boxes on the floor. "A couple of larger boxes are down in the loading bay. They told me y'all was leaving for the funeral, so I'll bring them up and leave them here with the others."

"Thank you, Rafe."

"Yes ma'am."

Vivien loved when Rafe made their deliveries. He'd worked with them long enough to know their routines and his way around the fitting area. And she never had to remind him to shut the storeroom door after he finished.

There was no denying he understood customer satisfaction. She'd witnessed one of the clerks next door in Better Dresses ordering him around, nitpicking about his every move as he made a delivery to her department. And through all her nonsense, he maintained an all-business composure and worked until the job was completed to the woman's satisfaction. Though she'd seen sparks of irritation flash in his dark eyes during the ordeal, he clamped his jaw tight and finished his job.

And she'd come to wonder if that was fair.

She pointed to the boxes. "Are those the dresses we ordered from Priscilla of Boston?"

Mirette craned her neck and glanced. "The mailing label says they came from Atlanta."

"Must be the gowns we ordered from Davison-Paxon." Vivien retrieved the scissors from her top desk drawer. "I wasn't expecting them until the end of the week, so that's nice they came today."

She smiled at Rafe. "Nice to have a surprise on such a sad day."

"Yes ma'am." He grabbed his dolly and wheeled it toward the back door. "I'll get them others up here soon as I can," Rafe called over his shoulder as he maneuvered out the door.

Vivien laid her black patent leather handbag next to her hat. "We shouldn't be doing this."

Mirette moved to her side. "Hard to stomach we went to the baby shower when Cathy was born, then her wedding, and now we have to go to her funeral."

The same heartbreak in Mirette's eyes ached within Vivien. "I called Glenna to check on Lenora. Dr. Hall gave strict orders she's not to go home or be alone for a few days."

Mirette laid her pincushion on the fabric cutting table. "I wish I knew something that would help."

"I offered to take them some food this week, but Glenna said the church ladies had been by and their refrigerator is stocked full of roasts and side dishes. And their deep freeze is full of casseroles. The only thing they can get into Lenora is iced tea."

Death left a hole in the heart not even the best casserole in the world could fill. "I'm going over after the funeral to sit with Lenora so Glenna can greet people coming to the house."

"I'll come with you. Between the two of us, we can give Glenna a long break."

Vivien squeezed her old friend's hand. "Thank you. Glenna sounded like she was about done in last night."

Mirette shook her head. "I can't imagine what they're going through. That family is so close they practically live in each other's houses."

How could anyone understand the death of such a sweet, beautiful girl? Not even age brought that kind of strength and wisdom.

Vivien blinked back more tears. "We'd better get going soon. I suspect the church is going to fill up fast."

Mirette walked to the storeroom and returned with a hanger for a wedding gown. "I've got to talk about something else, or I'm going to be bawling like a calf here in a minute. Who else called you last night?"

"Ruth Gaskins. Blessed me out again because Stacia eloped."

"Help me lift this gown off so I can hang it up before we leave." Mirette went and unbuttoned the bodice of the gown she'd been working on. "What did you say to Stacia anyway?"

Vivien bent over and gathered up the full tulle skirt as Mirette lifted the top of the dress. "She came in a-weeping-and-a-wailing while you went to lunch the other day. I sat her down in the mama's chair, and she proceeded to tell me that she didn't think she could stand having Martine as a mother-in-law. Howard didn't have enough backbone to stand up to her, and she didn't want her mother-in-law running her household."

Mirette pursed her lips and nodded. "Martine puts most drill sergeants to shame. The marines should recruit her."

"Be that as it may, I told Stacia that these things tend to work themselves out over time, and she and Martine could come to terms with one another once she was settled into her marriage."

Vivien sighed. "Then she tells me she never liked Howard enough to marry, just went with him because that's what her mama wanted."

She released the gown's skirt as Mirette fit the hanger into the top of the dress. "I told her I've never had a bride who didn't get cold feet, and they always thawed once they put their gown on, hooked their arm in their daddy's, and walked down the aisle to the man they loved. After that, she wiped her face, gave me a hug, and bounded out of here with her shoes."

Mirette straightened one of the gown's sleeves. "How did Stacia see that as an invitation to elope?"

Vivien buttoned the dress bodice so Mirette could hang the dress up on a rack. "I haven't a clue. Ruth pitched about four hissy fits over the phone. I cut in and said when Stacia comes back home, put her in the wedding gown, fix all the food, invite all the relatives, and have a party to celebrate her and Fred."

Mirette grinned. "What'd she say to that?"

"She hung up. If I'd known that was all it would take to get her off the phone, I would have said that at the beginning."

Vivien exhaled. Sharing the next phone call sliced through her core. "Then Bill Youngblood called to discuss what happened to Cathy."

"Do they have any idea who's responsible yet?"

"No, but he said he found something he wanted to talk to me about. Wouldn't go into details over the phone. We're supposed to meet here tomorrow after closing."

"No wonder you're so down in the mouth today." Mirette rubbed Vivien's back a moment.

She'd stayed awake far too late wondering if she could keep up with the wedding business anymore. She'd built her reputation on being able to make all her bride's wedding dreams come true. The last few days it seemed she couldn't please anyone, and everything she tried was going to pot.

Was she getting too old and losing her touch?

Vivien had no time to sit and stew over it as someone knocked on the glass of the salon's closed and locked front door. "Mirette, didn't you put up the Closed sign?"

"I did, but some folks don't read what's right in front of their noses."

Vivien walked to the front of the salon. A girl and her mother stood outside. The mother wiggled her fingers when she saw Vivien coming.

Vivien pointed to the sign. "We're closed for the afternoon."

The mother cupped her hand around her ear and scowled. Vivien undid the lock and opened the door. "We're closed for the afternoon to attend a funeral."

Both mother's and daughter's faces sagged into disappointment. "We just moved here from Tampa, and everyone told us there was no better salon around than Miss Vivien's to help plan a wedding."

Vivien glanced at her watch. "I've got a few minutes." She stepped back and ushered them into the salon. "Let's get you down in my appointment book so this doesn't happen again."

Mirette met Vivien with a we-don't-have-time-for-this gleam in her eye. Vivien countered with a yes-we-do look of her own. "This is my assistant and seamstress, Mirette."

While Mirette dipped her head in greeting, Vivien walked to the shelf where she kept the bridal guides. "I give all of my brides one of these when we start." She handed the book to the girl.

"Take this home with you. This guide has information for every step of your planning, from your dress, invitations, and flowers to your china and silver patterns, your crystal, and reception menus."

The girl opened the book and thumbed through a few pages. "Look, Mama. There's even information here about setting up my new house, and Wynton's interior decorating services."

Her mother pointed to a page. "And a list for florists, caterers, and jewelers." She met Miss Vivien's gaze. "This will be so helpful since we don't know a soul here."

Mirette cleared her throat in the background, and when Vivien turned around, her assistant held out her appointment book and a pen. Vivien turned to the first empty page, then held her pen poised over one of the empty boxes on the calendar.

"My next open appointment is on the last Monday in March."

"We'll take it," the mother said. "Thank you so much."

Once they were escorted to the elevator, Mirette met Vivien at the salon's front door with her coat, hat, and purse. "We'd better run before another one comes."

Vivien put on her coat, then settled her hat on her head. She faced Mirette. "Straight or crooked?"

Mirette reached up and readjusted the hat. "Now you don't look as though you're tilted."

"Can't have that." Vivien buttoned her coat. "I'll pull the veil down when we get to the church. I can't see through it well enough to drive."

Mirette nodded. "Good idea. I hate funerals, and I don't want to be attending yours anytime soon. I don't even want to be at my own."

"I don't know how you're going to work that one out, my friend." Vivien dug out the key to the salon's front door from her purse, then locked the door.

"I'm planning to get so old I just dry up and blow away on the breeze, like dandelion seeds."

They walked to the elevator and waited for the car to arrive at the fifth floor. "At least we've fixed it with the Lord and know where we'll both end up when we die."

A ding announced the car's arrival to the floor. Mirette motioned for Vivien to get in first. The elevator operator closed the gate behind them, then pushed the button for the first floor.

Mirette nudged Vivien with her elbow. "Promise me, you'll wait and let me go first."

There was no way she'd agree to something so morbid. "Only if I don't end up taking you out myself."

"I'll take that deal." Mirette slipped her purse to the crook of her arm and stared ahead, her eyes flickering with the old mischief Vivien knew all too well.

Gigi stood before the large mirror in the employee locker room, trying to decide if her suit jacket looked better buttoned or unbuttoned. Neither way seemed to work and it was starting to ratchet up her already-fraying nerves.

The real problem wasn't the suit but the girl in it. Why did she agree to work in Cosmetics?

"Because you'd go broke if you didn't." She chose to leave the jacket buttoned because it gave her the illusion of a smaller waistline. The other girls in the department were younger, thinner, and prettier, so she had to give herself some sort of chance.

Two of the girls she'd seen at Miss Vivien's the other day stood behind the makeup counter. They watched her walk toward the department for a moment, then one turned to the other and said something causing them both to laugh.

Gigi slowed her steps. She should have asked Audrey to walk her to Cosmetics and introduce her to these smirking cats. They would think twice about looking down on her if they knew she was friends with the most important woman in the entire store.

One of the girls, a tall redhead, scanned her from head to toe before she met Gigi's gaze. "May I help you?"

This woman's critical eye could have singled out so much in that glance. Gigi's large feet, her short, pudgy fingers, her thick wrists and ankles, or a handful of other flaws. The desire to turn around and run back to the locker room proved hard to resist.

Gigi stood straight because Mama always said that was the first step to making a good impression. "I'm Gigi Woodard. I'm supposed to come and introduce myself. I'll be starting here next week."

"Oh, you're the new girl." The brunette turned to her coworker, and they nodded in unison as if answering a silent question between them.

The brunette continued. "Jane is our manager, and she isn't here today, but we'll tell her you stopped by."

It was as if she were standing outside a fort, begging to come in, and these girls were the gatekeepers in charge of keeping unwanted folks out.

She might as well go back to Florida Delights and be bored out of her mind. "Nice meeting you both. I guess I'll see you next week."

"Sure," the brunette said before turning away to rearrange some boxes of facial cream on the shelves behind her. The redhead busied herself with dusting off the case displaying compacts.

Gigi left and headed to the cafeteria to meet Mary Jo for lunch.

When Mary Jo laid her lunch bag on the table, Gigi couldn't miss the dark circles hanging beneath her friend's eyes.

"Honey, you look terrible."

"I know." Mary Jo pulled out her chair and sat down. She pointed to the tea Gigi had gotten for her. "Thanks."

"Why are you bag-lunching today?"

"I need to pinch pennies for a while."

"What gives?"

"The prosthetic arm cost more than I realized because I forgot about tax and shipping. Then the car started making this strange noise while I was driving around yesterday and may need service soon."

"Oh my, Mary Jo." Gigi slid a cookie bar from her bag and passed it to her friend. "Lilla snuck me this from her latest batch when I walked in. She says hey."

Mary Jo mumbled her thanks and set the cookie bar aside. "What did you want to tell me?"

Gigi took a bite from her own cookie and closed her eyes as she chewed the warm, chocolaty softness. "Getting something fresh off the tray when Lilla's baking in the kitchen is the only thing I miss about working in the cafeteria." She wrapped up the remainder and put it in her bag. "I'll have to cut back on these. I'll be watching my figure a little closer from now on." Gigi patted her stomach.

Mary Jo looked up from her food. "Please tell me it's not for a man. You promised you'd wait awhile after what happened with Bobby last year."

The mention of her last romantic failure wasn't going to sink her excitement. "No. This is much better than a date."

The meeting with the two girls this morning did take a bit of shine off her news, but she couldn't hold it in any longer. "You can't say a word about this until after Monday. Promise?"

Mary Jo nodded slowly. "My brain is so tired I'll probably forget by the end of the day."

Gigi looked around to make sure no one near them was listening. "I'm being moved to Cosmetics."

"What?"

Gigi shushed her friend. "Audrey told me yesterday."

A slow smile spread across Mary Jo's face and into her eyes as she clapped her hands together. "Gigi, that's wonderful. Congratulations," she whispered.

"Can you believe it? Little-miss-hairnet with her giant feet is moving into one of the most glamorous departments in Wynton's."

"Stop saying things like that. You deserve it just as much as the next girl. Mr. Wynton wouldn't put you there if he didn't agree."

Gigi wrapped the remainders of her lunch and slid them into the bag. "You want to hear something silly?"

"What's that?"

"I'm scared to death. You of all people know how snobby some of those gals in Cosmetics can be."

Mary Jo pressed her lips in a thin line, then grimaced. "A couple of them were kind of icy and uppity when I was the perfume spritzer. Then again, Gigi, you're much tougher than I am. You'll have those girls shaking in their boots."

"They don't scare me." Sure, she could talk a good game to Mary Jo, but her first meeting this morning sure stomped on her confidence.

"I don't believe it. Look who's heading our way." Mary Jo pointed toward the cafeteria entryway.

Gigi swiveled to see Audrey coming toward them.

"I thought she swore she was never eating in the cafeteria again."

"She's not carrying any food. And boy does she look mad." Mary Jo reached for her glass of tea.

Though she looked mad as a wet hen, Audrey still walked with the grace of a dancer, a gift Gigi wished she could learn.

Her cross expression softened when she stopped at their table. "I was hoping I'd catch you two at lunch. Did you share your good news, Gigi?"

Mary Jo set her tea glass down. "Isn't it wonderful?"

Audrey nodded. "You're going to be nothing short of fantastic in that job."

"I wish she had as much confidence in herself as you do." Mary Jo answered Gigi's glare with a wink.

Audrey grabbed a nearby chair and joined them. "Just be yourself, and all the women in Levy City will be clamoring to have you help them."

Be herself. That was rich. Other than Audrey, Mary Jo, Miss Vivien, and maybe Mirette, no other woman in Levy City was willing to see her as anything but the twice-divorced, creeping-up-on-middle-age social failure she was.

Gigi glanced at the serving line in the cafeteria. Being a waitress or a server. That was the life she knew. Seemed to be the life she was destined to live, no matter how hard she tried to run away from it.

Hearing her name called brought her back. Both Audrey and Mary Jo stared as if waiting for an answer from her. "What? Did I grow horns or something?"

Audrey held out a copy of *The Levy Times Commercial* to Gigi and pointed to a story below the fold. "Have you read this yet?"

"No. I heard everything I needed to know here at the store."

Audrey pivoted to Mary Jo. "Did you see it?"

"No. Too close to home, and I don't want to scare my girls."

Audrey rolled the paper into a long, narrow tube and squeezed it with both hands. "Robbi Dever mentioned Cathy was a Wynton's bride. Three times. Not the greatest publicity, especially when we've got Bridal Week coming soon."

"Surely no one will connect what happened to this poor girl to the store." Mary Jo took a bite of her sandwich.

"Let's hope not." Audrey stood and returned her chair to its original place. "I'm sending Cathy's family flowers from the store, and I need to get the addresses from Miss Vivien."

"Is she good friends with the family?" Mary Jo asked as she cleaned up the last of her lunch and wiped the table with a napkin.

"Vivien knows Cathy's mother Lenora from Junior League. But that wouldn't matter. She and Miss Mirette keep files on all of their brides, including their family's information."

"Why does she do that?" Gigi grabbed her lunch bag.

"Her brides go on to become mamas, and she and Mirette attend baby showers and send flowers when the babies come home. She believes in giving full service in all stages of her brides' lives."

"That's amazing." Mary Jo pushed her chair back in and readied to leave.

Gigi rose too. "I've been gone longer than I should have been, though it probably doesn't matter. We haven't had any customers for days. It's been pretty boring."

Mary Jo nudged her on the arm. "But come Monday, you don't have to worry about that anymore, do you?"

Audrey tilted her head and nodded her agreement. "Valentine's Day is a week from Tuesday. You'll have girls clamoring for makeup to use on a special date with their fellas and boys hurrying in to buy their sweethearts perfume. You're going to be so busy the days will fly by."

She looked at her watch. "I've got to get back to my desk." Audrey headed to the exit, stopping only to toss the copy of the *LTC* in the trash on her way out.

"I've got to get back too. I'm covering hats, purses, and scarves until closing today. The other clerk went home sick with a headache." Mary Jo rubbed her own head as if she'd caught her coworker's ailment.

"I'll walk you out." Gigi pushed her chair under the table, and they walked side by side out of the cafeteria.

Once in the employee locker rooms, Mary Jo gave Gigi a firm hug. "I'm so proud of you. You study cosmetic trends and learn how to do them faster than anyone I know. You've got a knack for makeup. You were born to be in Cosmetics."

"Thanks."

Gigi opened her locker and placed her lunch bag inside. As she slammed the door shut, Mary Jo called a final goodbye and hurried from the room back to Women's Accessories on the main floor.

Gigi slid the neck of her combination lock through the hole in her locker's handle and clicked it shut. She caught sight of herself in the tall mirror on the wall across from the aisle where she stood.

"They're all sure you can do this. How do you think we'll do?"

She stared at her wide-eyed, silent reflection with the too-broad shoulders and special-order, large-sized shoes that cost more than her monthly apartment rent.

"Yeah, me too."

Gigi turned away. She headed back to Florida Delights to wait out the clock until she could go home.

Chapter 7

Vivien

The bride stood on one of the small platforms in the salon, rotating from side to side and cooing over the white cotton taffeta gown she wore. She stroked the ivory satin ribbons fashioned into tiny bows on each shoulder, where the cape-like silk train fastened to the gown. The V-shaped bodice hugged her waist above the long, bell-shaped skirt, making her look like the princess little girls dreamed of being one day.

"I think I love this one, Mama."

The mother's eyes misted. Sitting on her right was the bride's oldest sister, married in the prior year. She carried the air of the self-proclaimed expert as she inspected the gown to make certain every stitch, pearl, ribbon, and length of lace was perfect.

"This one is the prettiest on you so far." Her serious expression melted. As she showed her admiration by pattering her heart, the glow from the chandelier overhead flickered on her diamond engagement ring and gold wedding band.

The middle sister sat on their mother's left. A year older than the bride, she curled her lips into a sneer only a jealous sibling could muster. "I think that dress makes your hips look wide. And that train coming from your shoulder looks weird. Are you trying to be Queen Elizabeth with that thing?"

A mean-spirited satisfaction sparked in her eyes as she watched her little sister deflate.

Vivien had dealt with this situation a million times, and there wasn't a green-eyed monster born she couldn't stop in their tracks.

She positioned herself so the only face the bride would see was hers. "Would you like to try a veil on now?"

The girl nodded. "Do you think a short one would look better with this cape train, Miss Vivien?"

"I've got two different styles to try." Vivien walked to the rack where the veils were kept.

Robbi Dever sat in a chair off to the side of the bride and her family, observing and taking notes for her column. She waved Vivien over once she'd chosen the veils.

"That sister is presenting quite a sour pickle, isn't she?"

"I've got ways to sweeten her up."

Vivien held the first veil out for the bride to see. "This is a simple veil cap covered in plain white satin and embellished with tiny seed pearls around the edge." She moved the veil around so the girl could see the back. "The tulle veil flows from under this little satin bow."

Vivien straightened the hair comb on the inside and secured the veil to the bride's hair. She took a step back and allowed the girl to look at herself a moment. "What do think?"

"It's pretty."

There was no spark in the bride's eye, so this wasn't the one. "Let's put this back and try another."

She brought the second choice and held it out to the bride. "This headband style covers more of your head and frames your face."

Vivien pointed to the embellishments on the veil. "These cotton-silk pleats stand up a little higher, and these embroidered flowers all around the top have silver pearls sewn into the centers. Gives you a little more frill and sparkle than the other veil. These extra touches do make the veil a bit heavier."

The girl scowled as soon as she took a look, and Vivien removed the veil without comment. When it wasn't right, there was no use wasting time.

The problem sister snickered behind her but silenced when Vivien shot her a sideways glance.

"We got a new veil in yesterday that isn't on the floor yet. Let me go grab that one."

She returned from the storeroom, certain the new pick would be the one to make the bride smile and her mama and oldest sister cry. The problem sister was on her own to feel as she pleased, as long as she kept it to herself.

"This is a blusher veil. The headband is covered in pearls and lace and fits high on your head. These types go well with your pin curls. And the way the lace-trimmed tulle falls around your figure will show off your tiny waist."

Vivien fastened the veil to the bride's hair, then spread the soft lengths of tulle around the girl. Her eyes sparkled and her cheeks glowed with the look Vivien strove to achieve with every bride. She no longer saw herself as just a girl. She was a woman and soon to be a wife.

Vivien pulled a couple tissues for the bride, then handed her mama and big sister the box. After a moment, the problem sister snatched an extra tissue from the box and mopped her own eyes.

It was time to move away and give them a moment. Vivien ducked behind the large dressing screen camouflaging the checkout area, where she kept the sales slips, the cash register, and the point-of-sale machine she used to read customers' charge cards.

Robbi popped around the screen. "I see why you're considered the best in the business. What you did out there was masterful."

Vivien filled in the information on the sales ticket. "I love what I do, Robbi. When a bride's happy, I'm happy."

Robbi gazed at the screen. "Why do you keep the register hidden?"

"Taking the money is my least favorite part of the salon's business, and the less attention to it the better. I'd honestly do this for free if I could. But Mirette's got to eat, and I have to pay my mortgage."

She took a sales receipt book from under the tall white counter. Mirette came around the screen. "Did we find something that made everyone happy?"

Vivien held up the receipt book. "The Susanna fit the bill. That has been one of our most popular ready-made gowns."

"Even sour sister came on board?"

Vivien wiggled her fingers like a magician about to pull a rabbit from his hat. "Worked my magic on her and she came round."

Mirette pressed her lips together in a tight grin. "You gave her the 'be nice or be smitten by Miss Vivien's eye, didn't you?"

"Whatever do you mean?" Vivien winked at her assistant as she walked by.

She pulled a large white leather-bound book from a bookcase located next to the door to the fitting area. "All right ladies, time for our next step."

Vivien walked to the couch where Mama and the sisters now sat. The bride still stood before the mirror, smiling at her reflection.

"I'm not ready to take this off."

Vivien set the book on an empty spot on the couch. "I know, honey, but we have to get your measurements. Otherwise, you're going to be stumbling down that aisle because your skirt is too long. And those sleeves are hanging past your hands, so you look like you're playing dress-up instead of getting married."

She swept her hand toward the dressing rooms. "Go ahead and slip it off. Mirette's back there, and she'll help you."

The bride clapped her hands when she returned and spied the book in Vivien's hands. "Is that my bridal guide?"

"It is." Vivien opened the book to the first page. "This will help you with every decision you must make from now to the honeymoon. Mirette and I will also help you assemble your trousseau if you'd like."

It was then Vivien noticed the bride's eyes glassing over. At some point in this appointment, the excitement faded as the bride realized the volume of work ahead of her before her big day. Vivien placed the book in the bride's lap.

"This will be your best friend. There is information to help you with everything from your hope chest to your honeymoon luggage. The salon's number and my home phone number are on the front page. Mirette and I haven't encountered a bridal problem we couldn't fix, so don't hesitate to call."

The bride hugged her guide to her chest. "Thank you, Miss Vivien."

The family rose from the couch. "At least we know who our caterers will be," the mother said as she grabbed her coat from the nearby coat-rack. "We're using Cameron's again."

Vivien clasped her hands behind her back. "As you'll see in the guide, we're no longer working with Cameron's."

"Really? We loved working with them."

"Old Mr. Cameron became ill in July last year, and his son took over. Several of our brides have said young Mr. Cameron is very difficult to work with and the food wasn't worth what they paid. We have very high standards, so we had to take them out."

The bride's mother buttoned up her coat. "I had no idea." She pointed to the guide. "We'll choose another tonight. Catering has to be one of our earliest decisions. They book up lightning fast."

The bride fastened the belt of her own coat. "Mama, we have a year."

"And that's just barely enough time." Mama motioned for her brood to head for the salon's front door. "We'll talk about it in the car."

All but the problem sister waved back at Vivien before exiting.

When they were gone, Robbi pointed to the shelf where the guides were kept. "That is one important book. I'm betting Cameron's isn't going to be happy they've been thrown out."

"I didn't throw them out. Old Mr. Cameron and I had a long chat, and he agreed his son wasn't keeping up with the quality."

Robbi scribbled on a page in her notebook. "You have to maintain standards." She flipped the page closed. "I've got to rush to another gig, but thanks so much for letting me come in today. I'll call when I'd like to come again."

"Anytime, Robbi."

Robbi dropped her notebook in her purse and hurried out.

Vivien joined Mirette in the fitting area. "Did you get the skirt of Julie Morrow's gown hemmed today?"

Mirette flexed her fingers, but they were too stiff to bend. "I'm about three-quarters of the way done. Got a cramp in my fingers and had to stop for a while."

Their busiest season was beginning, and orders were piling up. Mirette hadn't lost her artistic touch, but she was slowing down, causing concern over whether she could keep up the needed pace alone anymore. Vivien weighed whether finishing gowns on her old sewing machine at home would alleviate some of the pressure. But she wasn't as quick as she used to be either.

She'd thought of asking Mary Jo for help, but she had an overflowing plate right now and couldn't take on another thing. A quick solution hadn't presented itself yet, so she'd left it with the Lord and hoped for a speedy resolution.

A male voice called her name. Vivien turned, drew in a deep breath, and then walked out to the salon floor. She found Mirette and the sheriff looking at the shelf where she kept the guides.

"Hello, Bill."

He switched his hat from one hand to the other. "Vivien, I'm sorry for having to call you so late the other night and for coming up here when I know you and Mirette are busy."

"You said you found something at Cathy's house you wanted to show me?"

He dropped his gaze a moment. "I wanted you to know first before it comes out in Robbi Dever's column tomorrow morning. She's been snooping around all week, asking my deputies, Cathy's neighbors, and whoever else she can find for news. We've been working hard to keep the details quiet, but I think one of the neighbors may have spilled too much."

He screwed his mouth into a look of disgust. "I wanted y'all to hear the worst of it from me first."

She crossed her arms. "I'm ready."

He paused before going on. "Excuse me for what I'm about to say in front of you and Mirette, but y'all need to understand."

Mirette scowled. "Quit hemming and hawing, Bill."

"Cathy was bludgeoned to death with a silver candelabra like the ones all the brides get as wedding gifts. When Miss Lottie found Cathy, she was dressed in her wedding gown. The label with your name on it had been torn out and laid across her chest."

Vivien and Mirette gripped each other around the waist and tried to support one another, but they still swayed like a pine tree bending to the force of a hurricane's winds.

Chapter 8

Audrey

Audrey sat at her desk, tapping her pencil's eraser against a folded copy of the latest *LTC*. With each strike her temper rose like the mercury in August.

She dropped her pencil into the container before she might have hit it so hard that it would have splintered all over her desk. Once again she unfolded the newspaper and reread the headline of Robbi's column below the fold: Bride's Death Ends Happily Ever After.

A voice pulled her attention away. "Hello?"

Audrey swiveled around in her chair to see a girl peeking her head into the executive suite. Her wide blue eyes surveyed the room.

She refolded the *LTC* and rose. "May I help you?"

The young lady walked into the room. Her brown hair was pulled back in a ponytail that swayed in rhythm with her steps. "Gosh, that's a beautiful suit. The emerald-green shade is just gorgeous. And the beige trim around your collar and cuffs makes it look so smart and sophisticated."

She held out a stack of paperwork. "Personnel sent me. I'm supposed to meet with Audrey Penault."

"I'm Audrey Penault." She spoke her name slowly, to ensure this girl heard the preferred French pronunciation of her last name. Audrey read over the paperwork. "Nice to meet you, Elizabeth Farris. You're new to Wynton's, aren't you?"

"Yes ma'am, I started last week. But I'm just Libby Farris. I never use my given name." She wrinkled her nose. "It's too stuffy."

While being called "ma'am" by the much younger girl pricked the ego a bit, the girl possessed a measure of poise and self-confidence necessary for the secretary role. The last seven girls sent in for the job all begged to be sent to another position after spending a day following Audrey around. "I was told you'd be here at nine this morning. It's after ten."

"Mr. Janess told me to come up a few minutes ago."

Audrey tapped the paperwork against her thigh. "You didn't know you were being sent up here until then?"

Libby shrugged one shoulder, then shook her head.

When the reality of the situation became clear, Audrey sat on the edge of her desk. "You aren't the first girl he picked to come here, are you?"

Libby's ponytail swayed again as she shook her head. "No ma'am."

"How many others were approached before you?"

"Nine."

Audrey pressed her lips together to keep from smiling. Points to Libby for having the gumption to come up and try.

She motioned for the girl to follow her to the sitting area in the office. It was time to see if she'd measure up to the job.

After settling her into a chair, Audrey retrieved her pen and steno pad to take notes to share with Mr. Wynton. She sat next to Libby and opened her pad to a fresh page.

"You noted on your forms that you type forty-five words per minute?"

Libby nodded. "I was one of the top students in my typing classes all through high school."

Audrey's hand flew across the page as she wrote the information in her neat shorthand.

"Golly, Miss Penault, you take dictation fast."

"How's your shorthand?"

Libby bobbed her head from side to side. "Fifty to sixty words per minute. Maybe."

This didn't bode well as Audrey made another note. Business stenographers needed to produce transcriptions of 100 to 120 words per minute. She herself averaged above 140, sometimes pushed higher when Mr. Wynton got wound up and spoke a mile a minute.

Audrey read over the forms again. Libby had been out of high school for a couple of years. She'd taken a correspondence course in secretarial work but held no jobs before coming to Wynton's.

Libby squirmed in the chair.

Audrey rose. This girl was underqualified, too young, and just not the right person. But she couldn't toss her out like an old shoe without giving her a fair chance either. "Let's do a typing test."

Once she had Libby settled at her typewriter, Audrey moved behind her and raised the chair up to a more suitable height.

Libby wiggled her fingers for a second, then held them above the keys. "I'm ready."

Audrey pulled a short memo she'd drafted earlier in the morning and set it next to Libby. "When I say go, I want you to type as much of this as you can in one minute. Ready?"

As Libby waited for the signal, Audrey couldn't miss how the girl's fingers shook as she held them poised above the keyboard.

"Go."

The typewriter's keys clacked as Audrey kept time on her wristwatch. As soon as the minute was up, she touched Libby's shoulder. "Stop."

Libby turned the knob and released her work from the typewriter's cradle, then handed the paper over to Audrey. "I made more mistakes than usual. I'm just so nervous."

"I'll keep that in mind." Audrey glanced over the paper. Quick estimation showed Libby's reported words-per-minute average was off by several words.

Audrey laid the typing aside, then got an unused steno notebook and handed it to Libby. "Let's do some dictation. That is a large part of my job."

Libby's dictation went no better. After a few sentences, it was clear she struggled with even simple sentences and would be lost with the more complicated directions Mr. Wynton often gave. Her knowledge of shorthand had some gaps, as she used incorrect symbols for some words and seemed to have mixed a few together in a statement Audrey couldn't decipher.

A wave of red crept up Libby's neck. Her ponytail no longer danced, but hung still as the girl dipped her chin and stared at her lap. The last thing Audrey wanted was to make the girl feel a failure.

She opened her desk drawer and pulled out a hankie, but Libby waved it away. "I don't know what got into me, Miss Penault. I'm really much better than this."

"These kinds of tests are always nerve racking, aren't they?"

"I didn't get the job, did I?"

At this moment, being softhearted like Mary Jo or experienced with crying girls like Miss Vivien would have been handy skills. Audrey didn't want to break the girl's spirit, but she had to be honest.

She paused, searching for the best way to say what must come next.

"Well, hello."

She jumped a bit as Mr. Wynton's deep voice sounded behind her. Audrey turned as he walked in the door. "You're back early."

He shifted his overcoat to his left arm, then held out his right hand to Libby. "I'm Mr. Wynton."

Libby shot a wide-eyed look to Audrey, who motioned for her to shake his hand. When she did, Mr. Wynton gave her trembling hand a hearty pump.

"And you are?" he asked as she pulled her hand back.

She again looked to Audrey but remained silent.

"Mr. Wynton, this is Libby Farris."

He smiled. "Nice to meet you. I know Audrey never allows just anyone to sit at her desk, so you must be the new candidate for her job."

Libby hung her head. "No sir, I don't think so."

Audrey scrambled to think of something kind to bolster Libby's spirit, but nothing worth saying came to mind.

Then Mr. Wynton spoke up. "That's nonsense."

Libby lifted her head and stared at him. "What?"

Mr. Wynton clasped his hands under his coat. "If you really want this job, you've got time to work for it. And I've got a feeling you'll do whatever you set your mind to."

The corners of Libby's mouth lifted, and she sprang from Audrey's chair so fast she sent it sailing backward. "I do want it."

"Good. I'd like you to come up every day for the next few weeks and follow Audrey around so you can learn her job."

Audrey's mouth fell open as Libby rushed around the edge of the desk and scurried to hug Mr. Wynton. "Thank you, Mr. Wynton."

She ran back to Audrey and locked her in a tight embrace around the waist. "You too, Miss Penault." She turned and hurried to the door. "See you in the morning, Miss Penault. And I'll be here at nine. Sharp."

Libby bounded out the door of the executive office with her ponytail swinging so hard it rotated like a plane's propeller.

Audrey swirled to face Mr. Wynton. "She is not capable of doing my job."

"I see a ton of gumption in that girl. She had the guts to come up here and face you, didn't she?"

"Yes sir. But—"

"She's young and obviously admires you, Audrey. She'll listen and learn from you. And she's not afraid of you." He grinned and headed to his office door, stopping for a moment as he turned back to face her. "Yet."

"But she can't type. And her dictation is terrible. She won't be able to get more than half of what you say."

He reached for the doorknob. "I ramble too much anyway. As long as she gets the highlights, she's fine."

He opened the door, then turned back to Audrey. "We need new blood up here on the executive floor. You and I aren't going to last forever, and we need to train up the next generation."

Mr. Wynton pointed toward the outer office door. "That girl is the future of Wynton's, Audrey. No one is better equipped to build Wynton's future than you."

He walked in and shut the door. Audrey went to her desk and grabbed the copy of the *LTC*. She glanced at the headline again, and heat traveled up her neck, warming her ears to the point she wouldn't be a bit surprised if steam started shooting from them.

She walked into Mr. Wynton's office holding the paper open for him. "This was in today's *LTC*." She pointed to the story below the fold.

He hung his coat in the closet and pushed the door shut. "What does it say?" He walked to his desk and sat down.

Audrey sat in her usual chair across the desk from him and read aloud: "'Bride's Death Ends Happily Ever After.' Then there was a lot of nothing about Cathy being homecoming queen in high school, marrying just a little over a year ago, and that Robbi was going to keep digging until she found all the truth about the murder. She made certain to mention her gown had Miss Vivien's label on it. And that the murder weapon came from Wynton's."

She crumpled the paper in her hands. "Robbi Dever's trying to tie Cathy Stevens' murder to the store. What should we do?"

Mr. Wynton leaned back in his chair and rubbed his chin before he spoke. "Right now, we do nothing." He looked her straight in the eyes. "And I do mean *we*."

He tapped the chair arm. "Robbi Dever is trying to build her column. We're a big name, able to grab her some quick attention. When all the fervor dies down, she'll move on to some other scandal, rake some other big name into her column, and we'll get back to business as usual."

"But don't you think—"

"The last time you got mixed up in something like this, you landed yourself in jail and I ended up in the hospital getting my stomach pumped."

He paused and the fire flashing in his eyes softened. "I don't want to put Cathy's family through any more sorrow than they already have by turning her death into fodder for a public feud with the *LTC*. For now, we keep our eyes on this. Nothing more."

Audrey flinched. In all her years of knowing him, he'd never spoken to her in so sharp a tone. "Yes sir."

She wouldn't defy him and go after Robbi publicly, but her mind wasn't going to stop churning through ideas to ward off the worst either. Her job responsibilities may have changed, but her pledge to protect Wynton's hadn't.

She would never allow anyone to bring harm to Wynton's without a fight.

Vivien shifted in the bucket chair reserved for mamas in the fitting area. Even with Sheriff Youngblood's warning the day before, listening to Mirette read Robbi's column out loud still wound her nerves into knots. Robbi left none of the horrid details out, including Vivien's label and the silver candelabra being part of the murder scene. And that was just in the first two paragraphs. The story went on to cover the entire bottom of the page, mixing tiny details with Robbi's personal editorial on how awful the entire situation was.

Mirette folded the paper into a square and tossed it into the nearby garbage can. "I see why Bill wanted to warn us first."

Vivien rose and pulled her charcoal-gray jacket into place. "I hate that Cathy's family has their tragedy spread before the entire city. It's got to be breaking their hearts."

She caught a glimpse of her reflection in the tri-paneled fitting mirrors. "If these circles under my eyes get any darker, I'll have to use my liquid paper to hide them instead of my typing mistakes."

Mirette waved her worries off. "Just pat a little more powder under there and you'll look fine."

She stood back and gave Vivien a once-over. "You look so smart in that suit no one will notice your tired eyes." Mirette adjusted the double-strand pearl choker around Vivien's neck, laying it above the neckline of Vivien's white silk chiffon blouse. "There. All put together."

"This is one of Marionne Leslie's new line for Wynton's." Vivien fastened the gold buttons down the front. "I loved how these resemble a woven rope. She always puts such nice little touches on her clothes."

Vivien pointed to the base of her midsection. "And her peplums at the bottom of her suit jackets hang in just the right spot to smooth a girl out around her hips. I can't wait to see what else she designs for the Wynton's collection."

"Is that the one that came with the matching swing-style overcoat?"

Vivien nodded. "The lining of the coat matches the lining of the jacket." She folded up the hem of the suit's jacket, exposing a white acetate lining decorated with a dark gray coat of arms. "The overcoat was the perfect weight for the raw, wet rain this morning."

"It was cold this morning. I fixed myself an extra cup of coffee just to warm my hands while I waited for you to come pick me up. My fingers are still stiff from the cold." Mirette balled her fists, then released them.

Vivien noticed it took Mirette's hands a little longer than usual to work through the move. The cold must have her arthritis acting up again.

It seemed almost disrespectful to think and talk of such everyday things like cold weather and arthritis when Cathy had been murdered three days ago. The sight of Lenora's ghost-gray face when she walked into the salon dredged up memories of another funeral long ago that Vivien had worked hard to forget.

"I hope Bill and his boys figure out who killed Cathy and put them away for a long time."

Vivien pointed to the copy of the *LTC* Mirette had thrown away. "If Robbi's stories help solve this, I can take a little negative publicity in front of my neighbors."

"When is the first appointment today?"

"Not until ten. You'll have time to work on the skirt of Ettie Vaughn's gown, which we should have finished by next week's fitting."

"Next week? I thought her fitting was in two weeks."

"No, she's coming in next Wednesday." Vivien flipped the page in her scheduling book. "Her appointment is at two."

Mirette rose slowly from her chair, taking extra time to unfold from her middle up. "Guess I'd better get busy then."

Yes, she needed to get busy. They had two other gowns needing alterations to be finished by the end of the week and then had to start on another bride's custom-made gown.

For the first time since they had started the salon, Mirette had fallen behind, and Vivien worried they might not meet the tight deadlines their wedding schedule demanded.

As Mirette headed toward the storeroom to retrieve the gown, a knock sounded on the salon's back door.

"Is Robbi coming in today?"

Vivien shook her head. "She comes in the front door."

The knock sounded again, and Mirette stopped in her tracks. "Do you think it's Bill? Maybe they caught the killer and he wants to let us know."

"That would be wonderful, but why would he come to the back door?" Vivien opened the door.

A young woman stood in the hall, grasping a large woven black bag with faded Bakelite handles in her brown hands. Her black hair was curled in a fashionable bob. She squared her shoulders and directed her dark eyes straight to Vivien.

"Are you Miss Vivien?"

"I am."

The women pointed to herself. "I'm Immogene Colten. Lilla down in the cafeteria is my sister-in-law, and she said to come see y'all. Rafe snuck me up here on the freight elevator so I could talk to you."

Mirette joined Vivien at the door. "What about?"

Immogene slid her gaze to Mirette, then back to Vivien. "Mrs. Bell tried to hire me to fix her daughter's wedding dress. But I flat out told her no. I'm not touching a dress made by y'all. She offered to pay me, but there isn't enough money to make me step on you two ladies' toes."

This must be the woman Merilee had bragged of on the phone the other night. "You must be quite talented if Merilee was willing to hire you to fix Mary Hadley's wedding gown."

Immogene shifted her bag to the crook of her arm. "I make clothes for several of the ladies around Levy City. I do suits, shirts, dresses for them and their little girls. Their husbands too."

She tipped her chin. "I made most of the gowns the ladies wore to the New Year's Eve ball here last year. Levy City girls' prom gowns too. They buy their fabric and patterns here at Wynton's, then bring them to me, or I make up one of my own."

The bulging sides of her bag stoked Vivien's curiosity. "May I ask what you have in there?"

Immogene spread the handles wide across her arm. She pulled a filmy pink fabric from within and shook out the wrinkles caused by being folded in her bag.

She laid the piece across her arm. "This is a sample of what I can do."

Immogene pointed to three rows of small rosettes made of chiffon and velvet, embellished with tiny silver sequins in the middle. Vivien and Mirette leaned in for a closer look.

There was no denying the talent behind Immogene's work. Rosettes were not a simple thing to make, and the folded petals of her creations rivaled the beauty of the real thing.

Immogene pulled out a piece of white cotton fabric smocked and embroidered with delicate blue and yellow flowers atop curvy green stems. Tiny black-and-yellow bees sat on the stems' leaves. "I can smock anything from baby clothes, little girls' Easter dresses, to lingerie for a trousseau."

She pulled a length of ivory satin from the bag and pointed to a section. "This is my other embroidery work. I can do leaves, flowers." She moved her hand to another spot. "This is a bird. I can do several different versions of this, big or small, on any type of fabric. Don't matter."

Mirette voiced her admiration in a whispered, "Well now, that's something else," echoing Vivien's silent opinion.

She'd worried about keeping up, and it seemed the Lord had provided them another seamstress with gifted hands and imagination. "Are you here looking for a job, Immogene?"

"Yes ma'am."

Vivien stood straight and looked at Mirette, then back to Immogene. "We don't normally hire out to other seamstresses. We do all our work here in the salon."

Immogene folded her pieces back in her bag. She met Vivien's eyes. "If you hire me, I promise you I can make anything you want. I do good work, I'm fast, and I'll always be on time. Lots of girls will be having weddings soon, and I know y'all have a lot to do. I can take some of it off your hands."

The clanking sounds of the freight elevator stopping on the floor echoed through the hallway. Immogene closed her bag as she stole a quick look down the hallway.

Unless they worked at Wynton's, Coloreds weren't allowed in the store without a note from a white employer. "You know I gotta leave before somebody sees me, or Rafe will get fired for sneaking me up here. But I need to know if you'll hire me before I leave."

"I'd like to talk with Mirette about it first."

"When you make your decision, you tell Lilla."

The sound of the elevator's doors opening echoed down the hallway.

"Thank you for talking with me." Immogene dipped her head once, then hurried down the hallway toward the freight elevator.

Vivien shut the door. "She is a talented seamstress."

"That she is." Mirette blew a whistling breath through her lips. "What a start to the day. I feel like I've been spinning on a merry-go-round upside down. I didn't drink enough coffee this morning to handle all this excitement."

Vivien headed out to the salon's sales floor. "Guess you can calm yourself while you finish sewing up Ettie's gown."

Mirette bowed at her waist, sweeping her hands out from her side. "Yes, your majesty." She bore a wide grin when she straightened. "Your service is my pleasure."

Vivien put her palms together, as if in prayer. "Let's hope nothing worse than Robbi Dever's columns happen today."

"Don't say that because worse will find a way to show up." Mirette walked into the storeroom to retrieve Ettie's unfinished gown.

The phone rang just as Vivien stepped onto the sales floor. As soon as she picked up the receiver, Robbi Dever's voice blasted back at her. "Vivien, we need to schedule a formal interview for my piece in the *LTC*."

"Robbi, we've got a very busy week ahead. I don't have time—"

"Give me a call, and I'll come over to your house to talk. That would probably work better anyway. We could relax and gab without all those interruptions in the salon."

She didn't have time to talk or be pressured into an interview. And after the piece in the *LTC*, she wasn't sure having her words pasted into details of the murder was the best idea. "I'll have to get back with you, Robbi."

"Fine. But if you don't call me back, I'll show up on your doorstep." She cackled into the phone before hanging up.

"Who was that?" Mirette called from the fitting room.

Vivien set the receiver back into the cradle. "Robbi. She wants to do a formal, sit-down interview now."

Mirette stuck her head around the door. "Good. And what's all that watching and scribbling in her notebook about? The *LTC* isn't big enough to need that much information. Makes me feel like I'm living in a fishbowl and she's a hungry cat."

Vivien laughed. "You should be used to it. We live in a Southern city. That is the epitome of being in a goldfish bowl."

Chapter 10

Gigi

Gigi stood gritting her teeth as she waited for two girls from Infants and Toddlers to stop yapping about a cake recipe and get out of the way of the locker-room mirror. Today was her first day in Cosmetics, and she had to make sure her own makeup looked right.

She couldn't blame the knots in her stomach on the extra-strength elastic in her new girdle. As she dressed this morning, yanking and pulling the fabric around her so she could connect the ten hook-and-eye fasteners, she worried her cornflakes might come back up.

The women kept yakking until one noticed her glaring at them. "I'm so sorry." She giggled as they moved to the side and made a spot for her.

A quick check rendered all was well on her outside. She grabbed her purse and hurried to clock in and report to her new assignment.

When she arrived in Cosmetics, a tall woman with jet-black hair styled into a smooth pageboy with tight curls around the bottom met her.

"I'm Jane Mitchell. You must be Gigi."

Gigi marveled at how precisely Jane's lipstick had been applied. The red shade complemented her royal-blue suit-dress. She wore a pearl-and-gold stickpin shaped like a tulip on the sailor-style collar of her dress. Her matching teardrop earrings danced below her ears whenever she moved her head.

Jane stepped forward and squinted as she stared at Gigi's face. "You need to work on using a bit less eye shadow, but you know how to match the right color with an outfit. Your eyeliner application is a little heavy."

Just what she needed, a boss with a watchful gaze that missed no flaws.

Jane circled Gigi once, then took Gigi's chin in hand and turned her face side to side. "Good use of blush and face powder."

She released her hold and stepped back. If she weren't such an elegant lady, Gigi wouldn't have been surprised if Jane kicked her shoes like men did to tires when mulling over buying a used car.

Gigi wished she'd grabbed something other than her red plaid vest and navy skirt from her closet this morning as Jane scanned her from head to toe.

"You're approachable."

"Is that good?"

"Cosmetics is one of Wynton's top two departments, and we must always be pleasant, helpful, charming, and able to assist our customers. And I prefer you wear a suit when you're on the sales floor."

Jane stared at her as if awaiting a response. Gigi hurried to comply. "Yes ma'am. I have a suit. Two suits actually."

"Only two? I guess that will have to do." Jane swept her hand toward the cases where the merchandise was kept. "You'll start out as a perfume spritzer. When you've proven you're ready, you'll move to a counter. You're lucky we're so shorthanded. We take whomever we can get right now. Follow me."

Gigi tried to overlook Jane's quip hinting at her being a second-rate employee as she complied.

Jane walked with quick staccato steps and stopped before a case filled with a variety of products. "You'll need to familiarize yourself with all the brands we carry." She moved behind the counter and slid open a glass door.

"Childress Drugs around the corner carries the lower-priced products you're probably more familiar with like Woodbury facial creams, Cashmere Bouquet talc and bath powders, or Cutex nail products."

She ran her hands across merchandise lined up in the case. "Here at Wynton's, we carry the more luxurious brands. Our customers want Estée Lauder, Revlon, Helena Rubinstein, and Charles of the Ritz."

Jane slid the door closed and moved on to the next case. "Here we keep our line of Max Factor, Elizabeth Arden, and Dubarry products. You'll need to be an expert on all of them."

She moved to another case. "We keep all our eyebrow brushes, powder, and lipstick compacts in here, as well as our foundations, facial powders, mascara, and lipsticks. You'll need to memorize all the shades, how to choose the correct one according to a customer's complexion, and how to demonstrate their usage. You can do that, yes?"

She tapped a nail painted with the same shade as her lipstick on the glass case counter. Jane wore the same expression Gigi's high school algebra teacher did when waiting for her to give an answer.

Algebra never once made sense to her. Makeup she understood. "Yes ma'am."

Jane's lips quivered as if she were holding back skeptical laughter. A we-shall-see expression sparked in her eyes, which set Gigi's determination to prove her wrong to a boiling point. "Very good, Miss Woodard. There are two things that you must remember." Jane looked her straight in the eyes. "This is very important, Gigi."

"Yes ma'am."

Jane went on. "First, being one of Wynton's top two most profitable departments means our clerks must meet the quotas. There are no excuses for coming up short. None. Do I make myself clear?"

"Yes ma'am."

"Second, we are a very close-knit family here in Cosmetics. If a girl can't find her place and get along with everyone, she's moved elsewhere or terminated. Understood?"

Gigi's resolve to succeed wilted like a week-old carnation. "Yes ma'am."

She gazed at the other girls around the department. They were prom queen and belle-of-the-ball types, with their hair pulled back in chic ponytails or Italian cuts with perfect pin curls. One wore her hair short in the same pixie Audrey Hepburn had.

She was ten years older, with a lot more mileage from two divorces and dumb choices. The other clerks dressed better than her, charm seemed to pour out of them, and they carried themselves with a classy air she didn't possess.

How could she fit in with girls like that?

Jane snapped her fingers near Gigi's ear, bringing her mind back to the moment.

She held out a decanter of perfume. "This is our scent of the day. Ready to make Levy City's ladies feel a little more exotic today, Gigi?"

Gigi read the label on the decanter. *Shalimar.*

Shalimar always had some of the most elegant ads in the magazines she'd gotten from Audrey. She sprayed a small dab on her left wrist, then rubbed the other over it, releasing the spicy citrus, vanilla, and flowery scent.

She waved her arm around her nose and breathed in the fragrance. "This is dreamy."

Jane's stern look softened. "Make our ladies love this scent on the spot, just like you did."

"Yes ma'am. I'll try."

Jane shook her head. "We don't try in Cosmetics, Gigi. We perform."

Jane showed her where she should stand and then returned to the counter at the other end of the department.

There was no time to worry over Jane's hint that she wasn't up to their normal standards or whether she'd ever make her quotas. An elderly woman headed her way. Gigi met her gaze. "Would you like a spritz of Shalimar? It will bring a breath of elegance to your day."

The women walked closer and then held out her wrist, and Gigi gave her a quick spray.

"That's lovely."

"This is our scent of the day." Gigi motioned to where Jane now stood at the perfume counter. "If you go to that nice lady waiting over there, she can help you take this lovely scent home with you. Make sure you tell her Gigi sent you."

"It's nice, but not today." The woman made her way down the aisle away from Cosmetics.

Gigi didn't know what to do next, so she spouted off the first thing that popped into her head. "Have a nice day, Ma'am. Enjoy shopping at Wynton's."

One of the girls at the perfume counter shook her head and then turned to another clerk and said something that made her laugh.

The pit of Gigi's stomach soured. None of these clerks, including Jane, believed she could do this job. She was too different from them, not loaded with charm and sophistication.

But she knew someone who could teach her that stuff.

And for the first time in her life, she was itching to learn.

Chapter 11

Mary Jo

Mary Jo turned the volume of Kenny's transistor radio up as she filled the sink with hot water to wash the supper dishes. She added a squirt of Joy and waited as the lemony-scented bubbles swelled above the water.

She did the dishes alone now. Kenny had slipped into the darkest mood she'd seen since the accident. He spent days on the couch, laying with his arm covering his eyes. The few times he did rise, he'd walk to the backyard, sit in one of the metal patio chairs, and do nothing but stare at the back fence.

Carrie Rose and Penny were tucked in bed, but she still heard their soft whispers and giggles floating down the hallway. Hopefully they'd float off to sweet dreams on those giggles—which was more than she could hope for.

She'd finish the dishes alone. Sleep alone. Raise their girls alone.

Dampness on her chenille slippers brought her back. A mountain of white froth towered above the faucet as water streamed over the sink's lip and down the cabinet fronts.

"Wake up Mary Jo, before you flood the whole house." She turned off the faucet, then grabbed a dish towel to mop up her mess as the last strains of Nat King Cole's velvety rendition of "Unforgettable" faded and a new voice blasted through the radio.

"Hello, Levy City. This is Robbi Dever on WZLC, and welcome to our new segment, *The Fashion Festival*, where we talk about what's news in the fashion world."

She couldn't care less about the newest trends. All the extra money she had managed to put aside before the final cost of Kenny's artificial arm came in was now stretched like a rubber band. There was no room to think of anything beyond doctor bills, food, rent, and keeping up with the needs of two girls growing faster than the dog fennel along the back fence.

And after what she wrote about Miss Vivien in the paper, Robbi Dever was the last person Mary Jo wanted to listen to.

The amazing part about Robbi's voice was how it came through the radio blaring like a car's horn. "Let's talk about what's new for spring and needs to be in your closet. First thing—"

The phone rang, and since it was the usual time for Gigi to call for a chat, Mary Jo clicked off the radio.

When she answered, Gigi wasn't waiting on the other end of the line.

"Hey, hon, it's Vivien. How are you? I haven't seen you in a bit."

Mary Jo stretched the phone cord and balanced the phone in the crook of her neck as she returned to cleaning her dishes. "Not too bad."

"Now we both know better, don't we?"

Mary Jo's cheeks warmed, and she wanted to hang up the phone and go crawl under her blankets and hide. Had Gigi blabbed to the whole town about her soured home life?

"Yes ma'am." She rinsed the last glass and set it in the drainer.

"Gigi says you've been living with the silent treatment from Kenny?"

Was there anything Gigi hadn't told Miss Vivien about her personal business? "Yes ma'am." Mary Jo wiped the last plate dry and draped the dish towel over the oven handle to dry overnight.

"You know, I went through something similar when my husband Carter came back from the war."

"You did?"

"He went for days without even acknowledging I was alive. He'd sit in his old easy chair in our living room and stare out at nothing. Didn't matter how hard the kids or I tried to get him to talk, he wouldn't even look at us."

"What did you do?"

"I hugged my kids more often so they knew they were loved, and kept doing what I had to do."

"How long did it take for him to come out of it?"

There was a long pause at the other end of the line before Miss Vivien answered. "He never really did. He died a few months later."

She'd never thought of anything like that happening to Kenny. No matter how mad she might be at him, she didn't want to lose him. "I'm so sorry, Miss Vivien."

"I moved past the tough stuff. You will too. For your kids and Kenny. Right now, you have to be the strong one."

The same words the doctor told her over and over. Hearing them from a friend didn't make them any less hard on her heart. "Yes ma'am."

"You have to be the one with the iron spine right now."

"I'm so tired, Miss Vivien."

"I know. No matter how long you sleep, you wake up exhausted. Every bit of energy you can muster gets sapped out of you before noon, and you still have to face the afternoon and evening. Everyone around you is demanding something from you and never asking what you need. Am I right?"

Hearing her feelings voiced out loud made her feel a little less alone. "Yes ma'am."

"And Gigi tells me your daddy is doing poorly, and your mama is calling for help all the time."

"She is."

"You have every reason to be worn out, Mary Jo. You'll make it to the other side of all this hard stuff, and then you can rest."

But what if she didn't want to get through it?

"May I confess something to you, Miss Vivien?"

"Go right ahead."

Mary Jo traced her finger along the curlicue pattern on the Formica tabletop. She was ashamed to admit what she was about to tell Miss Vivien. But if she didn't, she feared her head or her heart were going to shatter from the pain of it.

"Sometimes when I'm driving to the store after dropping the girls off at school, I play around with the idea to keep driving. Maybe find a new place to live where no one wants something from me."

The dam holding back her emotions burst and she sobbed softly into the phone. "I wasn't raised to be so selfish. I'm a mama and a wife. I must live up to my responsibilities. And I love my girls and Kenny so much. But I'm just so tired of all this."

Mary Jo set the phone down and reached for the damp dish towel and mopped her tears. When she was able to speak again, she picked up the receiver.

"I'm sorry. I just had to bawl a minute."

"You listen to me, Mary Jo Johnson. Every mama on this earth has felt the same way at some point. It's all part of the job. Motherhood and being a wife isn't for the weak-kneed."

"What do I do, Miss Vivien?"

"Hang up, go wash your face, pray for strength and wisdom, and go to bed. Tomorrow's a new day, and things might start getting better. If they don't, there's always another tomorrow coming. Eventually God works it all out."

Mary Jo dabbed at her nose. Miss Vivien's words weren't wrapped in sugar but they made sense and soothed because at least she listened and cared.

Which made her mother's penchant for throwing blame at her for not being better organized and at Kenny for being a lazy bum seem less important.

"Thank you, Miss Vivien." Mary Jo tossed the towel in the sink. "Gigi said you went to stay with Mrs. Baker the other night. How is she doing?"

Miss Vivien sighed into the phone. "She's a mess. And who wouldn't be?"

"I saw what Robbi Dever said in the *LTC* today. Gave me the creeps how she described Cathy's being hit in the head with a silver candelabra. And dressed in her wedding gown."

As soon as the words left her mouth, Mary Jo pressed her fist to her temple. Her brain was so fogged in she'd forgotten that Miss Vivien had designed Cathy's gown. She wanted to apologize for being so insensitive, but maybe saying that would only salt the wound more and embarrass Miss Vivien.

"Her death has been a shock to the entire city. We're all praying they find this person fast and lock him away forever."

"Has the sheriff told you anything about what they know?"

"Nothing beyond what's been in the papers. None of her neighbors saw a stranger hanging around or visiting Cathy. Her husband said he talked with her around nine the night before, and she was planning on going to bed soon after. The strangest thing is nothing was missing from her house. It seems the person responsible came there just to kill her and put the wedding gown on over her nightgown."

Mary Jo shuddered. "It's like something from a horror movie, isn't it?"

A bell rang in the background at Miss Vivien's end. "Hang on, somebody's at my door."

The phone rattled as Miss Vivien set down the receiver and went to answer. Mary Jo heard a low, muffled male voice speak. There was a long silence, and then hurried footsteps across the floor.

Miss Vivien picked up the phone again. "Mary Jo, I've got to go. Sheriff Youngblood is here. Another of my brides was killed."

The phone clicked off.

Mary Jo's hand shook as she placed the receiver back in its cradle on the wall. She looked in the living room where Kenny's snoring buzzed from the couch.

She walked to his side and shook him hard until his eyes opened.

"I need you to sleep in our room tonight. There's been another murder, and I'm scared."

The sullen look she'd seen in his eyes for the past week faded. He sat up and ruffled his hair with his one hand, then rubbed his face. "If somebody came here, I don't know what good I'd do."

Miss Vivien's words echoed in her mind. "*Be the strong one.*"

"We'd fight them together. Both of your old baseball bats from high school are under our bed. One for each of us."

Kenny stared up at her, then stood. He motioned toward the bedroom, then followed her down the hall and settled into the bed while she brushed her teeth.

With the late hour, she decided to skip setting her hair. She'd just pull it up into a ponytail for work tomorrow.

She felt nervous and almost shy as she lay down next to him. He turned out the light and rolled on his side away from her.

Silence settled between them.

"Thank you, Kenny."

"I'm going to sleep now."

Mary Jo pulled the covers to her chin, closed her eyes, and counted the hats and purses in the case at Ladies Accessories until she drifted off to sleep.

Chapter 12

Audrey

Audrey pulled into her parking space and waved to Nelson as he walked over to greet her. She gathered her purse and satchel in one hand, then grabbed the thermos of Maxwell House coffee and the cinnamon twists from Tiner's Bakery in the other.

He stood at the front of her car as she exited. The wrinkles in his brown skin seemed a bit deeper this morning. Had he not slept well? Or was this something she'd missed because her mind had been churning through the current lessons in office etiquette she'd needed to teach Libby?

"You're here extra early today. Big meeting with the boss?" He took the thermos and bag of pastries from her.

"No, another talk with my new assistant."

Nelson sat in the chair he kept nearby. A corner of his mouth curled into a half smile as he removed the top of the thermos and unscrewed the lid. "The girl's keeping you on your toes."

Audrey adjusted the cuff of her black gloves as he poured himself a cup of coffee. "I know this won't leave the garage. I'm not sure what Mr. Wynton was thinking when he hired her as my replacement. She's a sweet girl, but my goodness, she tries my patience sometimes. I spend most of my day reminding her of the simplest things over and over. I lie awake at night trying to come up with ways to help her."

Then there was the issue of time. With her mornings eaten up teaching Libby, she now worked late into the night in her new position as head buyer. In a few days, she'd be leaving for New York's fashion week and her first buying trip for the store.

Libby was nowhere near ready to take over as Mr. Wynton's secretary for a minute, much less an entire week.

She'd stood there so sure of herself when she told Mr. Wynton she could do both jobs. One way or another, she'd find a way to make this work, along with begging for a little divine guidance along the way.

Audrey locked her car door. "Enjoy your breakfast, Nelson. I'll see you tomorrow."

"You burning midnight oil again tonight?"

"Most likely. Guess I'll see you when I'm coming and going today."

"Better be careful. Them kind of hours don't make you any younger."

The truth in his words pulled at her heart as she forced herself not to wince when he worked harder than usual to remove his breakfast from the bag. Nelson's aging seemed to have sped up in the past few weeks, and she'd been so preoccupied she'd failed to see.

"Make sure you get your sleep today. Can't have both of us dragging around the store like a couple of mush-heads."

"No ma'am, we can't." He bit into his cinnamon twist, then stared across the garage as he chewed, his mind tuned to his own thoughts.

She wanted to push for more information, entice him to share what was happening. But Nelson would never cross such a line, and she must move on with her day. "Take care, Nelson."

She hurried on from the garage, her mind churning because Nelson wouldn't allow her to bridge the divide between them enough to do any good.

When she reached the executive suite, she found Libby sitting in one of the chairs in the waiting room. She popped up like water in a fountain.

"Good morning, Miss Audrey." Libby didn't just greet a person, she sang her salutations, a trait Audrey was still adjusting to.

"Wow, you look beautiful today. But you always look beautiful." Libby circled Audrey twice as she took inventory of today's look. "I love a suit with a peplum, don't you? It's such a feminine and classy look. And those pearl buttons and that royal-blue color look simply regal on you."

Libby stood on tiptoe and peered at Audrey's braided gold Monet necklace. "Ooh, it's perfect how that sits just above the neckline of your suit."

Audrey dipped her head quickly. "Thank you. And please remember, this is an executive office. You're an assistant, so those of us above you can call you by your first name. But you must call us by our formal names. I'm Miss Penault."

She walked to her desk and removed a stack of books from her satchel. She handed them to Libby. "I ordered these for you."

Libby read over each book's cover. She scowled when she looked back up. "I don't need these. I learned all this in my correspondence course."

Audrey expected this reaction and had practiced her answer multiple times last night so it wouldn't come out harsh and break Libby's spirit. For reasons he wouldn't share, Mr. Wynton believed Libby was Audrey's perfect replacement, and it was her job to shape Libby into exactly what Mr. Wynton needed.

"I want you to start with the first handbook and work on a section every night. You should do this until you've completed all three books. You also need to memorize the Gregg Shorthand Dictionary, and practice in the transcriptions studies book."

Libby's shoulders drooped as she glanced down at the books again. Audrey paused a moment, working to bring the right words to make her point without being harsh. "Libby, you have the potential to be a successful secretary. You're bright, you listen to instruction, and you aren't afraid to work hard."

Libby's eyes lit up from the compliment. "You really think so?"

"I do. But you must sharpen your skills to be able to do my job without me hovering over you all day."

She pointed to the books in Libby's hands. "Consistent practice is the only way you'll improve."

Libby released a long sigh. "Yes ma'am. I'll start right after supper tonight. Mama says I watch too much television at night anyway. She's always telling me to turn it off and read a book." She hugged the new manuals to her chest. "She'll love that I'm learning something for work. I guess I will too."

Libby deserved credit for not being one to lie down and quit. She set the books on the desk. "What are we going to work on first today, Miss Audrey?"

"Call me Miss Penault during business hours, please."

Libby tapped her forehead with the heel of her palm. "I keep forgetting that."

A soft tapping on the outer door interrupted them. Mary Jo stood in the entry, and from the worry-wrinkles puckering her forehead, she wasn't here for a social visit. "Do you have a moment?"

Before Audrey could answer, Libby headed for Mary Jo with her hand out. "I'm Libby, Audrey's new assistant."

Audrey met Mary Jo's wide-eyed surprise with her best I'll-explain-later look, then tapped Libby on the shoulder. When she turned around Audrey continued. "We don't rush up to people when they come in. Greet them first, ask how you might help them, and allow them to state their business. Then introduce yourself as Miss Farris and offer them help."

Libby's cheeks burned red as she pivoted to Mary Jo. "I'm so sorry." She held her hands to her temples. "There's so much to remember, and everything Audrey tells me seems to go in my ears and drain right back out before my brain soaks it all in."

Mary Jo took her by the hand. "I'm sure you'll learn all you need to know. I felt the same way when I started working here." She gave a final squeeze and released Libby. "You've got the finest teacher here at Wynton's."

Libby nodded so hard her ponytail swished back and forth. "Isn't Audrey just the ginchiest?"

Sappy admiration was something Audrey left behind when she quit fashion modeling. She'd have to plan another talk about proper office behavior with Libby later. For now, she needed the girl gone for a few minutes. "Libby, I need you to go to the supplies closet, please."

Libby set her focus on Audrey. "Yes ma'am. What do you need me to get?"

"A ream of typing paper, some more erasers because you've used up all I had in my desk. Five blue pens and five black pens. Get a pack of file folders too. Can you remember everything, or do I need to write it down for you?"

She looked at the ceiling, then recited Audrey's list. "Paper, erasers, five black, five blue pens, and file folders."

"Perfect. Go ahead now."

"Yes Au—Miss Penault."

As she walked past Mary Jo, she called over her shoulder. "Nice meeting you, Miss Penault's friend." She waved at them both, then bounded out the door, making Audrey half believe she was going to skip all the way down the hallway to the supply closet.

Mary Jo met Audrey's gaze and grinned. "You have an assistant now?"

Audrey pointed toward the hall. "She is more than I can explain right now. I could tell something was wrong when you came in. What's the matter?"

Mary Jo's grin melted away. "Miss Vivien called me last night to check on me. While we were on the phone, Sheriff Youngblood came to her house."

Audrey's gut twisted into a large knot. "Don't tell me."

Mary Jo grabbed Audrey's wrist in a crushing grip. "Another one of her brides was killed last night."

How could this be happening? "Who?"

"I don't know. She told me the news and hung up fast. It was so late I couldn't call her back. I'm going down to the salon to see how she is and at least give her a hug before the store opens."

Audrey pulled from her hold. "I'm coming with you."

"What about your assistant?"

"I'll catch her in the hallway."

When Audrey rushed from the office, she saw Libby was heading back, her hands filled with the requested items.

"Hold the elevator for me. I need to give Libby some instructions."

Mary Jo went ahead as Audrey motioned to Libby. She'd finally gotten the girl to walk at a more decorous tempo, and now she needed to hurry her along.

"Libby, hurry please."

The girl nodded and broke into a trot the rest of the way down the hall.

"Did I take too long?" she asked as she met Audrey at the doorway.

"No, you did fine. I need to. . .go take care of something on another floor. I want you to go in, put these things away where I showed you yesterday. Then, you are to answer the phones."

Libby gasped. "You're letting me use the phone?"

Not by choice. Audrey swallowed back the words and forced her next to come slower. "Yes. Now remember, you answer with 'Wynton's Department Store, Mr. Wynton's office.' Then you wait for the person on the line to tell you what they want."

Libby nodded. "I remember."

"Good. My message pad is right next to the phone. Write down the caller's name, their reason for calling, and a callback number. Once you have that information, thank them for calling and hang up. Say nothing else. Understand?"

"Yes, Audrey."

She didn't have time to correct her about calling her by her first name yet again. "If anyone comes to the office, tell them to come back when the store has opened. I'll be at my desk by then."

“Yes ma’am.”

She didn’t know what else to say, and leaving the office in Libby’s hands, even for a few minutes, made her blood pressure spike, but it had to be done.

“Good girl.”

Audrey rushed to the elevator, hoping she’d return to find the executive office still in one piece. Mr. Wynton kept telling her Libby was going to surprise her one of these days and be the picture of competence.

One could only hope. And then clean up the disaster later.

There was nothing worse than dealing with a hothead first thing in the morning. Vivien moved the phone's receiver to her right ear to give her left one a break from young Mr. Cameron from Cameron's Catering. He'd discovered she'd removed his business from her bridal guide and was mad as all get-out over the situation. She really didn't need this after news of Rayanne Steele's death.

Vivien took a sip of her warm tea as he spun off into another tirade. From the moment she'd answered the salon's phone, he'd spewed a whole list of colorful words and opinions at her, none of which were helping him earn back her favor. Above all that, she'd never heard a person go on as long as he had without stopping for a breath.

Mirette stood across the desk from her and pointed to her ear. "Is he still going?" she whispered. Vivien answered with a single nod as she covered the mouthpiece with her hand.

"Go unlock the front door. I'm going to hang up on him here in a few seconds. I've heard enough."

She removed her hand. "Mr. Cameron, I'm going to jump in here because the salon opens in two minutes."

He went to speak but Vivien talked over him. "I've let you say your piece. Now you're going to listen to mine. I don't remove someone from the guide for small reasons. My brides depend on me to supply them with the best people to fulfill all their wedding needs. These businesses need to be consistently dependable, pleasant to work with, and above all, able to deliver the utmost in quality service. I've been told you're not meeting these standards, I've seen this myself, and your own father agreed you're not maintaining your business's standards. As a result, you've been removed from the guide."

He sputtered his defense on the other end, but Vivien continued, drowning him out until he hushed once more. "Once you've been able to return to the high level of service and quality your business was once known for, you'll be reinstated. Until that time, we have nothing else to discuss."

"Does Mr. Wynton know you've kicked me out?" Mr. Cameron's words came through mushy, as if he'd clamped his jaws together so tightly only his lips had freedom to form his words.

Vivien lifted the tea bag from her cup and laid it on the saucer. "He is aware." And agreed with the decision wholeheartedly.

"This isn't the end of this, Mrs. Sheffield. I'll go to the *LTC* and let Robbi Dever know what you've done. She'll spill this all over the front page and folks will see how you've turned on one of the most beloved businesses and families in Levy City. We'll see how your precious Bridal Week goes when all the vendors in town refuse to work with you because of what you've done. You've been riding mighty high around here for a long time, but I'm not going to let you ruin our business. I'll ruin yours first."

It took every bit of manners Mama had pounded into her to keep from reminding him that her reputation had a far longer standing than his. The last thing she needed was to get in a "let's try to upstage one another" contest. She'd always found such things distasteful and just plain common.

"Mr. Cameron, I hope you have a nice day. I'm hanging up now." She set the receiver down and met Mirette's gaze.

"He is such a sweet little peach of a man, isn't he?" Mirette leaned against the corner of Vivien's desk. "He was yelling so loud I caught most of his little threat there at the end. Does he really think he can persuade everyone else in the guide to up and quit on us just because he told them to?"

"If he does we don't need to worry. All the other caterers, florists, and event hall owners in the guide benefit from being a part of Wynton's Bridal Week. They're also our friends and know we don't make decisions without good cause."

The phone rang as Vivien picked up her teacup and saucer. "I truly hope that isn't him again." She picked up the receiver. "Miss Vivien's."

Robbi Dever's voice blasted at her from the other end. "I'd like to come in today, to do that interview."

"Robbi, I don't have time to try to iron that out with you. I'll call you later."

Vivien ended the call and locked eyes with Mirette. "I wish I had my grandson's baseball bat here. Next time this phone rings"—she mimed swinging a bat through the air, then down on the phone—"bam."

"Sounds good as long as you don't use the thing on me too." Mirette poked Vivien in the side and then made her way to the fitting area. "I need to get the eight skirt panels on the Robbins girl's gown pieced together before lunch. Didn't you say her fitting is later this week?"

"She's coming in on Thursday. Did you finish the veil for her gown yet?"

"Took it home last night and put the lace trim on while I watched *The $64,000 Question* on TV. I hung the finished product up when I came in."

Vivien rubbed her forehead. "I saw you carry the veil in with you this morning." She opened her schedule book. "I need to get my head straightened before our girls start coming in. Otherwise, I'm not going to be worth a hill of beans on the sales floor today."

"Bill's visit last night still has you rattled, doesn't it?"

"There's no calming down and going to sleep after hearing such news."

Mirette nodded as she gathered up the fitting notebook where she and Vivien wrote down designs and details for each bride's gown. "I didn't sleep a wink after you called me. I couldn't get the images of what Bill told you out of my mind."

"Me neither." Vivien rearranged her long, rope-style gold necklace around the ruffled collar of her black-and-white polka-dot blouse, then adjusted her black patent leather belt along the waist of her long, black wool skirt.

"I kept picturing Rayanne Steele lying there in her dress, all those layers of ruffled lace along the skirt covered in blood, and our label right there across her heart." She drew a heart shape across her own front.

"I never would have believed a silver teapot could have been used as a weapon to the head. Then on top of that, her being found with our bridal guide clutched in her hands, as if she'd been reading it while she was—"

Vivien raised her hands and cut Mirette off before she could say more. "No more. It's just too heartbreaking."

"Have you spoken to her mother yet?"

"I'm going to call Helen Willis on my lunch break. And then I'm calling Marlene Steele, because we both know how Rayanne thought the world of her mother-in-law."

The salon's door chimes sounded. Vivien swung her attention to the entryway in time to see Mary Jo and Audrey rushing in.

Mary Jo hurried to Vivien's side and gathered her in a tight embrace. "Miss Vivien, I was so worried about you after we had to get off the phone last night. I don't know how you made it to work today." She squeezed Vivien's shoulders tighter.

Audrey stood off to the side. "What can we do?"

Vivien smiled at her over Mary Jo's shoulder. The difference between her two friends was as vast and wide as the acres of orange groves outside of Levy City. Mary Jo led with her heart and Audrey went straight to the practical. Right now, she needed both.

She pulled away from Mary Jo's hug. "Mirette and I have bride's depending on us. Besides, what would I do at home except pace the floor and fret until I drove myself crazy."

"Please don't read the *LTC* tomorrow. You know Robbi Dever will have a column telling all the gory details in there. She seems to be everywhere these days. I was listening to WZLC last night before you called, and she has a new fashion segment on there. How can a person go from murder in the morning to fashion at night?"

Vivien waved away Mary Jo's concerns. "Whatever comes up in the paper, I'll be fine."

Vivien turned her attention on Audrey. "There's nothing much that can be done right now. Bill and his men are working on both cases, gathering up everything they can find. He said whoever is responsible isn't leaving behind any clues to their identity or motive."

There was no sense in mentioning where her own thoughts had gone when Bill shared the details of the crime scene with her last night. After the shock of another girl's death eased, her mind went to stirring on a new thought.

For whatever reason, it became clear to her that whoever was killing these girls wanted her name associated with the murders.

There was no cause to worry about that now as she turned back to her friends. "Mirette and I are going on with our business, and I suggest you two do the same. Wynton's front doors will be opening in minutes, and this store isn't going to run itself now, is it?"

Vivien forced the corners of her lips into a smile she was sure didn't catch in her eyes. "Mirette and I are fine. Y'all go on now." She waved her hands toward the door as if she were herding them like a pack of cows.

Mary Jo pirouetted and headed for the door. Audrey stood a moment, staring at Vivien's face as if she were reading a message etched across her cheeks.

"Miss Vivien, if you need anything—"

"You're first on my list to call for help. You'd best get back before the boss gets in."

The quip about Mr. Wynton brought an unusual flash of emotion in Audrey's face. Her typical poise and confidence faltered a little as a trace of worry creased her brow.

In an instant, whatever might have been niggling at Audrey seemed to vanish as quickly as it had come. She lifted her chin, and a calm filled her dark brown eyes. "Yes ma'am. Hope you and Miss Mirette have a productive day."

She joined Mary Jo and they headed for the exit. Mary Jo kept her eyes forward as she relayed a story to Audrey. But Audrey paused for a moment and shot a look over her shoulder at Vivien.

Their eyes met and her concern was clearly broadcast in the few seconds she held Vivien's gaze. Her warning look wove itself among Vivien's own feelings.

Someone intended to turn up the heat on her, and the pot was only beginning to simmer.

The elevator dinged, announcing a stop on the fifth floor. Vivien lingered in case a walk-in had come. She could welcome them in and shower them with the full 'Miss Vivien' treatment.

When the doors opened she fought to keep her face calm as Robbi Dever waited for the operator to move the gate so she could pass.

Robbi came straight in the salon, hands held out wide. "Vivien, I had to come in today. With all that's happening around town, you need all the good news I can write for you."

It took everything within Vivien not to comment on Robbi's being the one who had put her in the bad news predicament in the first place.

Chapter 14

Gigi

When other girls played with crayons and coloring books, Gigi had sneaked into her mama's dresser and played dress-up with her makeup. When she turned sixteen, she hid lipstick and powder in her purse, then applied it in the girls' bathroom at school. She couldn't really remember a time when she wasn't copying how the stars looked in the fan mags or practicing in her mirror to get just the right look.

So why was she so scared of the Wynton's cosmetics sample case Audrey gave her?

The contents surrounded her as she sat on the small oval rug next to the bed in her room. Six different sizes of application brushes were lined up by her left knee. Lipstick tubes filled with every color of pink, red, coral, and one called "Desert Orange" that claimed to be kiss-proof, sat on her right.

Bottles of matching nail polish were grouped by the lipstick. A light-blue-and-gold Max Factor compact filled with an all-in-one cream plus powder, a concealer stick called Erace, and a container of pancake makeup sat in front of her crisscrossed legs. There were samples of eye shadows and mascara still in the case.

Gigi cradled her face in her hands. "Why bother learning all these names, and how to use them? Jane hates me, and I'm doomed to perfume spritzing for the rest of my life."

She'd been tasked with pushing the scent-of-the-day at the store, and three times those brands sold out in a single day. Almost every customer she spritzed and ushered to Cosmetics ended up buying something because of her talking to them about a product.

And yet Jane still blocked her from moving up in the department. *"You've got a few rough edges that need to be smoothed before I can feel comfortable with you serving our customers, Gigi. You must polish your personal presentation and salesmanship first,"* she'd said earlier in the day.

Gigi chewed her bottom lip all the way home on the bus to keep from crying.

She picked up a lipstick and tilted the gold-lacquered tube until the glow from the overhead light flashed along its side. Revlon's Fire and Ice, still one of the most popular Wynton's sold, and a shade that brought her many compliments whenever she wore it.

"What is the matter with me? I know how to use cosmetics better than anybody. Except maybe Audrey. My problem is I haven't learned how to act right with our customers when I'm selling the products."

Gigi rose and slipped her feet into her soft house slippers, then rushed into the hallway of her apartment building. Her muffled steps thumped down the stairs as she took them two at a time, hoping to get to the community phone before one of the other girls in the house beat her to it.

She rounded the corner to the large living room populated with old couches and chairs. Their landlady, Miss Anna May, had placed them there for all the girls to use when they needed a place to spread out and relax. Or entertain gentleman callers, because Miss Anna May did not allow men in any other part of the house, especially the upstairs rooms.

Gigi moved three bright pink pillows trimmed with wide ruffles out of the way. One of the consequences of living in a females-only apartment house was the presence of pink in every nook and cranny. But she wasn't complaining. Finding this room after her old landlord died was a blessing she thanked God for every night before she went to sleep in her tiny room.

She dialed the number, then bounced on the cushion as she waited for the sounds indicating that the other person had picked up on the call.

Gigi stood up when the ringing stopped and a voice answered. "Hello?"

She grabbed the receiver with both hands. "Audrey, this is Gigi. I need to talk to you. Right now."

"What's this all about?"

"I need you to come over to my apartment."

"Now?"

For some reason her knees decided to wobble, which didn't make sense because she wasn't nervous or scared, but rather getting more excited with her plan. Gigi plopped on the threadbare cushion of the couch and sunk into the ancient springs. "I need you to teach me something."

There was a long pause before Audrey answered. "And what would that be?"

One of the other girls came down the stairs, peered around the corner, and saw Gigi using the phone. She pointed to her wristwatch, as if to remind her of the house rules for calls.

Gigi moved the receiver away from her mouth. "I need ten more minutes, then you can have the phone."

The girl turned on her heel and headed toward the kitchen.

"Gigi, are you still there?" Audrey called from the other end.

"One of my housemates wants the phone. We have a rule saying calls can't go longer than thirty minutes, or you lose phone privileges."

"Did something happen at the store?"

Jane's words from earlier reached out and clawed at Gigi's excitement for her plan, planting weedy doubts where seeds of hope had been. "I need you to teach me how to act right. To our customers."

A long silence followed, and Gigi sprang up and paced around the couch, stretching the cord as far she could while waiting for Audrey to answer.

At last came a long sigh, and then Audrey spoke. "Gigi, I—"

"Please don't say no. I don't have any fancy manners, and snippy things come out of my mouth because I talk before I think. And I'm always using words that make me sound uncouth."

Audrey's response came in a high-pitched giggle. Gigi clenched her free hand into a fist.

"Don't make fun of me. I know I'm not as sophisticated as everyone else at Wynton's, and everyone in Cosmetics believes I don't belong there."

"Gigi, women who come to Wynton's cosmetics department need you. Please don't let Jane, or any of the other clerks there, intimidate you."

Audrey paused and Gigi's brain started racing. If only she could bring Audrey, dressed in one of her fancy suits with her hat and gloves, and have her tell Jane and all the other snooty clerks how great she believed Gigi was.

She almost missed working in the cafeteria now. At least Lilla was there and she'd had someone to talk to who actually liked her. The other clerks in Florida Delights were fun to work with and Mr. Spell was a nice man, but she needed something more permanent.

Audrey continued. "I'm going to tell you something, but you must keep it quiet for a few more days. Deal?"

Audrey was taking her into her confidence. This was unexpected, but when a body asked someone to turn them from a sow's ear to a silk purse, there had to be some give-and-take on both sides of the bargain. "Okay. Sure."

"On Friday, Mr. Wynton is going to announce that I've been promoted to head buyer for Ladies Fashions. I'm leaving for Fashion Week in New York soon."

Gigi's heart sank to the floor like a rock in a pond. "That's wonderful, Audrey. Even I know that's an amazing job. But it also means you can't help me, can you?"

"Au contraire. All you're really needing is a little polish. And *that* I will teach you."

Polish. The same word Jane had used. Gigi's heart snapped back into place and did the Bunny Hop inside her chest. Audrey would fix this and make sure she kept her job at Wynton's.

The girl waiting for the phone came and stood in the doorway. She rammed one hand on her hip and tapped her foot on the wood floors as she glared across the room at Gigi.

"You're the best, Audrey. See you at the store tomorrow. Bye."

She hung up, then jigged her way out of the room, past her housemate, and all the way up the stairs. When she entered her room, Gigi stared down at the products spread across her rug. She stuck her tongue out at the array. "I've got my own secret weapon. You wait and see what happens now."

Gigi walked to her nightstand and turned on the radio. Her new place had no TV, because the landlady believed television would lead to the ruination of American minds and ranted about the evils of watching the tube. Gigi had replaced watching her favorite shows with listening to the local segments on WZLC nightly, including Robbi Dever's fashion reports.

Listening about the clothes and Robbi's descriptions of what the Hollywood actresses wore was fun. Despite the fact that she didn't have any idea who the designers Robbi mentioned were or the meaning of some of the terms she used like *prêt-à-porter*, *bias cut*, or *haute couture*, Gigi still liked to sit and listen with her eyes closed and imagine what those beautiful dresses might look like. Which turned out to be more fun than sitting and watching TV and maybe proved Miss Anna May was right.

Maybe Audrey could help her understand those things too. She knew all about that stuff.

Robbi's voice blasted through the radio's speaker, calling her back to the show. "Good evening, Levy City. Welcome to Robbi Dever's *Fashion Festival*. Tonight, we'll be talking about what's new for spring, but first, I want to take a little detour down another clothing lane and discuss a new story I just heard. It seems another young woman, who was also a former bride of Miss Vivien's salon, was found dead last night. Again, this woman was dressed in her wedding gown, designed by Miss Vivien, whose own label was found on the body. I'll have all the details in my column, The Juice, where I squeeze a story until I've found all the seeds of juicy truth. As always, I'm on the first page of *The Levy Times Commercial* just below the fold. And now, back to what's springing up in spring fashions."

Gigi sunk onto the edge of her bed. Poor Miss Vivien. "She must be a complete wreck. Two of her brides. Dead."

Who did such things? And why?

She reached over and clicked off the radio. Celebrating spring fashions seemed disrespectful.

And she wasn't going to wrestle with her conscience for being disloyal and listening to Robbi Dever drag Miss Vivien's name through the mud.

Even she knew it wasn't fit for a person to act so to a good friend.

Chapter 15

Mary Jo

Mary Jo winced as the pin in her plastic corsage poked her finger. She worked to reattach the large red heart covered with fake roses to the lapel of her navy suit jacket. If she had her way, she would have tossed the thing the moment her boss left Ladies Accessories to deliver corsages to other employees.

Valentine's Day had been a favorite of hers since her sophomore year in high school. Kenny had surprised her with a beautiful golden sweetheart locket that year because she liked pretty things. He told her later he'd always get her pretty things because he loved the smile they brought to her face. And he'd made good on that promise.

Until the accident.

A display of heart-shaped candy boxes, trimmed with flowers or dolls dressed in long red or white dresses made of shiny satin, had been placed in the men's department across the aisle from where she stood. Her manager said they always put gifts there so husbands could find them easier. Wynton's even offered a Valentine's shopping guide for men to help them make the right choices and avoid ending up in the doghouse February fourteenth.

But right now, all she wanted was to march over there and stomp the display to pieces.

A man stood before the candy display, picked up one box covered with lace and velvet roses, and then set it down and turned toward Ladies Accessories. He made eye contact with her for a moment, then looked around as if searching for an escape route.

He shoved his hand into his pants pocket, and she caught a flash of gold on his left ring finger. Her manager told all Ladies Accessories clerks to be on the lookout for the lost husbands and be sure to assist them in finding the right gifts.

At least she could help another wife have a nice Valentine's Day tomorrow.

"Sir, may I help you?"

The man stiffened. "No ma'am." A thick, slow drawl seasoned his bass voice. He walked to a table filled with silk scarves, gloves, and an array of hatpins displayed on a black velvet form.

Men were the worst shoppers. They fumbled over anything feminine and were too stubborn to ask for the help they needed. Guiding them to choose practical yet pretty gifts while allowing them to feel in charge of the process worked best. "Shopping for your wife?"

The man removed his felt fedora-style hat and nodded as he focused on a pink-and-green flowered scarf. He ran his finger along the silky fabric.

"These Rodier scarves are always a nice gift." Mary Jo took a step back from him and motioned to the other tables filled with comb, brush, and mirror vanity sets, silver and gold compact mirrors, and key chains. "Look around. I'll be at the counter. Please ask me for assistance if you need it."

The man bobbed his head once and turned his attention to the hatpins.

Mary Jo returned to the counter and straightened up the shelf stacked with boxes of silk stockings and nylons. It was best to leave the man to his shopping.

Her patience paid off when he approached the counter. He carried the pink-and-green scarf and a gold hatpin shaped like a tulip with a large pearl nestled in its top. He held both as if they might break if he breathed too heavily.

"Can a lady wear these together?"

"Absolutely. This hatpin will look quite smart tucked into the folds of the scarf. And the colors in the scarf will go with so many outfits."

"And that's a good thing?"

Mary Jo fought back a smile while she nodded. The last thing she needed was to scare him off right before the sale because she made him feel silly. Men had the hardest time understanding female accessories.

"Yes sir. You've made a very smart choice. She can wear this pin in a hat, with this scarf, or even tucked in the lapel of a jacket. We girls like having lots of options."

"Do you have a box you could wrap this up in?" He laid the hatpin and scarf on the counter, then reached into his suit coat to retrieve his wallet.

"Yes sir. We have some lovely ones just for Valentine's Day." Mary Jo opened the doors in the cabinet behind her and pulled out a pink box covered in red hearts with Wynton's logo printed along the bottom edge. Gigi had teased the color matched a bottle of Pepto-Bismol when she saw Mary Jo unpacking them.

She now shrugged off her friend's crack as she grabbed two sheets of pink tissue paper to wrap the man's gifts in.

Mary Jo laid everything on the counter, then wrote out his sales ticket. Once he'd paid, she wrapped his purchases in the paper, then chose a wide red satin ribbon and tied the box shut with a large red bow.

"If you're needing a Valentine's card, our stationery department has several sweet ones to pick from. May I direct you to the floor?"

He shoved his wallet back in his jacket pocket and gathered his package. "I know where to go." The man took a few steps away, then swiveled back to face her. "Thanks." He settled his hat on his head and walked from the Ladies Accessories with long strides as if he couldn't get away fast enough.

She was filing his sales ticket when she heard her name called. Gigi came heading her way. "What are you doing here this time of day?"

"Jane made me take my lunch late."

"I wondered what happened to you. I saved you a seat and everything."

Gigi leaned across the counter. "We got a late delivery of perfume, so I had to unbox it and set up the displays while Jane and the other girls waited on customers. Couldn't leave until all the products were in the cases."

"None of the other girls helped you?"

"The other girls *never* help me." Gigi straightened and pointed to Mary Jo's corsage. "Have you and Kenny made up yet?"

Mary Jo grabbed the rag she used to polish the glass on the display cases. "No. The floor manager is making everyone wear these this week. You didn't get one?"

"No."

Mary Jo rubbed away a smudge her male customer had left behind. "Fake flowers aren't very romantic. Don't think my Valentine's Day will be either."

"I know mine won't be. I saw there's a Valentine's dance this Saturday at St. Vincent's church hall. Only three dollars a couple. They put on the best dances, and Billy Galvin's band is going to be there. He kinda sounds like that new guy on the radio, Elvis Presley." Gigi shrugged. "This will be the first year I haven't gone to a Valentine's dance in I don't know how long."

Mary Jo put the cleaning rag away. "You can come over and make Valentine's cards with the girls and me. The *LTC* printed the cutest ideas in the family section this week."

Gigi gave her a wide, fish-eyed look. "I'm washing my hair. I was going to listen to Robbi Dever's fashion segment on the radio, but I heard her talking about Miss Vivien last night and had to turn her off."

"I don't know why she has to say those things about Miss Vivien."

"Who's saying things about me?"

Miss Vivien stood a few feet away and had clearly heard their conversation. Mary Jo's cheeks warmed. How in the world did she get so focused on gabbing with Gigi that she failed to see Miss Vivien walk up?

"I'm so sorry. Gigi and I weren't gossiping about you, I promise."

Miss Vivien joined them. "Even if you were, I've reached the age where I'm too old to care."

Gigi swiveled around to face Miss Vivien. "What are you doing down here on the first floor?"

"I had a meeting with the floor manager. We're going over the details for the layout of the displays for Bridal Week."

"This early? I thought Bridal Week wasn't until April."

Miss Vivien waved her first finger in the air toward Gigi. "Early planning prevents later problems." She tapped the face of her watch. "I've got to get back to the salon. And you two better get back to work." Miss Vivien wiggled her fingers in goodbye as she headed for the main aisle.

Gigi tapped her fingers on the glass countertop. "I'm glad she's focusing on Bridal Week and not the other. . .you know."

"Me too." Mary Jo tilted her head toward a man who was standing a few feet away holding a large heart-shaped box of candy. "You'd better go. I think I need to ring him up."

Gigi mouthed a silent goodbye and scooted away. The man waited a few seconds and then strolled to Mary Jo's counter.

"May I pay for this here?"

She nodded and took a receipt book out. "Yes sir."

He slid the box onto the counter. "I want to make sure I get something nice for my sweetheart. She works so hard at home, and along with her birthday, I consider Valentine's Day her big day."

Mary Jo glanced up at him a moment. "What a sweet sentiment."

Moisture threatened to cloud her eyes, and she dropped her gaze back to the sales ticket.

Kenny once said things like that to her.

As she finished writing, he looked over at the case displaying the evening bags. "I'm planning on taking my wife out to dinner at the country club Saturday. Would one of those bags be something she could use?"

Mary Jo walked to the case. "Any of these would be lovely for a night out. Which one were you thinking of?"

He pointed a chubby finger toward a black faille drawstring purse with two slender handles. "How much is this black one?"

Mary Jo turned over the paper tag attached to the handle. "Two forty-nine."

"And what about the red one next to it, with the things around the sides?"

She touched the red silk clutch bag trimmed with tiny red ruffles along the flap. "Dollar ninety-eight."

"My wife loves red. I'll take that one."

"Yes sir." Mary Jo removed the purse and carried it to the cash register. "Would you like for me to put both in one large box?"

He clapped his hands together. "No, I want two separate gifts. Just to show her how much I love her."

"Of course." His bragging made believing he wanted Valentine's Day to be all about his wife difficult. Maybe he was just one of those rare men who talked about his feelings.

When she handed him both gifts, he smiled wide. "Hope you have a nice Valentine's Day too."

Her mouth wouldn't cooperate and slide into a smile, so she forced out a weak "Thank you."

It wasn't his fault her life at home smelled worse than a kettle of dead fish on a hot Florida day.

She watched him almost skip his way toward the entrance, and as she turned away, her eyes fell on the display across the aisle.

Maybe her customer had the right idea. Maybe Kenny needed to be the one being appreciated and spoiled a little this year.

She and the girls could make him cards. And Kenny loved chocolate. He always ate half of the candy in the boxes he'd bought her every year. Especially the cherry cordials and the ones with the coconut inside.

Who said she couldn't buy a box to share once the girls went to bed. The surprise might not bring a big reaction, but maybe he would at least sit with her and enjoy them and know that she still loved him to bits and never meant to hurt him.

She had two more hours before her shift ended. She'd use her employee discount, sneak the box home, and then hide it in the coat closet next to the washing machine in the utility room until tomorrow.

Mary Jo eyed the display, searching for the box she was going to claim as hers.

As soon as she was free, she scurried to the display. She grabbed her favorite box, one covered in red velveteen and edged with a red grosgrain ribbon embroidered with gold hearts.

Not too feminine, and for some reason it reminded her of the designs on a king's crown. Just right for the king of her castle.

She hoped he saw it that way too as she clutched the surprise and hurried to her car.

Chapter 16

Audrey

Audrey stood before the collection of dresses in her closet and sighed. How in the world could she find nothing suitable to wear for her trip to New York next week? Her closet was packed with enough clothes to start her own Ladies Wear department.

"Because you don't know who you want to be next week, that's why." She slid her entire collection of dresses to the side and flipped through them again.

She'd been away from modeling for almost five years. Returning to that world made her stomach percolate like boiling coffee. The runways would feature girls who'd lost jobs to her.

The goal of this trip was to forge relationships with the same designers she angered when she left the industry for business school. Negotiate deals with them to create exclusive designs bearing their brand for Wynton's. The challenge would be convincing them to see her as a businesswoman and not their favored model who walked away before crow's-feet and wrinkles forced her out.

Audrey slid the light knits suitable for Florida's climate down the clothing rod and focused on the clothes made of heavier fabrics. First up was a two-piece acrylic charcoal-gray suit with a belted jacket and a pleated skirt. The ensemble came with a matching overcoat.

She laid out a gray bow hat trimmed with a small black birdcage veil, her black T-strap pumps, and a matching purse.

"That would quietly whisper *sleek* without being stuffy." Demonstrating she'd not lost her taste or style when she'd left the fashion world was key.

Audrey flipped through her dresses, then landed on a dark green woolen suit with an hourglass fit. The black buttons running down the front were trimmed in gold. She had a leopard-print, peach basket-style hat and a faux-leopard muff that always looked smart with the dress.

"That's two outfits. Now for the rest of my trip." She still needed to choose a week's worth of suits for the days of meeting, greeting, and gazing at the fashion shows, then the same amount of evening gowns and cocktail dresses to cover the evening events.

Audrey's attention fell on the array of trunks and luggage she'd set out before she started looking through her closet. "I'll need to buy another trunk at the store." Maybe two if she had the time to sneak away and shop.

Mr. Wynton had insisted she take some time to look around for herself. *"I don't need to tell you of the value of shopping at the other stores. See what our competition is up to,"* he'd told her.

Shopping was her job now, and she could position herself as a walking advertisement. If something she bought received compliments from her neighbors, she could order it for the store and avoid buying things that wouldn't sell and causing Wynton's to lose money.

A knock sounded on her front door. "She's early." Audrey slid her closet door closed. "She must really be anxious."

She went to answer the door. "Come on in, Gigi."

Gigi started to step into the room, then backed up and wiped her shoes on the welcome mat. She met Audrey's gaze when she finished. "I didn't want to track anything in your house. The floors on the bus get awful dusty."

"I told you I'd be happy to pick you up." Audrey shut the door behind them.

Gigi clutched the tortoiseshell handle of her beaded purse. "Where can I put my bag down where it won't cause a problem?"

Audrey opened a small louvered door and motioned to the hooks on the wall inside the closet. "Hang your coat in here, and you can leave your purse on top of the glove chest."

Gigi slid her coat from her shoulders, stuffed her black gloves in one pocket, and then deposited everything in the closet. When she came back out, she stared at Audrey with wide eyes, as if she were awaiting her next instructions.

This was a side she'd never seen before, and Audrey wasn't quite sure how to address this scared-little-rabbit attitude.

It was hard not to think of the first time she babysat Mary Jo's girls, and how they cried until she'd suggested they play dress-up. The rest of that night turned out to be a nightmare, but at least for a few moments she'd managed to make them relaxed and happy.

She'd have to find the same magical something to help Gigi. "Let's go into the kitchen. I've got a fresh pot of coffee going, and I made a chocolate pound cake that just came out of the oven."

Gigi raised her nose and sniffed the air, then closed her eyes. "I wondered what smelled so delicious."

Audrey held her kitchen door open. "Have a seat at the table. I'll get the coffee and cut us both a piece of cake."

"I still can't believe you cook and bake like you do." After claiming a seat, she surveyed the room.

Audrey removed two cups from the cabinet and set them down on the table. "Why is that so hard?" She poured them each a cup, then slid the sugar bowl and creamer toward Gigi.

Gigi shrugged as Audrey handed her a spoon. "Are you on the level? You always look like you're dressed to be in a catalog, skinny as a rail, and never a hair out of place. And look at this kitchen. Spotless right down to the wallpaper, even though you baked a whole cake in it." She scooped some sugar from the bowl and stirred it into her coffee.

If they were going to get anywhere, Audrey would have to get Gigi past the idea that she was inferior to. . .well, just about everybody around her. This would require opening up more than she liked, but that's what friends did, and Gigi needed to know she was a valued friend.

Audrey swallowed a small wave of fear as she scrambled to form the right words. "Want to know a little secret?"

Gigi leaned forward. "You bet I would."

Audrey walked to her oven, opened the door, and slid out the dirty dishes she'd used to bake her cake. "I didn't have time to wash them all before you got here, so I hid them in here, to clean up later." She shut the door and then crossed her arms while she stared at Gigi. "I'm far from perfect, and maybe a little sneaky."

Gigi let loose a deep laugh. "You're human. Hooray."

The little confession worked and the rabbity look faded from Gigi's eyes. The bigger surprise was sharing her own shortcomings brought about a warm feeling for Audrey. She had to admit it was rather nice letting Gigi know she wasn't always the picture of perfection. Sometimes, she was just. . .Audrey.

Sharing dessert, talking, learning new things about each other. These were the feminine things she'd eschewed because for her younger self, they came too hard.

The earlier exchange made her want to experiment with another. "I have other secrets." She poured a small drop of cream into her coffee then watched the white swirls coil around as she stirred.

Gigi gulped down a bite of cake. "There's more?"

Audrey set her spoon on the edge of her saucer. "I'm trying to pack for my trip next week, and I can't figure out what I want to wear."

"I don't ever go anywhere, so I don't worry about that. Besides, if I did go, my whole closet comes with me because I don't own many clothes. Easy as pie." Gigi sliced off another bite. "Or pound cake."

Gigi closed her eyes as she chewed. "This is almost as good as Lilla's pound cake that she makes for the cafeteria sometimes." She washed her bite down with a sip of coffee.

"Gigi, how do you think I can help you?"

"Jane and the other girls know things I don't."

"What do you mean?" Audrey laid her fork across her plate.

Gigi pointed to her plate. "Like that. See, you put your fork down so daintily, without clinking it on the china or making a mess everywhere." She motioned to her own plate. "I put mine down on the tabletop, then realized I got crumbs all over the place."

Her eyes misted and she swiped away a tear trickling from her eye. "It's like some secret code they learned that I never knew existed. For instance, they know how to stand up straight, with their toes pointed out all ladylike and sophisticated. They even know how to hold their arms at their sides and look feminine."

Gigi stood. "When I stand up, I hunch my shoulders, and my arms dangle down like two wet noodles. And look at my hands."

She held them out for Audrey to see. "They're huge. Jane and the other girls in Cosmetics have these tiny hands and slender, girlish little fingers."

Gigi wiggled her digits at Audrey. "What woman is going to trust me to demonstrate the latest products on her when I've got sausages like these?"

She crumpled into her chair and buried her face in her hands. "They'd be worried I'd gouge out their eye with a mascara brush or smear lipstick from cheek to cheek like a clown's makeup."

As Gigi sniffled behind her hands, Audrey rose and grabbed a dish towel from the sink. She returned to the table and laid it before Gigi. Helping wipe tears, she could handle.

But the other problem presented a greater challenge. She'd rather poke herself with a straight pin than admit she hadn't a clue how to manage Gigi's insecurities.

Her friend had come to her for a solution. And finding solutions for problems at Wynton's had always been her top priority. Gigi was her friend, and she would find a way to fix this.

"First of all, you've got to stop picking at yourself so." She reached across and pulled one of Gigi's hands free, then pressed her own against it, palm to palm. "I want you to look at something."

Gigi opened her eyes, then gasped.

Audrey nodded. "Exactly. Your hand and mine are practically the same size. In fact, my fingers are slightly longer than yours."

Gigi snatched her hand back. "But mine are twice as fat."

Audrey swallowed back the frustrated sigh dying to escape from within her. "They are not. You've focused on all these flaws so long that you've blown them completely out of proportion."

Gigi spoke as she wiped her nose with a napkin, which muffled her words. "What does that mean?"

"You've made a mountain out of an anthill."

"I think that's supposed to say molehill."

The corners of Audrey's mouth twisted into a half grin. "Your tiny little flaws aren't large enough to be considered a molehill."

Gigi dropped her napkin over her plate. "That's easy for you to say, you don't have any."

"Will you please stop saying that? I have my own collection of flaws. Many, many of them."

"Yours are all on the inside, where nobody sees them, or judges you for them." Gigi squared her chin as if she were readying for what she knew was a silly argument but wanted to stir up anyway.

Audrey crossed her arms and rested them on the tabletop. "That's rich coming from someone who not even a year ago disliked me because I was uppity."

Gigi looked away as she fiddled with a button on her cardigan. "Mary Jo shouldn't have told you I said that."

"She didn't. Lilla did."

"Oh." Gigi dropped her hand to the table and ran her index finger along the smooth surface.

"Look, Gigi, I can help you learn to be a fantastic clerk in Cosmetics. But your biggest challenge isn't Jane or the other girls. You are your own worst enemy, and only you can change how you feel."

Audrey continued. "You know I went to finishing school, and Miss Evelyn, our headmistress, always told us that God made each of us unique for a reason. There are so many women in Levy City who would love to have you help them when they come to Wynton's. Do you know why?"

Gigi shook her head.

"Because when they look at you, they see a friendly face. Not a pretty girl focused on making her sales quota for the month, who looks down on them for not being more like her."

"Tell me something, Gigi." When her friend met her gaze, Audrey continued. "Why did you come to Wynton's in the first place?"

"I wanted a chance at something good."

"Then let's make certain you make the most of that chance." She gathered up their dishes and walked them to the sink. When she returned, she offered Gigi more coffee but was waved away.

When she'd wiped the table clean, Audrey motioned for Gigi to stand. "The first thing we're going to work on is poise."

"What does that mean?"

Audrey led her to the kitchen door and ushered Gigi through to the next room.

"What are you doing?"

"Teaching you how to walk and stand. Once you've got that down, I'm going to show you how to stand toe to toe with Jane and come off looking like a star clerk."

Gigi smiled wide. "I like the sound of that. Audrey, you're the best."

Audrey moved and let the door swing shut behind her. They'd see how much Gigi still liked her once the lessons and the evening were over.

Chapter 17

Vivien

There were few activities in the world better than sitting down with a new bride and helping her plan out the wedding of her dreams. Vivien had promised herself a long time ago that when she no longer got the butterfly flutters during a sit-down with her brides, it was time to take her name off the front of the salon and go home for good.

She opened the folder she'd made for her newest bride, Susan, and slid out a thin stack of papers. "I have all my new brides fill these out. Helps us plan out your big day and ensure everything comes out beautiful in every way."

Vivien held the first paper so Susan could see from her seat on the couch. Robbi Dever had bounded in as soon as the salon opened, and she'd claimed a nearby seat, scratching words in her notebook nonstop.

"This is for flower arrangements. You tell me what you'd like, and your choice of florist. We work with all of them here in town. If you're going simple, I'd suggest seeing someone from Wynton's own floral shop."

Susan pointed to the sheet. "Will this go in the bridal guide you gave me?"

Vivien tapped the book's cover. "This covers everything, including items you might borrow from the salon, like the runner for the church aisle, kneeling benches, large standing candelabras. I'm here to help you with each step."

Vivien handed her the book. "You are coming to Bridal Week, aren't you?"

"Yes ma'am."

"Perfect. All the things covered in the bridal guide will be on display, along with cooking demonstrations, things for your trousseau, items to help you set up your kitchen, tips on furnishing your new home, how to set up your invitation lists, and your gift registry."

Susan soaked it all in as she released a long breath that whistled through her pursed lips. She flinched when her mother elbowed her in the ribs.

"Stop puffing so, Susan. You sound like a steam engine."

Vivien patted the girl on the shoulder. "Do you have any questions?"

"No ma'am. But I'm about to bust from wanting to look at bridal gowns." Susan's cheeks dimpled from her wide smile.

"That is the part we all look forward to, isn't it? Do you know what style you'd like?"

"I can't describe it, but I'll know which one is my gown when I see it."

Vivien moved to the small table where she kept the latest editions of *Brides, Modern Bride,* and the newest magazine to hit the market, *Bride-To-Be*. She returned and held them out for Susan and her mother to look through.

"These will show you all the latest styles. I've got catalogs in the back, and we can order any gown you'd like. Mirette and I can also custom-make a gown if you don't see what you want. Take your time."

Her engagement ring sparkled under the salon's chandeliers as Susan opened *Modern Bride* first. She dropped her voice to a whisper. "I want to make sure I pick the right one. I mean, this gown is for the most important day of my life."

She turned a page, then looked up at Vivien again. "You keep all the wedding gown details secret, right?"

"Yes ma'am. We don't even allow the bridesmaids to see the gown until the bride says so."

"Oh good. I want my wedding to be perfect, right down to the surprise of my dress." Susan returned her attention to the magazine, stopping on a page while she and her mother discussed what details they liked or disliked on the dress in the picture.

"Take your time while I check on Mirette."

As she walked away, Robbi was thumbing through one of the bridal guides.

Mirette sat in her sewing chair pushing her needle in and out as she hemmed the light blue skirt of a bridesmaid's silk organza dress. "I should have this finished by tonight. All I have left is finishing the beading around the neckline and the edges of the sleeves."

Vivien peeked around the door frame of the fitting room to check on

Susan. "How's the other dress coming? The entire bridal party comes in on Thursday."

Vivien tapped her finger on the open page in her book. "Bridget Farraday has her first fitting this afternoon, so I'll need you to do her pinning then. And Helen Farmer is coming in to look at sample swatches tomorrow morning."

Mirette slid the fabric along her lap until she reached the next stretch to hem. "Are you trying to nicely tell me I'm falling behind?" She threaded her needle into the flowy fabric.

"I'm telling you flat out. We've got six new bridesmaids gowns coming in the day after tomorrow. And our appointment dates in March are almost filled."

Vivien met her old friend's gaze. "This is shaping up to be our biggest year yet, and we can't afford to muddle through on our reputation and good looks."

"Then you'd better stop nagging and let me get back to work." Mirette held up the hem of the dress as if to prove her point.

Vivien returned to the sales floor as Susan and her mother huddled together with their focus glued to a page. "You find one?"

Susan turned the page around for her to see. "This one, the Emelia."

Some folks thought naming the gowns was a strange custom, but for those who created and sold them, each dress carried its own distinct personality and traits. Naming the dresses made remembering and ordering them much easier.

"We have a sample of this beauty here in the shop." She walked to the armoires where the samples hung and pulled out the gown. She held the dress up as Susan and her mother rushed from the couch to get a better look.

"Mama, look at this Chantilly lace. Isn't it pretty how it drapes over the sides of the taffeta skirt, and goes all the way to the floor?" Susan circled the dress, lightly touching the smooth taffeta skirt. "This is so shiny."

"That's because it's organzine taffeta. This fabric picks up the lights and will shimmer as you walk down the aisle." Vivien held up the material for Susan's mother to see.

She was too busy looking at the lace covering the bodice to the neck, creating the oh-so-popular modest neckline the brides loved. "Susan, look at these tiny seed pearls." She touched them again, then pulled back as if she might break them. "This top is so dainty and pretty."

Vivien moved the dress to her other hand and pulled another from the rack. "This is Annalee, a gown with a softer, more romantic look. The lace covers the entire dress from the neckline, sleeves, and the acetate skirt."

Susan laced her fingers together over her heart. "I like this dress too."

"Emelia comes in white only." Vivien held the second dress up. "The Annalee comes in white, ivory, blush pink, or light blue. All four shades are beautiful."

Her mother scowled. "You only want white, right honey?"

"Might be fun to be different from all the other girls."

The big white wedding had come to be the in-thing, and though some brides dared to marry in light blue, blush, or ivory, Vivien and Mirette ordered most of their gown choices in white these days.

Vivien motioned to the couch nearest them. "Have a seat, Mama, and we'll have Susan come out and model the dresses for you in the big mirrors, under the lights."

When Susan was ready to show the Emelia, Vivien opened the door of the dressing room. "Let's go show your mama."

Susan lifted the front of the skirt and glided out the door. As she passed by, Mirette raised her eyes. "Now don't you look fetching."

"Thank you, Miss Mirette."

Susan walked to the wooden platform before the large, tri-fold mirrors. Her mother peered at her reflection as her eyes welled with tears. Vivien handed her a box of tissues, then spread the gown's skirt wide so both mother and daughter could see the full effect of the design.

"I don't think you could look more perfect if you tried." As all mamas did, she got up and walked around to see her daughter from every possible angle.

Vivien took a few steps back. "What do you think, Susan?"

"I really like this one." She chewed her bottom lip a moment. "But I still want to try on the Annalee, in the blush pink. Just to see how it looks." Susan watched her mother's face in the mirror.

"I don't see why. This dress is beyond perfect." Her mother may have been smiling, but notes of irritation played in her voice.

Mama and daughter not seeing eye to eye was nothing new. Vivien and Mirette held to a firm belief there was a dress for every bride, and a way to make her mama happy too. The trick was finding one in time to curtail a fussing match between a hen and a little chick ready to spread her wings and fly.

Vivien stepped in. “Let’s try the other one.”

“I don’t think we need to do that—”

“Mama, I want to see the other dress. Just for fun.”

Susan squared her shoulders, turned on her heel, and headed back to the dressing room. She flounced past Mirette, grousing under her breath.

“Didn’t have a meeting of the minds?” Mirette said when Vivien walked into the fitting area.

“Mama’s determined she’s going to like the Emelia.”

Mirette mouthed a silent “Oh dear” and returned to her sewing.

When they reached the dressing room, Susan clenched her fists and groaned. “What am I supposed to do, Miss Vivien?” She reached out and stroked the long lace sleeve of the Annalee.

“Try this gown on and if you like it, we’ll show your mama. Seeing you happy might help change her mind.”

Susan let go of the sleeve. “I hope so.”

A sparkle gleamed in a girl’s eyes when she’d found “the dress.” She’d stand straight, look at herself from all sides, and hold her head high. The greatest sign was the spark in the eyes when the critical voice living in every woman’s head silenced, and a quiet, confident one came through, uttering three simple words: *I look pretty.*

And it was as plain as a tail on a dog, when Susan tried on the Annalee, other words played through her head. “This dress makes me look like a pink Christmas tree topper.”

In times like this it was best to move the bride along quickly before she lost hope of finding something she’d look nice in.

“You wait right here. I have another gown for you to try.”

When she returned, Vivien held up a white taffeta gown embellished with silk roses around the waist. The neckline and long sleeves were edged in white satin ribbon trimmed with pearls. The plain skirt flowed to the floor in the wide bell-shape all the girls loved, with a ribbed bodice sure to compliment Susan’s tiny waist.

She’d also pulled a short tulle veil that flowed from a cap trimmed with the same ribbon and pearls. Vivien’s heart squeezed at the sight of her personal label sewn inside the gown. She battled to keep away thoughts of the two girls found with her name draped across their dead bodies.

Her focus needed to be on Susan as she reached out and stroked the soft fabric on the bodice. “I don’t even need to try this one on. This is my dress, Miss Vivien. I can feel it all the way to my heart.”

"Then let's go show your mama."

Tears and joy followed as Susan's mother approved the new pick. The fact that she would be wearing a Miss Vivien original pleased both mother and daughter. After the appointment time ended, they chattered like best friends about wedding details and how they were going to soften up Daddy when they told him the price of the gown.

Vivien had been so focused on helping Susan find her gown she'd forgotten Robbi was still in the salon and jumped when her voice blared at her. "Another happy bride with a Miss Vivien original," Robbi sang as she packed up her notebook and pen. "Your gowns seem to have a magic touch. Except for. . .oh, never mind me."

Robbi slung her purse on her arm, then waved at Mirette. "Happy sewing." She walked over to Vivien and grabbed her hand and shook hard like a politician stumping for votes.

"Vivien, it was a pleasure coming in here. Watching you take care of that girl was an experience."

She crossed the salon with her wide stride. "You're amazing, Vivien," she yelled as she exited and headed for the door to the stairs.

Adulation was something Vivien never aspired to. She'd learned long ago, hard work and building a good reputation were far less fragile than the public's love when life took wrong turns.

A wonderful silence settled over the salon with Robbi gone. Vivien switched gears to pursue an idea she'd formed during her morning drive to the salon.

"Mirette, I've got to run downstairs. If we have a walk-in, get them started and I'll be back shortly."

Mirette sewed a final knot, then cut her thread short. "What's going on with you? You're acting like you've got fire ants in your girdle."

"Nothing." Vivien hurried out the salon's back door and headed down the hallway to the employees' stairs. If Mirette knew what she was planning she'd be as mad as a hill of those fire ants that were supposedly in Vivien's girdle.

Chapter 18

Vivien

Vivien put a finger to her lips when Lilla looked up from the steaming pan of gravy she was stirring in the cafeteria's kitchen. Aromas of baking biscuits blended with scents of buttered carrots and roasted chicken.

Lilla lifted the giant spoon she'd been using and laid it on a small saucer streaked with remnants of an earlier batch of her well-loved chicken gravy. "You need something, Miss Vivien?"

"I want to ask you something."

"Let me turn these carrots down and get a pot of water for the rice boiling." Vivien sat on a nearby stool as Lilla turned on the burner beneath a huge silver pot. "You need me to fix you a plate?"

"No thank you." Vivien rearranged herself on the stool to ease a cramp in her back. It seemed her body was determined to remind her she wasn't a teenage schoolgirl who could sit on just any type of furniture these days.

"Lilla, I'd like to hire Immogene to come and work for me in the salon. Can you get the message to her?"

"Yes ma'am." Lilla opened a bag of rice and poured in the amount she needed with the expertise of one who cooks so well they no longer needed to measure.

"Tell her to come in tomorrow and go straight to the back door of the salon."

Vivien paused until Lilla located a lid to place on the pot for the rice. Once she had Lilla's attention again, she continued. "I'll talk with Personnel today, so she doesn't have to worry about store security snagging her in the hallways."

"Yes ma'am, I'll talk to her as soon as I get home tonight." Lilla opened a drawer and pulled out a clean spoon, then swished it around in her pot of boiling rice.

She turned the temperature down and put the lid back on the pot. "If you don't mind my asking, how are you doing? I hated hearing about those girls getting killed and them finding your bridal things there."

"It's been absolutely awful." It was nice to admit this to someone, let go of the burden of being strong in public and keeping her chin high.

Vivien had been careful to remain calm around her clients, and even Mirette. She'd never own up to sobbing every night once she changed into her bathrobe and put her feet up to work on new designs in her sketch pad. Tears stained those pages. If someone looked in her wastepaper baskets, they'd see a slew of used tissues.

The fragrance of the biscuits filled the room as Lilla opened the oven door and peeked in on their progress. "I don't like all those things that Robbi Dever's been saying about you in the *LTC*."

"I haven't read the paper in weeks." She'd decided not to read another word of local news until her brides' killer was caught.

Lilla moved to the corner of the room and picked up a folded-over copy of the newspaper lying on a cleared counter. "Her column this morning was about how the police keep finding your labels and dresses on the dead girls." She thrust the paper at Vivien. "Begging your pardon, but Miss Vivien, I think you'd better take a gander."

She'd rather not, but Lilla was being so kind. Vivien took the paper and read the headline.

Another Bride's Dreams Tarnished

Every detail of Cathy's and Rayanne's deaths was laid bare in black and white. Her labels ripped from the gowns and laid across each bride's chest, the silver candelabra and the teapot used to bludgeon the girls in the head, and the copy of their bridal guides laid nearby. As Lilla said, all the connections to her were front and center.

She folded the paper over and tossed it on the counter beside her. "I'm not—"

"You didn't read the other stuff." Lilla handed the paper back to her and pointed to the additional paragraphs.

Upon further reading, heat rose up the back of her neck, and she gripped the edges of the *LTC* so hard her fingernails left claw marks on the thin newsprint.

Young Mr. Cameron had come through on his threat to expose his being removed from the guide. His rant was placed at the end of the article—the last thing readers would see and plenty scandalous with all his various complaints against her snobbery, her unfair business practices, and how her age must be affecting her judgment.

The worst was his own conjecture about who was responsible and why these murders kept happening.

"*Miss Vivien has had full rule over the wedding business in Levy City for too long. It's clear she's been acting like a tyrant, a dictator, and someone has had their fill. It's time for her to retire and allow someone else to serve the brides in Levy City*," his direct quote read.

Having standards, exercising good business judgment, and relying on plain old common sense were now akin to being a tyrant. "Doesn't make me sound like a very nice lady, does it?"

Lilla took the copy of the *LTC*, walked across the kitchen, and dropped it in the garbage can. "Folks around here know what to believe."

She returned to the stove, slid on oven mitts, and took her biscuits from the oven. "You sure I can't give you one of these? They're good for settling an upset stomach."

"I couldn't eat now if I tried." Vivien slid off the stool and smoothed her full black-and-red plaid skirt into place. "Thank you for giving Immogene my message, Lilla."

"She'll be glad to hear it. What time you want her here in the morning?"

"Mirette and I get here around seven, so tell her to come at seven thirty. She can take the service elevator again and then knock on the salon's back door. I'll be waiting."

"You sure you couldn't meet her at the service door, down by the loading dock? That's the only one we can get into in the morning without trouble." Lilla removed the lid from the pot of rice and fluffed the contents with a fork.

"I didn't know about that."

"Thought you might not." Lilla put the lid on and removed the pot from the heat. "Immogene has to. For now." Lilla's eyes met Vivien's, and in them flashed a warning as well as something Vivien could only interpret as a mix of disgust and sadness.

"Tell her I'll be waiting at the employees' entrance, facing the garage. I'll walk her up the stairs myself. Then no one will have reason to bother her."

"Yes ma'am. She'll be there."

The door to the service line opened, and a young woman stuck her head in. "Lilla, we need the next round of everything." She exited as fast as she'd come, making the door swing in and out behind her.

Without a word, Lilla lifted a large metal pan filled with chicken breasts and legs, then made her way to the serving line door. She stopped and turned back to Vivien. "When you have time, let me know what desserts you need for Bridal Week. I know you like to plan early."

"I've got my list at home. I'll bring it to you tomorrow."

Lilla nodded and pushed her way through the door to the serving line.

Vivien hurried back to the salon. Reading Robbi's column had made her return later than she planned, and she hoped Mirette hadn't been hit with a barrage of walk-in brides while she was gone.

Her door chimes sounded but the salon was quiet, which always brought a moment of worry. Though they were a little backed up and the lack of customers gave them a chance to breathe a minute or two, her business owner's mind preferred a constant bustle of customers on the sales floor.

Mirette hurried toward her, her hands clenched and her face as white as bleached flour. "We got a phone call while you were gone."

"Did our one o'clock cancel?"

"Oh Vivien, I wish that were so." Mirette's bottom lip trembled, and she released a shaky sigh.

"Mirette, what on earth is the matter with you?"

Her assistant grabbed her by the hand and tugged her toward the fitting area in the back of the salon. "We'll talk back here."

Vivien allowed herself to be led to one of the bucket chairs and plopped down as Mirette took a seat in the other.

"Mirette, if you don't tell me what's going on, I'm going to—"

"Sheriff Youngblood called here while you were gone."

"What did he—" Vivien paused, as the tears brimming in her friend's eyes spoke volumes. "Oh, please no, not again."

Mirette laid her hand on her chest as her shoulders quaked with her sobs.

Vivien's throat constricted, and all she could force out was a hoarse whisper. "Who?"

Mirette swallowed hard before the words could come. "Leila Dyes."

Vivien's stomach churned, and she pressed her hand against her middle to hold off any eruptions. "When?"

"Bill said they found her late this morning."

A question loomed, and though she didn't want to know the answer, part of her pushed her to ask. "Was she dressed in her wedding gown?"

Mirette nodded. "And your card was set on her chest. Remember, she ordered her dress from Alfred Angelo. It wasn't one of ours."

Vivien smashed her fist against her lips, knowing full well her lipstick would be smeared. And she couldn't have cared less. Leila was a darling girl who'd been married less than a year. Rumor had it she and her new husband were hoping they'd be blessed with a baby soon because they wanted a big family.

One thing stabbing at her heart the most was knowing the cards she gave as a little encouragement to all her brides had been a part of the ugliness.

For all his blustering and whining in the *LTC*, young Mr. Cameron had been right about one thing. Whoever was killing her brides wanted the whole city to think this was all about her.

There had been no label to link her to this girl, so the killer chose the message she gave to all her brides as the link this time. Every bride she served went home with her dress nestled into its box, bundled in folds of pink tissue paper. She'd tuck one of her special cards, printed on light blue stationery festooned with tiny pink roses around the edges, in with the dress.

Printed on the cards was a simple message:

Wishing you all the best from this day forward
Love, Miss Vivien

The front-door chimes sounded, and Vivien rose from her chair.

"Our one o'clock is here." She slid out the handkerchief she kept tucked in her sleeve and blotted her nose and eyes.

Vivien caught sight of her lipstick smeared beyond the borders of her lips, and her mascara looking like a mud puddle in the corner of her eyes, in the fitting room's mirrors. "I can't go out there looking like this. I'll scare off both the bride and her mama."

She walked by Mirette and squeezed her shoulder, then moved to her desk. Vivien pulled out her purse and removed her compact. In a quick moment she'd fixed her smeared lipstick, cleaned up her mascara, and patted powder on her pale cheeks. When she finished, she put everything back and slid the drawer closed.

"We'll have to put this behind us for now, Mirette. Our next girl deserves the best we can give her." Vivien smoothed her skirt and adjusted the silk bow on her black blouse.

She exhaled, uttered a quick "Lord help us" under her breath, and then strolled out to the sales floor.

Her newest bride and her mother waited by one of the racks of gowns, looking over a dress the bride had pulled out.

Vivien blinked away a leftover tear and pasted on the phoniest smile that ever had graced her face.

"Welcome to Miss Vivien's. How can we help you?"

Chapter 19

Audrey

Audrey tried for the third time to read through her to-do list, without success. Libby had pulled one of the chairs from the waiting area close to her desk and sat filing her nails while chattering away about. . .something. One thing her assistant didn't come with was an off switch.

Leaving the office in her hands was a frightening prospect. Audrey had eaten almost half a bottle of Tums in the last few days alone. Mr. Wynton assured her the store wouldn't fall to the ground during the fourteen days she'd be in New York.

How much damage control would be necessary once she returned had kept Audrey up late for the past several nights. She'd spent hours compiling a folder for Libby. Information on things like what to do in case Mr. Wynton had to be out, how to handle when disgruntled customers called the executive suite, and the exact recipe for preparing Mr. Wynton's coffee. The folder was now several inches thick, and every minute she'd think of another item needing to be added.

The swishing of Libby's nail file stopped, as did the blue streak of blather. She popped from her chair and hurried to the door of the executive suite. "Hello, may I help you?"

Audrey turned to see Gigi standing in the doorway, staring at Libby. "Who are you?"

"I'm Libby, Miss. . .Penault's assistant. Do you have an appointment?"

Gigi stared at the girl, then switched to Audrey. "You never said you had an assistant. Is this part of the new job?"

"Not exactly." Audrey pushed back in her chair and directed Gigi to the waiting area. "Grab a seat and we can talk."

Gigi marched past Libby. "Excuse me."

When she was seated, Gigi pulled Audrey close, then tilted her head in Libby's direction. "Does she have to be here?" she muttered under her breath.

"Libby is going to help us." She waved her assistant over.

Libby's white crinolines under her wide blue skirt fluttered like curtains in a breeze as she scooted over to them. "Ooh, I'd love to."

Audrey didn't miss Gigi's eye roll or how her shoulders tensed. This wasn't going to be easy, but there was no other way to help her friend gain confidence around customers.

"We're helping Gigi with some employee training, so I need you to pretend you're a customer in Cosmetics."

Libby clapped her hands together. "This sounds fun. What am I going to buy?"

"We'll decide that in a moment." Audrey rose and pulled Gigi to her feet. "Let's practice what we went over last night at my house."

"You've been to Miss Audrey's house? I just know it's gorgeous, like a magazine isn't it? Oh, you have to tell me what it's like. I'm dying to know." Libby bounced on the short heels of her pumps.

Gigi put up her hands. "I'm not doing this."

She turned to leave but Audrey caught her by the arm. "Gigi, trust me."

Gigi clamped her lips together so hard they puffed under her nose. She exhaled with the force of a bull pawing the ground, ready to attack. Her fear and insecurities were about to boil over, requiring quick action.

"Libby, go stand by my desk. In a moment, you're going to approach Gigi as if she's the clerk at the perfume counter. You're shopping for something special, but you don't know what you want and you need her help deciding."

"Yes ma'am." Libby moved to the spot where Audrey pointed.

Audrey then turned to Gigi, who now stood with her shoulders hunched in as if she were carrying a sack of large rocks on her back. "Stand up straight, square your shoulders, and hold your head up like Audrey Hepburn in *Sabrina.*"

"That's one of my favorite movies. Wasn't she just dreamy in that?" Libby said behind them.

Gigi pivoted to face Libby. "Didn't you just love the dress she wore when she was waiting for David in the tennis court?"

Libby put her hands on her cheeks and shook her head. "And when

Humphrey Bogart found her on the boat at the end." She closed her eyes as she hugged herself. "I cried so hard."

Gigi patted her chest. "Me too. It's one of my favorites." She ran her hand over her hair. "I tried to cut mine like Sabrina's in the movie, but I ended up looking like I had a bad pompadour. It was awful."

Gigi's entire body drooped and any ounce of confidence she might have had seeped away. It was difficult to believe the hardheaded, say-it-like-she-thought-it girl could shrivel so quickly from the memory of a bad haircut.

Audrey formed a new plan. She tapped Gigi on the shoulder. "I love your hair *now*. As I've told you many times, you remind me of Marilyn Monroe in *Seven Year Itch*."

Libby's gasp sounded behind Gigi. "Miss Audrey, I love that movie too." She paused for a moment as her forehead puckered in a confused scowl. "You go to movies?"

"Yes, I do." She wasn't going to mention that she'd been to Hollywood more than once and turned down a chance to be in the background of a film. That information might send both Gigi and Libby into heart failure, and she didn't have time to fool with that.

"Maybe we could go see one together at The Tropics Theater sometime. Wouldn't that be fun? A night out, just us girls." Libby looked at Gigi. "You should come too. The more the merrier. We could share a jumbo popcorn."

"Yeah, maybe." Gigi nodded, then checked her watch. "My break is almost over."

"Let's try to practice, and then you can get back downstairs." Audrey steered Gigi to a spot in the waiting area, then turned to Libby. "All right, Miss Customer, you're up."

Libby scooted to the new spot where Audrey pointed, then straightened to her full height, as if she wanted to try her best to be at eye level with Gigi. "Excuse me, miss? I'm looking to buy some perfume, and I need some help finding just the right scent."

Gigi pressed her lips together, then rolled her eyes at Audrey. "This is stupid." She crossed her arms and humphed.

Audrey stepped behind Gigi. "Practice makes perfect. You want Jane to stand up and take notice of you, right?"

Though it was slight and Gigi caught herself in time, Audrey still saw her bottom lip tremble. She clamped her jaws together. Somehow she'd hurt Gigi's feelings, and now the entire lesson would be wasted.

Libby stepped forward and took hold of Gigi's hands. "If you could buy any type of perfume in the world, what would it be?"

Gigi pulled her hands back and clasped them into a single fist over her chest as she stared at Libby. "L'Air du Temps."

She'd pronounced it phonetically, and in a voice made soft to hide what she saw as her ignorance. Trying to find a way to correct her without hurting her feelings was going to take some doing. Tactics which now evaded Audrey's thinking.

"Aren't those French names nigh on impossible to say?" Libby turned to Audrey. "Miss Audrey, could you teach me how to say it correctly so I can help Miss Gigi?"

Audrey fought to keep her jaw from dropping. Libby's handling of the situation was genius. And completely shocking in its simplicity and smarts.

"Of course. It's pronounced *L'Air du Temps*."

Libby repeated the name a few times with surprisingly good results, then nodded to Gigi. "You try it now."

Gigi drew in a deep breath, but her practice was interrupted by a knock on the main door.

"I'll get that, and you go ahead and practice," Libby said as she skipped to the door.

Gigi was about to try again, but Libby's greeting the newcomer cut her off.

"Welcome, how may I help you?" Libby toned in the background.

"Well hello, Libby Farris. What are you doing here?"

"Hey, Miss Vivien." Libby tilted her head in Audrey's direction. "I'm her new assistant."

"I'm here to see Audrey myself." Miss Vivien stopped in the middle of the room and shot Gigi a questioning look. "Didn't expect to see you up here."

Gigi ducked her head and looked around, then checked her watch. "I'm going. If I'm late none of this will matter. . .not that it does anyway." She rushed past Audrey and into the hallway. Her running steps padded toward the elevator.

Libby puckered her lips and wiggled them from side to side. "She hasn't got a lick of confidence, does she?"

"Did I interrupt something? I can come back." Vivien started for the door.

Audrey held up her hand. "No ma'am."

For Miss Vivien to come in during the workday, something had to be amiss, making Libby a pair of little ears not needing to be there.

"Libby, I need you to go get some more cups from the storage closet."

"Again? I—"

Audrey dipped her chin and stared Libby square in the face. "Right away."

Libby's shoulders drooped and wilted like lettuce in vinegar. "Yes ma'am." As she slunk into the hallway, her muffled complaints of "Every time somebody comes in, I have to go to the supply closet" bounced off the walls and back to the executive suite.

Audrey went to apologize for Libby's behavior, but instead caught Miss Vivien staring into space, her eyes filled with a deep sorrow that seemed to well up from somewhere deep within. The depth of the pain sent a shiver down Audrey's back.

She possessed no instincts for dealing with strong female emotions, but Miss Vivien was her friend, and the urge to comfort swelled up, pushing her to act.

Audrey wrapped her arms about her friend. Miss Vivien's shoulders shook as small sobs escaped and spots from her tears dotted the front of Audrey's blue suit jacket.

Miss Vivien raised her head and brushed away her tears with her fingers. "I've gone and wet your Traina-Norell. I'm so sorry."

"You're forgiven, seeing you're one of the few who knows this is Traina-Norell."

Miss Vivien fanned her face with one hand. "That's from the '54 collection, isn't it?"

"Right again." Audrey hesitated as her mind reeled with what to say next. "As Libby is so fond of saying, Miss Vivien, what gives?"

The slight curling of her friend's lips eased Audrey's fears that her attempt to lighten the situation came off as bad taste.

"I came to ask you if you would hurry through a new hire request for me. Libby reminds me so much of Cathy Baker, Rayanne, and now Leila Dyes that this wave of sadness grabbed me, and I couldn't fight it off."

"I promise I won't tell anyone." Audrey held out a clean handkerchief she'd retrieved from her desk for Miss Vivien to use. "I hadn't heard about Leila yet. When?"

"Bill called to tell me a little while ago."

"I'm so sorry, Miss Vivien. I know what your brides mean to you."

"I feel like somehow it's all my fault. And every time I talk to Bill, I know he's holding back information, which he should. I have this nagging feeling there's a message to me mixed in all this, but I'm too dense to see it, and that is driving me insane."

"Don't blame yourself. We have to hope and pray Sheriff Youngblood will figure this out."

Audrey paused because it seemed like the thing to do before moving on to the other business where she could be of service. "I'll type up the application and have Mr. Wynton sign it today. He'll be back from a lunch appointment at the club any moment."

Miss Vivien pressed the hankie against the last of the dampness on her cheeks. "Thank you. And I'll wash your handkerchief before I return it."

Audrey walked to the filing cabinet near her desk, opened a drawer, and thumbed through the folders. "I'll get the application." Once found, she took it to her desk and sat down.

"I only know her name."

Audrey tapped the end of her pen on the desktop. "I see."

"No, I don't think you do."

"You're being rather cagey about all this, which isn't like you at all."

Miss Vivien straightened. "She's Lilla's sister-in-law."

"Do you mean Carletta, Immogene, or Minna?"

"How did you—I guess that doesn't really matter, does it? It's Immogene."

Audrey fed the application into her typewriter and filled in the information. "I hired her to make my gown for the New Year's ball one year. She's exceptional and fast. Orders must be going well."

"Through the roof." Miss Vivien sat on the corner of Audrey's desk. "I'll tell you this, only because I know it won't leave this office."

Being brought into another woman's confidence was not something she was used to. "Go on."

"Mirette and I are falling behind. We're both taking dresses home at night, but things are still piling up. With Bridal Week just around the corner, we need another pair of hands to keep things flowing. Otherwise, we'll fall short, and I won't have that, Audrey. I just won't."

Audrey removed the application from her typewriter. "I'll have this approved and delivered to Personnel before I leave today."

Miss Vivien squeezed Audrey's hand.

"Is it okay for me to come back in now?" Libby called from the hallway.

Laughter danced in Miss Vivien's eyes. "I'd better go."

There was a quick temptation to tell Miss Vivien she could take Libby with her, but Audrey resisted. "Come in."

Miss Vivien left the office, passing by Libby as she made her way back into the suite.

"Is Miss Vivien okay? She looked awful serious when she walked out."

"She's very busy today."

To make certain Immogene's application didn't get misplaced, Audrey added it to a stack she was taking with her.

"Libby, I'm going down to my office. Mind the phone and file the papers I laid out for you on my desk. When Mr. Wynton returns from lunch, buzz me. I need to talk with him about something this afternoon."

"Yes ma'am. I hope Miss Vivien doesn't work too hard. She looked awfully tired, and a little sad."

Audrey stared at Libby. For a young girl, she possessed an extraordinary ability to read people in a flash.

"Don't worry about her." Audrey pointed to the phone, which was now ringing. "You've got plenty to focus on right here."

"Yes ma'am." Libby lifted the receiver. "Mr. Wynton's office, how may I help you?"

As she walked to her office, Audrey couldn't stop wondering how much of an open book she'd been to Libby, and what the girl had read in her.

The message to see her manager couldn't have come at a worse time. Right in the middle of a sale that would help her meet the weekly quota.

"You need to get your things and head home, Mary Jo. Your father's sick and your mother needs you. Your husband said he'd get your girls from school."

Mary Jo switched into neutral. She couldn't move, think, or breathe.

"Go." Her manager waved her hands as if trying to sweep her out of the department.

If she didn't make it home and Daddy got worse, Mama would never forgive her. Once in the employee locker room, Mary Jo grabbed her things, including the box of candy she'd bought for Kenny. She ran to the time clock and punched her card, then wrangled her free arm into her coat sleeve.

She squeezed the steering wheel so tightly her knuckles ached as she sped to her parents' home. Doctor Hall's black Oldsmobile sat in the driveway, reminding her of a hearse. She grabbed her purse and ran up the brick sidewalk to the front door.

As she reached for the knob, the door swung open. Mama grabbed her by the hand and yanked her inside. She was still dressed in a light blue cotton housedress, the kind she often wore during the day when she was doing her housecleaning.

"Hang your coat on the rack. You know I can't stand clothing draped all over my furniture." Mama took Mary Jo's purse, and her hat, then stored them in a small credenza along the wall. "We don't want your free, fancy store clothes to get all wrinkled."

Her mother hadn't thought much of her receiving clothes in trade for being in Wynton's holiday fashion show last Christmas. Getting something for nothing was frowned upon in Mama's strict code.

"How is Daddy?" Mary Jo hung her coat on the hook next to Dr. Hall's black overcoat.

"How should I know? Dr. Hall won't tell me anything. He started choking and gasping for breath." Mama grasped her own wrists, as if holding onto herself for support. "His lips turned blue."

She paused, and her jaw trembled before she clenched it tight. "I saw red streaks on his handkerchief after one of his coughing spells. I've been praying like mad." She moved Mary Jo's coat to another hook on the rack.

"We have to have faith things will turn out." Mary Jo squeezed Mama around the shoulders the same way she'd hug the girls when they awoke in the night with fears of a noise or bad dreams.

Her mother jerked away. "What else would I be doing?"

The sharp tone seasoning her voice always had a way of slicing through Mary Jo and making her feel naughty and small. "Let's go sit down in the living room, Mama, and I'll fix you some tea or coffee."

Her mother huffed but did head to the other room. "Go see if he'll tell you anything."

"Yes ma'am."

Mary Jo tiptoed down the hallway to her parents' room. Through the open door, she watched as Dr. Hall bent low with his ear near Daddy's mouth. She took a single step inside, then stopped as a familiar twinge of uneasiness brought on nervous shivers.

Mama and Daddy believed their bedroom to be a private sanctuary for each other. When she was young and her chores included helping Mama with the family's laundry, she would run in, set her parents' clean clothes down quick as a flash on their dresser top, and then scoot back out to the safety of the hallway.

She knocked on the wooden doorframe. "Mama sent me in to see how Daddy's doing."

The doctor stood to his full height as he removed his stethoscope from his ears and draped it around his neck. A tuft of his salt-and-pepper hair stood up as if he'd been scratching his head.

Mary Jo stepped closer to the bed.

Daddy lay stretched out under the blue-and-yellow wedding ring quilt Mama had made for her hope chest when she was a young girl. His breaths came in too quick a rhythm. There was no color in his face, and he kept his eyes closed.

"How is he?" she whispered.

Dr. Hall's dark brown eyes met her gaze. "Not good."

He wouldn't want her to see him like this. Daddy was a quiet man who wouldn't voice his deep care for his children but showed it through actions of love. Like when he gave up a hunting trip in Georgia to help Kenny build the back porch on their house a few years ago.

"His heart's weak, and he's got pneumonia. Mae should have called me much sooner."

Footsteps thudded toward them from the hallway. Her mother appeared in the doorway. "That ambulance is here."

Dr. Hall moved past Mary Jo. "You two go sit in the front room. They'll need the space in here to get Harold wheeled out." He left them standing alone.

Mama went and clasped Daddy's hand. "I know I promised I wouldn't let them take you out of here, but the doctor ignored me. I'll come sit with you every day."

He didn't rouse as she kissed the wrinkled skin on the back of his hand. Mary Jo briefly turned away out of embarrassment for watching. Her stomach clenched.

There was no doubt Mama and Daddy weren't the types who showed off their love in front of others. Seeing Mama forget herself with such an intimate gesture made her mouth go dry.

Mama released him and wiped her hand on her apron. She squared her jaw and closed her eyes in what Mary Jo knew was another silent plea to God. She punctuated her prayer with a quick dip of her chin, Mama's way to show she was finished talking and expected things to be done according to her will.

She marched out of the room and Mary Jo followed her down the hallway.

"Mama, I want you to come home with me after they get Daddy settled in the hospital."

Her mother swung round on her. "I most certainly will not. I'm staying in my own house."

"You shouldn't be alone. I'll take off from the store and drive you to see Daddy."

Her mother stomped to the living room and parked herself in her rocking chair. She planted her feet, pushing back so hard Mary Jo feared the chair might flip over and dump Mama on the floor.

Dr. Hall entered with the men from the ambulance behind him. The sweet antiseptic smell of the medical profession assaulted her nose as he directed them to the bedroom. The gurney's metal wheels rattled as they hurried down the narrow hallway.

Mary Jo moved behind Mama's chair to be out of the way.

Mama pounded her fist on her rocker's arm. "I'm staying put. I can take the bus to the hospital." The one thing Mae Sellers allowed herself to take pride in was her own stubbornness.

Mary Jo had figured out how to outsmart her own toddlers when they refused to do what she'd asked. She now riffled through her mental bag of hardheaded-proof tricks as she came round to face her mother. "Have you ever ridden a bus?"

"You know I haven't."

"You'll have to share seats with folks you don't know."

Mary Jo settled on the couch and tried to ignore the soft strains of Daddy's moans drifting to them from the bedroom as the ambulance workers settled him on the gurney. "They don't let you save the seat beside you. Sometimes the buses are so full people stand in the aisles and hold on to the rails above your head." She knew this not from experience, but rather from complaints Gigi had made during their lunch chats.

Mama detested having strangers all around her, and it was plain to see the thought of being packed in like a box of crackers with others on the bus bothered her. But she was far from unraveling her resolve.

"What if your daddy's in the hospital for several days? You take off too much time from that job and they'll fire you."

"I'll talk to Mr. Wynton. I'm sure he'd understand." Or at least she'd beg Audrey to get him to understand.

"My, talking to Mr. Wynton all on your own. How fancy."

Mary Jo bit her bottom lip to keep from smiling. Mama relied on petty insults when none of her other tactics worked. "We'll pack your bag before we leave and stay until they get Daddy settled in the hospital. We'll go straight to my house after."

Mama set herself to rocking so hard the chair inched along the rug with each movement. Her silence signaled the first time Mary Jo had won a skirmish against her mother.

There was no time to revel in the victory as Dr. Hall and the other men carried Daddy's gurney down the steps. They had him loaded and headed to Levy City Regional Hospital in minutes. Mary Jo got Mama packed and in the car soon after the ambulance pulled away.

Once his patient had been admitted, Dr. Hall allowed Mama a few minutes to speak with Daddy, while he pulled Mary Jo aside.

"Keep Mae at home. Harold needs no excitement. Her coming would be too much."

"Yes sir." A mouse would have a better chance of keeping Mama at home than Mary Jo would. Mama respected no authority other than her own and Daddy's.

They drove home in silence. Mama refused any offers to sleep in the master bedroom and instead staked her claim on the living room couch. She laid back on the pillow Mary Jo brought and demanded Kenny open one of the windows to let cool air in so she could sleep. Then she needed another blanket, so she didn't get cold.

When Mama was tucked in and her breathing quieted to sleepy snuffles, Mary Jo remembered the box of candy she'd bought for Kenny. She'd put it in the trunk of the car when she left Wynton's earlier, with plans to sneak it into the house once he'd fallen asleep.

How could she have been so silly to have forgotten? The gift was to be the peace offering to help fix things, and now the entire box was probably unfit to eat.

Mary Jo snuck to the car when Kenny was brushing his teeth, grabbed the box, and hurried into the kitchen. She laid the box on the table, her hopes high the cooler night air had protected the chocolates from melting.

Upon removing the lid, her plans soured. The candy looked like a car had run over the box and flattened every piece. She lowered herself into one of the kitchen chairs and buried her face in her hands.

Kenny's lowered voice broke into her thoughts. "What's all this?"

She opened her hands like curtains and met her husband's questioning look. "Happy Valentine's Day."

Without saying a word, he went to the silverware drawer and took out a fork and spoon.

"Kenny, what on earth are you doing?"

He shut the drawer, then took the seat across from hers. "Did you eat anything tonight?"

"No. By the time we got home from the hospital and got Mama

situated, I wasn't hungry."

He reached across the table and laced his fingers with hers, the first time he'd been affectionate with her in weeks. "Go take a shower, put on something comfortable, and then come back here."

She shook her head. "I have to get up early to call into the store and let—"

"Mary Jo, they know you aren't coming in. Go clean up." He tilted his head in the direction of the bathroom. "When you get back, we'll eat this candy. You need something sweet to soothe what you've put up with today."

He smiled, and she melted in the glow of it. This was her Kenny. Her hero who always stepped in and made the ugliness go away. She'd missed him like the dickens, and tonight, he'd come back to her.

"I'd love to, but you saw what a mess this candy is."

He held up the fork and spoon. "That's why mankind made these."

She wanted to kiss him for being so wonderful, and just as the courage to do so welled up in her, the phone rang. Mary Jo jumped up to make whoever it was go away. "Hello?"

"It's Gigi. I wanted to check on you after I heard about your daddy."

Kenny turned in his chair and shot her a look asking for her to end the call.

"Hey, Gigi. He's in the hospital, and we've got Mama here with us."

At the sound of Gigi's name, Kenny swiveled around and put the lid back on the candy box. He pushed back with the box in hand, heading to the refrigerator.

Mary Jo touched his arm and shook her head as she covered the phone's mouthpiece. "Wait. Please," she whispered.

Kenny looked deep in her eyes, like he did back when they first got married. He settled down at the table and opened the box again.

"Whew, you've had a day. Did you hear about Miss Vivien?" Gigi called from the other end of the line.

Mary Jo's stomach flinched, but she kept her eyes on Kenny. "Another girl?"

"Isn't that awful?"

Mary Jo tapped on a coil in the phone's cord. "I hate hearing this happened again." She closed her eyes as Gigi went on to explain in more detail.

This was what being squished between rocks and hard places must feel like.

Knowing Miss Vivien was facing another bride's death was heartbreaking. But this call couldn't go on. She had Kenny back and nothing was going to steal away this moment, because she needed to enjoy the break before the next dark mood hit.

"I'm sorry, Gigi. I'm about to fall asleep on my feet."

"And here I'm going on and on. I'll see you tomorrow at the store and we'll catch up."

"I'm staying home, until Daddy gets better."

"Good. Call me if you need anything."

"Promise. Good night."

A wave of guilt blanketed Mary Jo as she hung up and joined Kenny at the table. She couldn't stop the notion that she'd dropped both of her friends like a hot potato tonight.

Kenny scooted his chair so they sat side by side, then handed her a spoon with a scoop of a melted cherry cordial.

"For my favorite Valentine."

Chapter 21

Gigi

Gigi's eyelids drooped and her head tipped forward as she sat on her bed, clad in her pajamas, robe, and pink fuzzy slippers. She took a break from filing her nails and turned to look at her alarm clock sitting on the nightstand.

"It's only seven thirty, and I'm dozing off?" She swung her legs over the bedside and bounced off the springy mattress. "I've got about as much to do as a snowshoe salesman in Miami."

With Mary Jo busy with her ailing father and caring for her mother, she never had time to talk on the phone in the evenings. And there was nothing on the radio but songs she'd already heard. Or Robbi Dever's fashion segment, which Gigi had abandoned weeks ago because she was always talking about the murders of Miss Vivien's brides. It seemed like she was stabbing her friend in the back if she listened.

If only she could meet a nice young man and go on a date or go see a movie. Even meeting for coffee, which she hated, would beat sitting in her room night after night with nothing to do but read magazines, set her hair, and file her nails.

Why did she have to have such rotten taste in men? Watching the other girls in the house fixing their hair and putting on their cutest dresses to go meet their fellas every night stirred up an ornery restlessness in her.

She missed the nights of being on the dance floor, the room a little too warm because of all the bodies packed on the dance floor. The laughter, the music, the fun of a man holding her about the waist, smiling, talking, swaying among the scents of cologne and perfume.

A soft knock on the door jarred her from her thoughts. "Gigi, there's someone here to see you."

She set her file on the desk and out of habit checked her hair in the makeup mirror she'd bought from Wynton's. Her other got broken in her move to the new apartment. "Who is it?"

"She said her name was Audrey Panall. . .or something."

Audrey? She never came by the apartment.

Gigi opened the door to find her housemate, Janet, dressed in a light blue quilted robe, her hair twisted in pin curls with a white silk cap wrapped around her head.

"She's waiting for you in the front parlor."

"I'll be right down."

Gigi worked hard to be pleasant to her housemates in hopes one of them might someday invite her to come along, but none did. They saw her as an old maid, too elderly to remember how to have fun. "Thanks, Janet."

"Sure." She walked down the hallway back to her room.

Gigi took the stairs two at a time, and when her slippers hit the polished floor at the bottom, her feet went out from under her and she went down in a heap.

The impact echoed through the room and into the parlor, causing Audrey to pull her attention from a painting on the wall in time to spy Gigi sprawled on her sitter, flopping like a turtle turned on its back.

"Oh, my gracious, Gigi, are you hurt?" Even in speeding to check on her, Audrey moved with the grace of a dancer, like Ginger Rogers or Ann Miller.

Ladylike and feminine. Jane and the other girls in Cosmetics would never give her a hard time if she could learn how to be more like Audrey.

Gigi pulled off her slippers and stood before her friend, rubbing all the places now screaming at her for being so clumsy. "At least I fell on a body part with enough cushion to take the fall."

Audrey motioned to the parlor. "I brought something for you."

Gigi peered around her and saw a white box sitting on the ancient coffee table. "You brought me a jewelry box?"

Audrey moved into the parlor and bent down to pick up an item on the floor next to the coffee table. She held up a large carton. "And a few other things."

"What do you want me to do with all this?"

"I have a plan." Audrey stacked the jewelry box on top of the other carton and walked to the stairs. She stopped and turned back to Gigi. "It includes you."

Gigi took careful steps to the stairs as she led Audrey to her room. Her landlady must have used too much polish on the floors when she'd cleaned.

"What's all this?" she asked when Audrey set the mystery parcels down on the rug.

"Put on your favorite outfit you wear to the store, and then we're going to play dress-up." Audrey moved to the door. "I'll wait in the hall until you're dressed."

All this made Gigi's head spin as bad as high school geometry did. "I don't have on a stitch of makeup—"

"Dress first, then we'll get to the makeup." Audrey closed the door behind her.

Gigi went to her closet and pulled out her navy suit and the white silk blouse she finally got out of layaway at the store. She left the jacket on the hanger. Once dressed, she opened the door and Audrey stepped into the room.

"Excellent choice. Now sit."

Gigi plopped down hard on her vanity stool, and the white fringe around the seat wobbled from the force. She watched in the mirror as Audrey picked up the samples case from the store. "I'll have you fixed up in a minute, then we'll move on to what helps every girl feel like a million dollars."

"And what is that?" Gigi wrinkled her nose into the snottiest expression she could muster.

Audrey stepped between Gigi and the mirror as she applied a pearl-sized dollop of pancake makeup on Gigi's cheeks. "Accessories."

When she moved out of the way a few minutes later Gigi squealed at her reflection. "I can't believe that's me. How on earth did you do that so fast?"

"Practice." Audrey moved behind Gigi with her head tilted like an artist reviewing their work. "You make an excellent canvas."

A knock on the doorframe interrupted them. "What's all the noise about?" Janet gasped and rushed to Gigi's side. "Honey, you look amazing."

"Audrey did this."

Janet jerked her attention to Audrey. "Could you teach me how to look this good?"

"No, but you can volunteer to be our model for Gigi to practice on."

"Split, sugar." Janet rushed to the stool and practically pushed Gigi from the seat.

Audrey motioned for Gigi to take her place, then held out the compact with the pancake makeup. She said nothing but looked directly at Gigi with an I-know-you-can-do-this expression.

"Put one small drop on your fingers, then gently smooth it over her skin." She waved her finger in a message to Gigi to get going.

Audrey took her through the finer points of shading, contouring, and blotting as well as other little secrets she'd picked up in her modeling days.

"Boy, Gigi, you're a natural at this. I never looked so nice." Janet cooed at her reflection.

Audrey shot Gigi an I-told-you-so-side eye, then walked over to the jewelry box she'd brought. "Now's the fun part."

She opened the box. "You first, Gigi." Audrey held up a necklace with three strands of large white beads, each separated by a golden leaf-shaped bead. "Let's see how this looks on you."

Gigi held the necklace in place as Audrey fastened the clasp behind her neck. "I have matching earrings too." She removed them from the jewelry box and held them out to Gigi.

"Gosh, Gigi. You look so sophisticated." Janet moved from the stool. "You should have a look at yourself."

Gigi ran her fingers over the necklace and then the earrings as she studied her reflection. "This suit never looked so good."

Audrey went to the larger box, now sitting on the floor. "Put your jacket on. I want to show you something else."

When Gigi turned around with her jacket in place, Audrey removed the necklace, then held out a mound of brown fur to her. "Your jacket has the perfect round neckline, so wrap this faux-fox collar around your neck."

Gigi complied, and then Audrey took a round rhinestone pin from the jewelry box and pinned the collar in place. Next came a fascinator, trimmed with a brown satin bow and a small swatch of fur matching the collar, that Audrey placed on her head. "Go have a look."

She didn't know what to think about the woman staring back at her, looking as if she were on her way to have lunch at the Grove or the country club. Gigi had no idea what going to the club was like.

If they were brainless enough to let her into one, she'd probably make a fool of herself by saying something out of place or breaking some rule of good manners.

She jabbed the collar with her finger. "Take this thing off."

"But you look—"

She balled her fists. "Get it off me, Audrey."

Audrey stepped forward and removed the pin, then unwrapped the collar from Gigi's neck. After both items were put away, she clasped her hands in front of her, released a breath, and stared, waiting for an explanation.

Gigi unbuttoned her jacket and laid it across the top of her vanity chair. "I don't want your cast-off clothes."

"These aren't my things. I found them in my new office." She waved her hand over the box. "They're samples, or merchandise I can't put out on the sales floor because they're missing labels."

She continued. "I brought them over for you to try. You can go through them, keep what you like, and share the rest with your friends." She gestured toward Janet.

Janet rushed to the box, knelt, and sifted through the contents. "There are some really great things in here, Gigi. They're all brand-new."

"What's all the ruckus in here?"

Gigi swerved to see another one of her housemates, Jewel, staring at them all.

Jewel crossed her arms. "I'm trying to listen to Robbi Dever's show on the radio, and y'all are making so much racket I can barely hear her."

Janet pointed to the box. "Gigi's friend brought over some items from Wynton's, and she's giving them away."

Jewel turned on her heel and headed for the door. "Keep it down in here. Robbi's talking about all the things going on with Miss Vivien and her brides, and I don't want to miss this." She walked from the room without saying another word.

The box and jewelry were forgotten as Gigi exchanged a look with Audrey, then hurried to turn on her radio.

Robbi's voice blasted from the speaker. "Well Levy City, it's happened again. Another bride who worked with our wedding maven, Miss Vivien, has met her 'till death do us part' earlier than she and her groom expected. The shocker is she met her untimely demise from the result of a crystal punch bowl being used to put her lights out permanently. Read more about it in my column, The Juice, in the *LTC*, just below the fold. Remember, if it happens, I've seen it, heard it, and now I'm telling you. I squeeze the juice from every story until we get to the seeds of the truth."

"Gigi, this is ghastly. Turn it off," Audrey commanded.

Ghastly was a nicer way to put things than what Gigi was thinking as she rose and turned off the radio. "Poor Miss Vivien."

Audrey grabbed her purse, then turned to Janet. "It was nice meeting you."

She then turned to Gigi. "Change your clothes and meet me downstairs."

The moonlight glinted on the surface of the lake. The darkness blanketing the neighborhood testified to the late hour as Audrey pulled her car into Miss Vivien's driveway.

"Are you sure she isn't going to be put out? It's pretty late," Gigi said over the top of the car once she and Audrey got out.

"She'll understand."

The porch light by the front door flickered on. Miss Vivien peeked through the ruffled curtains in her front room as Audrey and Gigi made their way past the flower beds filled with her prized petunias and roses.

The aroma of warm cinnamon and butter crept out the door when Miss Vivien welcomed them in. "Y'all are out late tonight."

Audrey scraped her loafers on the welcome mat, taking the extra time to calm her nerves while Gigi followed suit.

Robbi Dever seemed to think she was clever, poking fun of Miss Vivien, using a cutesy turn of phrase without any thought to the murdered girls and their families. If she hadn't been brought up more ladylike, Audrey would have kicked Gigi's radio out the window and enjoyed watching it crash on the ground.

"Why are y'all determined to grind your shoes into my welcome mat?"

Audrey met Miss Vivien's half grin. "We heard Robbi's show."

"Come on in. I've got fresh iced tea and warm coffee cake too, if you're hungry." Miss Vivien shut the door behind her.

"Thank you, but I'm too steamed at the moment to even think of eating." Gigi yanked off her cardigan.

A crooked grin spread across Miss Vivien's lips. "Y'all think I bake in the middle of the night for my health?"

Their footsteps echoed on the dark wood floors as Miss Vivien ushered them onto her living room couch. She sat across from them in a high-backed armchair, looking every bit as elegant in her white chenille robe embroidered with red flowers as she did in her best suit in the salon.

"You said you listened to Robbi's show together?"

"We were practicing with some cosmetics to help Gigi feel more comfortable in her new job."

"Jane and the other clerks have been giving you a rough time, Gigi?"

"Did Mary Jo tell you?"

Miss Vivien shook her head. "She didn't have to. I've worked with enough of those girls in the fashion show to know they're a difficult little sorority to break into." She shifted in her seat, rearranging the bottom of her robe to better cover her leg. "What has Audrey taught you so far?"

With Gigi's rejection of the fox collar, and her sudden outburst plus refusal to try anything else, Audrey was hard put to say she was doing much of anything to help. "The basic principles of poise, polish, and professionalism."

Miss Vivien propped her elbow on the chair's arm, then rested her cheek against her fist. "And how's that working?"

"I learned tonight that fake fox makes me itch."

"Me too. But's that's not why y'all sped over here, is it? You think I'm in a mess."

Miss Vivien uttered the words without emotion, as plainly as if saying steak was on sale at the grocery store. She crossed her legs and leaned forward.

"Robbi is a good lady to talk about fashion. She knows all about sewing and makes fashion talk fun, even if she doesn't follow trends herself. Trouble is, all she talks about now is me and my dead brides."

On the drive over, Audrey and Gigi talked of how Wynton's might stand up to the awful things Robbi Dever hinted at in her column and radio show. Seeing the tired look in Miss Vivien's eyes, the slight downturn at the corners of her mouth, and the small drooping of her shoulders erased all those good ideas.

"Has Sheriff Youngblood found anything pointing to the killer?"

If she'd known her last word would have made Miss Vivien flinch so, Audrey would have snatched it back. Instead, her friend looked as if she might burst into tears, a fit, or a combination of both.

"I'm so sorry, Miss Vivien. I shouldn't have said it that way."

"No reason trying to shine-up the truth. Bill and his boys haven't found anything. He says it's as if whoever is doing this pops out of the air, then disappears after the deed is done. They leave behind nothing. Except the clues pointing to me."

Audrey hesitated, then pushed forward with what she came to say because Miss Vivien needed to know what she'd figured out. "After Robbi's show, when she mentioned the punch bowl, I realized something."

Gigi whipped her head around and looked at Audrey. "What?"

"They're all items from Wynton's—"

"And my bridal guide." Miss Vivien finished Audrey's thought. "I know that guide like the back of my hand. When the teapot showed up as the second murder weapon, it was clear as day."

Gigi sat forward on the couch. "Have you told the sheriff?"

"They knew, but it still doesn't point them to anyone other than me."

Audrey slapped her palm against the couch arm. "Then we've got to find more evidence, send them in a different direction."

Miss Vivien traced the outline of a flower on her chair's upholstered surface. "While my tea brewed, and my cake was baking, I sat at my kitchen table and wrote down all the evidence to see if I could fit the pieces together. They won't."

She shrugged. "Bill says those poor girls opened the door to this person, and for some reason showed them their gowns. Then they were killed."

"But the weapons. Who would go digging through a stranger's home to find a candleholder, a teapot, and a punch bowl?" Gigi looked back and forth between Audrey and Miss Vivien. "Gives me the creeps to think about it."

"Me too, but as sure as the sun rises in the east, somewhere in that creepiness lies the answer we're all looking for." Miss Vivien rapped her knuckles in her lap.

"We're going to figure this out, Miss Vivien, and protect you and the salon."

"This is about more than just me and the salon. I don't want to see another young woman in Levy City die. If we don't stop this madman, every girl in town is going to be afraid to get married."

Miss Vivien paused and glanced at a large clock on the wall of her living room. "It's late. Audrey, don't you leave for New York in the morning? And Miss Gigi, you're never going to wow Jane or your customers if you show up with dark circles under your eyes."

The hint for them to leave being clear, Audrey rose. "I'm fine, been packed for over a week. Besides, I never sleep well before I travel."

Miss Vivien pushed up from her chair. "I don't either. I spend the entire night going over all the details. Are you flying out?"

"No ma'am. I've booked a private compartment on the train. But I will be flying home." To make certain Libby hadn't destroyed the executive suite or driven Mr. Wynton to distraction.

Miss Vivien walked them to the door, then gave them each a hug. "Thanks for worrying about me. Old age and the good Lord gives gals like me wisdom. We'll figure this out."

Audrey said little on the way back to Gigi's apartment. Too many thoughts churned in her mind, glomming together like wet mud and rocks in a cement mixer. One question kept popping up, begging for the clue they all needed.

"It's scary to think someone around us did these terrible things." Gigi voiced what had spun through Audrey's brain.

Audrey parked by the curb so Gigi could get out. "I'm afraid of what they've done too. But more afraid of what they'll do next."

Chapter 23

Gigi

There were enough people to start a stampede when she reached the bus stop. The whites waiting to board were bunched on the left. Some chatted together, while others stood alone, reading the morning edition of the *LTC*.

Probably Robbi Dever's awful column, with more bad news for Miss Vivien.

Gigi shifted her attention to the Colored riders who stood together several feet away. A young man dressed in the dark blue uniform shirt worn by Wynton's loading dock employees held the attention of the entire crowd around him. His story must have been a real humdinger because he kept waving his arms about his head, sending the entire crowd around him into fits of laughter so hard many were wiping their eyes.

If she could have gotten away with it, Gigi would have joined them just to hear the story. She needed something fun to think about rather than murder and Miss Vivien. From the moment her windup clock's alarm had jingled in her ears, her mind went racing with worries. She'd done a stupid thing in not letting Audrey help her last night, and sure as rain it was going to come back and nip her somehow.

The sounds of squeaking brakes mingled with the low-pitched roar of the bus as the vehicle rounded the corner and came to a halt before the bus stop. The men in the crowd waited, ushering the women to board first. The Coloreds waited, knowing they weren't allowed to set foot on the bus until all the whites took their seats.

Rosa Parks may have challenged the bus system in Montgomery, but in Levy City, the old ways stuck fast, and nobody pushed against them. Gigi shuffled into the line behind a woman dressed in her nurse's uniform and another who worked at Wynton's.

When she finally boarded, there was only one vacant space left in the middle of the bus, next to a man with his nose buried in the *LTC*. He didn't look up when she slid onto the seat next to him.

The Colored riders filed in, their eyes cast down as they passed the whites, who stared straight ahead. Since the whites filled all the available seats, the Coloreds stood in the aisle and grasped the metal rods above their heads and held on. They wobbled from side to side as the driver turned the bus onto the street.

A woman near her own age stood in the aisle next to Gigi. She carried a large, overstuffed woven bag on her arm. But that wasn't what caught Gigi's attention.

The woman wore a dark green suit as well made and fashionable as the ones Audrey wore to the store. Her hair was styled smooth with a row of neat curls at the bottom, and she wore a matching felt pillbox hat.

Gigi leaned close to her. "I love your outfit." Complimenting the woman would bring on the disapproving looks from fellow white riders, but if a girl took time to look nice, it was rude not to let her know.

The woman jerked to the side as the bus turned to the left. She straightened, then glanced at Gigi long enough to give a quick nod. "Thank you." The woman looked forward a moment, as if surveying to see if anyone noticed Gigi talking to her, then dipped her head low. "I like your outfit too. It's well made."

"Thank you. I bought it where I work."

The woman looked around again, then answered. "At Wynton's?"

Gigi nodded. "Did you get yours there too?"

"I made mine."

A man standing behind the woman poked her in the back. When she looked over her shoulder at him he shot her a warning look to hush. She rolled her eyes and turned to the front.

The bus moved into downtown, then pulled over to the curb in front of the store. Wynton employees rose to their feet. The Coloreds standing in the aisle moved like a giant inchworm, packing together like a tin of cookies as they moved backward to make room for the white riders to disembark. Levy City rules dictated Coloreds got on and off last.

Gigi gave the woman she'd spoken with a fast smile as she moved past, but she received nothing in response. She hadn't expected to. Even on a city bus, the rules for no interaction between the races were set in stone.

When Gigi stepped off, she headed for the employee entrance next to the parking garage. The crowd thinned as others walked past her. When they were far enough ahead, she stopped and turned to see the woman she'd spoken with on the bus.

Had things been different, she would have wished the woman good luck on her first day. In her heart, she still did.

After leaving her lunch and purse in her locker, she hurried on into the store. The hearts and pink crepe paper chains left over from Valentine's Day were now gone. The floor decorators were hanging green shamrocks to celebrate Saint Patrick's Day in a month. Audrey had said those employees stayed busy this time of year since there was a holiday every month from New Year's to the Fourth of July. And all those holidays provided Wynton's with the chance to offer merchandise to help their customers celebrate with sales. Sometimes it was hard to wonder if Audrey ever thought of anything other than retail and what was best for Wynton's.

The cosmetics department came into view. Gigi stood up straight to elongate her waist, and spread her shoulders, as Audrey had taught her. She slowed her steps and pointed her toes outward to make her stride more graceful. This made her wobble on the heels of her open-toed pumps like she was walking on the top board of a fence, but like Audrey said, practice made perfect. Unless she fell flat on her face.

Jane met her when she entered the department. "The new shipment of perfumes came in last night. You can restock the scents we sold out for Valentine's Day. Once you've finished, come see me, as I have a list of other tasks for you today."

Her gaze took in Gigi from head to toe. "Where did you get the new collar? The black velvet looks wonderful against your brown suit, and I love your pearl broach." She pointed to Gigi's brown velvet headband trimmed with a dotted-swiss bow. "Is this hat from Wynton's? It's darling."

Before Gigi could answer, Jane glided over to the makeup counter and took up a conversation in low tones with another of the clerks. They both stole glances at Gigi while they whispered together.

Better to ignore them, like a dull toothache. Gigi had forgotten she left her hat on when she left her other belongings in her locker, so she removed it and stashed it under the counter. After grabbing a pair of scissors, she sliced open the tape on the box of perfumes and was thinking about which scent testers needed refilling when Jane called her name.

She looked up to see Jane and another woman standing across the counter from her. The lady looked as though she were poised and ready to blast Gigi with a big bag of unhappy opinions.

Gigi rose, smoothed her straight brown skirt over her knees, and moved to the counter. "May I help you?"

Jane motioned to the woman standing beside her. "Gigi, this is Mrs. Hillary. She'd like to look at some perfumes."

Jane bowed her head and joined the other clerk. The way they both watched from afar triggered a warning to Gigi that she'd been set up somehow.

Mrs. Hillary pounded her palm on the glass top of the perfume case. "Hello, I'd like service, please."

Gigi snapped her focus back to her customer as heat traveled up her cheeks. She'd show them.

"Yes, Mrs. Hillary, I'd love to help you. What are you looking for?"

"I'm tired of Chanel No. 5, every woman I know wears it. I want something unique."

She took a quick look over the woman. Tiny, maybe stood five feet at most, and thin enough that a good gust of wind might blow her over. She wore a belted green crepe dress with a wide skirt held out by fluffy crinolines. The black lace gloves she wore matched her purse and gave her outfit a soft, feminine feel. But it was quite apparent she owned an iron will and was accustomed to being heard and catered to.

Not a woman who could pull off a dainty rose scent. No, she required something as robust as a rare steak cooked with grilled onions.

"I don't blame you for wanting something different. Who wants to smell like every other lady in the room?" Gigi brought out three choices.

She lifted the stopper from the first bottle and held it out for Mrs. Hillary to sniff. "This is Miss Dior. It has a spicier scent than most as it's a combination of lily of the valley, amaryllis, jasmine—"

"That smells like grass clippings to me." She wrinkled her nose and her entire face creased.

Gigi set the bottle aside and opened the next one. "This is L'Air du Temps." She spoke the name slowly, saying the words with the French flair Audrey had taught her.

Mrs. Hillary shook her head. "I wore that before I switched to Chanel."

"Youth Dew." Gigi didn't get the chance to even open the bottle before Mrs. Hillary held up both hands.

"My sister-in-law wears that. She and I don't get on very well."

Without a word Gigi set the decanter back in the case, then met her customer's pointed what-are-you-going-to-do-for-me-now look.

This woman wasn't going to beat her. Gigi put her hand on her hip and met Mrs. Hillary look for look. "You aren't leaving Wynton's without a new scent today, even if I have to conjure up a brand-new one for you." She dotted her claim with a firm nod, then looked over the array of perfumes she hadn't presented yet.

Audrey would have approved, and at the thought of her friend, a new idea beamed. There was a perfume she hadn't tried, but it might do the trick. Gigi searched the case for the blue Baccarat crystal bottle.

She wouldn't mention Cumby's Drug Store up the street carried the same scent, in a much cheaper blue cobalt bottle. Something told her Mrs. Hillary wouldn't set foot in there to purchase anything other than medicines.

When she spied the tester tucked behind the samples of the more expensive brands, her heart leaped. "This is Evening in Paris. A very sophisticated friend of mine wears this, and I have to say, I adore the scent."

It was Audrey's favorite, and Gigi worked to gather her thoughts to remember how this perfume smelled on her. "A lovely mix of violets, lilac, rose, and jasmine, with some other flowers added in to make this a pleasant, traditional scent." She handed over the glass stopper. "What do you think?"

After one sniff, Mrs. Hillary closed her eyes, and the closest thing to a pleasant look crossed her face. "Different for sure. I'll take it." The expression disappeared when she opened her eyes again. Her lips fell into a satisfied line as she unclasped the latch on her purse and pulled out her Wynton's charge plate.

As soon as Gigi rang up her purchase and wrapped up the perfume, Mrs. Hillary snatched her package and then marched to where Jane and the other clerk stood watching. "From now on, when I come in here, you send her—" She called to Gigi, "What's your name again?"

"Gigi."

Mrs. Hillary returned her attention to Jane. "You send Gigi straight over to wait on me. She's the only one around here who knows what she's doing."

Mrs. Hillary stomped from Cosmetics and headed down the main aisle.

Gigi put the cast-off choices back in the case, then wiped the glass clean. She fought against the urge to smile as wide as a crocodile, thinking how proud Audrey would have been.

"Looks like we may have a gatherer on our hands," the other clerk said.

Gigi kept her eyes down, unsure what the term *gatherer* meant. She'd ask Mary Jo later when they talked on the phone. For the moment, it was clear the clerk meant for her to hear, and she wasn't going to give her the satisfaction of ruining her day.

Her first sale was in the books. And she'd closed the deal by being plain old, hardheaded Gigi.

Chapter 24

Vivien

Vivien glanced at her watch for the fourth time as she blew on her hands. Her fingers stung and she was certain if she didn't get back to the warmth of the salon they were going to go numb. An icy, wet wind blew in through the opening of the loading dock. Five days ago the weather had been warm enough to not even need a coat. Now goose bumps covered her arms and down to her toes thanks to a blast of winter from the north.

The aroma of diesel exhaust filled her nose as a truck backed up to the loading bay. She'd come to meet Immogene at the service entrance, like Lilla insisted. Other Black employees filed in, but as the end of their line passed by, Immogene was not with them.

A man's voice boomed through the area and all the action stopped as heads turned toward the noise. One of the Black women poked another woman standing beside her.

"Immogene's been snagged by the security guard."

"I told her she wouldn't get in without a note. She fussed back at me, said things was all fixed and she didn't need one."

The first women tsked. "None of us gets in here without one on the first day."

That couldn't have been what happened. Audrey took care of the paperwork before she left on her trip.

The man's voice threatened as Vivien excused her way through the line of Black employees and headed through the service door. She found the guard standing on the bottom step, blocking Immogene from coming in.

"You've got no note, you're not coming in."

Vivien tapped him on the back of his shoulder. He turned around like a puffed-up rooster ready to spur an opponent but then deflated when he recognized her.

"Miss Vivien, what are you doing down here?" He grabbed the metal railing along the steps as if her presence had knocked him off-kilter.

"She's my new employee."

He stretched to his full height and looked down at her. "She doesn't have a note or a Wynton's employee card. She's not coming in without one or the other."

He appeared to believe she'd accept this as a sufficient reason. "Douglas Royce, you mean to tell me you believe I'd waste my time to come down here, stand in this biting wind, without my coat mind you, to fetch a woman who is not my employee?" She crossed her arms to let him know she wasn't going to budge. She was his elder, and he'd better act accordingly.

Vivien then motioned to Immogene. "I'll take you up to the salon myself."

She clasped Immogene by the elbow and maneuvered her past the security guard. The pink shade now coloring his cheeks may have been a mix of cold and a bit of embarrassment for being dressed down by a woman.

Her mother brought her up to be diplomatic when dealing with men, and she tried her best to follow suit most times. Mother also taught her when a woman reached a certain age, she lost all patience with nonsense.

As she ushered Immogene into the building, her conscience pricked at her until she turned around. "You're looking a little cold, Douglas. You'd best get inside before you catch something." Southern upbringing wouldn't allow her to walk away without trying to smooth things over.

His face softened into a more understanding expression. "Yes ma'am. Next time, make sure your Coloreds have the right paperwork before they show up."

Immogene stiffened at his remark. Vivien swung round to face Douglas. "Immogene's paperwork, signed by Mr. Wynton himself, was hand-delivered to Personnel yesterday by Audrey. Seems the problem was on your end."

Vivien urged Immogene into the store and escorted her up the employee stairs to the salon. Mirette met them on the sales floor. Her eyes filled with questions as she looked from Vivien to Immogene, then back to her friend.

"Vivien?"

"We discussed this last week."

Vivien guided Immogene into the fitting area. "There is a shelf inside the storeroom, you can put your things in there. Then come on out and we'll get you set up with your work today."

"Yes ma'am." Immogene walked into the storeroom.

Mirette waited until Immogene was out of sight before she lit into Vivien. "Did you tell me this before or after my morning coffee, because I recall no conversations about her working here."

"You know full well we're behind on the orders, and we need to get head-on into planning Bridal Week. Many hands make light work."

"And a kitchen with too many cooks renders rancid broth." Mirette pushed her lips into a fish-pout as she tilted her head to make her point.

Vivien patted her friend on the shoulder. "You've been hollering for an assistant for years. Now you've got the most talented seamstress in Levy City, next to yourself, working for you. I can't see why you're kicking up such a fuss. Next thing I know, you'll be pitching a hissy fit."

"I haven't pitched a hissy fit in years." Mirette pointed right at Vivien's nose. "You told me we were hiring someone in the future."

Vivien held her hands out to the side. "Well, like they're always saying these days, the future is now."

Mirette muttered *phooey* so that only Vivien could hear her.

"You said you had something for me to start working on?" Immogene stood in the doorway of the fitting area with a measuring tape draped around her neck. She'd removed her suit jacket and covered her clothing with a long handmade apron that featured pockets for holding her pincushion, a pair of scissors, and graphite pencils perfect for marking fabric.

"Immogene, I'll be right with you." Mirette walked to Vivien's desk and brought back the salon's inventory notebook. "I did a count of the bridal guides, to know how many to order, and I discovered we're missing one from the January shipment."

Vivien looked at the page. "Did we give one out and forget to write it down?"

Mirette shook her head. "No, they're all accounted for except the missing guide."

"How did we lose one?"

Mirette shrugged. "Don't ask me. I just do the sewing." She motioned for Immogene to follow her. "I've got a dress started on a form back here.

I'll show you the pattern so you can get started." She and Immogene disappeared into the fitting area.

The front-door chimes sounded, and Vivien whirled around to see Robbi bounding in, holding her huge alligator purse in her arms as if it were a baby. "Vivien, I know I should have called first, but I just had to come in and see how you're doing. This must be a horrible time for you."

Before she could answer, the entry chimes jingled again. When she saw Mary Hadley and Merilee Bell heading toward her, Vivien entertained throwing up her hands, running into the fitting area, and locking the door behind her.

They weren't on the books for an appointment, and both wore expressions sour enough to curdle milk. Whatever they came in for was going to fuel Robbi's lead paragraph in tomorrow's column or some funny turn of phrase on the radio tonight.

Vivien clasped her hands together and squeezed her fingers to the point of pain. "Good morning, ladies, how may I help you?"

Mother and daughter exchanged looks before Merilee spoke first. "As you know, Mary Hadley's nuptials are less than two months away." She paused. "We have something we need to talk with you about."

She turned to her daughter. "Go ahead, honey. Tell her what Mrs. Dyes said to you yesterday."

Vivien shifted her attention to Mary Hadley. She'd tried to contact Carol Dyes, Leila's mother, several times without success, and was becoming worried. They were all in the Levy City Garden Club and Junior League together, and Vivien wanted to give her condolences and get details for the funeral.

"Connie Pate and I went over Mrs. Dyes' to sit with her for a while. As you can understand, she's been prostrate with grief for days."

Mary Hadley spoke with a condescending tone she wasn't old enough to have earned, and every word she said scraped on Vivien's nerves like cat's claws on a tin roof.

"I'm so sorry to hear this."

Mary Hadley bowed her head to the side. "Of course. We all are."

She closed her eyes and released the slow sigh of one trying to deal with a complete idiot. "While we were visiting, Mrs. Dyes said something I thought you should know. With all that's going on around you, she's thinking of having a small 'family and close friends only' service for Leila."

Mary Hadley enjoyed what the underlying meaning of her statement brought. It appeared Vivien was being uninvited from Leila's funeral.

She met Mary Hadley look for look. "Considering the circumstances, I can't say that I blame her." And she meant every word.

A sickly sweet, phony-as-a-seven-dollar-bill smile spread across Mary Hadley's face. "And that brings us to my wedding." She exchanged a side-eyed glance with her mother. "Mama and I were hoping you'd respect my wedding as well and not attend."

Vivien kept her eyes on Mary Hadley. "Whatever you wish, honey."

"I also wanted to let you know, I won't be wearing the gown you made me. I'm sure you understand why, since your brides seem to—"

Vivien cut her off. "Mary Hadley, Mirette and I want you to be happy on your wedding day and wear whatever gown pleases you."

"Y'all never did get that dress right. No one we talked to could figure a way to fix it." Merilee tossed her head so hard her straw hat shifted and sagged over the side of her head. She shoved it back in place, but it took on a mind of its own and continued to slide down no matter how hard she worked to right it.

"I see." Vivien said. There remained nothing more to say, and hopefully the two of them would take the hint and leave.

Mary Hadley had more to say. "I can't leave without letting you and Miss Mirette know I hold no ill will against y'all."

She shrugged one shoulder. "I understand it must be difficult trying to keep up with the new styles and tastes. I respect the desire to hang on to the old traditions. They have their place, but they're just not for me."

Mary Hadley turned to her mother. "Mama, we should go. We have too many last-minute things and don't need to spend any more time here."

Merilee bounced her head in a goodbye. "Vivien."

The two of them walked out together, their wide skirts swishing in perfect rhythm with one another.

"I see this isn't a good time, so I'm going to go." In her usual long-legged stride, Robbi rushed from the salon, stopping at the elevators with Merilee and Mary Hadley.

"Is it safe to come out now?" Mirette called from the fitting room.

Before Vivien could answer, the salon's phone rang. She crossed the floor to reach it on the second ring. "Miss Vivien's."

"Vivien, this is Wally Carson."

"Yes, Wally, good morning. What can I do for you?"

"I don't know any other way to say this, but with all that's been going on with these"—he lowered his voice to a low-pitched whisper—"killings. . ." He cleared his throat before going on. "My wife's been after me to get our store out of the bridal guide, and off the roster for Bridal Week. My parents worked long and hard to build up Carson's Jewelers, and we can't afford to be mixed up with all this."

"Wally, I'm hoping you'll take a moment before you—"

"No, Vivien, we've been talking for a week, and I think this is for the best. Once Sheriff Youngblood solves the case and the worst of this has blown over, we'll talk about next year."

He hung up before she could get her defense in.

She looked across the room at Mirette. "Carson's just pulled out of the guide and Bridal Week."

Mirette took a step back as if she'd lost her footing for a second. "What?"

"Added to that, we've been uninvited to Leila Dyes' funeral, and Mary Hadley's wedding."

"Well that news is only half bad, though I'd really like to be there for Millie and Stanley. We dressed every one of their girls, and I feel like I know their whole family."

Mirette rubbed her forehead. "With Carson's gone, we'll have to get new guides printed and find someone else to come in and talk about engagement rings." She paused. "You could try to get a hold of that lady who works for Ayer Diamonds and goes all over the country giving lectures."

"Her name is Frances Gerety, and she's on the schedule. She's supposed to be bringing the film they circulate through the schools and church clubs. It's called *The Eternal Glow*." Unless she got wind of what was happening in Levy City and backed out, which Vivien wasn't going to express out loud to Mirette.

"Is that the one that talks about the history of diamond mining, cutting, and how to pick out a quality stone? I watched it on TV last year."

"Yes. Carson's was slated to do a talk about trends in engagement rings right after."

"What do we do now?"

"The same thing we Southern ladies always do. Stay calm and figure it out."

Chapter 25

Audrey

The icy wind's fingers slapped Audrey's cheeks and nose the moment her driver opened the cab door. Florida's milder climate had erased her body's memories of winter in New York City. She pulled on her cashmere-lined leather gloves and tightened her thick wool scarf around her neck before hopping from the cab's back seat. She handed her driver the fare and held back a giggle when he looked up with his eyes almost bugging out of his head.

"Thanks for the tip, lady."

"You're very welcome." She'd added an extra ten dollars in thanks for the man's patience in loading all her extra luggage into the trunk of the cab without grumbles. And he acted as a gentleman the entire time he drove her. Both actions deserved reward.

He pocketed the cash, then rounded the back of the car as he flipped the lid of the trunk. "You go on in and warm up in the lobby. I'll bring your bags in."

She flashed him her twenty-four-karat smile. "You are a kind and wonderful gentleman."

He ducked his head as if he were embarrassed by her praise, then hauled the first of her many bags from his trunk.

Audrey fought to keep the shivers from making her knees knock as she ascended the steps to The Plaza. Her heartbeat whirred like a pinwheel in a hurricane as she pushed her way through the revolving doors and entered the Fifth Avenue lobby. As always, her breath caught as she took in the arched windows over the French doors, the gold trim along the walls, and the black-and-white checkerboard tiles.

No hotel outmatched the glamour of The Plaza.

She walked to the cherry front desk and checked in. As she went to take her key from the desk clerk, someone screeched her name loud enough to echo across the entire lobby.

Every sinew in her body stiffened as a piece of the past she had walked away from was now running toward her.

"Audrey Penault, I still can't believe it's you." The woman's long white mink coat billowed around her as she held her arms out. "Prepare for an incoming squeeze."

Audrey braced herself for the embrace. As the woman's viselike grip caused her to grunt as her breath whooshed out, any hopes of a quiet evening sank. Once seen, there would be no more chances of hiding.

Audrey wriggled free. "Margo Morgan. It's been too long."

Margo took a wide step back and readjusted her matching white fur hat as she sized Audrey from head to toe. "Heavy wool coat, woven scarf, felt peach-basket hat. You're looking a little off-the-rack, darling." She rushed forward and seized both of Audrey's hands. "Please assure me you haven't fallen into hard times."

The clenching of her fingers hurt and Audrey pulled them free. "Trust me, all is well."

Margo clapped her hands. "Who are you modeling for this year? Dior? Givenchy? Or did Charles James snag you for evening gowns? You know you always looked spectacular in whatever they threw on you."

She'd spent her entire time on the train ride to New York preparing for this question. "I'm not here to model. I'm—"

"You're here as an editor for *Vogue*, aren't you? I heard rumors they had a new girl on board." Margo tapped the side of her head. "I should have known it was you."

Audrey shook her head. "I'm a buyer for Wynton's Department Store."

There was a level of relief in saying her new title. Margo would have turned purple and sprouted green spots if she'd known only a few weeks ago Audrey had been nothing more than Mr. Wynton's secretary. In Levy City, the position carried levels of prestige. Here in the New York fashion scene, it meant nothing.

The enthusiasm in Margo's eyes dulled. "You really did go and get yourself a business degree, didn't you? Must be such a dull letdown after all those years in Paris"—she motioned around the room—"and here."

The events of the past year floated through Audrey's mind. Margo's hair would stand on end if Audrey relayed how Mr. Wynton was almost poisoned by his no-good daughter-in-law, how she'd helped save the store from a buyout, and how their Christmas season was almost ruined by the murders of four employees. And she'd have to revive Margo with smelling salts if she mentioned her own stint in jail when being accused of said murders.

She stifled a grin as Margo looked over Audrey's outfit again, then wagged her finger in front of Audrey's coat. "Open it up, let me see how they've ruined you."

"Margo, really—"

"I insist. I'll have nightmares if you don't."

Audrey released a long breath as she unfastened the large buttons down the front of her coat. The expected measure of satisfaction came when she slipped it off and gave a slow twirl as Margo erupted in a song of *oohs* and *aahs*.

"No one could ever pull off a suit like you, Audrey dear." Margo circled her, taking in every detail of Audrey's plum-red Marionne Leslie suit, double-row pearl necklace, and diamond-and-pearl earrings.

"Whose is this? It's smashing."

"Marionne. This is her new line she's doing for Wynton's."

"How on earth did your little store rope her in? She refuses to design for any of the big stores here or in Chicago—not even in Hollywood."

Though the urge to brag a little about her being the broker of the deal with Marionne pecked at her, Audrey slipped back into her coat with the resolve to keep those details to herself. "She was happy to work with Wynton's, and we are beyond thrilled to work with her."

Margo cocked her head to the side as she tapped her chin with her finger. "Being back in the little old South seems to have seeped back into your voice."

Remarks against her drawl never stirred much in Audrey. The lilting, lyrical way her people, neighbors, and most of her customers talked was as much a part of her as it was them.

"It never seeped out, Margo."

Margo dug both hands into the deep pockets of her fur. "No, I suppose I've just forgotten. I'm used to your speaking perfect French."

A voice across the room called to Margo and she waved in response. "Look, I've got to run, but please promise me you'll come with me tomorrow night to a little cocktail party one of my friends is throwing. I'm dying to show you off and get you reacquainted with everyone. Eileen will be there, Dovima, Dorian, Jean, and Suzy. Even Richard and his new wife Evelyn. Did you meet her before you ran away?"

All the famous names she'd worked with. Eileen Ford, head of her former modeling agency. She'd shared runways with Suzy, and Dovima, and been on more photo shoots with Jean and Dorian than she could remember. They'd laughed together, and at times competed for jobs, but her inability to understand the inner workings of female relationships kept her from being close with them. She still followed their careers and inwardly cheered when she saw their latest pictures in the magazines.

And Richard Avedon. The one photographer she swore could look into her heart, find the deep emotions she kept hidden from the rest of the world, and pull them out in shots that were more art than ad, more about beauty of form than making a buck.

Her heart still pinched at hearing the names. All pieces of a dream she'd lived but that wasn't meant to last. She'd walked away, leaving behind a piece of herself in this world that kept her connected.

She'd made the choice on her own terms. And her new life suited her just fine.

Her trip through her memories caused her to take too long to answer Margo. "Never met Evelyn. He was still with Doe when I left."

"Please make sure to come with me. They've all missed you so. How long has it been, five years?"

"Almost ten."

Margo pulled her in for a hug, kissed each cheek, and then moved back. "Far too long. I'm glad you're back where you belong." She blew a kiss and hurried across the lobby to where a man in a long black overcoat waited for her.

Audrey saw that the bellboy had taken her luggage up to her room while she talked with Margo. She made her way to the elevators.

Seeing Margo and catching up for a quick minute was nice but jarring. Tomorrow would bring many others who'd known her before. Other fashion editors like Margo. Models she worked with in the fashion shows, modeling the clothes she planned to bring back to Wynton's.

And the designers. Many of them had begged her to come back and walk their runways again until she made it clear she'd traded the fashion stage for Wynton's executive suite.

When she reached her room, she changed into a pair of pink silk lounge pants with a flowy matching pink silk top and a lace robe, slipped her feet into a pair of silk slippers, and ordered a baked chicken meal through room service.

She retrieved her work satchel from the stack of her luggage and returned to the couch in her suite. In minutes, she had her calendar, sales reports for February, March, and April of last year, and her steno notebook ready.

She needed to plan upcoming sales for the store. Valentine's Day and Washington's and Lincoln's birthdays had passed, so she crossed those off her lists. A good retailer kept track of what sold best in which month, and she'd been studying Wynton's shoppers' buying habits for a while.

Children's hats sold well in July as mamas prepared for the start of school again in August. A good time for a sale in Cosmetics was February, as girls bought new products to dress up for their sweethearts and guys bought their girls perfume. China and glassware always went on sale after Christmas, in April during Bridal Week, and then in September to move inventory and make space for the holiday items.

Ladies Wear had many good months, one of which was fast approaching in April. The mass of clothes still in her new office needed to be cleared fast to make room for the new items she sought on this buying trip.

Her head was filled with plans and she'd filled pages with notes when the knock came, announcing her supper's delivery. Audrey stretched her neck and shoulder muscles, grumbling from spending too much time bent over. "Come in."

The waiter brought her supper in on a tray, then laid everything out for her on a small table. He pulled a chair back and motioned for her to sit. She complied, making certain to pay him a good tip before he slipped out.

He'd laid a copy of the evening paper next to her food, and as she cut off a piece of the chicken, she glanced over the headlines until one caused such a jolt she dropped her fork on the carpet, chicken bite and all.

Matron of Marriage Burying Brides

It couldn't be. Not way up here. Audrey went straight to the reporter's name.

Robbi Dever from The Levy Times Commercial

She shoved her food away, ran to the phone, and dialed Mr. Wynton. As soon as she finished talking with him, she was calling Miss Vivien.

Great news spread like molasses in January, and bad news spread faster than a fire in a haystack. If they were going to protect Miss Vivien, and Wynton's, someone needed to pour a bucket of water on Miss Robbi Dever as soon as possible.

The moment the phone rang, Vivien's heart went to town, pounding so hard she honestly believed it might force its way from her chest. She knew better than watching *Alfred Hitchcock Presents* alone in the living room without the lights on, but the day's events had put her in a mood, and sitting in the dark suited her.

She turned on the lights, then grabbed the receiver. "Hello?"

"Miss Vivien, it's Audrey. I'm sorry for calling so late, but I had to talk to you."

It was unlike Audrey to allow her voice to be laced with concern. Vivien walked over and turned off her program, then pulled the cord taut and returned to her spot on the couch. "Are you all right?"

"Not particularly. I saw a copy of the evening editions up here. Robbi's column was featured."

Vivien looped one of the cord's coils around her finger. "I saw it earlier in the *LTC*."

"No, you don't understand. This was in the New York papers."

She slumped against the couch's back. "Papers? You mean more than one?"

"Yes ma'am. Both the *Times* and the *Post*."

"Front page?"

"No ma'am, not the front page. The fashion section. Little blurbs summarizing the murders in Levy City. They named you specifically, as well as the evidence connected to the salon."

Vivien squeezed the edge of her chenille robe's neckline in her fingers. "Gracious sakes. How can this be?"

"I don't know, Miss Vivien. I know the papers in Atlanta, Tampa, and Jacksonville had the story yesterday. I've heard tell Miami papers are carrying it as well."

She'd lost count of how many glowing mentions she and the salon garnered during the New York bridal fashion shows in the past. A dear New York friend used to send them to paste in a scrapbook to look back on after she retired.

Would have been handy to have the scrapbook now, to display on a stand under her certificates on the salon's wall denoting her membership in The National Bridal Services, or NBS as those in the know called it, as well as the American Association of Professional Bridal Consultants, and the National Federation of Business and Professional Women's Club.

None of those were going to be worth a hill of beans if the murders, and the publicity about her connections to them, weren't stopped. "What a mess this has become."

"I talked to Mr. Wynton before I called you. He's going to speak to the owner of the *LTC* himself."

"That's only going to make her more determined than ever. Robbi's not the type to go down easy."

"Then I suppose our best bet is to beat Robbi to the truth so we can get you out of this mess."

Vivien released her hold on her neckline. "There is one thing I've been mulling over all day."

"What's that?"

"Bill Youngblood showed me my labels he found on the bodies. The edges weren't frayed, as if they'd been torn from the gowns. Instead, the edges remained intact."

"What do you think that means?" Audrey's voice held a new fire, and she was no doubt jotting down notes in her hotel room.

"They were removed with a seam ripper, by someone with a gentle hand and good sewing knowledge."

"You think the murderer could be someone in your business, like a tailor?"

"I do, and I also think our murderer isn't a man. I think it's a woman."

Audrey sucked in a breath that echoed all the way back to Florida across the phone lines. "You're sure?"

"I'm not ready to bet my life on it, but I'm thinking so."

"That makes sense." Audrey's mind must have kicked into a higher gear as her words came faster. "I've looked at the murder weapons. All from your bridal guide, all popular gifts on Wynton's bridal registry, and all of them symbolize what a wife's role entails."

"How so?"

A shushing sounded in the background, as if Audrey's skirts rustled as she sat down.

"Honey, are you in an evening gown?" Vivien asked.

"No, I'm just shaking out my red taffeta cocktail dress. While I was on the phone with Mr. Wynton, the bell boy brought up a last-minute invitation to a party for some of the designers tonight. It's a can't-miss, but I had to call you first before I changed clothes."

"Is that the long-sleeved one with the rhinestone belt?"

"Yes ma'am. It's so cold up here I brought my white mink cape to wear over it. Wish I could wear wool stockings too."

"You need to get going instead of wasting time on the phone here with me. There's nothing we can do tonight."

"Au contraire. Putting our heads together for a few minutes to stop Robbi Dever's train of destruction is far more important than an overcrowded cocktail party."

There was a catch in her voice Vivien couldn't miss. "Do I detect a bit of nerves?"

Audrey remained silent a moment. "No ma'am, not nerves, frustration. I don't like seeing my friends, or the store, attacked. Even if Robbi claims she's only chasing the truth. She could be a little less salacious about it."

Audrey was so like a bloodhound. Loyal, and when on the scent of something, nothing could call her off until she was good and ready. "What were you thinking about the weapons?"

"They all are a part of what a wife does. The candelabra is used for decorating and entertaining. The punch bowl is for entertaining. The teapot for hostessing. I think our culprit has a grudge against wives, and marriage. That's why they're after you. You've made your career helping girls become wives."

Vivien sat upright. "This all sounds sensible and plenty believable. But without proof, no one will care how many reasonable ideas we can present."

"No, but we now have a direction. A woman who maybe doesn't like marriage and who knows how to sew."

Audrey's no-quit attitude made sitting and pouting, as she had been, look far less appealing. Vivien propped her feet on the coffee table. "But who fits that bill in Levy City? Listen, hon, I'm old enough to know how to take care of myself."

"Yes ma'am. But remember what happened to the grandmother in *Little Red Riding Hood*."

"Oh, hush up."

Audrey giggled. "I'll be home by the end of next week. If I think of something else, you'll be the first one I call."

Keys jingled in the background. "I'd better get dressed. Good night."

"Good night, Audrey. Enjoy your party."

"Yes ma'am." She hung up.

Vivien set the receiver in the cradle, then melted into the softness of the couch cushions. Though meant in jest, Audrey's quip about the fairy tale rang with a bit of truth. Red Riding Hood's granny failed to see the wolf standing right in front of her.

Had she done the same?

Chapter 27

Mary Jo

The nerve of some people. Mary Jo sloshed the dirty plate into her dishwater a second time and gave the dish a hard scrub with her dishcloth. She clamped her jaws together to the point they ached. Mama sat at the kitchen table, reading the *LTC*'s evening edition out loud to her, and of course, she'd picked the very worst story.

That Dever woman's latest about the deaths of Miss Vivien's brides, complete with all the messy details. Honestly, with each passing day she found more ways to harp on about Miss Vivien's dress labels being found on the bodies and her bridal guides being part of the murders. She made out like Miss Vivien must be planning these murders herself.

She'd been glad to throw the paper away, or turn off the radio, unwilling to give Robbi her attention. Unfortunately, her neighbors in Levy City were enthralled by the news. Gigi said the *LTC* gained the highest number of sales in their history since Robbi Dever started reporting about the murders. The radio station announced they'd set records for people tuning in to her evening show.

Like Gigi said, the uglier the news the more people wanted to hear and talk about it.

Well, in her own home, she'd block the ugliness out. "Mama, aren't there any other stories in the paper tonight? Hearing all this talk of murder gives me the willies, and I won't be able to fall asleep. Remember, I need to rise early and get you to the hospital so we can bring Daddy home, and then I'm going back to work the afternoon shift."

Her mother humphed and snapped the page, ripping the spine of the paper in the process. "You wouldn't have to be at that store if you'd get that husband of yours out of this house and into a job."

For three straight weeks, from the moment she rose in the morning until she fell asleep on the couch after supper, Mama had done nothing but harp, fuss, and bash Mary Jo. That she could take it, was not in question. She always had. But the constant jabs against Kenny were a different matter.

"Do not talk about Kenny like that again."

Mama gasped. "How dare you speak to me like that?"

Her mother's jaw went firm as she set her lips in a determined pout, raring to spew her next round of nastiness at Mary Jo.

Mary Jo clenched her fists. This was her house, her kitchen, and it was unfair that Mama could choose to be as nasty as she wanted without any complaints from those she sliced to pieces with her words.

With hot words ready to spill over her mother, Mary Jo looked up to see Carrie Rose and Penny standing in the doorway, their faces white as flour.

"Mama?" Carrie Rose whispered. Her bottom lip trembled. Penny hid behind her sister, peered around her sibling's shoulder, then ducked behind her like a turtle pulling back into its shell.

"Why are you and Grandma fighting?"

Shame from scaring her girls cooled her rage. Mary Jo went and gathered them in a hug. "We're not fighting, just having a grown-up conversation." Though at the moment, neither of them was acting like proper grown-up ladies should.

Penny poked her head from behind her big sister. "Then why were you talking so loud, and cross?" As soon as she voiced her question, she ducked back behind Carrie Rose.

"I'm sorry we startled you." Mary Jo swiveled them both in the direction of their bedroom. "Time to brush your teeth and get ready for bed. I'll be in for kisses and a story in a few minutes."

She gave an extra push to get them moving down the hallway. When they entered the bathroom, Mary Jo stared at her bedroom door, where Kenny had sequestered himself as soon as he finished his meal and pushed away from the table.

She wheeled around and met Mama's beet-red face.

"You shouldn't lie to your children, Mary Jo. Teaches them to lie too." A self-satisfied smile swept across her mother's face.

Oh, what she'd like to say right now, but an admonition learned when she was a girl in Sunday school clamped her words.

Honor thy mother and father.

"Go on to bed, Mama. I'll finish cleaning up the kitchen, and then I need to call Gigi and see how things are at the store."

"Don't you call that woman this late at night. Your yakking and clucking will keep me awake."

"I'll close the living room door. You won't hear a thing."

"Mama, we're ready for bed," Penny called from her room.

Mama rose with such anger she sent the chair tumbling to the floor. She didn't even bother to right it but stomped into her makeshift bedroom and slammed the door behind her.

Mary Jo headed to the girls' room, and once they were tucked in, she returned to the kitchen and dialed Gigi.

Tears brimmed in her eyes when Gigi answered. "Hello, this is Gigi."

"I'm so glad you answered. I don't think I could have stayed on if one of your housemates did."

"What's the matter? You sound like you're about to cry."

Tears now washed down Mary Jo's cheeks. "Not about to, I am."

"Your mother again?"

Mary Jo slid out a chair and sat down at the table. Dirty dishes sat in her sink, but they'd wait until she finished talking with Gigi.

"She's been in a foul mood since breakfast."

"What put a bee in her bonnet this time?"

"She's mad because I'm going back to work tomorrow. She wants me to move in and help her take care of Daddy. The doctor told her twice it wasn't necessary, that a nurse will be coming by every day for the next two weeks."

Mary Jo propped her elbow on the table and rested her forehead in her palm. "I feel downright ugly saying this, but I can't wait to drop them off at home tomorrow."

"You've been an excellent daughter to her, so don't you go feeling guilty. Your mother is a handful."

Sounds of a door closing in the background sounded from Gigi's end. "Did you see the evening edition?"

"Mama was all too happy to read Robbi's column out loud while I fixed supper. How is Miss Vivien?"

"She's been so busy at the salon she hasn't had time to talk. I did hear from Lilla that Miss Vivien hired her sister-in-law, Immogene, to come in and help with all the orders. Lilla says Immogene is as good, or maybe better, at dressmaking than Miss Vivien and Mirette."

"Lilla's made a mighty big boast there." Believing anyone could outdo Miss Vivien was hard.

"Lilla showed me a coat Immogene made for her last year. I have to tell you, Mary Jo, I'm hard put to say Miss Vivien or Mirette could do better."

"Has the sheriff found any more clues as to who's behind all this?"

Voices sounded in the background on Gigi's end, and she waited until quiet returned before she answered. "Not one stitch of new evidence beyond the items pointing to Miss Vivien."

"I'm so worried for her, Gigi. This must be weighing on her like a rock. You know how she loves all her brides."

"There's one she isn't particularly fond of. Her name is Mary Hadley Bell. She's been kicking up all kinds of trouble and saying horrible things all over town about Miss Vivien."

"She's not a nice person at all. Kenny did some carpentry work on the Bell's house a few years ago when they redid Mary Hadley's bedroom. She about drove him crazy with her demands. He declared she was the worst spoiled brat he'd ever seen."

Her insides ached for a return to those years when Kenny was still whole and building things, she could be at home with the girls, and laughter filled their house rather than Mama's bitterness, Kenny's sadness, and her exhaustion.

Gigi giggled on the other end. "You should hear how Miss Mirette describes her." She erupted into full laughter that drew Mary Jo in and helped her laugh along.

"Is there any way we can help Miss Vivien? There must be something we can do."

"I wish I knew. There's something I've been meaning to ask you."

"What's that?" Mary Jo's eyes fell on the yellow sunburst-shaped clock on the wall, reminding her of the dried food sticking to the dirty dishes. She'd have to add more hot water and bubbles to her dishwater.

"One of the other clerks keeps calling me a *gatherer*. It's bad isn't it?"

"I'm afraid so. They call another clerk that when they feel she's brownnosing customers and the managers by outselling other clerks in the department."

Mary Jo rose from her chair. Mama would fuss about the waste and how Mary Jo must think money sprouted in her purse as easily as weeds in the yard.

"Hey Gigi, my dishes aren't going to wash themselves. Thanks for talking for a minute."

Mary Jo heard a female voice on the other end asking to use the phone.

"Oh gosh, I almost forgot to tell you. I got my first sale today."

"That's wonderful. Did Jane see?"

"Not only did she see, she sent the customer over to me, like she was testing me." Gigi paused, and then Mary Jo heard muffled voices on the other end.

"There's a line forming to use the phone. Good night and good luck."

Mary Jo hung up, then walked to the sink and turned on the faucet. As she swirled the new dollop of Joy dish soap into the warming water, movement beside her caught her attention.

Kenny leaned against the counter and smiled when she met his gaze. "I ate all the chocolates you gave me for Valentine's, but if you're not too tired, I'd like to share some saltines with butter and have a talk on the back porch."

Mary Jo dunked a plate into the water and scrubbed the surface clean. "I'm really tired. Can't we talk now?"

He scratched the back of his head, then lifted his shoulders in a nervous twitch. "I need to ask you something."

She washed, rinsed, and set the last plate into the drainer, then went to work on the silverware. "What is it?"

His expression darkened. "What would you think about quitting the store."

Mary Jo ran the forks and spoons under the faucet. "Kenneth Johnson, so help me—"

Kenny put his finger to her lips to stop her from going on. He enfolded her into a hug, bent at the knees, and rested his chin on her shoulder.

His lips were close to her ear. "You're overdue for a rest. It's time for me to get in the game and start learning how to use that new arm you ordered me."

He unlocked his arms and stepped back from her. "I want to hug you with both arms again."

He ruffled her hair. "I'm sick and tired of your mother chewing at you day and night about how we do things in our own house. Team Johnson is better and stronger than she thinks." Kenny cupped her face in his hands and lifted her chin so their eyes met. "Especially you."

Vivien sat in Mirette's driveway as she waited for her friend to lock her front door. She turned her car's heater off. Once the sun peeked above the horizon, the cold's chilly fingers no longer clawed their way through her stockings, causing goose bumps to rise on her skin.

Mirette opened the door and plopped on the passenger seat. "Sorry I'm late, moving slow this morning."

Vivien waited as her friend settled her purse and her large bag carrying the pieces she'd worked on at home by her feet. "Your arthritis acting up in this cold?"

"No." Mirette drawled out the word, then gave Vivien a stare cold enough to freeze a side of beef. "Thanks to your calling and telling me four more girls canceled their appointments, I was awake long after midnight."

She grimaced as she adjusted her position, groaning under her breath as she tried to bend her left knee. Vivien understood. Admitting they were slowing down in the race against the years came hard.

Mirette locked her door. "I'm concerned every engaged girl in town believes being associated with us means certain death."

Vivien backed her car into the street. "I'm bound and determined to do whatever it takes to prove them wrong."

"How are you going to do that?"

Vivien put the car in drive and headed down the street. "Haven't figured that out yet. But us old girls always find a way." She side-winked at her friend.

"I just cannot fathom that Happy Collins and the Lion's Club asked to be removed from the bridal guide. Happy's been our favorite florist for years, and the Lions know they have the best hall in town to rent for a wedding reception."

"When he called, J. W. claimed being removed passed by a unanimous vote."

Mirette grunted. "Unanimous because all their wives and daughters demanded it be so."

"Be that as it may, if this keeps up, the only thing we're going to have left is Wynton's bridal registry. We'll have to completely reorganize Bridal Week."

"Maybe we can pick Audrey's brain for ideas. She's good at all that sales and advertising rigmarole."

"She's in New York for the next two weeks, and then she's heading to Atlanta. Soon after, she'll be heading to the Paris shows."

"We both know, if you put a little bug about Bridal Week in her ear, she'll come up with something."

Vivien turned on her signal and waited on passing traffic before turning into Wynton's parking garage. "We'll see." It may have been pride or pure pigheadedness, but she wanted to come up with her own plan and not leave it to someone in the younger set. The world needed a reminder the old gals still had plenty of giddy-up-and-go when the situation called for gumption.

Later on, when they were in the salon, Mirette stood nearby, pinning a row of lace to the edge of a tulle veil. "What are you mumbling about now?"

Vivien propped her elbow on her desktop and cradled her chin in her hands. She tapped the eraser of her pencil on her empty appointment book. "Robbi Dever may have single-handedly put us out of business."

"It'd be nice if folks stopped paying attention to all her nonsense," Immogene said from where she sat stringing pearls together so they could be added to the veil Mirette was making.

Vivien pivoted in her chair to face her new employee. "She's brash, for sure. Always been that way."

"When you're built like she is, you're hard put to be a shrinking violet." Mirette put her sewing aside and rose from her chair, then arched her back. "I've been sitting too long." She twisted from side to side as she worked her kinks out.

The salon's entry chimes sounded, and Vivien and Mirette met each other's surprised gaze.

"Maybe one of our girls changed her mind," Mirette said as she returned to her chair and picked up the veil. “Immogene, I should have this finished in a bit, you ready with those pearls?”

“Yes ma’am.” She held up her already-threaded needle as proof.

Vivien picked up her scheduling book. “Mirette, you and I need to stop talking as if we’re one foot away from closing our doors. We’re not that bad off.”

“Yet,” Mirette said as she sat back down.

“There are still girls on the books, and I’ll hang my hat on that until every page of this calendar is blank. When that happens, I’ll worry,” Vivien said before walking to the sales floor.

Vivien found Margay Delmar and her daughter, Louisa, standing in the middle of the sales floor, still as statues and glancing at each other as if afraid to move.

“Good morning, ladies. Welcome to Miss Vivien’s.”

Margay stared like a seasoned hunter setting sights on a deer as she met the greeting. “Thank you.”

The Delmar family, including Margay’s husband, Leroy, were known for their tendency to keep to themselves. They had good reasons to be people-shy.

With their only child, Louisa, contracting polio when she was twelve, their family lived through quarantine and shunning. Local parents feared their own children might catch the dreaded virus from Louisa. Her being the only child in Levy City to come down with the virus didn’t help their standing among their neighbors.

Louisa’s affected left leg was stiff, and she had to swing it wide like a gate when she walked. These two deserved to feel wanted, welcomed. Vivien put every ounce of friendliness she could muster into the most pleasant, welcoming expression.

“I’m so glad you’re here. How can I help you today?”

Margay’s jaw relaxed and she looked as if she no longer believed they would be thrown out of the salon.

Louisa peered at Vivien over her thick, pointy glasses. “I need a wedding dress.” She spoke in a soft voice, but an air of no-nonsense peppered her entire bearing.

Vivien clapped her hands together. “Honey, congratulations. Who’s your lucky groom?”

“Vernon Pate.” She spoke with the same matter-of-fact tone as if she’d said she were picking up her mail at the post office.

Vivien clasped her hands together. "Well, aren't you something? He is a nice young man." She meant every word.

Vernon wasn't the best-looking boy in Levy City. He wasn't very exciting either, but he was working hard to build his plumbing business. Everyone in town who'd hired him claimed he was the best at unclogging drains and fixing leaky pipes.

And to his credit, he owned a heart big enough to see Louisa not as a cripple but as a woman worthy of spending his life with. These heart-warmers were the best things about the wedding business and would keep her there for as long as God was willing she do the job.

"This is the nicest thing we've heard all day." Vivien motioned to the nearest couch. "Let's go have a seat here and talk about what you'd like in a dress. Then I'll pull some samples for you to look at and maybe try on a few."

Mother and daughter followed her, each walking with the caution of one keeping an eye out for snakes in the woods. They sat close beside one another on the end of the couch, leaving a wide space for her to sit.

"I'm going to grab my notebook and a folder. I keep a file for all of my brides."

A shy grin wiggled across Louisa's face. "I always dreamed of being one of your brides."

Her mother laid a hand on her daughter's arm. "Don't get the cart too far ahead of the horse. We don't know if we'll find what we need here. We've had so much trouble already."

"Yes, Mama." Her face fell faster than an angel food cake, and the mix of disappointment and a bit of frustration pulled Vivien's heartstrings.

She returned to the couch and sat down. The notes and file could wait, for there was much more going on here than just searching for a gown. "Have you tried other dresses, Louisa?"

Disappointment and anger flickered in Louisa's eyes. "I've been to the secondhand store over on Tiller Street. We thought we could find something nice there that didn't cost too much."

Vivien switched her gaze between daughter and mother. "Didn't work out?"

A tear streamed down the side of Louisa's nose. "None of the gowns would work for me."

Vivien scooted a little closer and took Louisa's hand in her own. "You didn't like the styles?"

"No ma'am. The styles were just fine. They wouldn't work because of the way I walk." All that anger in her was ready to boil over and blow the lid off the pot.

Vivien switched her attention to Margay, whose own face beamed beet red. "I don't understand."

Margay swallowed. "She kicks her bad leg up and way out to the side now. The dresses we could afford were from back when the skirts on wedding gowns were narrower, and Louisa thought it looked odd when she swung her leg around underneath."

"Not odd, Mama, plain old ugly. I almost tripped in those long skirts because they were too tight for me."

"Those dresses must have been from the forties. They were more formfitting then." Vivien sandwiched Louisa's hand between both of hers. "You couldn't find any dresses with nice wide skirts?"

Margay squeezed the straps of her purse tighter. "All that extra fabric comes at a cost." She shot a quick glance at her daughter before going on. "We're still paying on her bills from the Crippled Children's Hospital down in St. Petersburg. How much do your gowns cost?"

Vivien focused on Margay. "Depends. They can go for twenty, up to fifty. Some custom gowns are even more."

Margay shook her head hard. "We can't come close to paying anything like that." She motioned to her daughter. "Let's go, Louisa. We're done here."

Louisa struggled to rise until her mother took her by the elbow and helped her stand.

"Vivien and I are whizzes at coming up with a gown for every budget," Mirette said from the doorway to the fitting room, where she and Immogene now stood.

"You bet your boots we are." Vivien resisted the urge to hug Louisa, knowing full well the gesture would be seen as pity. "What do you want to spend?"

Margay looked from her daughter to Vivien. "We couldn't go more than ten. We figured with all the things happening around town, you might be having a sale on your gowns."

Vivien didn't blame mother or daughter for thinking this way. If she were in the same spot, she'd do the same. "Right now we—"

Louisa cut in. "You don't have anything for us, do you Miss Vivien?"

"No, we don't."

She motioned to herself, then Mirette and Immogene. "Instead, we're going to design the perfect gown for you. When you walk down the aisle, no one will notice anything but how beautiful you are, inside and out. And we'll make the price fit your budget. I promise."

It was clear Louisa's head was yelling at her to be realistic, but an air of hope also shone from within her. "I told Mama you could help me."

Vivien stood. "I'll get you a file folder and my clipboard. Then you can tell me what you want." She gestured for Mirette and Immogene to come closer. "We are at your service."

Louisa opened her purse and pulled out a McCall's wedding gown pattern. "I bought this here at Wynton's, but when we opened the package, we saw the dress I liked was too difficult for Mama and me to make." She pointed to one of the pictures on the front of the package. "I want a long dress, like this one. With a full skirt so wide that when I walk my dumb leg won't even brush the sides. All the way to the floor, so no one sees my leg moving. Can you do that?"

"Without batting an eye," Mirette piped in. "What else do you want, honey?"

"A nice waist, and fitted sleeves that go all the way down to the back of my hands." The first break in her determined armor showed through as Louisa dipped her chin. "Is that too much?"

Vivien shook her head as she wrote on her clipboard. "Absolutely not. You keep going, sweetheart. We are all ears."

"I don't like lace. Can you put some other type of decoration on there to make the dress pretty? Maybe a big bow, or some ruffles and little flowers, like Jackie Kennedy's dress had? I saw a picture of her in *Good Housekeeping* magazine."

"I saw that article. She looked pretty. You will too," Mirette added.

Lace was all the rage, and most girls wanted yards and yards, from their hemline to their neckline. Vivien's thoughts whirred as she jotted down ideas for other fabrics, and then a last reminder to check their inventory of silks, satins, organzine, and tulle.

"What kind of neckline do you want, Louisa?"

She shrugged, then drew a line across her collarbone. "Maybe something up to here? I don't want to look daring on my wedding day." Her cheeks blushed pink.

"Jewel neckline," Vivien said as she jotted down the details.

"And it has to be white. I've been dreaming of a white wedding since I was twelve."

Margay squeezed her daughter's hand. "I've been dreaming the same thing since you were born." She looked at Vivien. "And seeing her standing in front of one of your big mirrors."

A vision of a gown formed in Vivien's imagination. She stopped writing and focused on Louisa. "We're in the business of making dreams come true here."

With how things looked, Louisa might well be one of her last clients, and she wasn't about to go out with a whimper. Vivien flipped to a clean page, then drew a quick sketch. When finished, she showed the picture to Louisa.

"What do you think?"

Louisa's face lit up as she swiveled her gaze from the dress to her mother. "That's my dream dress. You really think you can make this for me?"

Vivien set her clipboard on the sofa, then drew Louisa in for a hug. "You bet we can. That's what we do best here."

Chapter 29

Gigi

Gigi bit the insides of both cheeks to keep her true thoughts from showing on her face. Jane stood before her, delivering another lecture on customer service. Honestly, it seemed the woman believed her to be the most uncouth being to ever darken the doors of Wynton's.

"Remember your 'yes ma'ams' when waiting on our customers. And the 'yes sirs' to our occasional male customers. They all expect a certain level of decorum and finesse. You must practice these traits at home so they come as second nature to you when you're behind the counter or on the floor."

She stared a moment, then released a deep sigh as if yet again Gigi had danced with glee on her nerves.

Gigi jerked to attention. "Yes ma'am." If Jane weren't the boss, what she'd tell her. Mama spent years teaching Gigi the finer points of ladylike behavior. It wasn't her fault her daughter ignored most of the training because good manners cut in on her fun or was just too much trouble to remember. The gist of the lessons was still in her head, and she could follow them when she had to.

Mostly.

And if that wasn't enough, Audrey drummed all of the same stuff, plus extra, into her head. Even Miss Vivien gave her a copy of the Emily Post etiquette book she used to help her brides in the salon. Gigi had read through the first few chapters in the evening after work while her hair or nails dried. How much more polish did a girl need?

Every fiber in her tongue wished to shout "I'm not an idiot" from Wynton's top rafters all the way down to Jane's ears. Instead, Gigi plastered on a wide smile and clasped her hands behind herself so hard her fingers ached. "I'll do my best."

Jane waggled a finger at Gigi. "Better than best." She swiveled on her heel so fast her wide skirt swished, then walked to the other end of the cosmetics counter.

The other clerk, Christina, walked up to Gigi. "I'm heading to lunch. You take over for me."

"I've not run the makeup counter yet. Jane's only let me do perfumes."

Christina lifted one shoulder. "It's my lunch break. I'll only be gone an hour. How much damage could you do?"

She shot a fast glance at Jane, then returned her focus to Gigi. "You have to learn the entire department sometime. Between you and me, I think you're more than ready." She lowered her voice to a whisper. "I don't know why Jane is being so hard on you. Personally, I think she and the other girls are jealous because you're good friends with Audrey. They would all like to be as sophisticated and rich as her."

Gigi said nothing in response. Audrey was much more than the pretty package on the outside and her sporty red T-Bird.

"You go ahead, Christina. I'll keep things together until you're back."

"You'd better." Her coworker winked, then left to enjoy her break.

One hour. She could handle the time with no problem. Gigi positioned herself in the middle of the long counter, partway between the perfumes and the makeup and the shamrock decorations set out to celebrate the Saint Patrick's Day sales. Jane stood at the end of the counter near the shining compacts. She'd crossed her arms, and the "I'm watching" expression on her face didn't help calm the nervous twitters buzzing like hungry mosquitoes in Gigi's gut.

Gigi pulled the hem of her brown plaid vest into place over the waistband of her black skirt, smoothed the long sleeves of her blouse, and then checked the cravat-style bow at her neckline. Audrey told her over and over she was a natural for Cosmetics, and now was the time to prove her right and Jane wrong. In the most respectful way, of course.

A few moments later, a young woman around Mary Jo's age approached the counter. Gigi smiled. "Welcome to Cosmetics. May I help you?"

The woman met her greeting with a quick sweep of Gigi's appearance. She tapped on the glass counter above a powder compact. "Is that Revlon's 'Love Pat'?"

"It sure is."

The woman pointed to the white price tag next to the compact. "Is that the current price?"

"Yes."

The woman shifted her attention to another product nearby. "And this manicure set. Will it go on sale soon?"

"Yes, we will be having sales on both products soon. I—"

"This 'Futurama' lipstick. Is this the same one that was shown on *The $64,000 Question*? The one that comes with a refill that fits right in the tube?"

"Yes. This one goes for a dollar seventy-five. Best price in town. Guaranteed."

The woman pointed back to the compact and the manicure set. "Do you know how much they will be marked down during your sale?"

The woman moved down the counter to the perfume cabinet. She stood so close she could have pressed her nose against the glass.

The woman wore a simple blue suit similar to Gigi's own navy one. Her pumps bore scuffs on the heels and toes, one so deep the leather curled away from the nick.

"When did you say your sale was again?" the woman asked as she continued to stare at the perfumes.

"I didn't say."

She might not remember every page of the etiquette book, but she'd been mixed up with enough two-bit con artists to know when she saw one wearing heels and pretending to be a customer.

"Do y'all carry Emeraude?" the woman asked.

Gigi opened the case and removed a tester, then held the decanter out for the woman to see. She watched closely as the woman turned the bottle ever so carefully to view the price tag before she spritzed a drop on her wrist.

This woman was a shopper for another store, scoping out Wynton's prices and sales dates to help her own place of employment undercut the store and steal away customers.

Audrey had warned her of these tricks and told her the things to watch out for, like asking loads of questions about prices and sales, when everyone in town knew Wynton's posted the same information in the *LTC* at the beginning of the week. Another was buying several items at a time, like toys or clothes, and then returning them for a full refund a few days later after relaying the price information to their employer. The store worked hard to be on the lookout for these shoppers, and not being taken in by one was another notch Gigi wanted in her belt.

This woman probably worked at Hartner's, a small store on the other side of town. They were barely a step above a five-and-dime, didn't have half the inventory Wynton's had, and tried to undersell the store all the time.

Audrey called it the rules of retail, but it seemed underhanded and tacky. This was a game Gigi only knew a few rules for, but no matter what, she wasn't going to let Wynton's lose.

"May I interest you in something else?"

When the woman met her gaze, Gigi didn't smile. Her suspicions were as clear as if she'd written them on her face with a black China pencil.

"No thank you."

Gigi shifted on her feet. "All of our sales are advertised in the *LTC*, so keep an eye out. We're going to have some very good prices on all the items you've looked at."

The woman's mouth turned up at the corner in a knowing grin. "I'll do that."

She left the department without another word and headed toward Menswear across the main aisle from Cosmetics. The clerks there were far more seasoned, and she wouldn't have much success there either.

Gigi grabbed the bottle of cleaner and spritzed the woman's fingerprints from the glass on the case. People had to work, and she wouldn't deny anyone the opportunity to make a living. But sure as rain, anyone trying to double-deal to get ahead got nothing but a load of disgust from her.

Jane strolled to the counter as Gigi finished up her polishing. "You didn't make a sale with your last customer. She seemed plenty interested in our products, and we never want to discourage a customer from what they want."

Gigi didn't meet Jane's eyes as she finished polishing the glass. "She wasn't here to buy. She was here to nib into our prices. I'm convinced she was a shopper, maybe for Hartner's."

"And just what gave you that idea, Gigi?"

Gigi put the cleaning cloth and cleaning solution under the counter, then stood tall before her boss. "I had a feeling."

Jane opened her mouth to say something when one of the clerks from Menswear came rushing over.

"Did either of you see a woman come in here? Blue suit, straw hat?"

Gigi nodded. "She came by here a few minutes ago."

The man leaned on her freshly cleaned counter. "Did you sell her anything?"

"No."

"Good. We just snagged her as a shopper. Dale and I ran her off from our department. She kept asking about when our suits were going on sale. We think she came here to snoop for Worrell's Men's Shop."

Jane pointed to Gigi. "She was just telling me she thought she came here from Hartner's, trying to find out about our sales here in Cosmetics."

The male clerk's brows raised as he nodded toward Gigi. "Could be. We threatened to call Security if we saw her in here again."

He turned to Jane. "You've got a sharp one here." He waved his thumb toward Gigi.

"Don't forget to write a report." He waved again, then trotted back to his department.

Jane swung round on Gigi. "You've surprised me twice now." She stared a moment longer. "Why don't you go on to your lunch break early. Christina will be back in a few minutes, and I can watch the counters until then."

The compliment threw Gigi, but she threw off the shock to enjoy every minute of the reward. "Thank you."

She hurried to get her purse from her locker, then made her way to the shoe department. There was a darling pair of black patent leather pumps she'd put on layaway, and today she owed another twenty cents toward the cost. Wearing a size 11 shoe made it impossible for her to afford shoes any other way since she had to special order.

When she arrived, Gordon was assisting another woman. Gigi took a seat nearby, still close enough to see the lady customer was Robbi Dever, and she was holding out a loafer to him.

"You see Gordon, I've been chasing down so many leads for my stories that I wore a hole in the bottom of my shoe. You think you can put a new one on it for me?"

From where she sat a few feet away, Gigi could see the large hole in the shoe's bottom. The only way Robbi could have worn a hole that big was if she'd walked to China and back about three times.

"I'll talk to our shoe repairman and then call you with his answer, Miss Dever."

"If it's not fixable, order me a new pair, and call me when they come in. These are my walking shoes, and I can't chase down a story without good shoes."

Robbi elbowed poor Gordon so hard in the ribs he doubled over. "Yes ma'am." He coughed as he straightened.

She turned and made eye contact with Gigi, then marched to where she sat. "You're that waitress who's friends with Miss Vivien, aren't you?"

She thrust her hand and her fingers almost touched Gigi's nose. "I'm Robbi Dever of the—"

"I know who you are." Gigi leaned back in the chair, out of reach.

Robbi pulled her hand back, then dug in her giant purse, bringing out a notebook and pencil. "I'd love to get a quote from you for my column, maybe a little word of support. Miss Vivien could use a good word these days." She held the pencil to the paper.

The moxie of this woman. Standing there, acting as if she wanted to help Miss Vivien when she was the main reason for all the trouble. Plenty of things she'd like to say about Robbi came to mind. None could be printed in the paper, much less said out loud to another lady's face.

Gigi tapped the toe of her shoe on the floor to cool her temper enough to speak with a civil tongue. "If I think of something, I'll go straight to Miss Vivien myself."

Robbi shoved her things back in her purse, then pulled out a small business card. "If you ever feel the need to talk, here's my card."

She dropped her card in Gigi's lap, then went back and spoke to Gordon. "Thanks for the help. You're a peach."

Robbi threw him a salute-type wave, then took off from the shoe department with strides wide enough to cover an acre in a flash.

Gigi picked up the card, crumpled it into a ball, and threw the wad into a nearby trash can.

Audrey sat at a quiet table in the corner of a restaurant, reading over her notes and orders from the fashion shows she'd attended earlier in the day. She'd managed to gather an array of day and formal dresses, handbags, and a few smashing suits to bring back to Wynton's customers. For her first week's efforts, the results weren't too shabby, as Gigi was fond of saying.

Times and tastes were changing, and she'd managed to find something to fit all of Wynton's lady shoppers. Other store buyers she'd met mentioned their customers were moving out to the suburbs and becoming less interested in the big designer names or the downtown shopping experience. Wynton's still catered to the luxury tastes of the country-club set while also reaching the more modest styles of the penny watchers like Gigi and Mary Jo.

During each show, she tried to picture the women she knew in Levy City, how they would look in the outfits on the runway, what their dream outfits might be, and then make her buying choices accordingly.

There was an element of fun and mystery trying to guess what women might wear when Florida decided to be fickle in her weather choices, bringing about temperatures from all four seasons in a week's time. She had to pick the perfect number of warmer wools and cooler cottons to serve her customers' needs—and avoid buying too many clothes at full price that might end up on a clearance rack.

She was sketching an idea for the store's window trimmers to showcase the new spring line she'd purchased when the sound of a chair scraping across wood pulled her away from her work. When she glanced up, she had to work hard to keep from groaning.

A balding man wedged himself into the seat, adjusting his position so the extra folds around his middle could squeeze out through the spaces under the chair's arms. "Mind if I join you?" The edges of his bushy mustache curled along the outline of his thick upper lip as he smiled wide at her.

Having one of the slimier inhabitants of her former business bellying up and interrupting her work was the last thing she needed. "Mr. Hoverman, what an unexpected. . .meeting."

His paunch prevented him from leaning close to the table, so he placed his fingertips on the surface and wiggled them as if he were playing an invisible piano. "Didn't see you in any of the shows today. You doing print only now, or are you still walking?"

Audrey held herself stiff to stave off revulsion shivers. This man worked for a pulp-fiction magazine and had pursued her and other fellow models for years to pose for his sordid covers. Her agency forbade them doing any such jobs, which she would have turned down even if they hadn't. She'd vowed to avoid his type forever and a day and wasn't going to break said promise to herself.

She picked up her pen and finished the note he had so rudely interrupted, then returned her attention to the unwanted guest at her table. "No, I left the business. I'm working in Florida now."

He moved his tongue around his teeth as if trying to clean something from in between them, finishing with a loud smacking of his lips. "I hear the South has returned to your mouth, although you never did drop that accent like I told you. You would have gone further if you'd listened to me."

He threw back his head and released huffing guffaws until a deep, rattling cough interrupted his mirth. He'd been a chain-smoker in years past, and it seemed he had yet to drop the habit. "I'm not with those rags anymore. I've been hired to find girls for an up-and-coming design house down South. I could make you the star of the pack. You always were magic in a gown, especially wedding dresses."

Audrey returned her attention to her notes, scribbling out the names of the lines of day dresses she wanted to feature in the new window display. "As I said, I'm not in the business now."

Mr. Hoverman smashed his paunch into the table's edge and crossed his arms on the tabletop. He leaned forward. "You still look like you could throw on a Dior, hop on the stage, and bring the whole house down like you always used to."

He tapped a pudgy finger on the surface three times. "My new boss pays well, and I could put you at the top of the hiring list. Just say the word."

There were many words she'd like to say, but none of them were civil or ladylike. "Mr. Hoverman, let me be very clear—" since it seemed he was about as sharp as butter.

A man's voice cut in as she readied to give her unwanted guest a few pieces of her mind. "Miss Penault, I'm so sorry I'm late."

She looked up to meet the gaze of Joshua McKinnon, standing tall and polished as ever in a dark brown suit, perfectly set off with a wine-colored tie festooned with a stripe of yellow-and-black plaid across the middle. A dark overcoat was draped over one arm, and he held a brown felt fedora in his hand. Flakes of snow stuck to his blond hair.

He turned to Mr. Hoverman. "Excuse me, sir." He added an extra emphasis to his last word that made the man jerk his head around to face him. "I've got an appointment with Miss Penault, and since her time and mine are quite valuable, we'll be needing to start right away."

"Well, pardon me." Mr. Hoverman drawled his words, aping Joshua's own Southern accent. He wriggled himself free of the chair, then grunted as his legs struggled to lift his bulk. Once standing, he reached in his pocket. "Let me leave you my card."

Audrey held up her hand. "No need." She made certain to leave out the thanks her upbringing dictated. This was no time for the mixed message those kinds of pleasantries could bring on.

Mr. Hoverman grabbed the back of the chair to steady himself as he tossed his business card on the table by her papers. "First rule of business, honey. Never turn down a good contact."

He slammed his fraying black hat on and squeezed through the maze of tables and chairs, forcing other patrons sit forward to avoid contact with him.

Watching him walk away was probably the best thing that had happened all day. "Thank you, Joshua. What on earth are you doing in New York City?"

He sat in the chair next to hers, then motioned to her stack of papers and notebook. "You bring the store with you when you travel."

"I'm the head buyer for women's clothing at Wynton's."

"Congratulations on the promotion. How is the executive office running without you?"

Audrey set down her pen. "Since you're close with Mr. Wynton, I'll tell you. Not very well. I'm training my replacement. She's young, and Mr. Wynton sees great potential in her. I agree she has promise, but my-oh-my is she a handful."

"You talking about Libby?"

"How do you know her name?"

"I was introduced when returning a phone call to your boss."

She sat up in her chair. Her boss had mentioned nothing about this when she checked in with him earlier in the day. "Mr. Wynton called you? About what?"

"He relayed a question for Dad, who is at the hunting cabin right now. Nothing to worry about."

Her ears perked up at the tone in his voice. Not one of deception, but more of an effort to speak carefully to not trip any alarms. Her boss had sworn him to secrecy about something, no doubt.

He'd been much more close-lipped with her lately, and it was driving her to distraction. He wanted her to concentrate on her job here in New York.

During the day, she followed his wishes. At night, her brain went where it chose, and her thoughts bounced between worrying over Miss Vivien's plight and how much Alka-Seltzer Mr. Wynton consumed due to working with Libby.

Joshua pointed to her notebook and notes. "Pack all that up and let me take you to dinner. We can go to Divan Parisienne and have two plates of their best chicken Divan."

After dozens of cocktail parties, shopping and buying excursions, runway shows, and more wine-and-dines with vendors than she could remember, she'd planned on not speaking to another soul for at least the next twelve hours.

Audrey opened her mouth to plead out of the invite, but Joshua cut her off. "Not taking any answer but yes, even if I have to steal your notes and make you chase me down the street for them." His bright blue eyes sparked, and she half expected him to follow through with his threat.

Joshua never showed this exasperating side during the short time he worked at the store last year. He walked his fingers across the table toward her paperwork spider-style until she snatched them up and held her work against herself for protection. "I'd never give chase in these heels."

An idea dawned. "I have a suggestion."

"Let me hear it."

"Let's go to the Automat."

Joshua stared at her as if she'd asked him to jump over the moon. "You're joking."

Audrey pulled her coat from the back of her chair. "Not at all. I rather liked eating there when I first came to New York." She slid her papers and notebook into her new Marc Cross box bag. When Gigi was over at Audrey's house one evening, she recognized it as the same case Grace Kelly used in the film *Rear Window*. She almost split Audrey's eardrums with her squeals.

She handed her thick wool coat trimmed with a leopard collar to Joshua, then waited as he stood, held the garment out, and helped her slide her arms inside. Audrey drew her gloves out of one pocket and pulled them on.

"I think it would be lovely to revisit the old place, see if things have changed much."

He pulled on his own dark leather gloves and slid on his black wool overcoat. He wrapped a thick woolen gray-plaid muffler around his neck, then set his hat on his closely cropped blond hair. "Only you would go to the Automat dressed in leopard."

She settled her matching leopard fur bucket hat on her head, her purse in the crook of her elbow. Audrey tucked the case under her arm, then burrowed her hands into her matching leopard muff. She flashed her twenty-four-karat smile. "Give me one good reason why I shouldn't."

"Because some poor leopard is out there feeling underdressed." Joshua took her case in one hand, then took her elbow with the other and guided her toward the exit. "Let's go eat. I'm starved."

Audrey paused and removed one hand from her muff. "Your little leopard friend is just fine." She turned her collar up around her ears. "This is all faux fur."

While she snuggled her hand back in her muff, Joshua chuckled and linked his arm in hers as he walked her out of the hotel and into the night. The cold air slapped her nose and cheeks as a chilled shudder ran down her body.

"Invigorating, isn't it?" Joshua's warm breath clouded around his face as he positioned himself between her and the street.

Audrey's teeth chattered. "Maybe for a penguin, or a polar bear. My Florida blood is too thin for this kind of weather." Her face ached, and her toes went numb before they passed the fourth block down the sidewalk.

A bank's neon sign hung on the outside of the building along the way, projecting the time and temperature. Joshua must have noticed the number at the same time she did, as he blew out an icy whistle.

"Nineteen degrees? Whose idea was this again?" he asked as he nuzzled his face deeper behind his muffler. Her arm vibrated with the force of his own shuddering against the cold. "My Alabama blood isn't too fond of weather dipping below twenty."

They moved to the side as crowds of others passed them on the sidewalk, huddled into their own coats trying to keep warm. They crunched through a dirty dusting of snow collected outside the door of one of the shops.

Joshua quickened his steps and pulled her along. "The Automat's a few more blocks. You owe me at least five cups of coffee once we're there."

Audrey dipped her chin further into the top of her coat in hopes of blocking her nose and cheeks better from the cold. "Deal. We'll shake on it once we're inside."

Chapter 31

Mary Jo

The usual homesickness hit her on this first day back to the sales floor. Mary Jo had no appetite but still looked across the crowded cafeteria for the fourth time, checking to see if Gigi had come in yet. When she spied her friend, she leaped to her feet and waved, hoping she'd be seen.

Once Gigi reached the table, she hugged Mary Jo and almost lifted her off the floor. "I missed you."

Mary Jo patted her on the back. "I feel like it's been eons since I was here."

They released each other and sat down to eat. Mary Jo moved her tray to give Gigi more space to spread out her lunch. Expecting the usual bologna and cheese and one of Lilla's cookie bars, Mary Jo was completely surprised when Gigi instead pulled out a red-and-black thermos and an apple.

"You're having coffee only for lunch?" Mary Jo spread her napkin across her lap.

Gigi unscrewed the thermos' beige cup-lid. "Chicken soup." She dug deeper into her bag. "And a cathead biscuit. One of the girls in the apartments made this huge pot of chicken soup for her boyfriend, who's come down with the flu. Since it's going around so bad, he told her not to come over, so she got peeved at him and shared her soup with us."

The aroma floated to Mary Jo's nose as Gigi poured herself a cupful. "That smells wonderful."

"I tell you this girl put everything but the kitchen cabinets in this stuff. Said it will cure anything that ails you. I figure I'll eat it and keep myself healthy as long as I can."

She spooned a bite and ate it. "Thanks to me, Cosmetics has already met its sales quotas for the third time this month."

Mary Jo stirred a pat of butter into her mashed potatoes. "I'm so proud of you."

Gigi's cheeks turned pink as she ducked her head. "Thanks. I'm working as hard as I can."

"Are the other girls still giving you a hard time?"

"They don't talk to me. I'm being frozen out."

"Oh Gigi, I'm so sorry."

She pulled off another bite. "I don't give two cents about trying to be their friend. I'm here to make sales."

"What does Jane say?"

Gigi took a sip before answering. "She's been pretty nice to me, which makes the other girls more steamed."

Mary Jo's heart pinched. Breaking into a group of women as the new girl had to be one of the hardest things in the world. And it shouldn't have been that way.

"I told you they were a tight group." Mary Jo forked a piece of ham.

"Who needs them? I've got you. And Miss Vivien, Mirette, and Audrey." Gigi poured another serving of soup into her cup, then spooned a mouthful.

After swallowing, she pointed her spoon at Mary Jo. "Did you get Miss Vivien's invitation?"

"For what?" Mary Jo chased a pile of peas with her spoon until she could scoop them up to eat.

"She's hosting her ladies' club next week and wants you, me, and Audrey to come. They call it the TLC Club."

"Tender Loving Care Club? That's so sweet."

Gigi wrinkled her nose and shook her head. "She didn't tell me what the letters meant, but I guess that works. Anyway, the party is next Friday at seven. I'll bet her house is really swell."

"You've been to Audrey's, and she lives just across the lake from Miss Vivien."

"I've seen Miss Vivien's all lit up at night. It looks like a banquet hall."

Mary Jo wiped her mouth with her napkin. "With all this terrible stuff going on, is she really up for hosting a party?"

Gigi chewed the last bite of her biscuit, then swallowed. "You know Miss Vivien. She's cut from the cloth that never quits but keeps soldiering on till things get better."

Mary Jo laid her silverware on her tray. "I want to go. I've felt so bad about what's happened. One of the girls in Accessories told me she heard Miss Vivien's lost girls from her client list. They're too scared to buy a dress from her."

"That's so dumb. She isn't the one doing all the"—Gigi covered her mouth and spoke in a low tone only Mary Jo could hear—"murders."

"I wish we could find out a way to help her. Or at least stop Robbi Dever from talking about it all the time in the paper and on the radio."

Gigi wiped out her empty cup with her napkin, then screwed the lid back on her thermos. "There's other weird things happening around town she could talk about."

"Like what?"

"I overheard one of the women on the bus say that somebody threw eggs at the Bensons' house again."

"How horrid. Who would do such a thing?"

"Probably some teenagers up to no good. The only clue they had was the eggs came from Murphy's Dairy outside of town. They found an eggshell with their stamp on it."

"I know what I'd do if I found it was my teenager doing such. On the other hand, I have some better news."

Gigi raised one brow as she folded over the top of her lunch bag. "Better than your mother going home?"

That was great news, but she had more to share. "You'll never believe this, but Kenny decided he wants to learn how to use the new arm."

"He what?"

"And it's all thanks to Mama."

Gigi leaned forward on her elbows. "This I've got to hear."

Mary Jo pushed her tray to the side. "He told me he always hated how she chews at me about everything, always puts me down. After listening to her fuss about him not pulling his own weight and being a deadbeat, he got mad and said he has to prove her wrong."

She clapped her hands together. "He wants to go back to work as soon as he can find someone who'll take a chance on him. We both know it's going to be hard because people see him as a cripple." Oh, how she hated that word. "But we're hoping and praying there's somebody out there willing to at least let him try."

Gigi grabbed her hands and squeezed. "I'm so happy for you." Her wide smile faded as soon as she'd spoken.

Mary Jo noticed. "What's the matter?"

Gigi's shoulders drooped. "Nothing. I'm really happy for you."

"Then why do you look like I just shot your dog?"

"Because once he goes back to work, you'll go back to taking care of your house and watching *Howdy Doody* with the girls."

She drew a circle on the tabletop with her fingertip as realization hit.

Mary Jo slapped the table with her hand. "We'll have none of that moping." When Gigi looked up, Mary Jo continued.

"Miss Vivien, Audrey, and even Mirette would love to eat with you. And I'll come and meet you for lunch when the girls are in school. And if nothing else, you could always go back to sneaking in the kitchen and eating with Lilla. Although you'd have to be careful to not eat too many of those scrumptious cookie bars of hers."

Gigi shrugged as if knowing she'd best go along with Mary Jo's pep talk or risk having to sit through more. "Sure."

A man neither of them knew approached the table. "Are you Gigi Woodard?"

Gigi scowled. "Why do you want to know?"

He bent over in a nervous bow, then straightened and ran a hand over his forehead to smooth back a shock of jet-black curls. "I'm Ben Stafford from Accounting." He held out a check to her. "Personnel forgot to give you this, and your manager, Jane, said you were at lunch."

Gigi pulled back as if he were trying to hand her a snake. "What is this about?"

He laid the check on the table in front of her. "Wynton's gives out a 10 percent bonus to the first employee to make their sales quota before the end of the month. You won."

A pleasant expression crossed his face, part smile and part good humor, shining all the way into his green eyes. "Congratulations and well done." He dipped his head and started to leave, then swiveled back to face her.

"It was nice meeting you, Miss Woodard." He switched to Mary Jo. "And you too. . ."

"Mary Jo Johnson."

He raised his brows as if he recognized her name. "Ladies Accessories, right?" He gave her a quick bow. "Nice meeting you as well. I'm new here at Wynton's and know so few employees yet."

"Welcome to Wynton's," Mary Jo and Gigi chorused, then looked at each other and giggled.

"Thanks." Ben bowed his head once more, then made his way to the cafeteria's exit.

Mary Jo leaned across the table. "You could eat lunch with him. He seems nice."

Gigi stuck out her tongue as she picked up the bonus check. "I told you, I've sworn off men."

"Well, congratulations on the bonus. Shows Jane and all the others you're not someone to be trifled with. You're a serious saleswoman."

Gigi continued to stare at the check. "Yeah, I guess I am. And I know just what I'm going to do with this." She waved her check through the air. "I'm going right to the shoe department and paying off my new pumps."

Her mouth popped open. "I forgot to tell you who I saw there the other day. Robbi Dever. She brought in a shoe to be resoled. It had a big hole in the bottom, like something cut right through." She curled her fingers in a circular shape demonstrating the size of the hole.

"Then, she came over to me, said she knew I was friends with Miss Vivien, and gave me her card so I could contact her with something good to write in her column because Miss Vivien needed all the help she could get right now."

Mary Jo fell back against the back of her chair. "What unbelievable gall that woman has."

Gigi pushed back in her chair, then stood. "I crumpled up her card and threw it away."

Mary Jo lifted her tray and prepared to leave the table. "Good for you." She wiped away crumbs from Gigi's biscuit, then looked up when Gigi clicked her tongue against her teeth.

"I can clean up after myself, Mama." She winked at Mary Jo.

Mary Jo put the dirty napkin on her tray. "Guess you don't need a mama now that you're a big-shot saleswoman."

"Oh brother. One good month a big shot does not make. Jane let me go early, so I'd better get back." Gigi hurried through the thinning lunch crowd.

Mary Jo carried her tray to the belt, then made her way back to Accessories. When she arrived, a male clerk from Menswear was talking with one of the girls Mary Jo worked with. He held a rolled-up copy of the *LTC* in his hand.

"Sheriff Youngblood said he has no comment about what it meant," he said to the girl.

At the mention of the sheriff, Mary Jo hurried over. "What's going on? I heard you mention Sheriff Youngblood. Did they find another clue to the case?"

The young man unfolded the *LTC* and pointed to Robbi's column below the fold. "It's right here. According to Robbi, they found all the pieces to the glass punch bowl used as the weapon in Leila's murder except one. Sheriff Youngblood and his men searched Leila's house but never found it."

Mary Jo read the column twice, and by the third go-round, she worried her ham and mashed potatoes were going to come back up.

Vivien's hostess motto had always been no one went home hungry from her house, and tonight was going to be no different. The tables she'd set up and covered with her embroidered linen tablecloths last night now held enough food to feed an army instead of her flock of friends.

The full skirt on her brown taffeta dress rustled as she walked back and forth from her kitchen to the living room, carrying trays of food. Card tables were assembled around the room for the club's meeting, where budget, minutes from the last meeting, and the yearly community project would be discussed while the members ate. Afterward, the real fun began when each table ran games of Hearts for prizes, which Vivien had selected and stored away in baskets for distribution later.

She looked over the assortment of cheese and crackers, two plates of deviled eggs, ambrosia salad, chicken canapés, croquettes, and barbecued meatballs keeping warm in her chafing dishes. Her best silver serving spoons lay next to the dishes.

The two pound cakes she'd baked, one lemon, the other brown sugar and cream cheese, sat on the end of the table next to a bowl of her gooey strawberry topping. When the buzzer on her oven sounded, Vivien returned to the kitchen and removed a tray of apple tarts and set them on the counter to cool.

Mirette stood nearby, mixing up the juice and ginger ale to make the punch. "You can just pass me one of those tarts now, because as soon as the girls get here they'll be gone faster than you can say Jack Robinson."

Vivien removed a small dessert plate from the cabinet and passed her friend the dessert. "I've got homemade vanilla ice cream to go with it."

Mirette held the plate out. "Yes please, ma'am."

While Vivien scooped out a mound, her doorbell rang. She set the spoon in the sink and passed the dessert on. "Enjoy."

Mirette nodded as she ate a large spoonful of tart, then dug in for another as Vivien put the ice cream back in the icebox. She wiped her hands on her white tea apron adorned with tiny red-and-pink roses before she hurried to answer the front door.

The moment she swung the door open, Mary Jo wrapped her in a hug, then presented her with a small package wrapped in pink tissue paper tied with a black velvet ribbon. "I made you a little something."

"Now you didn't need to do that." Vivien took the gift.

She settled Mary Jo at one of the card tables set up in the living room, then sat beside her to open the gift. Inside was a tea apron made of chiffon and hemmed with a ruffle embellished around the top with a black velvet ribbon.

Vivien noted the tiny, straight-as-a-pin stitching, and the perfectly symmetrical ruffle. "Mary Jo, this is darling. Thank you."

She tilted her head to the side as if embarrassed. "It's just a little something I wanted to make for you to use tonight."

Vivien held the apron out. "I could sell these in the salon as bridesmaids' gifts, or even for a bride. This is just adorable."

She stood and untied her own, put it in the paper, and then fastened her new one around her waist. "This belt is so easy to tie, and wide enough to make a cute little bow."

Vivien slid her hand in the heart-shaped pocket trimmed with a mini-ruffle that matched the large one around the hem. "Mirette, come out here a second. I want to show you something."

"I can either come see you or stir up this punch. You can't have both, your majesty," Mirette called back from the kitchen.

Mary Jo giggled while Vivien shook her head. "Excuse me a minute while I show my poor, overworked assistant my sweet gift. I'm serious about carrying these in my salon. How long did it take you to make this?"

"I whipped that together last night, after the girls went to bed."

Vivien turned and headed for the kitchen. "When I get back, I want to talk about this more."

She walked across her foyer and down the hall to the kitchen. When she entered, she almost plowed into Mirette, who was carrying the punch bowl, filled almost to the brim, with both hands. The red liquid sloshed up the sides and back down like waves in a swimming pool.

"Good night, Vivien, you didn't tell me I had to make the punch and wear it too tonight." Mirette set the bowl down on Vivien's kitchen table.

Vivien held up her hands. "I wanted to show you something." She spun around before her friend as she lifted up the apron for her to see. "Mary Jo made this for me, and I was thinking we might pay her to make a few for the salon."

Mirette stepped closer. She lifted the apron's hem for a look. "These would sell."

The doorbell rang again. "You go, I'll bring in the punch."

Vivien held the kitchen door open, and Mirette moved through, headed for the living room with careful steps.

At the door, Gigi stood on the steps, a small potted fern in her hands. "I thought this might look nice on one of your tables tonight."

Vivien gave her a hug around the neck. "You're so sweet."

As Gigi walked in, Vivien rearranged the picture frames on a small credenza next to the door. "I'm putting the plant right here, so I'll see it every time I walk in, and think of you."

Gigi smiled as if the idea suited her. Vivien motioned toward the living room. "Let's go have a seat. Mary Jo and Mirette are in there."

After she gave a tour of her house, they sat and chatted about the store, the weather, Mary Jo's daddy's progress at home, and a dozen other things when Vivien's phone rang. She excused herself to answer.

When she returned, Mirette and Gigi were deep in a conversation about her new apartment. Mirette looked up and puckered her brows when she saw Vivien.

"What's the matter?"

Vivien walked over and took a seat at the table next to where they were sitting. "That was Merilee on the phone. She and Mary Hadley aren't going to make it—they had something come up."

"Then why the long face?" Mirette asked.

Vivien looked at her watch. "It's almost eight, and we're the only ones here."

Gigi and Mary Jo traded glances with Mirette, and then Mary Jo spoke up. "We've been running on so, I didn't realize the time."

Mirette rose from her chair. "I've been smelling this food all night. I can't wait any longer." She walked to the table and picked up one of Vivien's china plates.

Mary Jo and Gigi followed, and for a moment the room was filled with the sounds of serving spoons and forks clinking.

"This all looks amazing, Miss Vivien," Mary Jo said as she forked a meatball onto her plate.

Gigi stood staring at the chicken canapés. "What is this?"

"Chicken mixed with mustard, mayonnaise, and some other seasonings put on a cracker. It's called a canapé."

"Do I eat it with my hand?"

"You eat however you want, honey."

Vivien walked to her front window and peered outside. The street stood silent. No cars sat in the glow of the lights, nor were headlights coming from the main road as if possibly her guests had all run late.

Her parties had become events in Levy City, where neighbors and friends clamored to attend. Being invited to one of her gatherings was a symbol of having "made it" in Levy City's social circles in some folks' minds, though she always tried to invite folks from all walks and not just the upper crust.

The happy conversations from moments ago were now replaced by a concerned silence.

She now understood what being angry enough to spit meant. Maybe she should tell her friends to go home so she could throw on her robe and slippers and cry, scream, or mope around the house.

No. There would be nothing of the kind going on in her house. She'd lived through this kind of thing once before. No sense crumbling like a dried-up cookie because she'd been stood up—after all, friends still surrounded her.

She swung round and walked back to the living room, grabbed a plate, and cut herself a thick slice of pound cake. Confusion, pity, and worry shone in her friends' eyes when she joined them at the table.

Vivien spread her napkin in her lap and spooned three huge dollops of strawberries over the slice. "My mother once said meals should begin with dessert and put everyone in a good mood." She plopped the oversized bit in her mouth, then worked to chew it.

When she tried to swallow, the cake stuck like sawdust in her throat, but a few sips of punch helped push the rest down. She gestured to her friends' plates. "Eat up. No one says *we* can't have a party."

Gigi stared at her, then looked around the table at the others. Mary Jo kept her head down, and Mirette met Vivien with a firm set of her mouth.

"Go get those tarts and the ice cream then."

Vivien rose and brought the tray and the ice bucket with the ice cream to their table. She fixed each one a serving, then some for herself. "Don't feel sorry for me. I wanted a party with my friends tonight, and that is exactly what I'm having."

She cut a bite of tart, dunked it in the mound of ice cream on her plate, and held it aloft. "Here's to my dearest friends, minus Audrey, who's with us in spirit if not body. Let's eat up and worry about the calories another time."

"Here, here," Mirette said as she shoved a bite of tart in her mouth.

"Sounds wonderful to me." Mary Jo swung her loaded fork in the air as if raising a glass for a toast, then slid the dessert into her mouth.

The doorbell rang and Vivien laid down her fork. "Must be someone who had a change of heart." She rose from her chair and headed for the door.

Her heart skipped at least a dozen beats when she swung her door open to see Bill Youngblood standing on her top step, his uniform hat clutched in his hands.

Vivien gripped the edge of the door to keep herself from swaying.

"Vivien, I'm—"

She held up both hands to stop him. "Who?"

He stood silent, his face filled with compassion and pain. "Macy Whitten. Her father found her right before supper when he went over to work on the bomb shelter he's building for her and Jimmy."

Vivien's hands shook as she slipped outside and pulled the door closed to keep her friends from hearing. "Same scenario as before?"

Bill nodded. "The gown, the label, and one of those bride dolls you sell in your shop was in her arms. A cast-iron skillet was used as the. . .means."

Vivien grasped the doorknob in one hand as she leaned against the door for support. "Any clues?"

He closed his eyes as he shook his head. "The scene's clean." Sheriff Youngblood placed his hat on his head. "I wanted you to know before news hits the *LTC* in the morning. And Robbi's radio show. I'm really sorry for ruining your party. Sally wanted to come, but she's been down with the flu all week. She's lost her voice from coughing."

He scratched the back of his neck. "Come to think of it, I was supposed to call you on Monday to tell you she wasn't coming because she can't speak above a whisper. I've been so wrapped up in all this, I clean forgot."

Vivien opened her door. "I hope she's on the mend soon, Bill."

"Me too." He made his way back to his patrol car.

Vivien entered her house to her friends' laughter. Mirette must have been sharing some of her silly stories. They all turned her way when she entered, and the joy faded from their faces.

"Who was at the door?" Mirette rose from her chair and grabbed the back of it as she worked to get the kinks out and stand straight.

"Bill Youngblood. They found Macy Whitten this evening."

Mirette cupped her cheeks in her hands. "How many more of these are we going to have?" Her voice caught as a sob escaped her.

Mary Jo ran to hug her as Gigi left her chair and came to Vivien. She stood a moment, as if she were afraid to touch her, then took a step back and crossed her arms.

"We've got to figure out who's doing all this. People are blaming you, and that's not right, Miss Vivien."

Vivien gathered Gigi in her arms and patted her on the back. "Don't you worry about me, honey. I'll be fine. I'm just worried about all my brides. We've got to solve this so no more of them die."

Chapter 33

Audrey

There was something magical about walking into the Automat and seeing little had changed. White coffee cups filled the shelf next to the dolphin-shaped coffee spouts on the wall. Signs still hung above each section, denoting what type of food could be found on the shelves behind the rectangular windows. The scents of bread, rolls, pies, and hot and cold meals filled the space. The "nickel thrower" stood in her glassed-in booth, ready to break dollars into change and pass them through the small arched window.

Audrey claimed the last empty seats at a small circular wooden table near the door. She laid her hat, muff, and coat down on one of the four chairs as Joshua shed his own and deposited them on another.

"I love this place. You never know who's going to be here." Audrey tilted her head toward a group sitting along the wall opposite where they stood. "Those folks are new designers showcasing their first line this year. I met them last night at one of the parties."

She swept her eyes to another table where a stunning blond woman sat with a man whose temples grayed. "She's an actress, and he's some big Hollywood producer here looking for talent to take back to California. They were sitting a few seats down from me at the Traina-Norell show today."

Joshua leaned in and whispered next to her ear. "He looks like he's been around the block a few too many times."

His breath tickled her ear, and Audrey elbowed him lightly until he stepped back. "Shh. He's a very big name, from MGM or Warner Brothers. He's talking to one of my model friends about being in a movie."

Joshua looked around the room as the smells of baking bread and pie-crusts mingled with aromas of grilled onions. The heat came on, warming the room to a cozy temperature. "There's a table full of guys from the docks, and I'd bet those ladies seated in the front work at Macy's. All of us department-store people look alike. Tired and haggard."

"Speak for yourself." Audrey held up her handbag. "I've got a change purse full of nickels, and you can eat like you're a king in hog heaven tonight."

Joshua laughed at her. "Never in my life would I believe the word *hog* would be coming out of Audrey Penault's mouth." As always, he spoke her name with the French emphasis she preferred.

"I'm really a country girl at heart." She walked to the hot meals section and looked in the windows to see if any entrée tickled her dining fancy.

"Ah, but which country do you mean?"

"Florida's, with dirt, cows, horses, hunting dogs, and orange groves." She removed a handful of nickels and held them out to Joshua. "Feast away."

When she joined him at the table, he moved the array of plates in front of him to make way for her own. He pointed to her choice of beverage.

"Chocolate milk? I always tagged you for a champagne or luxury coffee girl."

Audrey pulled her chair out and sat. She spread the napkin across her lap. "In the last few weeks, I've sipped every fancy brand of champagne at cocktail parties, and coffee at the meetings at the design houses. Sometimes a girl just needs a little chocolate to sweeten her day."

Joshua spread a dollop of elderberry jam on a roll and raised it as if making a toast. "Here's hoping you have the sweetest of days from here on out." He finished with a large bite, then wiped away a small jam smear at the corner of his mouth in the most captivating way.

Audrey shook her head to clear her mind. A man using nice manners was in no way a good reason to stare at him while he ate. Best to switch gears and focus on the one thing they had in common. Business.

"You never did say what brought you to New York. Are you here for fashion week?"

He stirred his serving of pot roast with his fork. "Not exactly. I've been trying to meet with Marionne Leslie for two weeks."

Joshua went on. "We wanted her to do a line for us at Loveman's, but it seems Wynton's beat us to it." He stabbed a few strands of his roast with his fork. "I tried for two weeks just to get a message to her. Once she agreed to meet with me, I was met at her door by a butler who slipped me a note, written in the most beautiful script, saying she couldn't possibly think of signing with anyone other than Miss Penault from Wynton's."

While he slid his bite into his mouth and chewed, Audrey could detect wiggling at the corners of his lips as if he were either teasing or working hard not to laugh at her until he swallowed. "What's your secret?"

She stirred her bowl of vegetable soup, then buttered a roll. "Patience. I modeled for her once and called on behalf of the store. Three times with no success. Thankfully, she loves Mr. Wynton, so while she was vacationing in Miami I asked to talk with her." Audrey shrugged. "She liked my ideas."

Joshua laid down his fork and looked at her as if she were telling half truths. "What ideas?"

Audrey broke off a small piece of her roll and held it in her fingers. "You know better than to ask such a question. One never shares their best trade secrets in retail." She plopped the piece of roll in her mouth, then smiled at him as she chewed.

He pointed his fork at her. "Smart." Joshua reached for the pepper shaker sitting in the middle of the table, then dusted his bowl of green beans. "How much longer are you in New York?"

"Another week. I have some appointments with some smaller houses to order day dresses, and I'm meeting with another vendor to look at some mid-priced hats and ladies shoes."

"You're not spending time at the big names?"

The clinking of a plate being set in one of the windows as one of the workers replaced an item caught her attention. "I went to their shows earlier this week. I need to hit the mid-price houses too. Some of our shoppers aren't going for the big names as much."

She returned her gaze to Joshua. "They want quality, to look nice and fashionable, but they don't put as much thought into their designers. We still have the country-club set, but many of our shoppers prefer Lilli Ann suits to Chanel, what they see in the Sears catalog to Dior. New people from up North are moving to Levy City all the time. They want florals and tropical prints reminiscent of sunshine and the beaches. Flowy, light fabrics and bright colors were all the rage when I visited Burdines in Miami. Our shoppers still have more traditional tastes, but they also watch movies, and what their favorite stars are wearing, they want too. Especially our teens."

She continued. "Working with Marionne, Wynton's can provide the high-fashion look and style at a price that works for all our ladies."

Joshua pushed his plate aside and drew his dessert near. "I hate talking shop during dessert." He sliced off the tip of his pie with his fork. "I've known you for a while, and I want to know, what's your favorite color?"

His question was so strange Audrey missed stabbing her last sliver of pie and banged the fork tines on her plate. She put the fork down, sat back, and stared at him. "My favorite color?"

"Mm-hmm."

"What an odd thing to ask."

Johsua wiped his mouth, then folded his napkin and put it next to his plate. "No, it isn't. If I asked your shoe size, that would be odd. Your favorite color is just being curious."

"Curiosity kills, you know."

A man held the door open for a large group of people exiting the Automat, allowing a blast of cold air to rush in. Audrey shivered, then pulled her coat from the back of her chair and wrapped it around herself as she snuggled into the warm folds.

A slow, lazy smile crossed Joshua's face. "Curiosity's also a lot of fun."

Another group of patrons filed in from the outside, and Audrey turned the fur collar on her coat up around her neck. "Last month, I adored peacock blue. Today, my favorite is azalea pink."

Joshua's coffee cup clinked as he placed it on the saucer after downing the last drop. "And all this about your being a country girl. Truth?"

"Truth. When I was very young, I lived with Mother and Daddy on a farm outside of Levy City. We owned cows, horses, pigs, and some chickens. Mother hated the farm and spent most of her time in town at the cottage."

"Which is your current home?"

Audrey nodded. "Yes."

He leaned forward. "You're telling me you milked cows and slopped hogs." His brows shot up. "Don't tell me you plucked chickens."

Now he was being nothing short of ridiculous. "Also hunted, caught and cleaned fish, and I can field dress a rabbit. Which mortifies my mother."

He laughed, bringing up a caramel-apple type of enjoyment in her. Salty, sweet, maybe even sticky, but who cared about all the mess because it was warm and delicious.

And she'd bought him dinner. Mother would have fainted dead-out over such a breach of conduct. Her entire life, she drilled into Audrey that a lady never bought a man's meal. Doing so was the height of being unladylike and desperate.

He puckered his lips as he mulled her comment before launching a new question. "Tell me how a girl goes from running wild in the country to a runway in Paris a few years later?"

"Airplanes. And ocean liners."

Her fingers went icy cold. Audrey grabbed her muff from the chair beside her and burrowed them in the soft, furry tunnel. Nerves over wanting and not wanting to answer his questions may have added to their chill.

Joshua propped his elbow on the back of the chair next to him. "Why did you leave the modeling world? You obviously loved it. And don't give me all the riddles you tried on me the last time I asked you this."

He waved his hand over their empty plates. "We've broken bread together. Shared pie. You know as well as I, where we come from that means we're friends."

"I was still living in Paris, and one day I looked up at the Eiffel Tower and thought, it's just a bunch of metal. A few days later, I was modeling suits for Chanel when I looked in the mirror and thought, it's just another dress. I saw a print ad I was in, and it was just another picture. Somewhere along the way, the magic faded. I was tired of being someone else's product. I wanted to be the one figuring out what the world wanted and how to help them find it."

His eyes softened, and the look she'd grown to know so well flickered within. He was going to compliment her beauty, tell her she could step right back into the modeling world tonight, slather on the flattery so thick butter wouldn't melt in his mouth. She'd heard it oh so many times, and the disappointment swelled as she braced for the onslaught.

Joshua grabbed his coat from the back of a chair and slipped his arms through. "Makes sense to me, being you're Wynton's head buyer now. And I don't know of anyone in retail who knows their market better than you."

He squirmed until he was able to fit his coat on his shoulders and around his back. "I'm going back to Loveman's and do my own market analysis for our shoppers. We may need to make changes in our clothing offerings like you're doing at Wynton's."

For the first time in her life, a man other than her father and Mr.

Wynton saw beyond her face and realized she had a brain inside her skull.

Joshua checked his watch, then sighed. "My dad wanted me to call him tonight, and if I don't do so soon, he's going to be in bed and won't answer the phone. Once the sun sets, so does he." Audrey rose, and he rushed over to help with her chair. "I'll still be in town tomorrow if you'd like to meet for dinner again. My treat," he said as she pushed her chair under.

"I can't. I have a dinner, two cocktail parties, and then a date for coffee with an old friend later tomorrow night."

"Then I'm hailing a cab and delivering you to your hotel."

Later, when she'd hopped from the cab in front of her hotel, Joshua scooted over to the open door. "Thanks for one of the most informative dinners I've ever had. Good night."

He pulled the door shut, then waved at her out the cab's back window. Audrey watched until the cab turned a corner a few blocks away.

The cold nipped her cheeks, and she hurried up the steps, then made her way to the front desk.

The night manager turned round and met her with a wider-than-necessary smile as he greeted her.

"Do you have any messages for Audrey Penault, room 415?"

He bowed and walked along the array of open squares until he came to her room number. The manager removed the two pieces of paper inside and brought them to her.

She thanked him and proceeded to read the first as she walked to the elevator.

Call Mr. Wynton. Store Business.

The elevator doors opened, and she stepped in as soon as the operator moved the gate and let her pass by.

The sparkle of the evening faded as all the things Libby must have ruined came to mind. She flipped it behind the other paper and then tried to keep her face calm as she read over the words.

Call Gigi. Urgent. There's been another one.

Audrey leaped forward as the operator was closing the gate, forcing her way past him and out of the elevator. "Pardon me, so sorry," she called over her shoulder as she ran back to the front desk.

The clerk stared as she ran across the hotel lobby and stopped before his station. "I need to check out, immediately. And could you please send a bellhop to room 415 in fifteen minutes?"

He walked to her room's message box and pulled out another piece of white paper, then brought it back to Audrey. "I was told to give this to you when you returned to check out."

She took the paper and read the words.

I've booked a flight home tomorrow afternoon. Until then, I'll mind the store, and Vivien.

—TJW

Audrey met the clerk's gaze. "Will there be anything else, Miss Penault?"

She crumpled the note in her hand. Every fiber in her demanded she defy the boss, pack her bags, and head home, even if she had to get a ticket on a Greyhound and tie her luggage to the roof.

Mr. Wynton had spoken, and she must stay put.

Audrey raced up the four flights to her room. She had to call Miss Vivien.

Beams from the streetlights danced across the hood of Vivien's car as she turned into Mirette's driveway. As soon as she'd shifted into PARK, she flashed her headlights. A few seconds later her assistant's silhouette appeared behind the blinds covering her front door window. She moved slowly as she locked her front door and made her way down her steps to the car.

Once Mirette was settled in the passenger side, Vivien backed out of the driveway. "Have we lost our ever-loving minds, running around after midnight when we all have work tomorrow?"

Mirette pulled her robe tighter around her ankles. "You kidding? I haven't had this much excitement after nine since we sneaked into the store last year."

Vivien paused at the stop sign, twice looking in both directions before she pulled onto the street to head to Mary Jo's. "I don't know why Audrey thought this couldn't wait until she got home tomorrow night."

Mirette remained silent a moment. "Vivien, if she's come up with some idea to make this nightmare stop, I'd stay up for a week to hear what she has to say."

"I'd stay up for a month to make this end," Vivien said softly.

Mirette reached over and patted her arm. "I know you would, honey. We all would."

What had she done to cause all this? She'd prayed hundreds of times these past weeks for the answer so she could make amends and stop this madness. None came, and now dread filled her from the moment she awoke until the moment her brain stopped spinning at night and she slipped into fitful sleep. Every day she had to worry about which of her brides was next on this killer's list.

Mary Jo waited for them at the end of her driveway, and she bounded into the car as soon as Vivien came to a stop.

"I hope your husband isn't too upset with me calling so late and whisking you off on some crazy adventure," Vivien said as she pulled away.

"He fussed a little, then said it could be worse. We could be sneaking off to play poker."

Her jest brought a little measure of much-needed levity.

"I'm warning you both, Gigi gets grumpy when she's awakened in the middle of the night."

"How will that be any different from her normal mood?" Mirette cracked as they drove past the store on their way to Gigi's apartment house.

Vivien stopped her car in front of the building's sidewalk, then slid the gear into PARK. All the windows stood dark, with no signs of the inhabitants stirring, including Gigi.

"Are you sure she's up?" Mirette asked as she scanned for signs of Gigi being awake.

Mary Jo moved closer to the back seat window and looked out. "She said she'd be right out when I called her. Maybe she went back to bed."

"I'm shutting off the car before we wake the entire neighborhood." Vivien turned the key and switched her attention to the house. "Did the curtain in the front window just wiggle like someone was looking outside?"

"I hope it wasn't Jenny Vines peering out. She hates it when people stop in front of her building. She'll call the sheriff on us for sure."

"I'm giving Gigi two more seconds, and then I'm leaving."

Mary Jo grabbed the top of the front seat. "Wait, Miss Vivien, I think the door is opening."

Vivien moved to peer over Mirette, and indeed Gigi had emerged from the house. She tried to canter toward them, but the long skirt of her robe had wrapped around her ankles, forcing her to scurry to the car with tiny steps.

Mary Jo scooted over to make room when Gigi yanked the door open and hopped in. "I'm sorry. I fell back asleep waiting in the front parlor. Miss Vines was banging around, trying to get to the phone. She's upset y'all parked out here and was calling the sheriff but knocked a vase off the shelf, woke me up, and nearly scared me to death."

Mirette turned to look at Vivien, and though her friend's face was half hidden in the soft glow of the streetlights, there was no doubt a satisfied told-you-so look on her face.

"You'd better be hotfooting it out of here, Miss Vivien. She's plenty mad."

"I hear you, Gigi." Vivien stepped on the accelerator as she made a U-turn in the street to head back to her own house.

The leather in the back seat groaned as Gigi leaned back. "So tell me again why we're out in the middle of the night when we all have to report to the store in the morning?"

Mary Jo tsked her. "I told you on the phone, Gigi. Audrey has something very important she wants to tell us. Maybe she thinks it can help Miss Vivien."

"When did she call you, Miss Vivien?"

"About an hour ago. I tried talking her into waiting until tomorrow night when she was home, and she wouldn't hear of it."

Vivien pulled into her driveway. "I'll put a pot of coffee on. Y'all go get settled in the living room." She pointed to Mary Jo. "You make sure Gigi stays awake."

Both women smiled as they slid across the seat to exit Vivien's car.

Once the coffee was brewed and they each had a cup, the four of them squeezed in side by side on the couch as Vivien dialed the number Audrey had given her.

The hotel clerk who answered transferred them to Audrey's room.

"Miss Vivien?"

A yawn escaped her as she held the phone so they might all hear. "We're here, Audrey. What couldn't wait until tomorrow?"

"I spoke with Mr. Wynton earlier tonight. He's considering postponing Bridal Week until the police catch the killer."

Mirette shot her attention to Vivien. "Did you know this?"

"He phoned me right after he spoke to Audrey."

There was more they'd discussed during the short call. "We talked about shutting down the salon as well."

The group on her couch reacted just as she'd expected. Mary Jo shrieked, then covered her mouth. Gigi looked around the group with her jaw hanging open.

Mirette stared at Vivien with the eyes of a deer who knows it's been caught in the hunter's crosshairs without an escape. "Guess I need to start reading the help-wanted ads if I want to keep myself from being tossed into the old folks' home."

"No worries of that, my friend. I'll move you in here with me. I'm the only one who can put up with your cantankerous ways." Vivien winked when Mirette wrinkled her nose as if the idea smelled bad, then stuck her tongue out at her boss.

"I've had a thought," Audrey called from the phone.

"I'm having several at the moment, but good manners say I can't share them," Mirette mumbled under her breath, causing Gigi to burst into a fit of giggles until Vivien glared at the two of them with her best "Mom said hush" look.

"Go on, Audrey."

"Miss Vivien, you're right in thinking this person knows something about sewing, and the bridal business. We've figured out this killer is a woman, and the last murder proves that."

Vivien looked down the row at her friends, who all mouthed a silent *What?* to one another.

Miss Vivien motioned for them to be quiet. "Tell them how you came up with that, Audrey."

"The missing bridal guide. When was the last time a man stepped foot in the salon?"

"None, except Rafe when he makes deliveries," Mirette said.

"Exactly. And these crimes have a lot of hatred behind them. Toward brides."

Gigi leaned in closer. "How'd you come up with that notion?"

"Look at the weapons and how they were used. The girls were bludgeoned in the head, several times, with things brides receive as gifts. Those things don't have the same meaning to a man as they do a woman. And they're all found not just in Miss Vivien's guides but as a part of the entire bridal business. Most men wouldn't have any idea how to buy candelabras, or crystal, or even frying pans. They'd never give them a second thought. But women do."

Vivien's mind whirred as Audrey spoke, then jarred to a stop when another thought jumped out and screamed for attention. "I mostly agree with you, hon, but there's one man I can think of who has a strong vested interest in every single one of these objects."

Mary Jo clutched the corner of one of the couch's tufted-silk throw pillows. "Who, Miss Vivien?"

"Young Mr. Cameron, our disgruntled caterer. He uses silver tea services, crystal punch bowls, candelabras, and I'm positive he's got a cast-iron skillet or two in his kitchen."

Mirette nodded as she looked around the group. "And he's been mad-as-fire over our removing him from the guide."

"How did he get into the salon to steal a copy of the guide?" Audrey asked through the receiver.

Vivien tapped her hand on her knee. "He didn't have to. We dressed his daughter for her wedding last summer."

"That's right. He doesn't have the latest edition of the guide, but his daughter does have a copy." Mirette pounded her fist into the soft arm of Vivien's couch.

She clamped her jaws so tight her cheeks bulged a moment before she relaxed. "And all this time that shyster has been giving more tongue than a bloodhound on the hunt with all those letters to the editor of the *LTC* calling for Vivien to quit and close the salon to protect the brides of Levy City."

Gigi bounced up from the couch and tried to stalk away. She cracked her toe on the leg of the coffee table and went to her knees shrieking in pain.

"Is everything all right there?" Audrey called from the phone.

Mary Jo jumped to help Gigi, and Vivien picked up the receiver. "All is well, Gigi stubbed her toe trying to take her frustrations out on my coffee table."

Vivien glanced at the clock on the wall. "Audrey, we've got to hang up so I can get these girls back home for a little sleep before we all report to the store tomorrow."

"I do too. I have a show at nine tomorrow. Thank you for letting me share my thoughts."

Vivien looked at the faces of her friends gathered around, ready and willing to sacrifice to help her. A long time ago, she'd prayed for support like theirs.

If the salon closed, and her name meant less than mud, she'd start her career as a grandmother who spoiled her grandbabies rotten and drove her kids mad butting into their business.

For now, she hoped they could put their heads together and come up with a way to stop this killer and protect Levy City's young married women. And afterward, she'd enjoy a few more years doing what she loved.

Chapter 35

Vivien

March showed a preference for going out like a lion instead of the lamb as the damp, gusty wind blew across the crowd at Macy Whitten's graveside service. Many of the women in the group held tight to their hats with one hand as they waited for the pastor to utter his final amen.

Vivien's heels sunk into the soft ground as she and Mirette stood together, off from the group. There were stares and side-glances not meant to go unseen the moment they darkened the threshold of Levy City Methodist Church for the funeral. With four sweet girls now gone, the families and friends needed a body to direct their heartbreak at, a face or name to hold responsible for their pain.

She and Mirette became their targets.

Vivien leaned into Mirette, smashing against her purse. "I'm tired."

Mirette moved her handbag to her other hand. "This has been a long day."

"No, I'm tired of standing with my friends and neighbors mourning the loss of the future. Every one of these girls had parents who worked hard to teach them good manners, took these girls to church, made them do their homework, washed their clothes, fixed their meals. And now they've been robbed of the enjoyment of seeing them realize their dreams, have children, and just. . .grow old."

Nausea twisted her stomach, and she looked across the crowd to where Bill Youngblood stood in his sheriff's uniform, hat in hand as he delivered his condolences to the family or talked with family friends who must have been asking for any news. Bill spent much of the time shaking his head during these conversations.

She looked across the cemetery to the graves of the three other girls.

The vase at the base of Rayanne's headstone held fresh roses. The earth around Leila's stood barren. Not enough time had passed for the grass to grow over the freshly turned soil. Cathy's headstone stood next to an empty space reserved for her husband, like a cake topper made with a lone bride waiting for her groom to join her.

The mothers of the other dead girls came together and hugged Macy's mother, Carlene, as a group. They'd become a sorority of sorts, the only ones in attendance who understood the pain of an empty chair at family gatherings, an empty stocking at Christmas, and the coming years of dreading the calendar marking heartbreaking anniversaries.

Thank God they had each other. Going through something like this alone tore at a person's soul. The fiend responsible for this deserved the very worst the law could throw at them.

Vivien needed to move to a different spot to get her heels out of the dirt. "I've got to talk to Bill."

Mirette grabbed her by the hand. "Vivien, all we have are Audrey's speculations. He's not going to listen."

Mirette made a good point. What did she expect Bill to do with their musings? Without any real evidence, they were nothing more than thoughts bandied about at a late-night hen party. They'd be hard put to get a man to take them seriously without solid proof.

"He can hear what we think. Maybe we've seen something he and his boys haven't yet."

Mirette moved to block her way. "Vivien, please, let's go home. You're much too raw right now to talk with Bill or anyone else for that matter. We both know this cuts deeper than just the deaths of our brides."

She moved around her assistant. "Wait for me at the car, and we'll take our food over to the families."

Merilee Bell and Mary Hadley stood in her path, and Vivien said nothing as she moved around them. She could hear them whispering with other members from the Junior League, no doubt giving their opinions on her gall for showing up.

Vivien kept going and caught Bill as he was heading for his patrol car. "Miss Vivien. I'm glad you came."

"Mirette and I weren't invited to Leila's service."

He dipped his chin. "I'd heard that." From his wife Sally, no doubt, who was also a member of the League.

"Bill, Mirette and I can't take coming to another one of these."

He released a slow, pain-filled sigh. "None of us can, Miss Vivien. We're looking into new evidence every day, going over what we know to make sure we haven't missed anything."

Bill continued. "Our Mary Helen just got engaged. She and her mother were talking a mile a minute about all the wedding details and coming to see you at the salon. Since we found Macy, all that talk has stopped."

He turned to her, and the mask of a hardened policeman fell away, revealing the worried eyes of a loving father. "Forgive me for saying this, Vivien, but I can't say I'm not a little relieved they stopped."

"I don't blame you one bit, Bill."

She slid her hands into the pockets of her black swing coat. "The girls and I got together last night and went over some things we've learned. We may have information that could help you."

A voice rattled from the radio in his car. Bill put on his hat, then zipped up his leather police jacket. "I appreciate your wanting to help. I really do. But leave this to us, Miss Vivien."

He bowed his head in a quick goodbye, then hopped in his car and sped off, his tires kicking up the loose gravel in the cemetery's road.

Vivien turned to see folks splintered into groups. Some talked with the families and Macy's husband, Jimmy. Macy's father stood next to her mother, his face rock hard save for the twitching muscle in his jaw as he fought to keep his emotions at bay.

Those who loved Macy and her family came to give them hugs.

Long ago, Vivien stood alone before her father's grave in melting-hot sunshine, sweat streaming down her face rather than tears. She'd been the only one who had stood there while the city gravediggers lowered the simple pine box into the ground, listened to the soft thuds as they shoveled dirt to fill the hole.

The touch of a hand in the middle of her back jolted her from the past. Audrey slipped her arm through Vivien's as Mirette, Mary Jo, and Gigi stood on her other side.

Vivien wiped away a tear. "I didn't know y'all were here."

"We stood in the back," Gigi said.

Audrey tightened her hold as they neared the crowd. "We're going to walk you and Mirette back to your car."

Gigi stepped ahead of them and squared her shoulders with the bravado of a kid facing down his bullies on the playground. Mirette moved to Vivien's other side and Mary Jo took a spot behind them.

They were so sweet to try to protect her and Mirette from the glares and stares of the other women in attendance. Though she couldn't see their faces, Vivien knew narrowed eyes followed her as she passed by.

Her daughter was tucked away safe in another city, far from the reach of the killer. She didn't lay awake at night like they did, with their mama-hearts beating from both terror and sadness, praying tomorrow would be the day Bill Youngblood caught the culprit. Forever saddled with worry over their married daughters becoming the killer's next victim.

In their heartache, they'd forgotten how much she loved each of her brides and how much they'd made her a part of their families.

Vivien stopped walking and allowed her gaze to stray back to women in the crowd. They hovered around Macy's mother, Carlene. She'd draped herself over her daughter's coffin, hugging its girth as her wails grew louder and louder. Her husband tried to make her move, but she fought him off and collapsed to her knees as she buried her face in her hands.

An old verse from the book of Isaiah in the King James Bible Mama had read rattled her memory: "*Her gates shall lament and mourn, and she being desolate shall sit on the ground.*"

Vivien pulled away from Audrey's hold as she continued to stare at Carlene. "We've got to stop whoever's doing this. For all of them."

Wynton's always carried such a great selection of fabrics, ribbons, and buttons. Mary Jo perused the bolts stacked on the shelves, looking for material to make Easter dresses for Carrie Rose and Penny. Money from the sale of tea aprons she'd made for Miss Vivien was burning a hole in her pocketbook, and she could splurge a little and make outfits the girls would love.

Wynton's was dressing for spring, with Easter and April just two weeks away. The soft, flowy chiffons and cottons with bright, happy floral patterns caught her eye. As she tried to decide between pinks and yellows, she heard her name.

Gigi was coming toward her, a parcel of her own in hand. "You on a break?"

Mary Jo pulled out a bolt of a soft lavender print and unrolled enough to get a better look. "I skipped lunch so I could shop for the girls." She pointed to Gigi's bag. "What you got there?"

Gigi slid out a white record envelope from the box imprinted with Wynton's logo. Mary Jo leaned forward to read the words beneath the circle. "'Heartbreak Hotel,' Elvis Presley." She looked up at her friend. "Is this the singer you were telling me about? The one you saw on that show?"

Gigi's eyes widened. "Yes, I saw him on TV, on *Stage Show*. I've been wanting this record ever since it came out at the end of February. It keeps selling out in the record shop here at the store. I told Ralph to let me know when the next shipment came in. Thanks to my bonus, I still had enough left over after paying my rent that I could buy it today. This was the last one."

She pointed to the picture of a little white dog sitting in front of an old Victrola underneath the RCA Victor brand name. "I think their label is darling."

"My girls are asking for a dog for Easter." Mary Jo rolled the lavender fabric around the bolt and returned it to the shelf. "They want a collie like Lassie. That's their favorite TV show."

Gigi cracked the box lid open and slid the record inside. "Are you going to get them one?"

Mary Jo shook her head as she pulled out another bolt of flowered fabric. "Kenny likes the idea of a dog, and I've always loved dogs, but we'd need to fence in our backyard. Right now, Kenny's not able."

"He could once he gets better at using his new arm."

Mary Jo checked the price of the current bolt, then put it back. "That's going to take some time. He can't wear his prosthetic arm for very long because it doesn't quite fit right and rubs his scars raw. The doctor made him an appointment to go to a place in Tampa that can help fit it to him better, but that's not until late April. The girls want the puppy now."

She went to pull another sample, then ducked by the shelf as another woman entered the sewing department. Mary Jo poked Gigi, then gestured for her to look where the woman was standing.

"Isn't that Robbi Dever?"

Gigi wrinkled her nose in disgust. "Yeah, that's her."

They stared as Robbi looked through the assortment of threads. She raised her head, and Gigi pulled Mary Jo behind a rack of buttons to keep out of Robbi's view.

Gigi peeked around the rack, and Mary Jo stayed half hidden behind her friend as she craned her neck to see. "What is she doing?"

Robbi looked up again, and they both pulled back behind the rack.

Robbi caught the eye of the department's clerk, then snapped her fingers. "Willa, help please."

The woman smiled and made her way to Robbi. Gigi and Mary Jo squeezed in tight behind the rack as they spied through a small opening between two cards of buttons.

Robbi held up two spools of thread. "I tat lace for relaxation, and I was wondering if you had any of these in colors other than beige and white?"

The clerk slipped on her glasses and looked at the spools. "I think we've got some reds and greens left over from last Christmas in the cabinet underneath. Let me get the keys and we'll open it up."

"Marvelous."

Robbi walked around the department as she waited for the clerk to return. Twice she passed close to the rack, causing Mary Jo and Gigi to duck lower to keep from being seen.

"Gigi, I need to get back to work. My break is over," Mary Jo whispered in Gigi's ear.

"Me too. If I'm late, I'll never hear the end of it."

Gigi looked around them. "We could crawl out of here."

Had she lost her ever-loving mind?

Mary Jo pointed to her sapphire-blue silk dress, which was her new favorite because she loved the wide swing-skirt. "Not on your life. I have three crinolines stacked under this skirt, and the moment I go down on my hands and knees, they'd push my skirt up over my head." Mary Jo touched her leg. "And these are my last pair of good stockings."

"Well, we can't just pop up like a couple of jack-in-the-boxes and run for the exits either. She'll know we've been watching her." Gigi closed her eyes and pressed her lips into a tight line.

Another female voice spoke to Robbi, and this time she answered in a softer tone. Mary Jo peered through the space in the rack, then poked Gigi to get her to turn around for a look.

"That's Mary Hadley Bell."

Gigi nodded. "I've seen her around. What's she doing talking to Robbi Dever?"

They watched as the young woman reached in her purse and drew out a slip of white paper she handed to Robbi.

"Something I thought you might like to know." Mary Hadley snapped her purse closed and left the sewing department as the clerk returned with the keys.

"I wish I knew what that note said," Mary Jo said close to Gigi's ear.

When the clerk opened the case, she and Robbi bent down to look at the thread selection, creating a perfect diversion.

Mary Jo tugged Gigi's arm and they tiptoed behind the taller shelves filled with sewing machines as they crept away.

Mary Jo had never gotten herself into such a mess, and she could just see Robbi making some big to-do in the paper about her and Gigi spying on her in Wynton's sewing department.

Her brain spun with the worst possible things as she and Gigi hurried on. Mama would see the story and probably call her to read it over the telephone. Kenny would be mortified his wife's name was mentioned in such a tawdry way, and the girls would be teased at school because kids could be downright mean.

Her heart was thumping so hard she could barely hear herself think when they reached the elevator. Gigi mashed the button three times as they waited for the car to arrive.

Mary Jo kept looking back, expecting Robbi to come running down the aisle, her voice booming all over the third floor as she hurled accusations at them.

When the car arrived and the doors opened, they both dove in as soon as the operator moved the gate out of the way. Those doors couldn't close fast enough.

Her heart still drummed when the elevator started the downward trek. Mary Jo patted her chest, then looked over at Gigi, whose face was white as a slice of Sunbeam bread.

"Do you think she saw us?" Mary Jo drew in a deep breath for calm.

"I'm saying no and hoping I'm right."

Gigi's solution wasn't at all reassuring.

Vivien circled the dress form for the third time. She couldn't voice what was wrong with the gown she'd designed for Louisa, or what her eyes were seeing that didn't sit right.

"Mirette, did we make the bodice too long?"

Her assistant pulled her silver thimble from her thumb and set it in her chair. She unrolled her white measuring tape and stretched it along the dress piece. "Fourteen inches, same as what I wrote down the day she came in, and I measured her twice."

Vivien ran her hand along the plain taffeta skirt. "Is the gather at the skirt too tight, or uneven? The fabric isn't laying right at all."

"I don't know. Immogene stitched this up yesterday."

Vivien checked her watch. "Where is Immogene? She's almost two hours late."

Since all of their appointments for the day had canceled, Immogene's being late was a mere annoyance and not a crisis. With nothing else to do, Vivien stepped in to work on the dress. She was a little out of practice compared to Mirette and Immogene, but something was terribly wrong with Louisa's dress and she had to fix it.

This dress must be perfect.

"These darts down the front of it are just like the McCall's pattern she bought, but they're going to billow when she swings her leg out and accentuate everything she wants to hide."

The salon's phone rang. "I'll get that. Maybe one of our girls is going to reschedule."

Mirette unpinned the skirt from the bodice. "I'm not betting my paycheck on it." She removed more pins. "I'll see what we can do to fix this skirt."

"Please do," Vivien said as she lifted the receiver from the phone. "Miss Vivien's, Vivien speaking."

"Miss Vivien, this is Immogene. I'm sorry I'm late, but the driver put us off the bus this morning and left us at the corner outside of town. He must've radioed and told the other buses not to pick us up either because every last one of them drove right by us."

"Oh, my word. What happened?"

A long sigh echoed into the phone. "One of the regular buses broke down this morning, and when this other driver came to the Butler Street stop, there wasn't any room for the white people standing there to get on the bus. So he told all of us to get off and let the white people have the space on the bus. We told him we all had to get to work, and if we don't show up, we're fired."

"And then he forced all y'all off the bus?"

Immogene drew in a loud breath. "Yes ma'am. He threatened to take his tire iron after every one of us if we didn't get off. One of the men said he wasn't moving, and the driver went to hit him, but then we pulled them apart and we all got off. None of the other buses would stop to pick us up either."

She paused, then went on. "We walked to Bernard's gas station so I could call you on the phone and let you know what happened."

"This is ridiculous. I'm coming to pick you up in my car."

"No ma'am, don't do that. We called the store. They're sending a delivery truck over to get us."

"How many of you are stuck there?"

"Fifteen."

"I'm sure I could pack six of you in my car."

"No, don't come here. The truck is supposed to be on its way. I'll see you at the salon." She hung up before Vivien could voice any more objections.

"What was all that about?" Mirette said as she detached the skirt panel from Louisa's dress.

"Our entire town has lost its collective mind. The bus driver threw Immogene and the other Colored employees off the bus this morning. None of the other drivers would stop and pick them up, and now they are waiting for a Wynton's truck to come and get them down at Bernard's filling station."

"What a mess."

"I know. She said the truck was on its way, so hopefully they'll get here soon."

"The sooner the better. The later they get here, the more their pay gets docked for being late."

"You know what burns me up about this, other than the inconvenience to the entire store, those drivers could decide to stay in a snit for as long as they like. I have half a mind to march up to Mr. Wynton's office and tell him to give the bus office a call."

Mirette walked back to the dress form and fiddled with the bottom of the bodice she'd stitched together the day before. "Before you do that, go get your sketch for this gown. I want to check something."

Vivien went to her desk and pulled out her sketch pad. "You thinking we need to overhaul the entire design and start over?"

"No, this bodice isn't the problem. It's that skirt. If we could cover the thing with rows of lace from top to bottom, our problem would be solved. But then the simple top she wants won't look right next to all that embellishment."

Vivien looked over her sketch and then handed her pad to Mirette. "Louisa has such a nice figure. Broad shoulders, slim waist, and long legs. What if we stopped focusing on her bad leg, and built a new gown around all her good points, like we do all our other girls?"

"I don't know, Vivien. She was so specific with what she wanted."

Vivien took her sketch pad back. "She was specific about no lace, and a skirt wide enough to hide her leg."

"But we showed her that"—Mirette tapped the drawing in the sketch pad—"and that's what she's expecting."

"If you make her a gown that makes her feel beautiful, she's not going to care one whit if it's the original or not."

Vivien and Mirette swirled around to see Immogene coming in the back door. "The truck came right when I hung up with you. Darnell drove like lightning to get us here." She went to the storeroom and set her things down on the shelf, then returned to look at the skirt laid out on the cutting table.

She wrinkled her nose. "I didn't think that skirt was wide enough for her. The taffeta will bulge every time her leg pokes against it."

"Why didn't you say something about it yesterday?" Vivien asked.

"Y'all told me to sew it together, not give my opinion."

Seeing this side of Immogene came as a shock to both Vivien and

Mirette, and they shared a look before Vivien decided to clear the air. "Immogene, if you've something you want to say, consider this an invitation to speak your mind from here on out."

"Yes ma'am."

Mirette snapped her fingers. "I've got an idea." She went to the storeroom and returned with an armful of chiffon fabric, which she then draped over the taffeta skirt. "What if we used the taffeta, made a rib pattern on the bodice, and added an overlay? The chiffon would be flowy enough to ripple when she walked, and she'd look like a dancer."

"We could embroider designs on the chiffon to give it a little weight and help the fabric sit better over the skirt. I've even seen satin leaves sewn on chiffon. Looks real nice," Immogene said as she smoothed the chiffon over the taffeta.

Vivien unbuttoned her suit coat and removed it. She slid it over the back of her desk chair. "Where did you see that kind of work, Immogene?"

"My Mama taught me to sew things like that."

Vivien and Mirette traded surprised glances. They'd seen things like that too. In a New York show, and they were well aware of the woman known for that kind of work.

"Where did your mother learn?"

Immogene continued to drape the chiffon around the skirt, trying different types of gathers as she went. "She used to work for a lady in Tampa who had a shop. They made clothes for all the society ladies down there. The woman moved up North, and Mama sewed by herself until I came along. My daddy didn't like her working with a baby, so he took a job here and moved us all to Levy City." She pointed to the bodice pinned on the dress form. "We could build up a structure in the bodice, to play up your girl's tiny waist."

Vivien grabbed her sketchbook and made some notes based on Immogene's ideas. "Do you know what happened to the woman your mother worked with?"

Immogene shrugged. "No ma'am."

Vivien handed her book to Mirette. "I'll be right back."

She went to one of the racks on the sales floor, and when she'd found the gown she was looking for, she brought it back and held it up for Immogene to see. "Did your mother learn to make something like this?"

Immogene moved closer to the gown. She touched the soft organza rosettes and the satin leaves they sat upon. When Vivien tapped the label sewn into the gown, Immogene's eyes widened. "That's the name of the woman Mama was an assistant to in Tampa. How'd you know about her?"

"Ann Lowe is one of the best in our business. We've been following her work since she was down in Tampa, and then when she moved to New York. We've bought a few dresses from her shop on Lexington Avenue. Our well-heeled clients love her work."

"And we knew the moment we saw Jackie Kennedy's dress that Ann made it, even if they didn't give her the credit in the news articles," Mirette added.

Immogene folded the length of chiffon and held it in her arms. "They did Miss Lowe wrong, and she couldn't do nothing about it." Her smile faded. "I'm surprised you two would say such."

She searched Vivien's face, then Mirette's, gauging their reactions to her statement as if she wanted to see what they'd do next.

Vivien draped the gown over her arm to keep the hem from touching the floor. "Mirette and I appreciate good work, no matter who does the making."

Immogene looked her right in the eyes. "You don't worry a Colored woman might do better than y'all, or steal away your business?"

"Girls are getting married every day. There's plenty of work for all of us." Mirette traded Vivien's sketchbook for the dress. "I'll put this back, and you two artists decide how we're going to fix Louisa's gown."

As she walked away, Immogene pointed to the gown. "If I made a gown for your salon, all my own work, would you let me put a label with only my name on it in the dress?"

Vivien opened her sketchbook back to the page with Louisa's original dress design. "My husband Carter took me down to Tampa once for Gasparilla. Ann made all the costumes for the Gasparilla court. They were out-of-this-world gorgeous with all the tiny little extras she put in like ruffles and fabric flowers. Then, when we went to one of the parties, oh my goodness, the gowns she made were so elegant. She'd dressed all of Tampa's high society that night."

She'd never forgotten the work on those gowns. "Everybody in that room knew who made those gowns, and I thought it was unfair."

"Did you say something to the other ladies?"

"No. We didn't bring things like that up back then."

"Don't much do it now, either." Immogene still bore the challenging look in her eyes, making it difficult to decide how to answer her.

Vivien chose the truth. “No, we don’t.”

Immogene pointed to the gown Mirette took back to the rack. “Mama said nobody made flowers better than Miss Lowe.”

It was hard to discern if her change of subject was meant as a peace offering to smooth the tension of the earlier exchange, or just that she’d made her point and moved on. “Immogene, I think you come closest to the best of what Mirette and I have ever seen.”

She held her head up with the confidence of a queen addressing her court. “Thank you, Miss Vivien. I work hard.”

“We’re glad you’re here. Mirette and I needed some new talent in here and new ideas. And when you’re ready to design a gown, we’ll have a conversation on how to work out that label business.”

Immogene was loaded with both. She wasn’t going to cause the too-many-cooks-makes-rancid-broth trouble Mirette warned of, but she was certainly going to stir the pot up on how things needed changing.

And maybe it was time for her and Mirette to pick up their own spoons and learn something new from Immogene.

Chapter 38

Audrey

The scratching of a pencil on paper caught Audrey's ear as she sat in the front row of the showing of Claire McCardell's summer and fall collections. She turned to see the woman sitting beside her, hiding her hand beneath her handbag, scribbling on a piece of paper.

Audrey craned her neck to see if the woman held one of the show's programs, listing the names of the dresses and their numbers. She did, but unlike Audrey, she'd not selected any dresses. Instead, she'd drawn small pictures and written detailed descriptions of each garment from the runway on separate, smaller sheets of blank paper.

The woman was a sketcher, employed by a smaller house to copy the designs from the big names and take them back to make knockoff copies. She looked around the room to see if one of the spotters paid to stop such activities had realized what was going on.

How this woman managed to get a seat in the show remained a mystery. Being granted a ticket to any of the big designer's shows was no easy task. Most American store buyers had to rely on contacts with buyers from Paris who held offices in New York to get tickets. Audrey still had contacts from her modeling days, and after a few phone calls she'd secured seats at all the best shows from Paris and the United States.

A tall man with shoulders so wide he looked as though he wouldn't fit through the door appeared at the sketcher's side. He bent down and spoke in a low tone, then snatched the drawings. His long fingers stretched around her arm like a clamp as he lifted her from her seat and escorted her from the room.

Audrey's focus went back to the runway. McCardell's sportswear fit well with what Wynton's ladies' tastes leaned toward. Casual while still formal and elegant. She'd checked off the numbers of everything she'd seen so far and planned to buy all the shirtwaist dresses as soon as they appeared on the stage. Those flew off the racks at Wynton's as fast they stocked them.

A tap on her shoulder from behind startled her. As she turned to see who'd touched her, Joshua slid into the seat vacated by the sketcher. "I knew I'd find you here. Claire's clothes seem custom-made for Florida."

Audrey kept her eyes on the runway as she answered. "She's a favorite at Wynton's."

"I thought you said you were focusing on the more midline priced clothes."

Audrey put a check by the number of the latest creation, a darling little gray cotton day dress with a tie belt and black buttons running down the front. "I've bought all we needed. This is for our fall stock."

"I didn't see you at the shows at the end of last week."

"I went home to attend a funeral."

Joshua leaned in close. "Not another. . .situation, I hope."

She jerked to face him. "What do you mean?" Audrey turned her attention back to the stage so she didn't miss the next dress coming down the runway.

"I know difficult things are happening down there again."

She checked off another dress on her card. Joshua's father and Mr. Wynton must have been talking about what was happening with Miss Vivien. He had mentioned her boss had a question for his father.

Audrey nodded without looking at him. The clothes saved for the show's finale were now leaving the runway, and she clapped along with the other attendees. Next, she needed to hand in her card to one of the saleswomen and make an appointment to return and review her choices, place her orders, and set up shipping arrangements.

Before she could rise from her chair to complete her business, Joshua nudged her with his elbow. "Free for lunch? We could try to make Divan Parisienne or go back to the Automat. Your choice, my treat. I owe you a meal."

Her heart sank a notch. Lunch with him sounded delightful, but she'd packed her day full of buying for the store and meetings with prospective vendors. "I'd truly love to go, but my day is packed."

He reached in the inside pocket of his jacket and pulled out a business card. Joshua motioned to her pencil. "May I?"

She handed it over. He turned the card over and wrote something on the back. "Here's the number of my hotel, and my room. When you're hungry enough to take a break, call me. I'd love to talk over some ideas I had for Loveman's shoppers like you've used at Wynton's."

Audrey took his card. "I promise the moment I'm free, I'll call." And she meant it.

He handed the pencil back to her. "I'll try not to starve before then."

They stood together, and Audrey noticed over his shoulder a saleswoman was freed up. She waved and the woman nodded and moved toward her.

"Thank you for the invitation, Joshua. I've got to try to get my card turned in and run to my next appointment." She tucked his card into the pocket of her blue Jeanne Lanvin suit.

"Of course. Good luck."

When the saleswoman drew near, Joshua greeted her, gave Audrey a final bow, and then walked from the room.

When she finished her order and was walking from the show's meeting room, Audrey removed his card and read over the printing on the front.

Joshua McKinnon
Executive Vice President, Loveman's Department Store
Birmingham, Alabama

"Good to have friends in high places," she whispered to herself as she wrapped her suit's matching shawl around her shoulder and headed to her next meeting.

When at last she'd finished her day and returned to her hotel room, Audrey lay on the couch with her feet propped up on the opposite end. She loved her blue patent pumps, but they murdered a girl's feet after she'd stood for over three hours at a party. Three hours of being trapped in a group of people she didn't know from Adam's house cat, listening to their conversations about who traveled where for Christmas, who had the best parties at their summer homes, and who was seeing whom on the sly.

She laid her head against the soft cushion. "Those parties are one of the many things I don't miss about this world." Mainly because they were more Mother's type of fun than hers.

At least the meeting with a prospective vendor went well, and she could return with a good report for Mr. Wynton. With all the storm surrounding Miss Vivien's, being the bearer of better news brought a sense of satisfaction.

In between all the meetings, shows, and parties, her thoughts always trailed back to Miss Vivien. "And there's not one thing I can do until I get back to Levy City." Which dug in her craw more than anything. She had slipped back for the funeral, thanks to Mr. Wynton's plane reservations, but she had a job to do for the store here in New York.

Audrey sat up and opened her case to file her new paperwork away. She bumped the corner with her knee and sent documents sliding down to the floor, where they fanned out like a peacock's tail. When she bent down to pick them up, she noticed a business card lying among the stack.

"Whose is this? I put Joshua's in my wallet, and all the other cards I collected went into my files."

When she had the card in hand, she read the front.

HARRISON P. HOVERMAN

"If I remember correctly, back when you wrote those tawdry novels, your name used to be Clive Hoverman. I'd bet neither is your real name. You've probably got a list of aliases as long as my arm."

Audrey crumpled the card, but then remembered he'd said he now worked for a wedding gown designer. In Florida.

She rushed to her purse and pulled out her wallet. Once she'd found Joshua's card, she went to her phone and dialed the number.

"My mother would have a fit if she knew what I was getting into."

The ringing on the other side stopped as the clerk at Joshua's hotel picked up.

"Joshua McKinnon's room please. This is Audrey Penault calling. Please tell him it's urgent."

Chapter 39

Audrey

As soon as the knock on the door came, Audrey grabbed her long white mink cape and her red purse, which matched the dress she was wearing. She had a role to play tonight, and she must look the part.

When she opened the door, Joshua's brows went up. "Is that what they're wearing to daring midnight capers these days?"

Audrey turned her room's lock, then deposited the key in her bag. She swung her cape around her shoulders. "You don't believe a red grosgrain Dior cocktail dress and a white mink cape are appropriate attire to meet with a weasel?"

He bowed and motioned toward the door. "No ma'am, I do not. The only place you won't stick out is dinner and dancing at the Copacabana."

"That's a little too wild for me."

Joshua fell into step with her as she rushed down the hallway. "And meeting with a man to look at wedding gowns in his hotel room is tame?"

"No, but I'm going there anyway."

He offered her his arm as they walked down the long hallway toward the exit of the building. "I must say, running around with you is never dull."

Joshua walked her from the building and hailed a cab.

Audrey gave their cabbie the address, then settled against the seat. The city lights flashed inside the interior as they sped through the city to the seedier side of town where Mr. Hoverman was staying.

When the cab blew past the expensive New York nightclubs, Joshua whistled under his breath. "There's the Copa. I've only been there once. How about you?"

"In my modeling days, we'd go there for dinner and dancing."

"I remember our dance at the New Year's Ball last year. I'm sure you were a sensation at the Copacabana."

She turned to him. "If you dare say I'm as light as a feather on my feet, or I dance divinely, or any such drivel as that, I'm going to grind the pointy heel of my pump right into the toe of your nice loafers."

He held up his hand in surrender as he laughed. "No ma'am. I've not forgotten your aversion to flattery."

Joshua lowered his hands. "But I was going to ask you if there've been any advancements in the murder cases plaguing Miss Vivien."

Audrey's cheeks warmed. How vain she must have sounded, jumping down his throat in fear of a compliment. And yet, she'd not worried how anyone thought of her in a long time.

"I talked with her last night, and things are worse. Her brides are canceling their orders, and her vendors refuse to participate in Bridal Week."

Joshua scowled. "A rather drastic move."

"Our local paper isn't helping the cause much."

The cabbie slammed on the brakes, sending her and Joshua jolting forward. "I've seen those columns by Robbi Dever. Definitely stirring the pot."

"Boiling it over is more like it."

Their driver honked his horn, then pressed the accelerator, sending them smashing against the back seat. "And no clues yet?"

"Just common denominators."

He grew quiet and looked past her as he seemed to be thinking over what she'd said. "Do you have any thoughts?"

"Miss Vivien and I think the culprit is a woman, someone who knows how to sew. And obviously hates weddings and wants Miss Vivien out of the business. There are a few people angry enough to want revenge on her, but we can't pin anything to them yet. Bill Youngblood—you met him last year. . ."

Joshua nodded. "I remember him."

"He's combed through evidence hundreds of times, but with no witnesses, fingerprints, or connections to anyone but Miss Vivien, he's stopped cold."

He went quiet, as the wheels in his head seemed to be turning while he took in what she'd said.

"You were in intelligence and investigations during the Korean War, weren't you? What do you think?"

His attention snapped back to her. "Where did you hear that?"

"Cissy bragged you up as some kind of military intelligence man last year when she hired you to run Wynton's security."

He made a face as if the idea were a huge exaggeration. "I'm good at hiding, so I was sent to watch things. Main thing I did was write a lot of reports that very few people read. Really boring stuff."

Joshua played down his work, and acted uncomfortable with talking about the war, as most of the men she'd known who fought in Korea did. Unlike the soldiers from World War II, these men came home to no parades, accolades, or heroic titles. Just like Joshua, they seemed to wish for nothing more than to put the experience behind them and not speak of it again.

"Thank you for coming on this spy mission with me tonight."

He tapped the face of his watch. "I'm a little afraid we'll be out past my bedtime, although I'm more concerned of what we might find when we get there. That location isn't where they hold garden parties, for sure."

"You know it?"

He crossed his arms. "The more colorful people hang out there."

The exact kind of place she'd expect Mr. Hoverman to stay in. "Well, you said you were good at hiding. If we come upon something unsavory, you'll know what to do."

"I'd like to hide right now."

Her teasing hadn't gone over as she'd hoped. "Joshua, I can't stand the thought of going to another young bride's funeral or watching my friend be brought down by another's evil acts. I won't stand by and let this happen, and from what I've seen, you wouldn't either."

He reached over and patted her on the arm. "You know what your trouble is?"

"What?"

"You've got a giant brain in that head of yours. One smart enough to know when it should listen to your heart."

Audrey swiveled in her spot and stared at the profile of his nose and chin in the dark, noticing for the first time how strong both were. "Thank you."

"Oh, that compliment gets a thank you, does it?" His usual teasing tone returned.

She turned around and stared out the window for the rest of the drive.

Joshua paid their fare, giving the driver instructions to wait for them.

The cabbie turned off the car and pulled the front of his cap over his head as if he were going to nap. He buried his gloveless hands within the folds of his coat.

The snow had stopped, and the cold air frosted the tips of her ears. In her hurry from her hotel room, Audrey had forgotten to grab a hat. She pulled the card from her pocket. "We're looking for The Tolbert Hotel."

Joshua tapped her on the arm and then pointed in the direction to their left. "Over here."

Their steps crunched as they walked across the uneven pavement. When they reached the front of the building, they located a delivery buzzer next to the door.

"I'd like the honors." Audrey reached and pressed the button.

A few moments later, Mr. Hoverman himself opened the door. He smiled wide at her. "Miss Penault." He pointed a round, fat finger at Joshua. "Who are you?"

"Her personal assistant."

Audrey held up his business card. "You invited me to stop by and look at your inventory."

Mr. Hoverman pursed his lips and twisted them to the side. "When I mentioned modeling our gowns, I didn't expect to be giving you a private showing. I was surprised to hear from you."

"Mr. Hoverman, like I told you, I'm a buyer for Wynton's Department Store. We do have a bridal salon."

He grunted. "One that's not doing so well, or so I hear."

Mr. Hoverman wasn't one she'd pegged for reading the papers much. Being low enough to make light of Miss Vivien's plight fit him to a T.

"We're always looking for new designers, and I've been so busy I couldn't get around to seeing your stock until tonight." She gestured toward the door. "Thank you for allowing us to come for a look."

He smiled so wide his plump cheeks rippled like an accordion. "Yeah, sure. Come on in."

Joshua went in first, forcing Mr. Hoverman to take a step back before Audrey entered. "We'll follow you," he said as he fell in behind their host, keeping himself between Mr. Hoverman and Audrey the entire way.

They walked through a lobby filled with couches and chairs bearing rips in their upholstery. The stuffing spilled out of the many rips and tears. The aromas of cigarettes and mold mixed with Mr. Hoverman's overuse of cheap cologne.

Audrey followed Joshua into the elevator. He wedged himself between her and Mr. Hoverman, then clasped his hands in front, looking ready to spring into action if needed.

When the elevator stopped on the second floor, Joshua motioned for Mr. Hoverman to disembark first and then led Audrey out.

The scent of cheap cigars and perfume was trapped between the walls of the hallway. Audrey took care not to catch her red satin heels in the spots where the green-and-black linoleum had worn through.

Hoverman took them to a room whose door stood open. "I don't have our full collection in here, but you can see a few of our top designs."

Both men moved to allow Audrey to step in first, and Joshua followed close on her heels. Hoverman closed the door after he entered.

The room contained a small unmade bed pushed against a wall covered in yellowed wallpaper. Other than an old, dusty chest of drawers, the room held no more furniture.

"The bathroom's down the hall if anyone needs it," he said as he pulled a rolling rack filled with gowns into the middle of the room.

Hoverman held up a wedding gown made of silk satin, with long sleeves and a high neckline. A large white bow with long, trailing ribbons was fastened to the front of the dress. "Nice, huh? Very simple, elegant, and modern."

Mr. Hoverman pulled another from the rack, a tea-length with a shawl collar. "This length is all the rage, but our designer took it to a new level by making a matching headscarf to use in place of a veil." The scarf was pinned on the dress, and he held it out for Audrey to see.

He held up the bottom of the gown. "Instead of straight across, she made a scalloped hem trimmed with a homemade lace. Not something you'd see anywhere else."

"And who's your designer?"

Mr. Hoverman hung the dress back on the rack. "She wishes to remain anonymous. For now." He grinned as if he relished the chance to be mysterious.

"Your designer doesn't want to be known?" Joshua asked.

"Not at this time."

Audrey fought to keep her face, or any other part of her body, from reacting. She swallowed twice to ensure her voice would be calm when she asked her next question.

"What is your brand name?"

"Rose Regals."

He spent the next twenty minutes pulling gowns from his rack, extolling their detailing, their modern designs, even calling one dress a bride's ticket to leaping into the Atomic Age.

The brand was the only thing she'd come for. It might turn out to be no help at all. Or it might lead them to someone who'd be very happy to see Miss Vivien fail, making room for themselves in the wedding business.

For her plan to work, she needed a dress in hand to set Sheriff Youngblood on a new trail. "I'd like to put in an order for the tea-length." Audrey rubbed her hands together to ward off the chill creeping in though a nearby broken window.

"I'll get my receipt book." Hoverman plopped on the bed, which groaned and sagged under his weight. He grunted as he reached under and pulled out an ancient briefcase whose faux-leather sides peeled like a shedding snake.

"Can you box this up for us?" Audrey asked as she looked over the gown once more.

His pleased expression melted. "What?"

"I'd like to take this with me. Tonight."

His eyes shifted between her and Joshua. "These are samples. Not for sale."

"Mr. Hoverman, you don't understand. I want to buy this gown tonight, to feature in our upcoming Bridal Week. I'm more than willing to pay extra to have the gown now."

The possibility and satisfaction of making a quick buck flashed in his eyes. "I think my employer would be amenable to that."

Though it was shocking he knew the word *amenable*, his willingness to make what might have been an under-the-table deal came as no surprise. "Thank you, Mr. Hoverman."

With the transaction finished and the receipt in Audrey's hand, Mr. Hoverman reached out to shake her hand. Joshua stepped in and clasped the man's hand. He gave one hard pump before releasing and stepping back beside Audrey.

Hoverman put his receipt book back in the case, then closed the lid and snapped it shut. "My new employer will be thrilled. Thanks for your business, I hope we can work with Wynton's in the future."

He wrapped up her purchase by pulling his own clothes from a battered cardboard box, wrapping the gown in sheets of wrinkled tissue paper, and securing it with a string that looked like it should be tied to a kite.

When Audrey had her purchase in hand, Joshua pressed his hand to the middle of her back. "We'd best be going." They skipped waiting on the elevator and scurried down the stairs and outside where their cab awaited.

When they reached the car, Joshua tapped on the window, awakening their snoozing driver. "Take us back to the hotel, please."

The driver started the engine as Audrey and Joshua slid into the back seat. When they arrived at her hotel, Joshua went to pay the driver, but she clasped his arm before he could remove his wallet.

"It's my business expense." Mother would again be aghast, and Mr. Wynton would treat this as part of her travel budget and reimburse her. And she'd promptly donate it to any expenses needed to keep Wynton's Bridal Week on the schedule.

"I'll see to your door," Joshua said as they walked up the steps to the hotel's entrance.

"There's no need. I—"

"My dad and my mother raised me right. I'll see you to your door."

When they reached her room, he waited as she took her key from her purse.

"Miss Penault, you're no doubt the most boring woman I've ever met."

"Why, Mr. McKinnon. That's the nicest thing I've heard since you complimented my brain."

He yawned, making her follow suit. When she'd recovered, she put her key in and unlocked her room's door. She turned back to him.

"Thank you for helping me tonight, Joshua."

"Always a pleasure, Audrey."

He gave a slight bow and turned and walked down the hallway.

Chapter 40

Gigi

Gigi peeked her head inside Wynton's cafeteria kitchen, checking to make sure no other employees were there with Lilla. She'd missed their daily talks, and she could use some common sense wisdom right now.

Lilla sat on one of the tall stools at the counter, eating a bowl of stewed tomatoes and white rice. She was off in thought as she dunked a corner of her fluffy, buttery corn bread in the juice and took a bite. Whatever was on her mind must have been serious from the look on her face.

Gigi's bologna and cheese on Wonder Bread didn't hold a candle to Lilla's lunch, but it was the end of the month, and she always ate cheap until her next paycheck came.

She knocked on the door to avoid startling Lilla, who jerked her head around to see who was at the door. "Come on in, stranger."

Gigi closed the door and walked to the empty stool Lilla pulled out for her. She set her bag down. "I need to get myself some tea, I'll be right back."

When she returned, Lilla's bowl stood empty. Her friend had no assigned lunch break and often ate fast to get back to cooking for the cafeteria. Lilla sipped at a cup of steaming coffee as Gigi took her seat.

"What are you baking today?" Gigi took a deep whiff. "My tongue is watering."

Lilla set her cup down. "Applesauce spice cake with cream cheese frosting. Mary Margaret wants me to expand our dessert offerings."

"Why? The whole town comes to Wynton's for your peanut butter bars and apple pies."

"Don't have to tell me that. All week folks have been poking their heads in here, asking me where the peanut butter bars and the pies are."

She shrugged. "Gotta do what the boss lady says, for now. I heard Mr. Wynton has hired a new cafeteria manager and Mary Margaret's going to be moved up to the stationery department."

Gigi unwrapped her sandwich. "Who's the new manager?"

"Bob Steele. He was the assistant manager of the Grove."

The name sounded familiar, and then Gigi gasped. "Was he married to Rayanne Steele? One of the—"

Lilla nodded. "His wife was one of the brides who got killed."

"Oh my, that poor man."

Lilla took her dirty lunch dishes to the sink and rinsed them. "He's supposed to be a nice, quiet fella. Be a big change from Mary Margaret."

Gigi took a bite of her sandwich and thought how much better things could be for Lilla and the others with a new boss. "Hey, Lilla, were you caught up in the trouble on the bus yesterday?"

Lilla pressed her mouth into a tight line of disgust. Anger burned in the depths of her dark eyes. "Bernard dropped me off early at the store on his way to the station. He had a busy day, and when Immogene and the others showed up, the whole place went crazy."

Gigi set her sandwich down. "I heard the driver ran over a nail on Warm Springs Road and was stuck there for over two hours."

"None of that gave the other driver the right to throw folks off the bus. They were there first and paid their fare, which they never got back. Immogene's husband called the bus line and asked them for a refund, and the lady he spoke to on the phone laughed at him and hung up."

Gigi shook her head. "That's stupid."

Lilla sat silent a moment. "Wasn't stupid to Immogene. She lost money," she said softly.

Gigi reached out and clasped Lilla's hand. "I didn't mean to make short of what happened. It's awful they got treated that way."

"Mm-hmm, it was." Lilla sipped her coffee. "All those folks forced to show up to work late."

Gigi crumpled the wax paper she'd used to wrap her sandwich. Most times she never thought about the differences in her skin color and Lilla's, or the other Black employees. But then something like this went and happened. The divide between Black and white split further, with her standing on one side wishing she knew how to build a bridge to the other and make all this stop so they could just be people together.

Lilla rose and took her dishes to the sink. "Bernard fixed eight flat tires that day. He said one of the construction trucks building those houses out in the new subdivision must have dropped a whole carton of nails on the road and they didn't get them cleaned up very well. One of the folks was that Robbi Dever lady from the paper."

She went on. "Mary Hadley Bell brought in her daddy's big Oldsmobile too. She drove in with the tire all flapping, jumped out, and commenced to tell him he was to fix her car right away. He's a grown man, running his own business, and she talked to him like he was her dog."

Lilla dried her dishes with more force than was necessary. "He told her he had six cars ahead of hers."

Lilla turned to look at Gigi over her shoulder. "Bernard said she put her hands on her hips, told him she wasn't going to be seen standing around a Colored's station all day long, and he was to do as she said, or she'd call her father."

"What did he do?"

"He said she could go right ahead, it wasn't going to change her having to wait. She could borrow his phone to call for a ride or take the bus home. Then he pointed out the way to the bus stop up the road."

Gigi laughed. "I can't imagine Miss Hoity-Toity getting on a bus. How'd she get home?"

"Robbi Dever had her car towed in shortly after, and she offered Mary Hadley a ride back into town in the wrecker. He said they were all chummy, calling each other by their first names."

Together. Robbi and Mary Hadley had been together at Wynton's the day she and Mary Jo saw them in Sewing.

"Is Bernard afraid her daddy will come down hard on him?"

Lilla shook her head as she put the clean dishes away in the cabinets. "He's done work on Mr. Bell's car before. He doesn't like to stir up much. His wife and daughter wear the pants in that house. He stays out of their way."

The noises in the cafeteria grew louder, as Lilla opened the oven to check on her cake. "My man doesn't say much bad about people, but he said he was sure glad when those two women drove off together with the tow-truck driver."

She shut the oven again. "Sounds like the big rush is on, so I'd best get back to work."

Gigi watched her friend work. Lilla held herself differently now. Her jaw set harder, as if underneath the calm and pleasant attitude she put on for the world, she was fed up and about to go off.

Gigi packed up the last of her lunch. "I'm sorry."

The oven's buzzer went off, and Lilla scowled as she turned off the timer. "What're you sorry for?"

"How you, and Bernard, and Immogene get treated. It's not right."

Lilla opened the oven door and moved back from the rush of heat. "No, it's not." She reached in and brought out one of the cakes and set it on the counter to cool, then did the same with the other. "We're ready to make things change."

Gigi moved closer to make sure no one could hear them. "Are y'all planning something like those protests going on in Alabama? The newspaper said they were still boycotting the buses in Montgomery, and then I heard about that other lady, Autherine Lucy. They had to let her into the University of Alabama back in February. The Klan burned crosses on the campus, and they had all kinds of violent riots going on because people didn't want her there."

The story about Autherine hadn't made the *LTC*'s front page, like all the bad news surrounding Miss Vivien did, but was back on page four, tucked in between news about an upcoming cattle auction at the fairgrounds and the projected prices for oranges later in the year.

The news may have been hidden, but it still stirred worries for Lilla. Gigi grabbed Lilla's hand. "People might do the same thing here. I don't want to see you get hurt."

Lilla patted Gigi, then pulled her hand free from her grip. "Right now I'm planning on getting back to work, and you should too."

She cut a small piece of cake, wrapped it in a napkin, and handed it to Gigi. "Tastes better without the frosting." Lilla smiled, then patted Gigi on the arm. "Thanks for coming by to see me. I miss you since you went and got all fancy with that new job."

"I miss you too."

Gigi would have loved to invite Lilla to her new apartment, but that was something both knew she could never do. Her landlady, Miss Vines, held to the old ways, and she'd never let Lilla set foot through the front door unless she was the help.

Gigi put her lunch away in her locker and returned to Cosmetics with an extra five minutes to spare. Jane liked when her employees returned early, and she met Gigi with a deep nod as she settled in behind the counter.

"Miss Woodard, we have a young lady coming in at one for a makeup demonstration. I'd like you to take care of her. She's wanting a new look for her upcoming wedding, and I think you're the perfect person to work with her."

"Yes ma'am."

Gigi went to the cabinet to get one of the sample makeup kits like the one Audrey taught her to use. "What's her name?"

"I'm sure you may already know her. Mary Hadley Bell."

It took everything within her not to throw the case down and run from the department screaming like a banshee.

Chapter 41

Gigi

Gigi drew in a few deep breaths as she watched Mary Hadley walk toward Cosmetics. She hoped God Himself would clamp her jaws shut and keep her from saying all the things she shouldn't.

Audrey had drilled her on how to be a supreme professional, poised in all situations that might arise, and display nothing but polished behavior. But none of that prepared her for the strong temptation to tell off the snotty, spoiled brat now sitting before her, smelling of Shalimar, which she'd learned only two days ago cost as much as a whole month's pay.

She unclenched her fists behind the counter, then stretched her face into what she hoped was a pleasant expression and not the look of a boxer ready to land a punch. "How may I help you?"

"Is Linda working today?"

"No, she's off today."

Mary Hadley looked away, sighed as if just being in the same space as Gigi was too much to bear, and then rolled her eyes. "How about Amy?"

"She doesn't work on Thursdays."

Was she going to go through the entire list of girls who worked in Cosmetics before she accepted Gigi's help?

"I know Jane is here, I spoke with her on the phone."

"Jane is at lunch. She won't be back for an hour." Gigi opened the makeup sample kit, pulled the foldout trays, and spread out the cloth where she would lay the brushes.

She held up a jar of cold cream as she met Mary Hadley eye to eye. "I'm ready when you are."

The corners of Mary Hadley's lips turned up so high her nose crinkled. "Judging by your own makeup, you don't have the fine touch I need. I'm going to a very important meeting tonight, and I need to look dazzling."

Dazzling was it? A vision of painting her up like a clown came to mind, tickling Gigi, but she held her laughter as she reached under the counter and brought out a copy of *Vogue* Audrey had given her. She thumbed through the pages until she came upon the picture of a model Audrey had used to teach her some new techniques.

According to Audrey, the woman went by Doe, which was short for some long, fancy name Gigi had forgotten. Her style and look, Gigi remembered. Mary Hadley's dark hair and creamy-white complexion, nice high cheekbones, and fuller lips made her a good match for the makeup palette used in the picture.

She showed the picture to Mary Hadley. "Would you like to try this look?"

The girl's sneer melted from her face. She touched the page. "You can do this for me?"

"Of course."

Mary Hadley put her hands in her lap. "Fantastic."

Gigi draped Mary Hadley with the small cape used to protect the customer's clothing from any drips that might fall during the process, then spread a small dollop of cold cream across Mary Hadley's face to give her what Audrey called a fresh palette.

"Let's try Helena Rubinstein's liquid makeup first. I like this product because it gives you a more natural look and conceals all those little flaws like dark shadows and lines, without being too thick and apt to melt off when it's warm. Which, for us Florida girls with our changeable weather, is so important all year round."

All those hours of studying the ads Audrey sent her and practicing with her housemates on how to talk about the products while applying them now paid off. Her hand never shook as she smoothed the foundation on and patted a light dusting of powder over it to create the matte look they all loved these days. A swish of brown eye shadow helped to bring out the blue-green shade of Mary Hadley's eyes.

When it came time to apply the eyeliner, Gigi took her time, making certain she drew the perfect little flicks at the ends to create the oh-so-popular doe-eyed look Hollywood actresses helped make a must-do.

"I think on your cheeks, I'll use just the tiniest touch of pink to go with your black hair. Give you an Elizabeth Taylor kind of air."

Mary Hadley soaked in the compliments like a dried-out sponge.

Every time Gigi praised her, the girl sat up straighter in the chair and stared at her reflection. Gigi continued to mumble, "So pretty, so beautiful, nothing short of perfect."

It was enough to make a person want to spit up. Daddy had a saying for girls like Mary Hadley. He shared it when Gigi was twelve and came home from school sobbing her eyes out because two classmates called her a man-girl on account of her big feet and hands.

Daddy had hugged her and told her those cute, tiny girls were a perfect example of how beauty was only skin deep, but ugly went all the way to the bones. Over her life, she'd come upon a lot of other pretty faces who were bone-ugly on the inside. Mary Hadley sure seemed to be one of them.

When it was time for the final touch of mascara, the temptation to accidentally poke Mary Hadley in the eye was a fleeting thought. As Gigi looked over her work, she was overcome by a stronger realization. Audrey had told her she was born to do this job. And she was starting to believe her.

Gigi handed Mary Hadley a tube of lipstick. "Jane tells me you're getting married soon."

"Mm-hmm."

"Did Miss Vivien make your dress?" She knew the answer but also heard how much trouble this girl had stirred up in the salon. Mirette said she was the first bride they ever worked with that they'd wished had chosen to elope instead.

Mary Hadley rolled her eyes. "That dress was dreadful. I found a seamstress who offered to make me another, but she couldn't put together what I wanted in time. She fixed the gown from Miss Vivien's. But now I don't know if I'm going to wear that dress or not. And with all this nasty business with her brides going on, I think Miss Vivien should close down her salon. Permanently."

She raised her eyes from the mirror. "I'm sorry, I'm going on without any thought to your being friends with Miss Vivien. I meant no offense. I just think she isn't keeping up with the new trends. After all, this is the Atomic Age, not old age."

Heat rose up the back of Gigi's neck as Mary Hadley giggled at her own joke. She'd probably get in trouble for sharing her opinion, but for the moment, she didn't care. "Miss Vivien's a smart lady. She'll figure all this out."

Mary Hadley's brows shot up. "Does she have some idea of who's behind all this?"

"She had many ideas. All her friends do." Gigi passed a tissue to Mary Hadley to blot her lips.

Jane returned from her lunch break and situated herself at the next counter over, so Gigi hurried to drive the conversation back to the products. "The right shade of lipstick finishes off your look, especially on a day as special as your wedding."

Mary Hadley's eyes went to Gigi's bare ring finger. "Are you married?"

She'd tilted her head when she asked, watching Gigi's reaction with a side-eyed expression hinting she already knew the answer and liked putting Gigi on the spot.

Gigi crumpled the tissue in her hand and tossed it in the trash can behind the makeup counter. "No."

She loosened the ties and removed the cape from around Mary Hadley's shoulders.

Mary Hadley turned her head and gazed at herself from all angles in the mirror. "I'm going to make such a splash tonight." She looked up at Gigi. "You surprised me."

She sat there as if waiting for Gigi to bow to her praise. Picturing how fun it would be to dump this woman from the chair into a heap on the floor forced Gigi to suppress a giggle. "You're all set."

Mary Hadley rose, then tossed her head. "Wrap up everything you used on me, and put it all on my daddy's charge account, Richard Bell. This will probably be the last time I use it."

Gigi retrieved a box from under the counter, then removed the cosmetics from the case and packed them up. As she tied the string around the lid, Mary Hadley held out a charge plate.

Gigi took it, then filled out the receipt. "You're certainly going to wow them at your meeting tonight."

"Oh, I'm counting on that."

As Mary Hadley almost pranced her way out of the store, the memory of Miss Vivien sitting alone at her house when all her friends chose to stand her up, including Mary Hadley and her mother, hit Gigi. They had called ahead, almost as if to rub it in that they weren't coming and knew the others weren't either. Miss Vivien said they were going around town turning all the mothers against her, and after spending a short time with the girl, Gigi believed it.

She didn't even try to hide her dislike of Miss Vivien, and it was plain as day, Mary Hadley would be happy to see her gone.

Chapter 42

Vivien

After the mess on the bus, Vivien and Mirette decided they'd pick Immogene up and have her ride to work with them. This allowed them to talk over ideas for the construction of Louisa's gown, and Immogene was free with her opinions, which Vivien was still getting used to.

This morning, she rode quietly in the back seat, looking out the window. When Vivien glanced at her in the rearview mirror, her new assistant was staring out the window, and it was apparent her mind was a million miles away from Levy City.

"I'm going up to the executive suite to meet with Mr. Wynton this morning, so y'all can work on the dress without me."

Mirette shifted in her seat to better face Vivien. "Is there trouble?"

Vivien turned into the store's parking lot. "No, I need to talk something over with him."

She headed for the parking garage and waved at Nelson as she stopped at the garage entrance. By the time he'd made his way to her car, she had the window rolled down. Vivien gestured to Immogene in the back. "Immogene will be riding in with us now."

Nelson's gaze swiveled to back seat, and he and Immogene shared a quick glance before he returned his attention to Vivien. "Yes ma'am. Go on in."

He stepped back and walked back toward his chair.

"Miss Vivien, you can always drop me off at the back of the store," Immogene said from the back seat.

"There's no sense in wasting time driving circles around the store."

"I'm not supposed to be in the garage."

Vivien pulled into a spot and slid the gearshift into PARK. She turned around and faced Immogene. All of Wynton's garage guards were Black, so Immogene's statement made no sense. "And why is that?"

Immogene gathered up her purse and her sewing bag. She stuck her chin up as if she were readying for a fight. "The people who park here trust Nelson and the others because they'll be fired if their cars are damaged. With the rest of us, they're afraid we'll mess with their fancy cars."

Vivien turned around and gathered her own things and turned to Mirette. "There is a lot more going on around here than we ever knew."

She opened her car door. "We are all entering through the side door, so come on, Immogene."

When they entered the hallway, a woman from the jewelry department saw them and narrowed her eyes at Immogene, who stood tall as she walked on Mirette's right side.

The woman looked at Vivien. "Is she with you?"

She'd spoken as if Immogene, a grown woman, were a child lost from their parent or a stray dog in need of an owner. "This is Immogene, and she is my new assistant in the salon. We're on our way up to the shop now."

Vivien moved around the woman while Mirette and Immogene slid past her on the opposite side. They made their way through the main floor to the employee stairs.

Immogene paused a moment. She rotated as she looked up at the chandeliers hanging from the ceiling, seeing the balconies on every floor, then ran her hand along the fluted column near her. "My friend Carla is one of the night maids. This is just like she described it."

Once they'd made it to the salon, Vivien put her purse and hat in her desk, then made her way to the executive suite.

It was a jarring sight to find Libby seated in Audrey's chair, tapping away on her typewriter. Her ponytail swayed each time she shifted her attention to the notepad on her left. Vivien knocked on the doorjamb to announce her arrival.

Libby swiveled in her chair. "Miss Vivien, good morning." She pushed back and rose, gesturing toward the chairs in the waiting room. "Have a seat, and I'll let Mr. Wynton know you're here."

She buttoned the top button of the cashmere cardigan she wore over her crimson silk dress, then walked to her boss's office, her bouncy steps causing the crinolines under her wide skirt to swing. Her soft knock brought a low response from within.

Libby opened the door wide enough to slip her head through. "Miss Vivien is here."

She stepped back and waited until Mr. Wynton appeared in the doorway.

He smiled as soon as he saw her. "Vivien, come right in." He turned to Libby. "Hold all my calls, until nine. Audrey's supposed to be calling then."

"Yes sir." She went back to her desk and returned to her typing.

Vivien entered the office and sat in the chair Mr. Wynton pulled out for her in the sitting area off to the side of his desk. He sat across the coffee table from her and lifted a coffeepot resting on a turret. "May I pour you a cup?"

She waved him off, then met his gaze. "No thank you, Tom."

The leather sofa creaked as he sat down and leaned back. "What did you want to talk about?"

She'd been awake most of the night and didn't want to say anything to Mirette and Immogene in the car until everything was said and done. "I want to know what your plans are for the salon and Bridal Week."

He stared at her a moment. "We have no vendors willing to work with you. I've had mothers all over town calling and begging me to force you to shut down the salon until these murders are solved. The Women's Auxiliary is threatening to boycott the store for Easter, Mother's Day, and all holidays afterward if I don't."

He rubbed his hand on his knee. "There isn't a jeweler, caterer, photographer, florist, travel bureau, or even limo driver in the state of Florida willing to come to Wynton's. I've even called some in Georgia, and they've heard about the murder through Robbi's columns being picked up by their local papers. No one will come within a hundred miles of us right now."

Vivien propped her elbow on the arm of the leather wingback chair and rubbed her forehead. "I'm scheduled for an interview with Robbi for the *LTC*. Maybe that would be picked up like the others, give me a chance to tell my side—"

"Robbi called me at home last night to say she can no longer interview you. Having you in her column would be too damaging to the paper."

Vivien leaned against the padded arm of the chair. "And yet she writes about me daily in her column and goes on and on about me during her radio show, linking me to all the murdered girls. Tom, that doesn't make sense."

He held up his hand to calm her. "I'm on your side, Vivien."

"I know you are. But we have to think about these families, don't we? I'm the reason their daughters are being killed. The whole city can't take this out on the person responsible and I'm the only target they can see."

He leaned forward and rested his elbows on his legs as he clasped his hands. "There are a lot of things that are unfair—"

"Like the fact that I have to walk my new assistant, Immogene, up to the salon every day to keep security from snagging her, or that I have to drive her here myself in case the bus drivers decide they aren't transporting Coloreds tomorrow? More than a dozen of Wynton's employees were affected by this, Tom. You say you care about *all* of your employees. There are things going on around here that would curl your tail if you knew."

He jerked back as if she'd struck him. "If you're talking about the store, Audrey keeps me abreast of everything, and we are making changes. Slowly."

Mr. Wynton continued. "As far as the buses go, I'll make a call, but I doubt it will do much. It's beyond my circle of influence."

He rose from his seat. "But I will send a warning to the security guards to leave Immogene alone."

She stood to face him. "Thank you, Tom. As far as the salon, I made up my mind last night that I was closing. I love what I do, but I love my brides more."

Vivien grabbed the top edge of the chair and squeezed. "Mirette, Immogene, and I are still coming in. We have a gown we promised, and we're going to finish this girl's dress in time for her June wedding."

He got up from the couch and walked with her to the door. "Bill Youngblood agreed this is our best option. Levy City has buried too many girls. We've got to make this stop."

"I can't believe we're letting this murderer beat us, Tom."

The memory of the mamas huddled together at Macy's funeral turned up the fire heating her anger. "I just hate giving in to whoever's doing all this." Because this was exactly what they wanted.

Mr. Wynton opened the door. "We all do."

"I'll go down and tell Mirette and Immogene." She turned on her heel and walked from his office. When Libby bid her goodbye, Vivien could only muster a half-hearted wave as she headed back to the salon.

Upon her return, she found Mirette and Immogene looking through the selection of sheer fabrics. Vivien said nothing as she entered the fitting room.

Mirette pointed to the cutting table, where pieces of organza, chiffon, and tulle were laid out. "Immogene and I are deciding what to use for the overskirt. Our thought is we could combine those flowers she's so good at with my embroidery and maybe edge the overlay with gros point lace to give the skirt more interest."

Vivien went to her purse and dug out her key ring. Without a word, she walked from the fitting room, turned off the sales floor's lights, and locked the salon's front door.

"What'd you do that for?" Mirette called from the fitting room.

Vivien stood in the middle of the sales floor, looking around at the sitting areas, the platforms where brides modeled gowns, and the silhouettes of the mannequins in the salon's front windows dressed in this month's highlighted gowns.

She'd been so angry last night and maybe too focused on her pride or stopping whoever was behind all this. Standing there in the dark, her anger faded as she faced what was lost.

There would be no more happy tears, hugs, and squeals filling this space. This little world of femininity, where the talk of lace, seed pearls, and satin became as important as the world events on the front page of the *LTC*. Where mothers saw their daughters grow up to become the brides they'd dreamed they'd be, and realized their little girls were going to be wives.

It was never really about her reputation as a designer, the gowns, the mothers of the brides, flowers, candelabras, or white runners going down the church aisle. This was a place where the gift of lifetime love between a man and a woman was celebrated.

"Vivien, what is going on with you?" Mirette was by her side, and in the light coming from the fitting room, she could see her friend's face creased with concern.

"We're closing down the salon." Her throat went dry the moment she opened her mouth, and her words faltered.

"What?"

"Mr. Wynton and I decided."

"What do we do now?" Immogene asked from the fitting room doorway.

Vivien crossed her arms and pressed them against her midsection to give herself strength. Bursting into tears wasn't going to solve anything. They needed to keep going, stick to their plans. "I told him we were going to finish Louisa's dress."

"How're we going to do that if the salon's closed?" Mirette asked softly. "Louisa can't come in for fittings."

"We'll work on it here, and when time comes for fittings, we'll take the dress to her."

Vivien lay her arm across Mirette's shoulders and walked her back to the fitting room. "We will come to the salon, normal as ever, and do our work."

She closed the fitting room's door, then looked in the faces of both her assistants. "When we arrive, we'll come in the back entrance, through the loading dock and up the stairs to the delivery hallway. The door to the salon remains locked, and we don't open this fitting room door while we're in here."

"We mustn't mention who this gown is for either," Mirette added.

"Exactly." Vivien pointed, thrilled her old friend always picked up her slack when she'd forgotten something.

"And don't either of you worry about getting paid. I've always put a little of the salon's profits away, in case we had a situation like this one come about. We'll have this mess solved long before my rainy-day pot empties out."

Vivien clapped her hands together with enthusiasm she didn't feel. "Ladies, we can do this. We'll give Louisa's dress our complete attention. Levy City's young people aren't going to stop falling in love in this town, and when this mess is over, we'll reopen the salon."

A knock sounded on the salon's back door. Immogene gasped and raised her hands in the air. "That about sent my heart out of my chest."

Mirette patted her own chest. "Mine too."

Vivien drew a deep breath to calm her own pulse's racing. "I'll see who it is. Could be one of our last orders arrived and Rafe brought it up."

She opened the door to find Gigi instead of Rafe. "When I came up here and found the front door locked, I knew something was wrong. Lilla told me about these back hallways, so I snuck in here when nobody was looking."

"What was so all-fire important you had to come up here and scare us half to death?" Mirette asked as she patted the spot over her heart again.

Gigi gazed around the group. "I think Mary Hadley Bell's mixed up in all this. She's up to no good. Women like her always are."

Chapter 43

Vivien

Vivien drove her car into her designated space as president at the Junior League Headquarters. She took a second to fluff her hair and make certain her lipstick wasn't smeared on her teeth. With all she had swirling about between and the mothers of Levy City who were also in the League, she needed to present herself as best she could for the meeting she was about to run.

The lot was almost full, which seemed odd. The meeting wasn't scheduled to start for another hour. She always arrived early to help and talk with the ladies on the setting-up committee. As she entered the meeting room, conversations hushed. All eyes turned to her, and there wasn't a friendly spark among them.

She walked to the front of the room, set her purse down, and removed her shawl. She'd picked her favorite dress to bolster her spirits, a plum-colored silk taffeta with a wide, swishy skirt. She'd chosen to accessorize with the double string of pearls and matching earrings Carter had given her for their anniversary. He was always her greatest fan, and tonight she needed to feel his encouragement and love as she faced a group of hostile women she'd once considered friends.

Vivien picked up the gavel and rapped it on the wooden lectern used in their meetings. "Since we're all here, let's call the meeting to order. I'd like to—"

Merilee Bell sat in the front row. She jumped to her feet. "Vivien, I want the floor."

"Merilee, you'll have to wait until we get—"

Sarah Cameron, wife of young Mr. Cameron the caterer, stood up. "I think we should let Merilee speak."

A din rose as other women joined in, demanding the same.

Vivien silenced them by pounding the gavel again. "Are we going to throw decorum to the wind tonight?"

"There are things that must be said, Vivien, and this is the time and place." Merilee looked around the room as others nodded.

Vivien set the gavel down. "All right. Speak your piece, Merilee."

She puffed herself up and pivoted to face the group. "In light of all that's happened, I move that Vivien Sheffield step down as our president and we rescind her membership immediately."

"Come again?" Vivien looked around the room. From the many nods and whispers, it seemed the group agreed.

"The League is about community improvement and leadership. Vivien is not supplying either right now."

Sarah Cameron stood. "She's making our entire chapter look terrible. Can you imagine what other members around the country think when they read those newspaper articles about her? What does that say about us as well?"

Another woman stood. "Vivien, you've got to understand, we don't mean any harm. We have to protect our reputation."

Vivien scanned the group. Most of her friends were on their feet, talking amongst themselves or trading comments across the room with one another. Those who sat with their heads down and hands in their laps pained her the most. They disagreed with the call for her ousting, stayed out of the fray, and would not join in the soft mudslinging.

They also remained silent.

Looking around the room, she noticed none of the mothers who'd lost a daughter to this madness had come. Others argued for them, made claims in their names, argued for sympathy for their dreadful situations.

These murders were tearing her beloved town apart.

She pounded the gavel so hard she feared it might break in two. "Order."

Sarah Cameron walked to the lectern, then spoke in a volume only she and Vivien heard. "You brought this on yourself. Did you think you could go around like a queen, deciding who gets to conduct business in this town according to whatever puts a bee in your bonnet?"

Her face grew crimson as she clenched her fists. "Do you realize how much business my husband lost? All because you spread your nasty opinions all over town. It broke his poor father's heart, Vivien. He thought you were his friend, and then you go and try to ruin the business he spent his life building. The very thing he wanted to leave behind for his son."

"Sarah, my decision was based on—"

"The bank doesn't care what your decision was based on. They want mortgage payments. Payments we can't make because my husband's been blackballed all over town."

Vivien reached out to comfort her. "I'm so sorry, I had no idea."

Sarah slung her hand away. "We haven't booked anything beyond a few retirement dinners. Weddings are our bread and butter. And you've ruined any chances we have."

The noise continued in the room, and Sarah stalled, as if the sound of it broke her train of thought. Her chin quivered as she spoke again. "Being the town's pariah doesn't taste good, does it?"

Sarah returned to her chair and sat.

Her words shook Vivien to her core. Had she been too picky and particular with the guide? Did she put too much stock in preserving the standards for the salon or act out of pride rather than thinking of the consequences of her choices?

It was hard to believe the Camerons' business had soured in a couple of months. Then again, with the salon shut down, she might find out how quickly the same could happen to her.

Vivien pounded the gavel again. "Ladies. Please. We must have order."

When her request was ignored, she walked over to the wall and cut off the lights. The din in the room died down as all the attention turned to her.

Vivien flipped the switch back on, then looked at every face in the room.

"I love this city. I love this organization and what we've been able to accomplish over the years."

It was only then she realized she still carried the president's gavel. She tapped the head against her leg to help her concentrate on what she needed to say next, and not the emotions boiling within her.

"You are all dear women, and my good friends. We know each other's secrets—like how old we all are—and like good Southern women, we'd never tell a soul any of them."

Several in the group sat, as if the shock over what they had done was settling in.

She zeroed in on Merilee Bell, who was the only one still standing. "I'm happy to step down. Out of love for those four sweet girls, I will go."

Vivien walked to Merilee, handed her the gavel, gathered her things, and left to a cacophony of whimpers breaking out around the room. Seemed the realization they'd been sold a rotten apple brought on a roomful of buyer's remorse.

Once she'd arrived home and had a good cry on her bed, she dialed Mirette to tell her the news.

"They voted you out?" she said when Vivien delivered the news.

"No vote. Merilee brought up the idea, and the room evolved into pure chaos. I resigned and left."

"Good grief, what were they thinking? And what is Merilee up to?"

Vivien stretched her legs along the length of her bed. "She's been trying to get us to bend the rules and allow Mary Hadley to join. We don't take girls younger than twenty-three, and Mary Hadley's only twenty. And we both know how she hates being told no."

"The two of them got it in their heads to take advantage of all this tragedy? Vivien, I can't fathom how a body could want to do such a thing."

"To be honest, I'm hoping I'm wrong. Merilee isn't cold or mean-spirited. A little too much for putting on the dog, but she's not heartless. Mary Hadley was the only child she was able to have, and Mama can't say no to her baby."

Mirette huffed into the phone. "Mary Hadley takes advantage of her mother."

"She takes advantage of everyone. Maybe marriage and someday a family will make her grow out of it."

"Those are the things we old ladies pray for, aren't they?" Mirette yawned.

"Hey, my friend, thanks for letting me whine to you so late. I'll let you go. We have a lot to accomplish tomorrow if we're going to finish Louisa's dress in time for her wedding."

"They did you wrong, Vivien."

"Maybe it was time for some new blood." Vivien untucked her bedspread and wriggled underneath. "Good night."

"'Night."

Vivien set the receiver in the cradle, and before she could turn out the light, the phone rang again.

"This is Vivien."

"Miss Vivien, it's Audrey. I'm sorry for calling at such a late hour, I just got back in. Mr. Wynton told me about y'all's decision concerning the salon, and I had to make sure you're all right."

"I'll weather this just fine."

"There's another thing. I think I may have found a clue to whoever is behind the murders."

Vivien sat up straight. "What is it?"

"Have you ever heard of the brand Regal Rose wedding gowns?"

"No."

"I think whoever is designing these gowns wants you out of business. At all costs."

"Do you have any clue as to who?"

"Not yet, but at least now we have physical proof of a motive."

This was unbelievable. "You bought one of these gowns?"

"Yes. I've got a flight back to Florida tomorrow. We'll talk more then. Good night."

Vivien hung up and leaned back on her pillows.

She turned off her bedside lamp and looked up at the dark ceiling in her bedroom.

Dear God, please let this be the beginning of the end of this nightmare.

How could a married woman get so nervous over going on a date with her husband? Mary Jo stared at her reflection in the vanity table's mirror as she applied her lipstick. No matter how much she brushed it or applied hair cream, her hairdo hung in weird waves that made her head look lopsided. When she tried pulling it up in a ponytail, her skin seemed to pale. And tying her hair back with a scarf made her look like she was trying too hard to be fashionable.

It didn't help that Kenny liked to listen to the radio while he showered. Robbi Dever was on, but she couldn't go in and turn the thing off because he still didn't like her to see him without a shirt on.

So she clamped her jaws together and raked the brush through her hair one last time as Robbi rattled on in the background.

"Hooray, Wynton's has finally put our community before business and canceled Bridal Week. You know, I also discovered the Junior League ousted Miss Vivien from their chapter, ending her reign as their president. I'm glad to know Wynton's is following their lead."

Heat crept up Mary Jo's cheeks, and she yelped as she scraped her brush over the tender skin on her left ear. She set the brush down as Robbi went on.

"And yet, Levy City, there's more to this story. Vivien's closest circle of friends, whom we all know will stop at nothing to protect their friend's sterling image, have taken it upon themselves to try to dig up evidence that just isn't there. Yours truly has exposed all there is to know here on The Juice, where I keep squeezing until I've found every seed of truth in a story. We'll be right back after these messages from our sponsors."

Wasn't that just the bitter icing on the cake? Insinuating that she, Audrey, and Gigi were trying to lie for Miss Vivien.

Oh, that woman. What she'd like to tell her.

"Mary Jo, I'll be ready to leave in five minutes," Kenny called from the bathroom.

"Turn off the radio."

When she heard the welcome click of the button, she turned on her stool to see Kenny's reflection in the mirror as he buttoned his shirt himself.

Mary Jo dabbed at her eyes with her fingertip. Thank God he'd come to terms with using the prosthetic arm and was now working harder than ever to master how to use it. A few months ago, she'd been terrified of losing both her husband and her marriage because she'd bought him that thing. After a few adjustments and training at the clinic, he'd made progress.

And that was good.

She gave her hair a final fluff, then rose to finish dressing. They were going to the drive-in. No one would see her hair anyhow.

The sound of the doorbell sent the girls into a flurry of squeals. "Aunt Gigi is here."

"Let her in." Kenny's voice echoed down the hallway from their bedroom.

A duet of "Aunt Gigi" filled the house, followed by Penny yelling, "Aunt Gigi, you smell like a garden."

Mary Jo hurried to put in her pearl earrings and pin the matching broach on the collar of her pink sweater. With it not being spring yet, the color was a little bright. But Easter was a week away, the weather had warmed a little, and it went like a dream with her favorite black pencil skirt.

"How do I look?" She twirled in front of the bathroom doorway as Kenny slicked his hair back with Brylcreem.

He whistled. "I'll have the prettiest date at the drive-in. We'll be making out more than those teenagers parked around us."

She blushed as she waved off his remarks. "Oh you. I'll go say hey to Gigi and give her all the instructions."

"Don't know why you bother with all that. She won't follow any of it." Kenny walked to their closet and slid his feet into the new penny loafers she'd bought him from the store. Tying laces was still a challenge, but the new shoes allowed him to look slick and be more independent at the same time. And they'd added another little pep to his step.

She would have paid a gold mine for that. Luckily, she used her Wynton's employee discount instead.

"I know. That's why the girls love it when she babysits."

He grabbed his wallet and put it in his pants pocket, then grabbed his black-and-red-checked flannel jacket from where she'd laid it out for him on the bed.

Mary Jo grabbed her black purse and gloves on her way out of the room.

When she reached the living room, both Carrie Rose and Penny held large packages wrapped in silver-and-pink paper. Mary Jo pinned Gigi with a look. "What's all this?"

Gigi raised her hands in surrender. "Don't blame me. Auntie Audrey brought these back from her trip to New York. She dropped them off at my apartment on her way home. I'm to tell you she saw these in a window, and they begged to be brought home to two sweet little girls."

"Mama, can we please open them now?"

"If you don't, I think you're both going to burst."

The girls tore into their presents, then both gasped, as did their mother.

"Oh my goodness. Those are Miss Revlon dolls." She traded disbelieving looks with Gigi.

Carrie Rose opened the box and pulled her doll out. "She looks just like Auntie Audrey." She held up the doll, who was dressed in a red-and-white polka-dot dress with a wide skirt.

Carrie Rose lifted up the edge of her doll's skirt. "Look, Mama. She even has crinolines just like yours."

"My doll has hearts on her pink dress. Look, Mama, isn't she pretty?" Penny shrieked as she pulled her doll from the box.

Mary Jo nodded, then cupped her hand around her mouth as she leaned over to Gigi. "What was Audrey thinking? These dolls are too grown up for my girls. They're wearing high-heeled sandals and pearls. And they have grown-up figures, if you know what I mean."

Gigi giggled. "I know exactly what you mean."

The girls slid to the floor and began a conversation between their new dolls.

"I'm going to name my doll Arabella," Carrie Rose said as she pretended to walk her doll across the floor.

"I'm calling my doll Cindy because her real name is Cinderella."

"You'll need to play carefully with those dolls, girls. And we'll have to write thank-you notes to Auntie Audrey tomorrow."

"What's all the hubbub out here?" Kenny said as he entered the room. Both girls stood and ran to him, shoving their dolls up for him to see.

"Wow, those are really pretty." He turned a questioning look to Mary Jo.

"Audrey sent them. From New York City," Mary Jo said as she pulled on her gloves.

"How fancy. You girls will need to take care of these dollies. They seem very grown up."

He turned to Mary Jo. "We'd better leave now, Mama, if we want to make it there in time to get our hot dogs and fries before the movie starts."

Mary Jo held her arms out. "I need goodbye kisses."

Both girls ran to her and planted a wet smooch on either cheek, then returned to their new dolls.

Gigi gave her a gentle shove. "Out the door, Mama."

Mary Jo still needed to relay the instructions. "I forgot to tell you—"

"I'll find food, they won't die, and we'll be fine. Go have fun." Gigi fanned her hands as if she were sweeping Mary Jo out the door.

After Kenny pulled the car into their chosen spot at the drive-in and hooked the speaker onto the door's edge, he motioned to the box containing their food.

"Let's eat."

The hot dogs tasted better than she remembered, and Mary Jo laughed when a drop of relish and mustard stuck in the corner of her mouth and Kenny wiped it away with his napkin.

It was heavenly to sit in the front seat with her sweetheart, sharing fries and drinking Cokes, and forget about amputations, ailing parents, and not being the mama she'd always dreamed of being. Things were getting better every day.

When the big screen lit up and the newsreels started, she snuggled up to Kenny like she used to when they were high school sweethearts. He kissed the top of her head as the coming attractions played.

She placed all their empty cups and food wrappings on the carrying tray and hung it on the outside edge of the passenger-side door. A teenage boy came by a few minutes later and took it away.

"Oh look, *Lady and the Tramp* is playing next week. The girls would love that."

Kenny nodded. "Let's make it a date then."

Their conversations stopped when the main feature, *Meet John Doe*, came on. Mary Jo was pulled in right away. As the story unfolded, she found herself sitting up straighter, with her fingers clamped on the dash, listening to every word.

"Hey, you're really enjoying this, aren't you?" Kenny whispered in her ear.

"Don't you get it? This is exactly what she's doing."

Kenny twisted around to face her. "Who are you talking about?"

"That awful Dever woman. Just like Barbara Stanwyck's character, she's using her column and radio show to spread lies and fool Levy City."

"Honey, that's how some news works."

"No, she's been claiming she finds all these details, but she doesn't. I know who's been helping her. And I'm starting to think something else too."

"What is that?"

Mary Jo settled back next to Kenny. "I'm not sure yet. I need to talk to Audrey, Gigi, and Miss Vivien. Because if I'm right. . ."

Her pulse thumped in her ears so loud she almost couldn't hear the movie.

"Oh boy, if I'm right."

Chapter 45

Gigi

Gigi rushed up the employee stairs to Miss Vivien's. She had news. Lots of news.

Being a Wynton's employee gave her—what was it Audrey called it?—carte blanche or something or other, to be in the salon even though it was supposed to be off-limits. She used the delivery entrance to avoid being seen. She'd made it off of Jane's doghouse list, and she wanted to keep it that way.

Gigi rapped on the door four times, the number they'd all agreed upon to signal their arrival. The whole thing felt like a spy movie and added an extra layer of excitement. Not that they needed any more with all that had happened over the last few days.

It was a shock when Immogene opened the door. None of Wynton's Black employees were allowed to stay after hours once they'd finished their shifts. "They're all waiting in the mother's sitting area." She poked her head into the hallway, checking both directions before closing the door. "Did you see anyone in the hall when you came up?" she asked as Gigi walked in.

"No, why?"

"We heard a door slam a little while ago, and since Better Dresses next door is closed for the day, nobody's supposed to be in the hall."

"Maybe it was Rafe making deliveries up here?"

Immogene shook her head. "They didn't have any on the floor today."

She motioned for Gigi to follow her to where the group was sitting.

Audrey and Mary Jo sat next to each other, deep in conversation. Probably about those dolls Audrey sent the girls. Their mama hadn't quite gotten over them.

Miss Vivien waved Gigi over to an empty chair between her and Mirette.

"The last time you put Mirette and me together, we got in trouble," she joked as she took the offered chair.

Mirette poked her in the side. "If our luck's any good, we'll do that again."

Miss Vivien wagged her finger at Gigi. "If y'all don't behave yourselves, I'm going to put Immogene in the middle of you."

Immogene shook her head as she put up one hand. "Don't put me in charge of making Miss Mirette behave. I don't have that much patience."

"Neither do I, so let's move on to why we wanted to talk with all y'all." Miss Vivien crossed her legs and looked around the group with the air that she meant business.

"Before we get into all the ugly stuff," Audrey interjected, "I've got something for each of you."

She drew out a large box that had been sitting behind her chair, folded back the flaps, and reached inside.

The first item she brought out was a thin jewelry case covered in black velvet. She handed it to Miss Vivien. "A little something I picked up for you in New York."

"Honey, you didn't need to bring me anything." Miss Vivien opened the box and whispered, "Oh my." She held up a double-strand Aurora Borealis Rainbow crystal necklace. The beads lived up to their name as they twinkled in all the colors a person could think of.

"Audrey, this is gorgeous. Thank you."

Audrey ducked her head as she pulled another box out and passed it to Mirette. "Since y'all wear black or dark colors here in the salon, I thought these would look nice."

Mirette took hers from the box and fastened them around her neck. She moved to see herself in the mirror. "I love them."

Next, Audrey pulled out two red velvet jewelry cases and handed one to Gigi and one to Mary Jo. "Saw these and thought of you."

Inside each one was a Trifari rhinestone-and-gold short-chain necklace. "Those will go with any type of neckline you wear."

Gigi ran her finger along the curving gold links, then tilted the necklace to watch the rhinestones glitter underneath the lights. "Thank you." The gift was one of the nicest things she'd ever owned.

Mary Jo jumped from her chair and ran over to hug Audrey around the neck. "You shouldn't have. This and the dolls for the girls. It's too much."

Audrey pulled out a rectangular box tied with a blue bow and handed it to Mary Jo. "For Kenny. One of the fashion shows I attended gave out samples. It's one of those new cotton summer shirts for men."

Mary Jo hugged the box to herself. "He'll love it."

Gigi was about to tell her news, when Audrey reached in and pulled out one more jewelry box and gave it to Immogene. "For you. But don't tell Lilla about it yet, because I got her the same thing, and I want it to be a surprise."

Immogene stared at the box, then went to hand it back to Audrey. "I can't take this."

Audrey eyed her a moment. "Immogene, consider that a part of your work attire. Something you can wear when you come to work here in the salon." She switched her attention to Miss Vivien. "Once we get you up and running again."

Gigi bit her tongue to keep from sighing with frustration. It was nice of Audrey to bring them all souvenirs from her trip, but she felt worse than a kid at Christmas watching others open their gifts. What she wanted to share was burning a hole in her tongue, and she couldn't wait much longer.

Immogene opened the box. Her face remained stone cold as she lifted a strand of pearls out and held it between two fingers, allowing the lengths to dangle. After a moment, she laid them back in the box and closed the lid. "Thank you. This was very nice."

Gigi bounced in her chair like the lid on a boiling pot. "Can I talk now?"

"I guess so, since you look like you're about to pop." Miss Vivien rested her elbow on the arm of her chair.

"The other day I had to wait on Mary Hadley Bell. She came in to get her makeup done, and while I was working, she told me she was getting all dolled up for a very important meeting where she wanted to make a big splash."

"She is such an unkind person," Mary Jo said as she looked around the group.

Gigi went on. "Mary Jo and I saw her come up to the sewing section, and she gave Robbi Dever a note, and said it was something she'd want to know. That very night, Robbi Dever blabbed all over the radio how Miss Vivien was thrown out of the Junior League."

Miss Vivien scowled. "You think Mary Hadley told her about it in that note?"

Gigi nodded. "Robbi went on the radio at eight, and you said you were the only one who left the meeting at eight fifteen. How else did she find out?"

"She's right. I heard Robbi say she knew when it happened on the radio last night," Mary Jo said.

Mirette wrinkled her nose at Mary Jo. "What were you doing listening to her show?"

"Kenny had it on. It's a long story. But I have something I thought of at the drive-in last night. I think I know how the killer is choosing the girls."

Gigi swung around in her chair to face her friend. "How'd you figure that out?"

"We went to see *Meet John Doe* last night. In the movie there's this newspaper reporter who writes this fake letter and it causes all kinds of commotion. Anyway, I got to thinking about all the columns Robbi wrote to get attention, and the letters to the editor Mr. Cameron wrote, and how bad I felt that all we ever read about Miss Vivien in the *LTC* is negative. Then I remembered they also publish the wedding announcements."

Miss Vivien gasped so loudly Gigi feared she might pass out. "What is it, Miss Vivien?"

"One of the services we provide here at the salon is I write their wedding announcements and send them to the *LTC*. If the bride wishes, I mention that we designed her gown, or that she bought it from the salon."

Miss Vivien cupped her face in her hands. "That's how the killer is finding my brides."

Another thought hit Gigi. "How did the killer know? Most of those girls have been married for a while. Their announcements were in the paper years ago."

"The archives," Audrey said softly. "All papers keep copies of their old editions."

"I'm sure Sheriff Youngblood's looked through those already." Mary Jo looked at Miss Vivien. "Don't you think?"

"If he had, he wouldn't tell us. He doesn't want us girls fiddling around in his investigation."

"Harland Brown's worked at the paper for as long as I can remember. I bet he'd know if someone had been digging through the old announcements," Mirette added.

Gigi sprang from her chair like a kernel of popcorn in a hot skillet.

"We could go over to the paper and ask. And it's almost time for Robbi's radio show, so she won't be there to see us poking around."

Vivien moved to her desk. "We'll take my car."

The others stood, and then Gigi saw Immogene remained in her chair. "Aren't you coming with us?"

"I'm going home. I can't afford to get mixed up in this." She stood, slipped the handle of her bag on her arm, and headed to the back door. She stepped into the delivery hallway and turned back to the group. "Good luck, y'all. Find the truth and help Miss Vivien. I hope I see y'all here tomorrow, and not in the paper because the police took you in for messing around at the *LTC*." Immogene closed the door behind her.

"I have to speak with Libby before she leaves, so I'll meet y'all there." Audrey hurried out.

Miss Vivien's keys rattled as she gathered her things and looked around the group at her friends. "Y'all ready?"

Gigi slid on her coat. "Ready as rain."

Libby was tapping away at the typewriter when Audrey walked into the executive suite. She set down the box and walked to the desk. "Excuse me, Miss Farris, may I have a word?"

Libby twirled around in the chair. "Miss Audrey, you're home." She ran around the desk with her arms spread open, almost tackling Audrey to the ground when she grabbed her up in a tight hug around the waist.

"You were gone way too long." Libby gave her another hard squeeze.

Audrey unhooked the girl's arms and stepped out of her crushing embrace to gather her breath. "It's nice to be missed, but it shouldn't be so painful. You nearly crushed the life out of me."

Libby put her hands to her mouth. "I'm so sorry, Miss Audrey. I'm just happy you're back." She released a long sigh. "Running this office is exhausting."

"I'm well aware of that. Did you keep up with all the things I left for you like the new employees list and filing the sales reports?"

Libby pointed to the filing cabinet by Audrey's desk. "Mr. Wynton went over the sales reports with me yesterday. They're so interesting, seeing what sold well and what didn't. We had a long talk about how the buyers use those to decide what things to purchase for the store."

She pointed to Audrey. "He told me you're the best he's seen at picking up on trends early. Gosh, you're so smart."

Being away for two weeks had dulled her patience for her assistant's excitement over pretty much everything. "Did you file the sales reports?"

Libby nodded and sent her ponytail wagging. "Uh-huh. They're in the cabinet. And I sent little welcome-to-Wynton's cards to the new employees. We only had two this month, so it didn't take that long."

Audrey noted Libby's saying "we." If nothing else, her assistant had come to feel a sense of belonging in the store. The first step to growing a loyalty that transformed good employees into great ones.

"I'll check on the other assignments I left you tomorrow. It's late, and you'll be needing to leave soon." She reached into the box and pulled out a large box tied with a pink ribbon and handed it to Libby.

"I brought you something from New York."

Libby grabbed the box from her and tore off both ribbon and lid in one motion. Her eyes widened like two saucers as she lifted the light blue cashmere cardigan and a silk scarf decorated with yellow-and-blue stripes from within the tissue paper. "Oh my."

Libby turned teary eyes to Audrey. "These are so beautiful. Thank you."

Audrey held her hands up when Libby moved as if she meant to grab her in a viselike hug again. "You're very welcome. A young lady working in an executive office needs a nice cardigan and scarf. You'll look very professional in both."

Libby hugged both to her chest. "I'll wear these every day." She then shook her head. "Well, not every day. That would be silly because they'd get soiled, and people might think I was weird or something always wearing the same thing. I can't believe you thought of me when you were on your trip. That's so nice of you, Miss Audrey."

Libby would have been bowled over by how many times she'd been thought of during the trip. "It was my pleasure."

Audrey pulled her gloves from her purse. "I'm leaving, and I think you should as well."

"See you tomorrow." Libby folded the gifts and put them back in the box. "My mama isn't going to believe Audrey Penault brought me a gift all the way from New York City."

"You have proof now I would and did." The others were waiting for her at the *LTC*, so Audrey hurried out of the office before Libby grabbed her again.

The sun had set, leaving behind a narrow ribbon of pinkish orange on the horizon as Audrey pulled her T-Bird into the parking lot of the *LTC* building.

When she joined her friends, Mirette and Vivien were in the middle of bickering while the others stood by.

"We would have been here a lot sooner if you'd been a little more adventurous with your speed, Vivien."

"Mirette, the last thing we need is a speeding ticket. There's good reason why Bill Youngblood took away your driver's license and impounded your car. If I lose mine, neither of us will be able to get anywhere."

Mirette clicked her tongue against her teeth. "I didn't go that fast."

Gigi poked Mirette in the side. "I heard you were going sixty down Percy Avenue. You almost took out Mr. Darby and his dog when they were crossing the street at the light."

Mary Jo gasped. "Miss Mirette, you little speedster."

Mirette fanned both hands at Mary Jo to shush her.

Audrey looked around the small parking lot. "Who's the night guard for the *LTC* now?"

"Not a clue," Vivien answered as she put her keys in her purse.

"Whoever it is, he's headed this way."

Vivien clicked her purse closed. "We need to get into the news office tonight. Who's our best sweet talker?"

"Audrey," the other three said in unison.

Audrey swept her gaze at the group. "Y'all are too kind."

The guard strode up to the group and shined his light in Audrey's face.

Vivien stood next to Audrey. Hopefully, her being an older lady would help them seem less suspicious, but the whispering and giggling coming from the other three wasn't helping their cause.

Vivien snapped her fingers in her best mom-hushing-the-kids cadence. The point seemed to be taken as the troublesome trio went silent.

He kept his flashlight pointed at Audrey's face. She raised her hand to block the onslaught of the extra-bright glow.

"The paper's closed, ladies." He shined the light around the group.

Vivien stepped toward him, putting herself in the line of the light. "We wanted to talk with Harland Baker about something that might be in the archives."

Gravel crunched under the guard's heavy boots as he shifted his feet. "He's getting the early morning edition ready, and he doesn't like people coming in."

Mirette stepped toward the guard. "Tell Harland it's Mirette and Vivien, from Wynton's salon. We just want to look up something."

"He's not going to budge, ma'am."

Audrey shifted her feet in the loose gravel, and the guard jerked the light back her way. "Could you at least ask him? This is very important to Miss Vivien and Wynton's. I'm sure Harland would want to help one of their top contributors to the paper. We buy more ad space than anyone else in town."

There was hope he'd understood the *LTC*'s reliance on selling ads to keep the presses running. Audrey flashed her best smile, and there was no question they were getting inside the building.

"Yes ma'am. I'll walk y'all in."

"That's marvelous. Thank you."

Vivien motioned to the others. "Y'all come on before Audrey's magic wears off."

Audrey's eye roll at her comment wasn't missed by the others as she heard muffled snickering behind her.

The guard led them into the building, doing his best to shine his light to guide their way around the many holes in the lot.

Once they were inside, the guard excused himself. A few moments later, Harland walked into the lobby. His eyes went straight to Miss Vivien. "I'll take you to the archives, but you're only to look through the wedding announcements. I keep a tidy records room, and it's going to stay that way. We understand?"

They collectively nodded their heads. When Harland went ahead to lead them to the archives room, Mirette tugged on Vivien's sleeve. "I see why he's still a bachelor. Fus–sy."

Audrey kept her attention straight ahead, hoping and praying Harland didn't hear.

The room looked as if no one ever entered. Filing cabinets four drawers high stood side by side in straight rows, looking like metal soldiers standing at attention.

Harland walked to one row and patted the top of the first cabinet. "These first two hold all our wedding announcements. The dates are written on the tags at the front of each drawer."

He looked over their group. "Did you need a whole hen party to look up a few announcements?"

Vivien swept her hand around the group. "They're here for moral support."

Harland grunted and shook his head. "Women. Who are you looking for?"

"The girls who were killed. Cathy Stevens was June 1953; Rayanne Steele was May 1954; Leila and Macy were June of last year, 1955."

He pursed his lips. "They've sure been popular since they died."

"Harland, what on earth are you talking about?" Mirette walked toward the first cabinet.

He glared at her as if she'd asked him if he lived on the moon. "Robbi Dever came in here back in January, looking for names of girls to interview for that series she was doing on Bridal Week. Then that really snotty Bell girl came in here a few days ago, treating me like I was ten years old. She riffled through a whole mess of my files. The place looked like a bomb had gone off after she left. Took me three days to get all the papers cleaned up and put in their proper place."

He went on. "The sheriff and his crew came in here right after the murders started, then came back after each girl was killed. I asked him what he was looking for, and he said they'd know when they saw it." Harland shrugged. "Guess whatever he wanted is still missing since they haven't caught anybody yet."

"Thank you, Harland. We will make sure to leave the archives just as we found it," Audrey said, hoping he'd take the hint and leave them be. There was much on her mind, and she didn't want to share it with anyone outside of the group.

She kept her peace until he was out of the room with the door shut behind him.

Gigi was the first to jump in. "What does all this mean?"

"Robbi Dever picked the same girls the killer picked." Miss Vivien's heels clacked on the polished wood floors as she walked to the row of filing cabinets. "In January, before any of this nightmare happened." She looked down the row. "Here's the one we want."

Mary Jo grabbed Gigi's arm so hard she yelped. "Do you think she's the—"

Vivien held her hands up to force a pause. "Now hold on. This is all coincidence at this point."

Gigi pulled free from Mary Jo's grip. "Exactly. Where does Mary Hadley fit in with all this? Maybe she's the killer."

"I wouldn't put it past either one of them," Mirette said as she pulled up an old wooden rolling desk chair and sat.

"Robbi's been many things in her life, but I don't see her being a killer, even if Mirette thinks so." Vivien walked to where her assistant sat and patted her on the shoulder.

"What did she do before she worked for the *LTC*?" Mary Jo asked.

"She got a home economics degree from some ladies college up north. When she graduated she took a job with the government and lived up in Washington, DC, working for some program to help women in poor areas. Her mother used to talk about it all the time."

"Robbi grew up here?" Gigi asked.

Mirette nodded. "She did and came back home with her tail between her legs after her government job was cut."

"Levy City High hired her to be the home economics teacher but then fired her after a year."

"What happened at the school?" Mary Jo asked.

Mirette twirled around in her chair to face Mary Jo. "She couldn't cook and wouldn't teach the girls anything except sewing, budgeting, and how to get into college. Robbi can sew like nobody's business."

Audrey walked over to the group. "Of course, I remember now. After she got fired, she went to New York and worked as a seamstress for a wedding gown designer. Robbi even designed her own line one year."

"That's right. Mirette and I attended Bridal Week in New York City that year. Robbi's line was very forward-thinking," Vivien said.

"And she got booed off the stage."

Vivien frowned at her friend. "Mirette, it wasn't that bad. They didn't boo—the crowd just didn't react at all."

"They went silent. No one clapped the entire time her dresses were on the runway."

"And if I remember, yours came out next and the crowd never stopped clapping throughout your entire line," Audrey said.

"I had completely forgotten about that." Vivien looked down at her friend. "Those shows made us both about half-crazed from nerves."

Mirette nodded.

"What happened to Robbi after that?" Gigi asked.

"Her mother passed away, and she came home to bury her and settle her affairs. A few months later, she went to work for the *LTC* as the girl-about-town reporter."

Mirette huffed. "And here we are."

"Which is right back at the beginning, with nothing to help you, Miss Vivien," Gigi said.

A door closed behind them and they all turned to see who'd come in. Harland marched to the file cabinets, then pushed his horn-rimmed glasses up on his head as he scanned the space. "I came to make sure y'all kept things clean."

"Harland, you said Mary Hadley Bell came in here. What was she looking for?"

"I didn't ask. She and Robbi came back here one morning cackling together like they were about to lay a dozen eggs. I lit out and went to the printing press where it was quiet."

Miss Vivien shut the drawer she'd been looking in. "I think we're finished here. I'll drop Gigi off at her apartment house and take Mary Jo back to the store. I'm going home to take a hot bath, put my feet up, and watch *The Ed Sullivan Show.*" Vivien waved her hands to herd her friends out the door.

Mary Jo held up an envelope. "Who's RRD?"

Audrey spun around and saw she was holding up an empty envelope. "Where did you find that?"

"I saw the corner sticking out from under one of the filing cabinets."

Harland grunted and walked back to the door. "Robbi must have dropped it."

Audrey went and blocked his way, keeping him in the room. "How do you know it's hers?"

He narrowed his eyes and grabbed the doorknob. "She's always getting messages in those envelopes from some secret source she has. The letters are her initials, Roberta Rose Dever." Harland gave Audrey a final glare and stomped from the room, slamming the door behind him.

"Oh. My. Word," Miss Vivien whispered as she motioned for Mary Jo to give her the envelope.

Mary Jo complied. "What are you thinking, Miss Vivien?"

"Robbi's mother's name was Rose."

She turned to Audrey. "You remember the question you asked me the other night? About those gowns you found?"

"Yes ma'am."

"You know what we have now, don't you?"

Audrey nodded. "Yes ma'am, I do."

Mirette pushed up from the chair, then groaned a moment as she forced her back to straighten. "You two going to share what this is all about?"

Gigi crossed her arms. "Yeah, what is the thing that you have, Audrey?"

She looked around the group, ending with Miss Vivien. What she had might be nothing, or it might be everything.

“What I have. . .is bait.”

Chapter 47

Vivien

Silence in her car weighed heavy as Vivien drove past the lake toward home. The mirrored beams of moonlight swirled through the coffee-black water like heavy cream as she passed along the shore before turning onto the street to her house.

The scents of four different perfumes now battled for dominance in her car's interior, making her miss the bustle and noise of her friends being there with her. Vivien shrugged as she pulled her car into the garage. "I know, Mama, I'm not supposed to get attached. But I've broken your rule ever since I first met Mirette."

Her phone's ringing met her as soon as she came through the door leading from her garage to the kitchen. Vivien lifted the receiver by the next ring. "This is Vivien."

"You must have taken the scenic route home," Mirette teased from the other end.

"You know me too well. The lake looked awful pretty under the moonlight tonight."

"Do you think what we found out at the *LTC* is worth anything?"

Vivien hung her car keys on the hook by the garage door. "We could talk to Bill and see what he thinks."

"He'll claim we meddled in his case. Until we can take him a written confession from Robbi or Mary Hadley or whoever else is the killer, he's not going to listen to us."

She couldn't believe she heard the clinking of a spoon sounding from Mirette's end. "You are not drinking coffee this close to midnight. You're not going to be able to do a lick of work tomorrow."

"It's hot tea, your majesty. I wanted something warm to help me wind down from running around town like a night owl."

"Let me call you back. I'm going up to my bedroom." Vivien hung up the phone, then carried her shoes in one hand and her purse and shawl in the other. She used her elbow to flip the switch and turn off the kitchen light.

She padded up the stairs in her nylons, then deposited shoes and everything else in their proper place. When she settled on her bed to call Mirette back, her face tingled from Noxzema and the scrubbing with Pond's cold cream.

"Took you long enough to call back. I almost fell asleep waiting," Mirette grumbled.

"You know I won't go to bed without a fresh face. Fighting back those wrinkles is a never-ending battle."

"Poo. I gave up on that years ago, and I go to bed a lot happier. I got to where I couldn't stand the smell of Noxzema."

The best part of their nightly talks was their conversations went off in any direction and nothing was off-limits. Daddy had once told her discussing religion or politics was the best way to lose a friend, but she and Mirette had talked, argued, agreed, laughed, cried, and at times stopped speaking to one another over everything under the sun.

Daddy had been wrong where Mirette was concerned. He'd been wrong about so many things.

Mirette called to her. "Did you fall asleep on me?"

"No. I guess Audrey's reminding me of Robbi's tough breaks brought back memories of other things."

"Vivien, you don't need to be letting your mind go back there. What happened to Robbi that time in New York wasn't our fault, and neither was the other."

She'd lived with shame, being shunned, and feeling the dirt under society's shoes for something another had done. Thanks to Mama not allowing her to wallow, but instead pushing her to find ways to write her own story for her life, she'd moved past those feelings.

Or had she? Was all the work building her reputation as "Miss Vivien" more about fighting against being called "Jailbird's girl" or "Robber Rick's daughter" when she was thirteen?

"Mirette, do you think Robbi grew to hate me because she lost her career as a wedding gown designer?"

"People do awful things when their feelings get hurt."

"What happened went beyond hurt feelings. On top of coming home to bury her mama, Robbi had to face the entire city knowing she'd failed at something for the third time."

"But Vivien, from envy and revenge to murder?"

"Mirette, you and I both know how deep some feelings go with us females."

Her friend released a deep sigh. "Sadness does strange things to people, doesn't it?"

"It's more than that, Mirette. It's sadness that doesn't see any hope on the other side."

"Well, I'd like to be on the other side of this sad conversation. Let's change the subject and talk about those gifts Audrey brought back to everyone. That girl loves to shop, doesn't she?"

"Funny thing is, I've been wanting one of those crystal necklaces for a while but always was too busy to look at the store for one. It was nice of her to think of us, wasn't it?"

"You didn't catch what she said?"

Vivien paused a moment. "No, what?"

"That we could wear them and sparkle while we worked. She's expecting the salon to reopen and telling us to as well."

"Of course we're going to reopen. This isn't going to last forever."

"Speak for yourself. Old ladies like me never know when we're going to meet the proverbial bucket and give it a grand kick."

"Bro–ther. You, my friend, are far too mean to die anytime soon."

"If the Lord calls though."

"He has my permission to take you."

A loud screeching sounded from Mirette's end of the phone, followed by a loud crashing noise. "What on earth was that?"

"I think a car hit another car outside in the street." Crinkling sounds came through as Mirette lifted her venetian blinds. "Oh no. Vivien, I think someone has been run over out in front of my house."

"Get off the phone and call Bill as fast as you can."

"You call him for me. I'm going to check on the person in the street."

Vivien jumped from her bed. "Mirette, don't go outside. You stay put until the police get there. I'm calling them right away."

Vivien pressed the button and ended the call, then dialed Levy City's sheriff's office. The young man who answered was almost as upset as she once she'd relayed her message. He promised to be at Mirette's in minutes.

Vivien ran to her closet and pulled on her robe, then her long overcoat. She slipped on a pair of her loafers, which were going to look ridiculous with her robe, but who cared at a time like this? If she ended up on the front page of the *LTC*, no one would care anyway. They'd all think she'd gone mad from her latest trials.

Once on the road, she drove at speeds Mirette would have lauded. When she turned the corner to her friend's house, her headlights illuminated two large humps in the road. Vivien turned off her car and left it right in the middle of the street without bothering to shut the door.

She ran to the first body. It was Mary Hadley Bell. A trail of blood streamed from her forehead. Her body lay twisted like a broken doll.

"Oh no."

Vivien stepped over her and hurried to Mirette. She knelt and lifted her friend's head into her lap. "Mirette, can you hear me?" She shook her arms gently. "Mirette."

She touched her neck, felt a light pulse. Vivien pulled back her hand, and in the yellow gleam of the streetlight, she saw red. Lots of red.

"Oh, Mirette. Please don't die. Stay with me, honey."

Vivien screamed for help and her pleas echoed between the houses lining the street. Windows lit up along the block. She hollered again as she lay Mirette down, then stripped off her overcoat.

Her friend was from the old school of manners and would have been mortified for the neighbors to see her in her bathrobe. Vivien wrapped her coat around Mirette, then held her against her again.

Nella Campbell and her husband Don were the first to reach the scene. Nella covered her mouth with her hand when she saw Mary Hadley's body. She pointed. "Is she. . . ?"

Vivien nodded. "Don, go call an ambulance. The police should be here any minute."

Her arms shook from supporting Mirette's deadweight, but she wasn't letting go until help arrived.

The neighbors crowded around. Someone brought a wool blanket and laid it over Mary Hadley.

"We need to call Merilee and Richard and let them know," a voice said, but Vivien never looked up to see who had spoken. She couldn't take her eyes from Mirette.

"You hang on, you hear me? If you die on me now, I'm going to give you what for when we meet again at the pearly gates."

The deputy rolled up in his car. His kept his bright headlights on, and their glare hurt Vivien's eyes so she looked away.

"Make way, folks. Please, move back."

He came and knelt in front of Vivien. "Is she alive?"

"Yes, but she's fading. I feel her pulse getting weaker."

"We called the ambulance, Officer. Should be here soon."

The deputy rose without a word and went to where Mary Hadley lay. "Did anyone see what happened?"

Voices chattered around the group, but no one came forward to speak.

Vivien went to speak, but her throat closed around the words. She swallowed, then coughed to clear their way. "Mirette and I were on the phone. Tires screeched, and she heard a thump. She told me someone had been run over."

Tears flooded from Vivien's eyes, and she didn't care. "I told her not to come out here. I told her to stay put."

She bent her head over Mirette. "Why didn't you listen to me? Just this once?"

In the distance, the ambulance's wailing siren played above the crowd's murmurings. Growing louder and louder by the second. The deputy directed people out of the way.

"Mirette, help's here. Don't you go." Vivien leaned in close to her friend's ear. "Don't you leave me."

Chapter 48

Vivien

Vivien sat by Mirette's bedside. Dried bloodstains created a polka-dot pattern on the front of her overcoat. The deputy, the ambulance drivers, and even Mirette's nurse begged her to go home, change her clothes, and get some sleep.

How was she supposed to sleep? As soon as she closed her eyes, allowed her thoughts to drift, the images of Mary Hadley and Mirette lying in the street rushed in. She'd declined coffee, yet the sweet young nurse brought a cup. It now sat on the bedside table growing colder by the moment. Like Mirette's hand.

Vivien rubbed her friend's skin. "We've got to keep these million-dollar fingers of yours warm. This mess will end soon, and we'll open the salon. I might hang some crepe paper and big giant bows all over the place, in the brightest purple I can find."

Vivien squeezed Mirette's hand. "Mirette, honey, you've got to wake up. Open your eyes for me. The doctor says the sooner you wake up, the better."

He'd said many other things too, like severe concussion, damage to her brain, and the chance she might never regain consciousness. The kind of blow to the head Mirette had received could cause a myriad of problems, especially in someone of her age.

"He called you elderly, Mirette. You've got to wake up so you can tell the little know-it-all off. We old girls have to stick together, remember?"

The time sitting hunched over caused an ache to creep up her back and explode in spasms across her shoulders. Vivien released Mirette's hand and stood, arching her back to relieve the pain.

In normal circumstances, she'd be asleep in a minute in the kind of dull-gray lighting of the room. For now, time seemed to stop even though the large round clock on the wall ticked away. And sleeping was something she did in another lifetime. A time when the world made sense and horrible things like murder and hit-and-run incidents didn't happen.

A soft knock invaded the silence of the room. Vivien glanced over as Mary Jo peeked around the door. She crept in and engulfed Vivien in a hug.

"What are you doing here?"

Mary Jo squeezed harder. "Sheriff Youngblood called Audrey and told her what happened. She called me and went to pick up Gigi. They should be here any minute."

"We are here." Gigi strode into the room and sandwiched her with a hug from the other side. "Miss Vivien, I'm so sorry."

Audrey closed the door once she'd entered. She didn't join in the hug, but went to the bedside and looked down at Mirette. "How is she?"

Vivien patted both Gigi and Mary Jo before wriggling free from their grip. "She was beaten about the head. I don't remember how many stitches they put in to close the wound, but it was a lot. They had to shave part of her head, and we all know how much she'll hate having a bald spot."

"We'll get her a great hat. Or a turban," Audrey said softly.

"Those bandages already look like she's wearing one," Gigi said as she walked around and stood on the other side of the bed.

"How bad is it?" Mary Jo asked.

"They don't know. She needs to wake up so they can evaluate her." Vivien reached down and grabbed Mirette's hand again. "Honey, the girls are here. They want to talk to you. You need to wake up and tell us you're fine."

Vivien's voice caught. Her knees went to gelatin, and she swayed before collapsing in the chair. "Whoever did this cracked her skull open. Bill and the doctor both said she was hit with something large and heavy to do this kind of damage. Like maybe a tire iron."

She pressed her fist against her lips until she could calm her sobs. "Why? Why would someone attack her?"

"Because she knows who killed Mary Hadley, and they had to make sure she kept quiet." Though she spoke in a whisper, Audrey's voice fell loud in Vivien's ears, as if she'd been yelling at the top of her lungs.

"I can't believe this is happening." Mary Jo smoothed a wrinkle from the sheet. "We're not going to find out who did this to you unless you wake up and tell us, Miss Mirette."

"Maybe she's just being stubborn, to tease all of us." Gigi tried to smile to help make her point. The corners of her mouth trembled and wouldn't curl upward.

"I wouldn't put it past her. You know how she gets," Mary Jo said.

Vivien took hold of Mirette's hand once again. "I've known all her moods for a long time."

"How long have you known Miss Mirette?" Mary Jo asked.

"The easy answer to that would be how long haven't I known Mirette."

Another spasm ripped across her back, forcing Vivien to let go of Mirette so she could stand and stretch again. "My father was a loan officer at the bank, and when I was thirteen, he was convicted of stealing loan payments."

The gasps around the room came as no surprise. No one ever figured their friend was the child of a jailbird. Vivien continued with her story. "Daddy went off to jail, Mama went to work as a cook in a restaurant. I was the eldest child and stayed home to care for my two younger brothers and my baby sister Elizabeth. We called her Bitsy."

She went on. "When my brothers were old enough, they went to work to help support the family. Mama had taught me to sew, and I was mending the family's clothes. I made a few dresses for Mama and my sister. My first designs were for Bitsy. I'd draw pictures of ladies and cut them to make her paper dolls. Then I'd draw dresses for her to put on them while I cleaned up our house."

Vivien sat down in the chair. "Bitsy got scarlet fever when she was six and died. My brothers had left home to fend for themselves by then, so Mama got me a job working with a lady who owned the local millinery shop back home."

She tilted her head towards the hospital bed. "Mirette worked for her too. From the first moment we sat in the shop's back room sewing hats together, we knew we were meant to be lifelong friends."

Vivien folded her hand around Mirette's. "She helped me open my first shop. After Carter died, she was the one who jerked a knot in my tail and told me I had to keep going, no matter how sad or angry I was. I had a little girl and boy to raise."

The room seemed to instantly grow cold. Vivien rubbed away the chills on her arms. "If I was running short on food, she skipped meals so she could fix us a pot of beef stew with anything extra she had in the icebox or her cupboard. And buy a loaf of bread so my kids wouldn't go to bed with empty stomachs."

The emotions she'd dammed up inside broke through, and Vivien could speak no more. Her eyes and nose ran like a river from the flood of tears.

Audrey moved to her side and held out a white linen hankie embroidered with pink roses. Vivien mopped her tears. "I met Carter when I went to meet Mama at the hotel to walk home together."

She blew her nose, then continued. "We both married wonderful men and buried them. Mirette moved here and we started our first shop and then moved into Wynton's. I never expected things to end like this."

Mary Jo rushed to her side. "Miss Vivien, we aren't going to give up. Miss Mirette's too feisty to give in to this. You're always saying what a grump she is when she doesn't get her Sunday afternoon nap."

The door opened and Merilee Bell tiptoed into the room. "I had to come see you. I didn't know what else to do."

Chapter 49

Gigi

The moment Mrs. Bell entered the room, Gigi moved to the door with the intention of throwing the woman out. The last thing Miss Vivien needed was that woman coming in and slinging blame for her daughter's death all over the room. But Audrey caught her by the arm and pulled her back as the two women embraced.

"Merilee, I'm so sorry about Mary Hadley. When I got there. . .I'm so sorry."

Merilee nodded. "I know. Bill told me what happened." She looked at Mirette's silent form. "I hope I'm not intruding."

Intruding? The way she and Mary Hadley behaved, invading was more like it. Gigi clenched her fists and counted to ten to keep her tongue from going off. This wasn't the time or place to make a scene. Audrey must have noticed her getting ready to pop off again because she lowered her brows in that ladylike way she had of disapproving without letting the whole world know.

"Not at all. Come sit down." Vivien led her to the empty chair.

Merilee lowered herself to sit, then tucked her purse against her middle. "I couldn't stay at home. Richard's gone into his study and shut the door."

She looked around the room as if she wanted the group's approval. "You know how men are when things like this happen."

Vivien rubbed her back. "How are you holding up?"

Merilee's knuckles went white as she gripped her purse strap. "Every five minutes, my mind keeps reminding me this is real, and my baby girl is gone. I cry and then go numb. Over and over."

Vivien looked around the room. "Y'all can go on home. This room wasn't meant to hold all of us."

"Kenny is walking the girls to school tomorrow. I'll leave in a little bit to go home and shower." Mary Jo set her purse down on the small table by the bed.

Audrey gestured toward the door. "I'm going to ask for some more chairs." She looked at Gigi and Mary Jo. "Come help me?"

"I'm happy to stand. Helps me stay awake." Gigi crossed her arms to show she was cemented to the floor and staying put. Audrey gave her a long look then left the room, and Mary Jo followed her out.

Vivien turned back to Merilee. "Why was Mary Hadley in Mirette's neighborhood tonight?"

"Vivien, she's been acting so strangely these past few weeks. Lying about her whereabouts, going out at indecent hours. This morning when I asked her what she's been up to, she ordered me to stop prying."

She released a long, shaky sigh. "I owe you an apology for the way we both went on about her dress being wrong. It wasn't." Merilee shook her head. "I think she enjoyed seeing how far she could push the two of you into pleasing her. I should have stopped her from being such a pest."

"Oh, Merilee. Mirette and I have done this for so long we took none of that to heart."

"Thank you for being so kind. I couldn't believe it when she told me she'd taken the dress to Robbi Dever to fix."

This news hit Gigi like a brick in the face. "Robbi worked on her dress?"

Both women jerked around to face her as if they'd forgotten she was still in the room.

Merilee nodded. "Immogene wouldn't touch it. That last time we came to the salon, and Robbi was there, she told Mary Hadley she wanted to interview her for the Bridal Week series she was writing."

"Did they meet?" Miss Vivien asked.

"Robbi took Mary Hadley to lunch at The Grove, and they were there for hours. When Mary Hadley got back home, all she seemed to talk about was Vivien."

Heat rushed up Gigi's neck. "What was she saying about Miss Vivien?"

Merilee looked down at her lap. "That she went around like she was the queen of Levy City, fooling people into believing she cared about her brides, when her real goal was turning weddings into a money tree for herself."

Those words pressed the accelerator on Gigi's anger, and she could hold her tongue no longer. "What an ugly thing to say. Everyone knows Miss Vivien would—"

Miss Vivien put her hand up. "Gigi, please."

For Miss Vivien's sake, she'd hush. If Merilee started saying terrible things again, Gigi would toss her out like yesterday's trash.

Merilee put her hand over her heart. "Vivien, I'm so sorry about all the ugly things I said to you in the salon. And the horrible way I acted at the last Junior League meeting."

Miss Vivien switched her attention to Mirette. "The League and my reputation aren't worth a hill of beans to me right now."

Merilee continued. "I was terrified the killer was coming after my girl next. We all were. Except Sarah Cameron. She just wanted revenge because their business was going down the drain. Her husband is not much of a businessman. He's misused funds, and they're about to lose everything."

Merilee scowled. "I don't know why I brought up such a gauche thing at a time like this. What's the matter with me?"

Gigi was ready with a long list of items to answer her question, but Miss Vivien spoke first. "You're grieving."

The door opened and Audrey entered with a folding chair in each hand. She set the first one up for Miss Vivien and put the other against the wall and sat down.

Mary Jo unfolded the two she brought on the other side of Mirette's bed. She took one and pointed to the other until Gigi sat beside her.

Merilee opened her purse and drew out a business card. "This was in Mary Hadley's purse when Bill brought it back to the house." She handed it to Miss Vivien.

"At supper tonight, Mary Hadley announced that she'd broken her engagement to Ben and was going to New York City to model wedding dresses for this man. Richard and I of course blew up, but she rolled her eyes and said she wasn't going to be forced into giving away her best years or her brain to a man. When I asked her where she got such ridiculous ideas about marriage, she ran out the door before we could stop her."

She snapped her purse shut. "I don't know when she met this man."

A new truth zapped Gigi. "I do."

All eyes turned to her. "Mary Hadley came to Cosmetics a few days ago and wanted me to do her makeup. She kept talking about this important meeting she was going to that evening. It was the same night as the Junior League meeting."

All Mary Hadley's primping and gazing at herself that day now made sense. "She kept commenting how she had to look her best."

Vivien read the name on the card. "I've never heard of him." She passed the card to Audrey.

Audrey glanced at the card. "He works for Regal Rose."

Merilee nodded her head so fast her entire body rocked in the chair. "Yes, Regal Rose. That's the company Mary Hadley said she was going to model for."

"But why was she in Mirette's neighborhood so late at night?" Audrey asked as she handed the business card back to Vivien.

"She and Ben bought one of the new homes they built on the other end of Mirette's street. Mary Hadley went there in the evenings to set up house."

The nurse opened the door. "Ladies, y'all have to go. Doctor's orders."

Merilee stood and hugged Vivien. "Please call me with any news about Mirette."

"I promise."

While she walked out, the nurse held the door open and mouthed a silent *Get out* to the rest of the group. Gigi walked to the bed. If only Miss Mirette would pop those eyes open, say something funny in that way of hers, and tell them all she took a great nap. She reached down and patted her blanket-wrapped shoulder. "You need to wake up and tell us who did this to you, Miss Mirette."

Miss Vivien met Gigi's gaze. "She liked you so much."

Audrey leaned her chair against the wall and went to Vivien's side. "She *still* likes Gigi and will tell her when she wakes up." She picked up the chair again.

"Ladies, now." The nurse swept her hand toward the hall.

Gigi grabbed her chair and walked around the end of the hospital bed behind Mary Jo, then stopped as the other two filed out the door. "God has his eyes on Miss Mirette."

Miss Vivien patted her heart, and turned to focus on Mirette.

No one spoke as they walked to the parking lot together. The silence pressed down on them like the hot air that made a person feel they'd melt before a big summer thunderstorm hit.

Mary Jo flashed her lights to say goodbye as she pulled out of the parking lot.

"We've got to catch who did this." Gigi said aloud when she slid into the passenger side of Audrey's T-Bird.

"I have a plan." Audrey slid her key in the ignition and started her car.

Gigi leaned back against the red-and-white seat. "Good. It will be nice to squeeze the seeds of truth out of Robbi Dever for a change."

A hard thumping on the top of her hair brought Vivien around. She'd fallen asleep resting her head on her arms at the edge of Mirette's bed. Her neck and back cramped as she sat up and tried to shake away the sleep.

"Vivien, you stink," a scratchy voice called.

She sat up to see Mirette looking at her. "Good gracious, you're awake."

"Quit your caterwauling. My head is throbbing." Mirette rubbed her hand over the bandages wrapping her head. "Oh, lawsy-may, you let them put me in a turban. You know how I hate those things."

Vivien ran to the door and opened it. "Nurse, come quick. She's awake. Mirette's awake."

She rushed back to her friend's bedside. "How are you feeling?"

"Like a train ran over me, backed up, and ran over me again. What happened?"

Vivien slid into the chair beside the bed. "You don't remember?"

"If I did, I wouldn't be asking you. I think you need to be in this bed, and they need to send me home."

Vivien took Mirette's hand. "You listen here, you stubborn old goose. You've had us all terrified these last few days." Her voice caught, and she stopped a moment to gather herself. "We thought we'd lost you."

The corners of Mirette's mouth turned up slightly. "It's nice to be loved."

The nurse rushed in, her hat askew from running down the hall. She checked Mirette's pulse, then laid her hand back on the bed. "I'll call the doctor." Before she hurried out, she righted her white nurse's cap and secured it with a bobby pin pulled from her hair.

"What's all the fuss about?" Mirette's voice sounded dry and raspy, as if she'd been yelling for hours.

"You were attacked, hon. You've been out for three days."

Mirette's eyes fluttered open. "Three days? What in the name of Pete happened to me?"

Vivien grasped Mirette's hands within her own. How much to share with her friend wasn't clear. Giving her small doses seemed the best idea until the doctor came. "You had an accident."

"Did I fall down my front steps and crack my head open?"

"No."

"Did that old shelf in the garage finally give way and take me down with it? It's been rotted through for years."

Vivien's stomach churned as the vision of Mirette and Mary Hadley lying in the street replayed in her mind. She drew in a long breath to usher in calm. "No, it wasn't the shelf."

On the final word, Mirette heard a tremor in Vivien's voice. She looked straight at Vivien. "What happened to me, Vivien?"

"We were talking on the phone—"

Mirette cut her off. "I know that part. What happened after? Tell me."

"You heard a noise, a car slamming into something. I told you not to go outside to look, but you did. I don't know what happened after that. When I arrived, you were lying in the street. Someone had knocked you in the head, and you were unconscious."

Mirette sank her head into the pillow, and the room fell into silence. Her eyes twitched back and forth as if she were rewinding the scene in her mind, trying to find the spot where the truth hid.

The doctor opened the door and walked in with the nurse close on his heels. Vivien moved to make room for him by the bed. He put his stethoscope in his ears and listened to Mirette's heart, then took a small flashlight out and shined it at her eyes.

Mirette held her hand up to block the light. "Is blinding me necessary?"

He rested her palms against his own and pumped them in the air, then dropped them and whisked back the sheet. The doctor tapped a small hammer against each of her knees, then spread the sheet back over her.

"For now, things look passable. Due to your age though, I'd like to keep you under observation for a few more days, just to make sure nothing serious develops. You've got a concussion, and I want to keep you calm and quiet for the next few days."

He grabbed the clipboard hanging on a hook attached to the foot-rails, scribbled a few notes, and walked from the room. The nurse tucked the sheet around Mirette from the waist down to her feet.

Mirette pointed to her throat. "Could I have some water? I'm dry as a bone."

The nurse clasped her hands in front of her. "I'm so sorry, I can't bring you anything yet. The doctor wants to make certain you're fully awake and alert before we start any fluids."

"Talking with you isn't enough?"

Mirette's grousing didn't budge the nurse. "No ma'am. The doctor was very clear."

The nurse folded the ends of the sheet into hospital corners and tucked them under the mattress. "I'll give you five more minutes to visit." She checked her watch and left the room.

Mirette pointed to her throat. "Feels like my throat is full of sand." As if to prove the point she coughed. She crumpled the top edge of the sheet in both hands. "I think I'm remembering something, but it doesn't make sense."

Vivien sat on the edge of the bed. "Tell me."

"Maybe it's real, maybe not, but I keep having this picture of looking up from the street and seeing a long raincoat, and a row of handmade lace hanging beneath the hem. Does that make any sense?"

Vivien patted her on the arm. "None of this does yet. I'll promise you one thing: This stops now. I'm calling the girls, and we're going to solve this."

Mirette's eyes drifted shut. "Good, go home and call them now. Then take a shower. You know I love you to bits, but you stink to high heaven. And I really need some quiet."

✦✦

Vivien didn't realize how much she needed that shower until she sat on her bed with her wet hair twisted into a towel. Spending all those days at Mirette's bedside with nothing to do but pray and think gave her the time and opportunity to go over all the clues they'd found so far.

A rather nasty story unfolded before her, in need of justice and a quick trip to the end. She dialed the executive suite because she didn't have Audrey's new office number.

"Hello, this is Audrey Penault."

The sound of Audrey's voice shook Vivien for a second before she gathered herself to deliver the first of her good news. "She's awake."

"Oh, thank God. How is she?"

Vivien wiped away a drop of water trailing from her hair with her fingertip. "Saucy and groggy. The doctor decided to keep her for a few more days to make certain she's not going to have any long-standing effects from the injury. He said she's got a concussion."

"Does she remember anything?"

"Not much. I need you to call the other girls and tell them to meet me in the salon after work tonight."

"I'll let Gigi and Mary Jo know."

"Thank you. I've been going over things in my mind, and I don't like the answers I landed on."

"There are things we need to share with you too."

Vivien sat on one of the couches as she waited for her friends, absorbing the empty silence. She'd asked Audrey to drive Immogene home early to keep her out of the fray.

She raised her gaze to one of the chandeliers. In the murky gloom, she couldn't see the fixture but knew it was there. The same went for the person responsible for all of the heartache that had cut her, and the rest of Levy City, to the bone.

For better or worse, whether she ended up richer or poorer, she was going to end this once and for all.

When Mary Jo arrived, she came in the back door and went straight to the dress form where Immogene had been working on Louisa's gown.

"What beautiful work, Miss Vivien." She pointed to a row of the champagne-colored crepe rose petals Immogene had attached to the chiffon overskirt. "I've never seen anything like these."

"Immogene has a great eye for putting something different in just the perfect place. I honestly believe she'll be running her own shop someday. She's a smart gal."

Mary Jo circled the gown. "Y'all must have a dozen or so crinolines under there to make this skirt stand out so far."

Taking a moment to talk shop eased the jitters rising up each time she thought about her plan. Vivien went over and lifted the gown's hem. "Immogene and I fashioned an inner boned bodice made of faille and attached it to an old-fashioned hoopskirt to give the gown more structure underneath. Our bride had polio and needs the skirt to be out of the way of her affected leg so she can walk. It also holds the dress out so Immogene can decorate it with her special touches."

Mary Jo leaned closely and studied a cluster of embroidered leaves made with ivory thread. "The stitching on these is exquisite."

The salon's back door opened, and Audrey entered, carrying a large dress box. She smiled as soon as she saw Vivien. "I've got a present for you."

She set her load on the cutting table, then opened the flaps and drew out a tea-length wedding gown. Audrey held the dress up for Vivien to get a closer look.

Her heart added a dozen extra beats to its rhythm when she spied a row of tatted lace. She checked the label sewn in the back of the dress. "I knew it."

Her eyes met Audrey's. "Mirette said the last thing she remembered was someone standing next to her, and a row of homemade lace peeking out from under their coat."

Mary Jo raced over to the dress, and as soon as she spied the trim, she clapped her hands. "We've got her."

At the same moment, Gigi burst in the door. She tossed her lunch bag and purse onto the cutting table next to Audrey's box as she rushed over to Mary Jo and Vivien. "Who did we get?"

Vivien pointed to the lace on the gown's skirt. "The one woman in Levy City who tats lace like this."

"Will someone please explain to me how the lace on this dress proves who the murderer is?" Gigi held her arms out as she looked around the group.

"In due time, Gigi dear." Vivien took the gown from Audrey. "Sit down, y'all. This may be a long night."

A good dose of common sense told Vivien she was crazy. As she drew in a deep breath, she caught a glimpse of herself in the fitting room's three-way mirrors. She bore the same squared shoulders and jaw-clenching determination John Wayne and Alan Ladd showed in the movies when they faced down the gunslingers terrorizing their town.

Unlike them, she had no guns to stop the killer. She had friends and hopes in a half-cocked plan. "Robbi Dever will be here in twenty minutes."

"What?" Gigi looked like her eyes were going to pop from their sockets, while Audrey and Mary Jo stared without speaking.

Vivien held up the gown. "I want this on one of the mannequins in the shop's window so Robbi will see it. Mary Jo and Gigi, get the other gown out of the window and on a hanger before she gets here."

"Yes ma'am," Mary Jo said as they rose to follow her orders.

"Audrey, turn on all the lights. Robbi Dever's evil acts will no longer be hidden."

Someone opened the back door and called out. "Miss Audrey?"

Audrey mouthed a silent apology for her assistant, flipped on the lights, and went to the door. "Libby, what on earth are you doing down here?"

"You told me to always be aware of things around the store and jump in to help when a situation looks bad. And if this isn't one of those situations, I don't know what is." Libby crossed her arms without her usual ponytail-wagging head nod.

Vivien hurried to shut the back door. "Libby, what do you think is going on?"

"That gown Miss Audrey brought down here isn't from Wynton's. It came in a ratty old box, and I know you would never put something cheap like that in the salon. Call me the cat killed by curiosity, but I know something's going on. I'm here to help."

The last thing they needed was Libby's well-meaning but misplaced devotion to duty. Not to mention hearing the ugly details concerning murder, lying, and whatever else came out when they confronted Robbi.

Gigi and Mary Jo came back carrying the gown from the window. Vivien pointed to the first dressing room. "Hang the dress in there for me."

She addressed Libby. "Right now, the best thing you can do is—"

A knock on the salon's front door sounded. "That's Robbi," Gigi hissed as she and Mary Jo hurried toward the fitting room to get Vivien's gown out of sight.

Audrey took Libby by the shoulders. "Go hide in one of the dressing rooms, and stay there until I come and get you."

"Yes ma'am."

Audrey rotated the girl toward her intended hiding place and then gave her a gentle push. "Hurry."

Libby trotted to the nearest room and closed the door behind her.

"Gigi, you and Mary Jo get the two white bucket chairs from the fitting room and put them near one of the sitting areas on the sales floor."

They hurried to comply as Vivien turned to Audrey. "You and I can sit on the couch."

Robbi knocked again, this time a little louder.

Vivien glanced over her shoulder and saw Robbi move to the display window where her gown now hung. Her eyes went saucer-wide as she gazed at her dress. She lowered her head like a bull preparing to charge a matador. Her jaw squared as if she were ready to spew words strong enough to break the window's glass.

"She's seen the dress."

Gigi and Mary Jo set their chairs near the couch and sat down.

"Are we ready?"

Gigi, Mary Jo, and Audrey took their places.

"Then let me welcome in our guest."

Vivien's silk skirt's swishing brought to mind those cowboy movies again, with the rustling of her dress replacing the jingling of the spurs as the hero and the villain closed in on one another in their cinematic standoff.

She opened the door. "Thank you for coming."

Robbi stalled in the hall a moment. "That dress in the window is new."

Vivien took care to keep her best poker face on while Robbi pretended to study the Regal Rose gown. "Audrey brought that back from New York. She said the gown came from a new design house here in Florida."

"Whoever they are, they've got some nerve moving in on your territory." Robbi moved to the salon's entrance. "Nice dress though. Very modern."

"I've been thinking the same thing myself."

Robbi's eyebrow twitched, and she seemed to be fighting to keep the corners of her mouth from curling into a grin as she walked past Vivien into the salon.

She went to the sitting area and took a seat on the couch end opposite Audrey. "Is this little party for me?"

Gigi gestured for Vivien to take her chair as she moved to the couch to sit with Audrey.

Vivien sat, then crossed her legs to keep Robbi from seeing how shaky they'd become since she entered the salon. "We know, Robbi."

Robbi stared with an expression as blank as a snake's eyes. "What do you know?"

"We know you own Regal Rose and that you made the dress hanging in my window."

"Not a crime."

Mary Jo narrowed her eyes as she stared at Robbi. "It is when you kill people to help your company get going."

Robbi tipped her head back and laughed. "Honey, that's quite a story."

Vivien dug her nails into the chair's soft upholstery. "You killed innocent young women."

Robbi stopped laughing. "You took quite a sharp turn there, Vivien. Why would you say such?"

It was hard to remain calm, to keep from shrieking like a madwoman and calling Robbi every terrible name in the book and maybe making some new ones up on the spot. "I want to know why you've been preying on my brides."

Robbi looked around the group, then settled her attention on Vivien once more. "Your brides." She leaned forward and rested her elbows on her lap and her chin on her hands. "How sweet of you to claim all those girls as your own. I've heard you filled one hallway in your house with pictures of every bride you've dressed. Must be quite a large space. Although, you could afford a palace. You're Miss Vivien after all. The queen of Levy City."

"Mary Hadley got that insult from you, didn't she?" After Gigi's outburst, Robbi whirled around and looked at her.

"Who is Mary Hadley?"

Mary Jo pointed at her. "Don't you sit there and pretend you didn't know her. Mrs. Bell told us you had lunch with her, and that her daughter ended her engagement because she believed she'd be modeling gowns for you in New York. She had Mr. Hoverman's card in her purse. We know he worked for you."

Robbi waved away Mary Jo's comment. "Young girls get such silly ideas sometimes."

It didn't escape Vivien's notice that Robbi glossed right over knowing Mr. Hoverman. "Old ladies get silly ideas too. Like how a certain someone stole one of my bridal guides and chose murder weapons from it. And then she used a seam ripper to remove my labels from those poor girls' gowns to ensure my name would be associated with their deaths. Or how she only chose brides who went to college and then became housewives."

Robbi snickered as if Vivien said that pigs could dance like Fred Astaire. "Vivien, you do go on. Since you're hinting I'm the person of whom you're speaking, how would I know if they went to college? I've been away, didn't know those girls at all."

Gigi slapped the couch cushion. "You looked at the wedding announcements at the *LTC*. I remember reading one that mentioned where a girl went to college. We know you went through the files. With Mary Hadley."

Vivien nodded. "Beyond the normal things all young women their age have in common, I couldn't see the common denominator among those girls. Cathy, Macy, and Rayanne all wore one of my gowns. Leila's was an Alfred Angelo. And then this morning, I got to thinking about how these poor girls were killed. By blows to their head."

She went on. "Mary Hadley's words cleared away my fog. She told her parents she wasn't going to give her best years, or her brains, to a man."

Vivien paused, letting her words hang in the air. "Unlike my dead brides."

Robbi crossed her legs. "Ladies, you're enchanting. You've spun more tales than the Grimm brothers. But I'm a reporter. I run on cold, hard facts."

"Here's a fact. We have a dress that we know you made, with your signature lace," Audrey said.

She pulled a receipt from the pocket of her slim brown skirt and read the order out loud. "You've bought several spools of DMC Cordonnet Ecru thread over the past few months. Mary Jo and Gigi witnessed you buying this same thread at Wynton's."

"I have a second fact, Robbi. Mirette woke up today." Vivien had waited all day to say this, to watch Robbi's eyes for signs of fear that her last attempt at murder hadn't succeeded.

All she saw was the anger of a hardened heart. Vivien continued. "She remembered ecru tatted lace hanging beneath the hem of her attacker's overcoat. Same as the lace on your gown hanging in my window."

Robbi laughed again. "This is all circumstantial. Bill Youngblood would throw you out of his station if y'all showed up and told him these tales."

"Gigi gasped. That hole in the bottom of your shoe came from a piece of glass. The same piece missing from the punch bowl, the one Sheriff Youngblood never found. Ben in Shoes can verify you brought the shoe in to be fixed and prove this isn't some tale."

"I've got a tale for you, Vivien. All these years, I've lived in your shadow. Mama used to tell me to practice my sewing and maybe I'd get good enough to come work at Miss Vivien's salon. After that show in New York, she nagged day and night for me to swallow my pride and ask you for a job so I could save face."

Robbi cackled. Goose bumps rose on Vivien's skin as the sound rippled around the room.

She went on. "If Mama had only known you were the daughter of a jailbird."

After all these years, that jab still stirred shame. Vivien winced.

Robbi sneered at Vivien. "That's right, I know all about Daddy's sticky fingers. And you can bet your bridal guide I'll write that story in my column." Robbi paused, never breaking her gaze with Vivien. "I'll spread it all over the bridal world. Moral of the story, don't step on Robbi Dever. I bite." She turned a smug grin Vivien's way. "It's time for you to go away, Miss Vivien. I'm the future of bridal fashions, and the future is now."

She glanced at Gigi. "As far as Mr. Hoverman goes, he and I parted ways."

"Did you kill him too?" Gigi asked.

"If I did sweetie, you won't find him." Robbi unfolded her long legs as she rose from the couch. "I'm tired of talking fairy tales, and this little party is boring."

"Maybe I can liven things up a bit." Sheriff Youngblood emerged from the delivery hallway.

Robbi turned on Vivien. "I underestimated you."

Bill walked to the couch and stood next to Robbi's seat. "Miss Vivien and I had a long visit this morning."

For the first time, Robbi displayed a flicker of fear when Vivien started to speak. "We talked about envelopes with your initials on them, sent to the *LTC*, filled with pages of graphic details of the murder scenes. From a source who seemed to have a ringside seat and a flair for catchy headlines."

When Bill gestured for Robbi to get up to go, Vivien had to ask one last time. "Why, Robbi?"

Her question brought a smile displaying every tooth in Robbi's mouth. "To dethrone the queen. You want to know how I got my big feet inside those precious brides' homes? Two little words. *Miss Vivien*. I said I wanted to write a story extolling all your wonderful virtues, and they couldn't sling those doors open fast enough."

Robbi looked around the group. "They jumped at the chance to show me their gowns. I asked about the guides, had them show me their favorite gifts from the book. When they came out to model their dress for me, wham. They never knew what hit them."

"And Mary Hadley?"

Robbi grunted. "A necessary dope. There was nothing wrong with the dress you made her. That girl didn't want to get married. She wanted to be her." Robbi pointed at Audrey.

"When I told her she was too country for New York City, she threatened to run to her mother with the truth. She won't be running anywhere now, will she? I fixed her dress so her mother would tout me to her friends. With you on the bad list, I could take over and save the day for Levy City's brides."

Sheriff Youngblood took Robbi's arm. "I'd say you're on the bad list. Permanently." He turned to the group. "I got here late, so I'll need to sit down with y'all to get all the facts for my report."

"I've got it, Sheriff."

Everyone turned as Libby crawled out from under Vivien's desk. She held up a clipboard. "I wrote down everything that was said in this room."

Audrey moved to her and took the clipboard. "Libby, your shorthand is perfect." She read the notes, then looked up at the sheriff.

"She took down every word." Audrey handed him Libby's work.

He tapped the page on top. "You know I can't read this chicken scratch. I need you to type this up for me, Audrey."

"Libby will. She's Mr. Wynton's new secretary."

Libby's mouth gaped open. "Really?"

Audrey flashed her one of those electric smiles of hers. "I don't think anyone could fill my chair better than you."

Sheriff Youngblood walked Robbi to the back door. "Miss Dever, I'd like to escort you to my station and have a little talk. I'm just dying to see what we'll squeeze out of you."

When they were gone, Mary Jo rose from her chair and circled the sitting area. "I can't believe Robbi Dever killed four girls so she could get rid of her competition." She swerved her attention to Vivien. "No offense."

Vivien waved off Mary Jo's comments. "You're telling the truth. It's ugly, but true."

"And y'all thought *I* had an inferiority complex." Gigi looked around the group until Audrey gigged her in the side. "What was that for?"

Audrey pinned her with a look. "I'm not going to sit here and let you put yourself in the same category as Robbi Dever."

Mary Jo shot Gigi a quick smile. "She set you straight."

She and Gigi shared another smile.

Vivien leaned back in her chair and closed her eyes. "Mirette's going to be so disappointed she missed all this drama. She's become very fond of soap operas."

Vivien stood in the middle of the sales floor and gazed around the salon. The entire space seemed to be holding its breath as the time leading up to the salon's reopening ticked away.

"Why are you standing out here wasting time when we have Louisa's final fitting in thirty minutes?" Mirette said behind her.

Hearing her assistant's complaint was better than gold. "It's so nice having you back. It just wasn't the same place without all your grousing."

She squeezed Mirette around the shoulders, then stepped back and gazed at her friend. "I never realized you had the features to pull off a turban."

Mirette patted the base of her silk head covering. "It keeps me from looking like a cantaloupe. I still don't understand why that doctor saw fit to shave almost my whole head to put in a few stitches."

Twenty-two stitches, stretched from Mirette's crown and down to her left ear. Vivien thanked the good Lord every day that her dear friend was spared the worst from Robbi Dever's attack.

"We've come a long way from those days of making a gown and praying some girl would buy it, haven't we?"

Mirette groaned. "Stop talking like we're about to die. My bucket's got enough dents from Robbi trying to kick it in for me."

"I'm thankful she didn't know your head is the hardest part on your body."

Mirette stuck her tongue out. "You're a regular comedienne this morning."

Vivien followed her into the fitting room. Immogene was pressing the gros point lace around the neckline of Louisa's gown when the back door opened.

Audrey entered carrying a cake, followed by Gigi and Mary Jo, whose hands were filled with forks, napkins, and plates. As soon as they closed the door, they broke into a song to the tune of "Happy Birthday": "*Happy reopening day to you, happy reopening day to you, happy reopening day, Miss Vivien, Mirette, and Immogene, happy reopening day to you!*"

Audrey set the cake on the small table next to the chairs in the fitting area. Mary Jo set down the plates and pulled one of Lilla's large kitchen knives from the stack of silverware she'd brought. "Who wants cake?"

"This early in the morning?" Vivien said as she fought back tears.

Mirette grabbed a fork and plate. "I'm a recovering invalid. I'll take the first piece."

"I can tell from here that's one of Lilla's cakes. Too fluffy and moist to be anybody else's. You can give me the next slice." Immogene unplugged her iron and set it aside.

She fluffed the skirt of Louisa's gown, then ran her hand across the overlay. "I don't think this could have turned out any better."

Audrey moved in for a closer look. She pointed to the small chiffon rosettes. "This I love. I saw work similar to this in New York, at Ann Lowe's shop on Lexington Avenue."

Immogene smiled at Audrey's compliment.

Audrey continued to study the gown. "You three have created a beautiful dress here. Are you going to feature this gown in the bridal fashion show?"

Vivien forked a piece of cake. "No. This dress was quite possibly the most challenging thing we've ever made and belongs to a very special young lady."

She slid the bite into her mouth, then closed her eyes as a perfect combination of soft cake and sweet icing exploded in her mouth. "This is definitely one of Lilla's."

Immogene nodded as she swallowed. "Nobody bakes better than my sister-in-law."

Gigi scraped up a glob of icing on her fork. "She should go into the catering business. Everything she makes is fabulous."

Immogene wiped her mouth with a napkin. "That Mr. Cameron called her not too long ago, asking if she'd come work for him. He'd made a deal with that Dever lady to cook for the Bridal Week celebration she was planning. She told him no on the spot."

Gigi dropped her fork on her plate. "Robbi Dever was planning her own Bridal Week?"

Vivien set her empty plate down. "She admitted that to Bill during questioning. Her plan was to run me out of town, then come to Mr. Wynton with her new line of gowns and a proposal for a new, more modern take on Bridal Week. She'd talked a few of our vendors into coming along by promising them free advertising on her radio show."

Vivien laid her napkin on her plate. "Apparently, she also shared she'd named her brand after her mother. Rose was her middle name too."

Mary Jo shook her head. "After committing murder, stealing, lying about Miss Vivien in front of the entire city, and being envious, she honored her mother. I guess it's nice she didn't break all the commandments."

Vivien pointed to her watch. "Ladies, this party was so sweet, and I really want to eat every last bite of this cake, but we have a bride due here in five minutes."

"We do love how y'all thought of us." Mirette hugged Gigi, then Mary Jo.

They pointed to Audrey. "It was all her idea, even the song."

The salon's front doors chimed. "That's Margay Delmar and Louisa. Y'all have got to skedaddle. We promised them both we'd keep her dress a secret until her wedding day."

Audrey went to pick up the cake, but Mirette clamped her wrist. "Leave that right there, missy."

She and Audrey shared a look before Audrey broke into a wide smile. "Yes ma'am. Libby may sneak down here for a piece. The phone started ringing as I was leaving the executive suite, and she couldn't come with me."

"She'd better come fast because Immogene and I aren't going to let it sit there and go to waste, are we?"

"I know that's right," Immogene said as she worked to transfer the gown from the dress form to a hanger. "I'll go put this in the room for Louisa."

"Thank you, Immogene." Vivien licked a dot of icing from her fingers, then wiped them on a napkin. "Won't do for the new-and-improved Miss Vivien to go out with sticky fingers."

"We've had enough of that in this salon already." Mirette collected Louisa's veil and followed Immogene to the dressing room.

Mary Jo and Gigi slipped out as Vivien went to the sales floor. Audrey stayed behind to clean up and get the chrome dome back on the cake.

Vivien met Margay and Louisa at the fitting-room doors. "Louisa, you are absolutely glowing."

"I didn't think it was possible to be so excited and terrified at the same time, Miss Vivien. Is my dress ready?"

"Mirette and Immogene are in the dressing room waiting to help you into it."

While Louisa made her way to the room, Vivien directed Margay to one of the mama's chairs.

"Miss Vivien, once she got polio, I thought we'd lost this dream." She pulled a crumpled hankie from her purse. "I've been a mess all morning."

She wiped her nose. "Thank you so much for letting us come in early. A crowd of girls and their mothers were gathered at the elevators when we came in. I think the salon is going to fill up fast once you open the doors."

Louisa walked out of the dressing room. "Mama, watch." She walked the length to the platform by the three-way mirrors. "They did it. The gown doesn't show my weird leg at all. I look like I'm floating when I walk." She stepped onto the platform before the mirrors, then twirled around, looking at her reflection.

Margay buried her face in her wet hankie. Vivien retrieved a handful of tissues and handed them to her.

"Miss Vivien, that's the most beautiful dress I've ever seen." She crossed the room to her daughter. "This overskirt. . .these little flowers and leaves are prettier than anything I've seen in a garden. She looks as graceful as a swan when she moves."

"I must say I've never seen a girl bring out the beauty in a gown as well as you do." Louisa blushed at Audrey's compliment while Vivien settled the veil onto her head and draped it around her shoulders.

Vivien then moved back to stand with Audrey and Mirette, giving mother and daughter a moment to themselves.

Audrey leaned in close. "Miss Vivien, y'all outdid yourselves with that gown."

When Vivien turned to thank her for the praise, she caught the fleeting glow of a certain spark in Audrey's eyes as she watched mother and daughter admiring the details on the gown, hugging and wiping their eyes together.

"Oh. My. Stars," Vivien whispered to herself.

“What’s the matter with you?” Mirette said as she pulled one of the mama’s chairs over and sat down.

“Nothing. Everything is wonderful.”

She turned her attention back to Louisa. “Ain’t love grand, Mirette?”

Author's Notes

The 1950s were a great time to be in the wedding business. The dark times of war had passed, and the country was determined to push toward a more hopeful future. Young ladies dreamed of being brides, and department stores created the full-service bridal salon to meet those needs.

There was so much more to the business of weddings and running a salon than I ever realized. While I was writing this book, I had to keep reminding myself this was a story and not a tome on the history of the bridal business or department store bridal salons. I had to leave behind so many fascinating details in my research notebook but wanted to share a few here to give a taste of what I learned.

The traditional wedding had become the ideal in the 1950s, creating a fast-growing national bridal market. Men had become more equal partners in the wedding than in the past. The double ring ceremony, where both the bride and the groom exchanged rings, became one of many new traditions couples included in their ceremonies. Many of these traditions are still present at weddings today.

Like Miss Vivien's, the department store bridal salons became the hub of all things bridal, and worked to meet a bride's every need, even those she didn't realize she had. They were trendsetters, devising different ways to help brides plan their big day. Well-informed bridal consultants guided girls through the choice of their wedding gowns, gift registries, invitations, and even honeymoon plans. Salons gave free, often leather-bound bridal guides to their brides to help clients through each step from the engagement to settling down to life after the honeymoon. These guides also offered lessons in bridal etiquette, beauty and hairstyle tips for the big day, or choosing just the right floral arrangements. Stores held Bridal Weeks showcasing all the products related to brides, weddings, and housekeeping, as well as offering demonstrations on interior decorating, cooking, cleaning, and home budgeting.

Salons kept an inventory of items a girl might need for her ceremony—including large candelabras, white runners for church aisles, candles, and arches for flowers. Others put together emergency kits containing smelling salts for overly nervous brides or mothers, nail polish, spare nylons, aspirin, makeup, or any other items that could be used to ensure all went smoothly on the big day. The bridal consultant and salon owner often assisted in choosing a venue, figuring out seating arrangements, and setting up and decorating for the wedding ceremony. They prided themselves on being able to handle any problem, including cold feet, squabbling family members, unexpected weather, jilted brides, and the occasional elopement.

The wedding gown reigned as the top thing on every bride's list. In the 1950s, girls had many choices. Salons offered ready-made gowns off the rack that could be ordered to fit. Brides could also make their own gown. Popular sewing pattern manufacturers of the day like *McCall's* and *Vogue* sold patterns to fit all the current trends, whether it was the long, full-skirted ball gown or the chic tea-length style that became popular in this era. Brides ordered from favorite stores like Carson Pirie Scott in Chicago, Priscilla of Boston, Alfred Angelo (which started in Philadelphia but was later headquartered in Delray Beach, Florida), and Davison-Paxon in Atlanta.

Couture gowns were also a choice for the brides with a larger budget. Many designers emerged during the 1950s, and one of the most talented was the African American designer Ann Lowe. One of her most famous gowns was worn by Jacqueline Bouvier in her marriage to John F. Kennedy in 1953. The gown garnered much attention and was featured in many magazines, but due to her skin color, Ann did not receive credit for the design until years later. Determined to succeed in what she loved most to do, Ann continued to dress the higher-end ladies of society, becoming the first African American woman to own and operate a couture dress shop on Madison Avenue. Though she gained success and a large group of clients in the early years of her career, her high-society patrons did not want it known that their gowns were made by a Black woman.

Ann Lowe developed a distinctive style for all the gowns she designed. Known for her ability to create realistic flowers and other natural details as embellishments, she created gowns that are not just something to wear but also beautiful works of art. Many are featured in exhibits at the Metropolitan Museum of Art and the Smithsonian. I knew very little about her when I started researching but soon grew to be a huge fan of her dresses. My words do not do justice to her talent, and I highly recommend those who love high fashion and stunning gowns to look up her work. You won't be disappointed.

I was surprised that in one stage of her career, Ann designed dresses for wealthy clients in a community near Tampa, Florida. She lived in the house of a wealthy family, designing gowns and costumes for their daughters for social events like Gasparilla, debutante balls, and coming-out parties. She honed her skills here in Florida, becoming the favorite seamstress of many well-to-do families. In time, she opened her own small shop, setting up a workroom in the back of her house where she taught dressmaking classes to neighborhood women, bringing some into her business. Ann moved to New York in 1928, where she went on to open her own shop. She later expressed she loved all the families she'd worked with in Tampa dearly, but she wanted to move on and make her mark in the fashion world. She most certainly did just that.

Sharp lines had been drawn during this time between Blacks and whites. Segregation, racism, and unfair social practices continued. But those ways were facing more challenges, and like Ann, many African Americans were standing firm and pushing against the boundaries. Autherine Lucy overcame the establishment to become the first African American student to attend the University of Alabama. In 1956, students in Tallahassee, Florida, organized their own bus boycott to protest the racial segregation in the city. Browder v. Gayle, a case related to the Montgomery Bus Boycott, overturned the segregation on local buses. Others were working to establish themselves as business owners, doctors, nurses, teachers, and writers to serve their community in helping others overcome. The struggle wasn't over, and many, like Lilla, had decided the time had come to force change. Like Mr. Wynton and Vivien, many were becoming more aware of this struggle and starting to question the old ways. The early threads of change were being woven together in Florida, but the worst was far from over.

The inclusion of a character suffering from polio was based on something from my own life. One of my relatives contracted polio when she was a child and was left with a lifetime disability. But being of strong stock and filled with an iron will, like Louisa, she went on to marry, raise children, and live a full life, doing whatever she put her mind to and doing it well. Polio was a heartbreaking disease, and the children's hospital mentioned in this book was, in fact, based on the American Legion Hospital for Crippled Children, which opened in St. Petersburg, Florida, in 1926. Founded as a place to care for children with polio or other crippling conditions, this hospital treated children of all races, cultures, or religious beliefs, regardless of their ability to pay for the care. During the 1950s, the peak of the polio outbreak, the number of services available to their patients included surgical facilities, a school with a full-time teacher, a library, and physical and educational therapy. This hospital still exists today and is now known as Johns Hopkins All Children's Hospital.

I loved getting into the importance of radio during this time. In the 1950s, there were over 2,000 AM radio stations around the United States. Many were local stations that filled the airwaves with scripted shows similar to Robbi's, sharing everything from crop prices, the weather, local church choirs performing hymns, news and happenings about-the-town, to color commentary during local high school sporting events. In a few years though, the rising popularity of performers like Elvis caused stations to focus on more music and less talking. By the end of the decade, the days of seeing crowds of listeners walking around with a small transistor radio tucked in their shirt pocket and a headphone stuck in their ear faded. With TVs being more readily available and affordable, audiences tuned in to the new variety of programs to watch. Radio's hold over the public's attention waned.

It was fun to find out that many of the wedding traditions I thought were from generations ago actually originated during this time. Yes, there was a growing, thriving business being built around wedding venues, engagement and wedding rings, catering, gowns, and bridal gifts. Many complained that bridal consultants, department stores, jewelers, and other companies changed something meant to be sacred into nothing more than a moneymaking scheme. But to most in the wedding business, their work meant far more than just the dollars to be made guiding girls from engagement rings to the church ceremony. There was a deeper meaning for them, and Miss Vivien echoed this when she saw another bride enjoying her bridal moment.

"Ain't love grand?"

Acknowledgments

Having the opportunity to let my mind wander into the world of Wynton's again was more fun than I imagined. Thank you Becky and the Barbour family for believing in these ladies and the stories they want to tell. I've loved spending more time with Audrey, Miss Vivien, Mirette, Mary Jo, and Gigi.

To my fabulous agent, Linda. Thanks for all you do, and for supporting this project from the very start.

I owe great thanks to my Word Weavers Tampa chapter. All the cheers, all the suggestions, and all the encouragement you heaped on me and this story helped me find my way to those two magical words we all live for. *The End.*

To Jen, a tower of patience. You kindly sat through all my texts filled with whining and complaining when I got stuck during the writing process. Though I deserved a kick in the pants at times, you sent cheery words to get me going again. Thanks for keeping me accountable and sane.

To Katherine, Denise, and Evelyn. You kept me straight and helped me see the past through a different lens. Thank you.

To my Aunt-Sis, Barbara. Thanks for introducing me to great stories when I was young. You helped launch my imagination into wonderful places.

To Gail. Thanks for sharing all the wedding pictures. They were a wonderful little glimpse into this decade and a truly fabulous resource.

Dear Sue. Thanks for letting me drag you to a vintage bridal gown exhibit, staying engaged as I obsessed over every inch of lace, silk, satin, and tulle in sight. And afterward, you still had the patience to listen while I droned on about veils, dress styles, and fabrics. Best research buddy ever.

To Sharron, Jan, Crystal, Sally, Marianne, and Melissa. Thanks for all the texts and messages cheering me on and checking in when I dropped into my story world and forgot to check in with the real one. You reached out at just the right time.

To the Buckman girls. Thanks for many years of laughter and friendship, and for allowing me to live vicariously through all your awesome adventures. Buckman rules!

To my guys. Love you to bits.

And a huge thanks to God for. . .everything.

Donna Mumma perfected storytelling in her first-grade classroom, spinning tales exciting enough to settle a roomful of antsy six-year-olds. She is an award-winning author who loves to blend history, mystery, and a dash of hope in stories that explore ordinary people who learn extraordinary life lessons. Donna is an active member of Word Weavers International, serving as president for the Tampa chapter as well as a mentor for chapters around the country. She was recognized as the Word Weavers traditional groups president and mentor of the year in 2022. She also serves as a line editor and contributor for Inkspirationsonline.com, a site featuring devotions written for writers by writers. An avid believer in education, Donna earned her M.Ed. in elementary education from the University of Florida. A native Floridian, she loves sharing life with her husband, her adult children, and her energetic collie, Duke.